WELCOME TO MY NIGHTMARE

Chris mustered up his courage and approached the corpse. He peeked under its collar but could see no bite marks on the rotting flesh.

As he gazed at the body's withered hand, his peripheral vision picked up a slight movement. He stepped back swiftly.

A pair of glassy eyes stared back at him from the skull-like face—eyes that had sprung wide when Chris wasn't looking. The corpse's mouth opened, and it proceeded to wet its lips with the ooze from its gray tongue.

"Go . . . away," it whispered.

Other Avon Books by
John Peyton Cooke

THE LAKE

OUT FOR BLOOD

JOHN PEYTON COOKE

AVON BOOKS ◆ NEW YORK

OUT FOR BLOOD is an original publication of Avon Books. This work has never before appeared in book form. This work is a novel. Any similarity to actual events or persons, living, dead or undead, is purely coincidental.

AVON BOOKS
A division of
The Hearst Corporation
105 Madison Avenue
New York, New York 10016

First Avon Books Printing: March 1991

AVON TRADEMARK REG. U.S. PAT. OFF. AND IN OTHER COUNTRIES, MARCA REGISTRADA, HECHO EN U.S.A.

Printed in the U.S.A.

RA 10 9 8 7 6 5 4 3 2 1

This book is for
GORE VIDAL

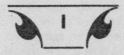

THE FEAST OF BLOOD

THAT first night, Chris Callaway dreamed of someone tapping at the window. . . .

"Who is it?" his dream-self mumbled.

The rapping persisted, but no answer came.

Chris rubbed the sleep from his eyes and peered out into the darkness. The moonlight shining through the window and French doors gave the bedroom a somber cast, but his view of the moon was obscured by the far bedpost. The figure lurking outside on the balcony was hidden as well.

"Is that you?" asked Chris in a stage whisper. His excitement was tempered by the thought of accidentally waking his parents.

The plate glass of the French doors rattled, but still no one responded.

The air in the room was stifling, every door and window shut tight and locked. Chris felt strangled by the oppressiveness, and loosened the top few buttons of his nightshirt. He reached for the oil lamp on the night table, struck a match, and lit the lamp, turning the wick up enough to give the room a warm glow.

It was then he noticed the necklace of garlic he was wearing, along with the silver crucifix pendant. Since he hadn't worn them to bed, clearly they had been his parents' doing. They were the ones who had sealed the room, Chris realized, and they'd probably smeared cloves of garlic around the edges of the doors and windows as well.

Damn them!

Chris peered around the bedpost, yet his view of the visitor remained obstructed by the half-closed curtains, so he threw aside the bed covers and got up. His sweat-soaked nightshirt clung to his skin as he hurried to the French doors, drew the curtains farther open, and fastened them to the wall with the silk sash.

Abruptly, the rapping ceased.

As Chris had expected—as he had *hoped*—there beyond the threshold of the balcony stood the vampire, draped in his black woolen cape.

The vampire's face held an air of majesty and beauty despite his skin's ashen luster. A high forehead rose above his gaunt features, with raven-black hair plastered flat against his skull, displaying a prominent widow's peak. His hand, holding the cape against his chest, showed an ancient ring embedded with a large ruby that shone with a supernatural gleam of its own. Over the vampire's shoulder loomed the silhouette of the Carpathian Mountains, rising high above the smoking chimneys of the village.

In his haste Chris began to unlatch the door, but suddenly the vampire fixed his gaze upon him, and with his eyes commanded Chris to wait. Sneering, the vampire pointed down at Chris's chest and hissed his displeasure. He ordered Chris to rid himself of the hideous *things* he wore against his breast.

"Yes, Master," said Chris with a nervous grin, hoping the vampire wouldn't be angry with him.

Staring deeply into his visitor's black eyes, Chris removed the string of garlic and the crucifix from around his neck and tossed them into the far corner opposite the bed. Then he fumbled with the latch until the door eased open, letting in a quick gust of cool night air.

"Please, Master," Chris begged. "Please come in."

The vampire burst into the room, grabbed Chris by the shoulders, and tossed him onto the bed. Transfixed by his gaze, Chris lay still, breathing heavily, and waiting. He had already been bitten on two separate evenings, which was why his parents and their doctor had tried to protect him this night: once he had been bitten a third time, he would become a vampire himself, one of the undead, and lost to them forever.

Which was exactly what Chris desired—*and time was of the essence!*

The vampire's eyes compelled him to pull his nightshirt up over his head and throw it on the floor. Suddenly naked, Chris attempted to cover himself with his hands, but the vampire's eyes commanded him to lie still and relax, and all would be well. He felt a new calmness wash over him as he dropped his arms onto the bed and waited. The vampire grinned in approval, baring his sharp canines.

"Master, do it now! Kiss me, please!"

The vampire flung himself upon Chris and dug his teeth into his neck. Chris's blood gushed forth, past the vampire's sucking lips. He became dizzy as he felt the throbbing in his neck, the tingling in his limbs.

The vampire was drawing the life out of him!

When he was finished, the vampire pulled Chris from the bed and bade him kneel on the Persian rug. Chris felt so spent he thought he'd topple over, but the vampire kept a steady hand on his shoulder, holding him up, readying him for the ultimate feast. The vampire unbuttoned his own shirt of blood-spattered white silk, and with a sharp fingernail sliced open his skin from chest to navel. A bright glistening redness flowed out, inches away from Chris's hungry mouth. The vampire grasped him by the hair and pressed his face into the dripping wound, commanding him to drink.

Chris did so eagerly, without reservation. The taste was divine, and as he drank he felt the vampire's blood filling him up, coursing through his veins, restoring him to life.

"Eternal life," whispered the vampire. "Drink! Drink deeply!"

Chris couldn't get enough of it. It spilled over his chin and down his chest, trickling onto his penis, which had grown harder and harder the more he drank and now stood fully erect, engorged with blood.

"Now you are undead," said the vampire. "Undead, do you hear!"

Undead! thought Chris with excitement. *Undead at last!*

Suddenly, there in the doorway stood his parents and the doctor, shrieking and gasping in horror. The doctor wielded a crucifix at arm's length and took a timid step forward.

The vampire merely laughed, then leaped across the room and flung himself upon the intruders. . . .

Chris awoke at this point, and when he realized it had only been a dream, felt strangely disappointed. Then he went back to sleep.

THE MARK OF THE VAMPIRE

WHEN Chris put in his contact lenses and looked in the mirror the next morning, he noticed two fresh bruises on his neck. After many weeks of being sick, the discovery failed to surprise. Instead, Chris was amused at how closely the marks on his neck resembled the bite of a vampire, or at least how he had always imagined a vampire bite might look in the flesh.

He could barely recall the vampire dream. Most of the details had already escaped his recollection, and he was left with the vague notion that he'd been thrust into a 1960s British horror movie, complete with blood, gore, and fangs.

As Chris's brain started chugging to life, he realized he actually remembered little—if anything—of the night before.

Late the previous afternoon, he had fixed macaroni and cheese for dinner, lain in bed, and watched Chicago's favorite six o'clock news team. They had reported that the mayor was bickering with city public health officials over the content of a proposed drug education program for the public schools, the weather tomorrow would be sunny and humid, and the Cubs had blown their winning streak one month into the season. Then he had grabbed his remote and turned on the VCR to watch an episode of "The Frugal Gourmet" that he'd taped some other evening, wishing throughout that he'd had the energy to cook some real food instead of packaged macaroni and cheese; the Frugal Gourmet had fixed himself garlic and egg soup and gone to great lengths to explain that Spanish food was *not* Mexican food, "You see?" After that, Chris's memory failed him utterly, except for brief flashes from the vampire dream. He couldn't even recall turning off the TV, much less getting undressed and going to bed.

Chris assumed that he must have sleepwalked through these motions and gone to bed early, though it was disconcerting being unable to remember precisely. Most likely he'd taken a dose of Demerol and forgotten that, too.

Lightly touching his neck, Chris felt soreness at both bruises. They were virtually identical in size and appearance, but on closer examination they looked decidedly unlike bite marks. In Chris's present condition, a bite on the neck would have caused profuse bleeding on his pillow and would have taken perhaps weeks to heal properly. The thought was ridiculous, so he put it out of his mind.

Since taking ill, Chris had both bruised and bled with ease. The drug prednisone, which he'd been given as part of his remission therapy, had contributed to the already weakened coagulability of his blood. His gums bled when he brushed his teeth, and he often suffered nosebleeds for no apparent reason. Chris had picked up several new bruises in recent weeks, but what disturbed him the most was that they were all much larger than they should have been and took far too long to heal. His doctor had warned him this would happen.

"Yeah, you're looking great," Chris said aloud, but the sarcasm in his tone went unnoticed by his reflection, which simply smiled stupidly back at him.

He hardly recognized himself anymore. The prednisone had also made his body retain water and given him what were known as Cushingoid features. Unfortunately, "Cushingoid" did not mean that Chris looked like the great British movie actor Peter Cushing, who, in his oft-repeated role as vampire hunter Professor Van Helsing, had destroyed Count Dracula on numerous occasions in bloody Eastmancolor.

Rather, "Cushingoid" meant that Chris's face was now bloated and puffy, a pale round moon-face with dark rings circling the eyes. All the chemotherapy he had undergone had left him practically bald as well, though oddly enough the prednisone had also caused him to grow new hair in strange places.

A year ago, a friend who was trying to get into Chris's pants had told him he looked like a young Donald O'Connor with his fresh Irish face, sandy red hair, and freckles. But now Chris felt he looked more like old Uncle Fester from the Charles Addams cartoons. Deep down, he failed to see the humor in his own sad joke. Chris didn't like what was happening to him, which was, in a word, leukemia—cancer of the blood.

His legs were stiff as he stepped into the shower. The muscles ached, and he could feel a dull, throbbing pain coming from the shinbone and femur in both legs. Although the bone pain was far less severe than he'd experienced before, Chris knew he should take some Demerol today just in case it got worse. The painkiller worked best when taken before any pain really set in.

Chris was in between cycles of his remission-induction therapy, the so-called rest period. Every two weeks, he had to go to the hospital to get a small shot of vincristine, a drug that had been derived from the highly poisonous periwinkle plant. The injection was quite an intense experience; the tiny dose of two milligrams was all it took to give an immediate rush of euphoria. Chris wished he could have it more often, yet he understood that any higher dosage or greater frequency would likely destroy his entire nervous system. The prednisone made him euphoric at times, too, but at other times considerably depressed. It was toxic as well, though nowhere near as dangerous as the vincristine. Chris was put on prednisone for the five days of the drug therapy cycle, during which he had to go to the hospital each day to get a shot of cytarabine in his thigh. These, in combination with cyclophosphamide taken orally, wreaked havoc on his bone marrow and his lymphatic system, which

was a good thing when you were dealing with acute lym-
phocytic leukemia. But when the five-day therapy cycle was
over, Chris's body was a wreck and he was put on a nine-
day rest period before starting all over again. He had just
finished his fourth week out of six, and had an excellent
chance of getting it into remission, though remission was
easier to induce in children than in twenty-two-year-olds.
After remission, Chris would be put on a sixteen-week program of drug maintenance therapy, and only after that would
he truly feel back to normal. Then, provided the disease
remained in remission, he could expect to live another five
years.

And after that? Chris thought. *Aye, there's the rub!*

He rinsed himself off, then turned off the hot water and
opened the shower curtain, but suddenly felt faint and nearly
blacked out, so he stood still for a moment trying to catch
his breath. He always left the door to the bathroom open
while showering to keep the room from fogging up and to
let fresh air come in. Soon his vision cleared, as the blood
came back to his head, and he reached for a towel.

"Knock, knock," came a voice from the living room. It
was Tim Duffy, but then who else would it be? Tim wasn't
asking to come into the bathroom, but rather, as usual,
warning Chris he'd entered the apartment.

"Be out in a sec," answered Chris in his weakened voice.
The lymph nodes beneath his jaw were still slightly swollen,
a constant pressure on his pharynx and vocal cords. As he
dried himself off, he could feel his heart beating at a pa-
thetically fast rate. Hot showers always did this to him.

"And here I was all set to barge in and scream 'Up and
at 'em!' or 'Rise and shine!' "

"Please, Tim." Chris wrapped the damp towel around
his bloated waist and came out of the bathroom, each step
sending small pains up his legs. His heart refused to calm
down. "You're getting more and more like my mother every
day."

"Sorry."

"You should be."

"I just get a kick out of waking you up, and here you've deprived me of it. It's not like you to be up so early."

"Ten-thirty?"

"That's early for you these days."

Tim Duffy was "a man of size," as the politically correct would say. Although Chris himself had grown slightly obese since first taking prednisone, he had a long way to go before he looked like Tim. When regarding Tim's rotundness, Chris was reminded of a eunuch in Rome's heyday (not that he'd ever seen one firsthand, or even been to Rome for that matter, much less in antiquity), though in personality Tim was probably more agreeable than your average eunuch. When asked, Tim's lover, Bob, had assured Chris that Tim was indeed no eunuch. Chris was embarrassed that he'd even brought up the subject, but Bob had looked as if he had been asked before. Tim's double chin, pasty face, beady eyes, and black curly hair must have left a similar impression on other people, or at least on other curious gay men.

Tim set down a couple of bags of groceries in the kitchen, then traipsed into the living room and yanked open the vertical blinds of the front window, letting bright sunlight stream into the apartment. Chris squinted at the sudden bright glare reflecting off the hardwood floor.

"You're one of these types who likes privacy, I see." Tim had said this before, and seemed to think it was funny, but Chris truly did value his privacy. Living in a garden apartment, it was all too easy for passersby to gaze through the windows at night.

"No one can see into your and Bob's windows up on the third floor, I suppose."

"No need to get defensive, darling boy."

Chris didn't think he was being defensive, but he let it go. Tim had bandied about such categories and labels for the two years Chris had known him. Bob, Tim's significant other for the last fourteen years, was a psychologist, and therefore so was Tim, though a graphic artist by trade.

"Mmm! What is that I smell—liver?" Tim asked with a mischievous grin.

"I don't know what you smell, but it's not liver. Last night all I had was macaroni and cheese. I hate liver."

"Well, I still smell it."

As Tim began putting away the groceries, Chris made his way to the kitchen and sat on a bar stool. He was breathing hard, his body working overtime to get the oxygen that his pounding heart was demanding.

"Want to see my vampire bite?" Chris asked.

"I'd rather bite you myself, dear." Tim was putting a head of lettuce into the Tupperware lettuce crisper. "Let's have a look."

Chris tilted his head to the side, exposing his neck. "Just a couple of bruises, is all, but kind of keen, huh?"

Tim's face waxed sympathetic as he examined the bruises. Then he sighed heavily and said, "You and your vampires," as if he were a mother dealing with a precocious child.

"I know, what are you ever going to do with me?" Chris enjoyed playing the part of the flirtatious cute boy, though he kept forgetting he was no longer cute.

"What indeed!" Tim started transferring several bottles of mineral water from the sack to the refrigerator. "Those gross pictures on your walls—I mean, look at this place! Vampire City!"

Tim was right. Chris had decorated the walls with posters of Christopher Lee, Bela Lugosi, and Klaus Kinski all portraying vampires, plus a poster of Conrad Veidt slinking about in black in the German silent film *The Cabinet of Dr. Caligari*, looking vampirish though he wasn't exactly playing a vampire. It was no secret Chris enjoyed vampire novels and vampire movies, and he invariably dressed the part for Tim and Bob's annual Halloween Screamfest. Yet while Tim and Bob became "Halloweeny" only once a year, Chris's interest in such things persisted year-round.

"Listen, hon, Bob and I will be flying off to Houston in a couple hours. It's just for a few days, remember. Are you sure you can take care of yourself okay?"

"Sure," said Chris. "I'll stock up on garlic, whittle some

stakes and stuff. Could I borrow your rosary and a crucifix?''

"Why don't you just let them take you? You love them so much. You'd probably enjoy it, sucking blood, turning into a bat. I bet you'd get a real kick out of it." Tim sounded utterly disgusted.

Chris laughed, then continued with the joke. "Did you notice how pale I am? I've lost a lot of blood and I feel weaker today, too."

Chris was being honest, though; the last time his doctor had checked his red blood count, it had been low, though not yet low enough to require another transfusion. Chris had needed a transfusion at the beginning of treatment, because the leukemic cells had devastated his blood. When he was low on red blood corpuscles, it made him breathe harder and his heart beat faster, trying desperately to get enough oxygen to his body. The lack of oxygen made him weak, but the pumping of his overworked heart made him weaker.

Of course, Tim knew this was all part of Chris's condition, so Chris wasn't surprised when Tim ignored his implication that a vampire had sucked out his blood. Tim, being the amateur psychologist, probably figured Chris was merely seeking attention, which was true. Being severely ill while living by himself had made him desperately lonely. Chris relished his daily visits from Tim, and felt warmed by Tim's protective, maternal way with him.

"And what's this?" Tim asked, picking up a plastic videocassette case from the kitchen counter. "I might have known—*Dracula, Prince of Darkness*. This stuff isn't good for you. Worshiping bats is not healthy."

"Let me see," said Chris, taking the videotape from him. Without a doubt, it was what Tim said it was, but Chris was at a loss as to what it was doing in his apartment. It was a rental videocassette from a store at least three miles away. Even though he couldn't remember what he'd done the night before, he knew he couldn't have possibly walked or even taken the El down to this out-of-the-way video store and rented this tape. Chris didn't have the energy for such excursions. But, considering Tim's suspicious nature, the last thing Chris needed was to let him in on the mystery.

"Sure, a friend of mine rented this for me," Chris claimed. "I was going to watch it today."

Tim probably hadn't noticed where the tape was from, much less wondered how Chris had come by it. Tim was no dummy, but still, things seemed to blow right past him when his mind was focused on more important tasks such as putting away the groceries. Chris was sure his simple explanation was sufficient.

Oh well, however he had ended up with the movie, he was going to be sure to watch it later in the day; it was one of his favorite films. Chris went into the living room to put the movie on top of the TV.

"Ow! Jesus!" Chris's knee gave way for a second, but he caught himself by grabbing onto a chair. The ache in his bones was growing worse; if he didn't take his painkiller now, he'd be in agony before he knew it.

"What's the matter?" Suddenly, Tim was concerned.

Chris sat down carefully in the chair, putting the videotape in his lap. "Could you go get the Demerol? I think this is going to be one of those days."

Within a minute, Tim had brought the medicine spoon with a dose of liquid Demerol jiggling inside. Chris put it to his lips and drank it down, knowing the effect would come gradually. Tim took the medicine spoon from Chris and handed him a glass of water to wash the Demerol down with.

By now, Tim must have known everything about attending to Chris. Chris had been through some much rougher times several weeks ago and had needed more regular attention than he did now. Tim had taken it upon himself to be Chris's nurse, errand runner, and chauffeur for the frequent trips to the hospital. Tim had moved his office/studio to his upstairs apartment two years ago. He was almost always around at any time of the day Chris might need him.

"Is there anything else you need?" Tim asked.

"No, thanks, I'm all right. You go ahead and finish with the groceries."

Chris counted himself lucky to have Tim, whom he considered an empathetic soul, as a friend. Clearly, Tim felt for Chris because he'd been stricken with leukemia. But Chris conjectured that Tim's motivations ran deeper than that. It wasn't mere friendship that fed Tim's actions, nor was it sexual desire; Tim and Bob had had a healthy monogamous relationship for years that showed no signs of weakening. What drove Tim was his belief in the family unit. He had grown up in a large family and had never kept his sexuality secret from them, yet he'd maintained great relationships with his parents and siblings, and continued to attend mass with his family whenever possible.

Chris, however, had had an altogether different family experience. Like Tim, Chris had been raised Catholic—or, as he preferred to think of it, South Side Chicago Irish Catholic—but there the similarities ended. His only brother, Patrick, had been killed by a hit-and-run driver when Chris was an infant and Patrick was five. Chris, of course, had no memory of the accident, but it had nonetheless haunted him as he grew up. Once he reached his teen years, he could no longer get along with his father, while his mother sat by like a docile goat, never willing to come to Chris's side in any argument. His dad was sole ruler of the household, and that was final. Chris put up with the Catholic schools his parents sent him to, but never caught the religious bug and at age sixteen refused to set foot in church again. This put him in immediate disfavor and nearly got him kicked out of the house when he faced the Wrath of Dad. The eventual kicking out finally did occur two years later, when Chris told his parents he was gay. Anymore, Chris tried not to think about his parents; they were no longer a part of his life.

"You were low on pasta, but now you've got gobs. There's some cottage cheese in the refrigerator; now don't forget and let it go bad. And I finally got you your Spaghettios—God only knows why, but I did. Promise me you'll at least eat some greens with them. There's lettuce, and there's frozen broccoli and spinach in the freezer, and some frozen dinners, too. Plus, I got you some mushrooms. After Bob and I get back next week, we'll come over and I'll treat you to my creamy mushroom garlic spaghetti.''

"Sounds great.''

Tim seemed to think he was filling a gap by providing the familial love he thought Chris needed, taking care of Chris the way he felt a mother should take care of her son and being a strong shoulder to cry on.

Outwardly, Chris denied he needed such love and attention, but deep inside he was grateful to Tim for all he'd done. Chris's parents refused to believe he was suffering from leukemia; they were certain he had AIDS and that Chris and the doctors were simply lying to them. But even if his parents ever offered to take him in and take care of him, Chris would refuse. He didn't want his last few years on earth to be living hell.

Unfortunately, he also knew Tim couldn't continue taking care of him forever. No matter what Tim might say about himself, he had his own life to live. Chris didn't feel he truly deserved the attention. After all, he was going to die anyway in a few years, no matter what Tim did for him today.

"Now, do you need anything else?'' Tim asked once more. "I've really got to run. Bob has us flying out of Midway instead of O'Hare, all the way on the other stupid side of the city.'' Tim was folding the grocery bags and putting them in the pantry.

"I'm fine. Go ahead and go. But could you take out the trash when you leave?''

"Sure thing, sugar. And remember, if you've got an emergency, my mother's number is right here by the phone.''

"Thanks. You're a peach.''

"You've got that right, hon.''

AN UNEXPECTED GUEST

AFTER Tim's departure, Chris set himself up comfortably on the living room couch, propped up slightly with pillows, with a pitcher of ice water on the coffee table and the Dracula film ready to run in the VCR. But now he realized the movie would have to wait. He was likely to zap in and out of consciousness for the next several hours, and at the present moment he was already drifting. He tried for a while to keep his eyes open, but the effort was too great, and soon enough his lids were falling and his eyeballs were rolling up in their sockets. His heart was beating steadily and his breathing was regular. He let the remote control to the VCR slip from his fingers and onto the carpet, and then his head lolled back against the pillows. The Demerol had begun tugging at Chris's brain, pulling him down into the land of dreams. . . .

The next thing Chris knew, he was in total darkness, crowded close together with many other people. Around him, all was wet, and he realized he and the others were swimming underwater somewhere. He was unable to perceive the surface of the water, and got the impression that the place they were in was cavernous in size, perhaps completely filled with water. No matter where he turned, he bumped elbows with someone else. His vision was improving gradually, and he was able to make out shapes, which was when he realized he didn't have any elbows, or

15

any arms or legs for that matter. And the people around
him weren't people; they were giant creatures with rounded,
transparent outer shells protecting a dark interior mass. Chris
had seen these creatures somewhere before . . . he knew it
now; these things were different varieties of white blood
cells, each with two or three visible nuclei, and he was with
them down in his own bone marrow.

Some were granulocytes, some were monocytes, but most
seemed to be lymphocytes. Chris himself seemed to be a
lymphocyte. All the other cells were pushing at him from
all sides. They squeezed him out of the huge mass of white
blood cells and into a small blood vessel, where the crowding was less severe. In the next moment, he saw a granu-
locyte circle itself around a smaller approaching object,
envelop it with its milky skin, and then proceed to swallow
it inside and dispose of it. All around him swam multitudes
of red blood corpuscles, but they were looking pale, as if
they needed oxygen.

Chris saw all manner of strange foreign objects traveling
down the bloodstream: bacteria, viruses, and who knew
what else. He knew that he should be doing something about
them; he should be spraying them with antibodies so the
granulocytes and monocytes would eat them. But he felt
helpless, paralyzed. He was incapable of performing his
functions. All he could do was float through the bloodstream, watching everything go to hell.

Now he knew that all those cells crowded in the bone
marrow weren't lymphocytes after all, and neither was he.
They were all lymphoblasts, leukemia cells. Chris saw many
more of them floating alongside him now through the
plasma. None had the nicely rounded outer shape of a lymphocyte; they were all jagged-edged, looking damaged and
corrupted. Some were already splitting into two cells,
though they weren't supposed to. These lymphoblasts were
too young to be reproducing, too immature, yet they continued doing it, regardless of the consequences. They had
already filled up the bone marrow and were now traveling
all around the body, to places where they didn't belong,

crowding out all the other blood cells and keeping them from doing their work.

Chris could feel his body stretching, pulling him apart. One of his nuclei had begun separating from the others. Soon he would be making another lymphoblast just like himself and letting it loose on the blood to wreak havoc. The pull was getting stronger. He was snapping apart, but some of him was going with the new lymphoblast, which presently wrenched itself away from him and floated out to join the others. . . .

Chris's eyes sprang open, and he suddenly found himself back on the couch in his living room, groggy and not altogether there, but back to reality nonetheless. That had been one strange dream, but not unlike others he'd experienced while under the influence of Demerol.

Chris was thirsty, and drank half a glass of water. He saw by the clock on the VCR that he'd been asleep for nearly two hours, though it felt like less. It was past time to fix some lunch already, if he had the energy to get up. Then, provided he felt awake enough, he'd eat his lunch while watching *Dracula, Prince of Darkness*. But first he decided to continue resting on the couch for awhile. Lunch could always wait. . . .

Orderlies in blue gowns were wheeling Chris down the hallway. He lay on his back on the bed, mesmerized by the fluorescent light panels as they whizzed by overhead.

"What's going on?" he asked. "What happened?"

The orderlies gave no answer but continued staring ahead as they maneuvered the bed around the corner and into a private room. One person, a female nurse, remained behind with Chris while the others left. She clutched his wrist, checking his pulse. The lines on her face deepened.

The doctor walked in. He asked the nurse for Chris's stats, and the nurse told him she couldn't find a pulse.

"Nonsense!" said the doctor. He plugged his stethoscope into his ears, ripped open Chris's shirt, and tapped the end of his instrument along Chris's chest, listening to the heartbeat and the wheezing of the lungs. "Nurse!"

"Yes, Doctor?"

"Give me your arm."

"Yes, Doctor."

The nurse held out her arm. The doctor grabbed her by the forearm and thrust her wrist into Chris's face.

"This man needs blood," he said.

Then Chris bit into the nurse's arm, finding some nice, full arteries. The nurse stood by, stoic as she performed her duty. Chris sucked on the wound, drawing her blood into himself, gulping it as it spurted down his throat like the thin stream of a drinking fountain.

"Go on," urged the doctor. "Drink!"

The nurse let out a small moan, as if she were about to faint. Chris could feel her arm growing weak. Her blood pulsed ever faster, until finally she collapsed. The doctor caught her, removed her arm from Chris's teeth, and set her into a nearby chair.

"It's not enough!" shouted the doctor. "My God, it's not enough!"

Chris lapped up the blood that had spilled over his chin.

"Here!" The doctor rolled up his sleeve and offered his arm to Chris. "Take this."

Chris bit down hard, puncturing a large, juicy vessel. The hair on the doctor's arm tickled Chris's nose as he sucked out the blood. He drank to the fullest, slurping noisily, clutching the muscular arm that had been offered to him. Finally, the doctor collapsed as well and fell away to continue bleeding on the floor, joining the pool of blood that was still dripping from the nurse's arm.

Suddenly, Chris found himself feeling much better. He got up from the bed, wiped his face with some gauze, washed his hands in the sink, tucked in his shirt, and walked from the room, continuing down the hall and out of the hospital, into the waiting night. . . .

* * *

When Chris woke up again, the sun had set. The lights in his apartment reflected off the front window, keeping hidden what lay in the darkness beyond.

"What time is it this time?" he mumbled to himself, finally focusing on the VCR and finding it was nine o'clock.

The last thing he could remember, he had been about to fix lunch; then he must have fallen back asleep and dreamed once more—yet another vampire dream!

This was getting to be a little strange. Although Chris loved vampires, he was hard-pressed to recall ever having dreamed of becoming one before last night. The other odd thing was that these dreams weren't nightmares but good cathartic dreams, the kind that left him feeling better afterward. While Chris didn't mind the catharsis, it bothered him that it had come only after his dream-self had killed two people. He remembered, too, that in his first dream last night, the older vampire had attacked his parents as well as a doctor. That, at least, made a sick kind of sense. Chris's parents had practically disowned him, and by now he had no great affection for his doctors, who seemed to do nothing but make him feel worse. Chemotherapy, for one, was not fun, and any doctor who ordered or performed bone marrow aspirations deserved whatever pain a vampire might be able to inflict upon him. The mere thought of a bone marrow aspiration made Chris's butt sore. No wonder he was turning into a vampire in his dreams. In his current shape, it was the only way he could extract his revenge on sadistic doctors and uncaring parents.

A pair of headlights shone through the front window as a car pulled up in front of the building. Chris sat up on the couch to take a look. It was a pizza delivery car, and the driver was getting out and walking straight for Chris's door. The delivery boy disappeared from his line of vision right as the doorbell rang.

"Just a minute," Chris said. He got up from the couch carefully and walked to the door stiff-legged and groggy.

Opening the door, he found a lanky redheaded teenager holding a ten-inch square pizza box.

"That'll be eight dollars," said the delivery boy.

"I didn't order any pizza."

"Isn't this 1425 West Nelson, apartment one?"

"Sure, but—"

"We even called to confirm it—" The delivery boy broke off and abruptly shifted his gaze to some point beyond Chris's shoulder, his mouth agape. Chris turned around to see what the guy was staring at.

It was a half-naked young woman.

"I ordered the pizza," she said. She stood in the doorway to the bedroom, leaning against the door frame, clad loosely in an open bathrobe of Chris's. Her small, firm breasts had pushed aside the folds of the robe and stood out, displaying a small tan line. She sauntered across the living room to the entryway, past Chris, and handed the pizza boy a ten-dollar bill. "Keep the change." She gave the boy a wolf's grin as she shut the door in his face.

Chris stood there holding the pizza, trying to figure out if he knew this woman.

"What am I doing here, you're about to ask," she said. Now the wolf's grin was directed at Chris.

"That's about right." Chris thought he recognized her from somewhere. He wondered if she were on TV, or if perhaps she was one of his many faceless co-workers from the financial services company. Not having been to work in weeks, Chris figured he could easily have forgotten a few of them. Somehow, however, he couldn't picture this girl wearing "professional dress," the conservative outfit working women had adopted as if it were part of a national dress code. No, this woman looked like one of the club denizens Chris had run into when he used to be able to go out dancing.

"Don't worry, Chris. Everything's all right. I'm here to help you."

"How do you know my name?" he demanded.

She ignored his question.

Her short boyish hair was sheared a half-inch long on

one side and dyed the flat black tone preferred by the ul-
trahip. She wore thick black eyeliner and mascara along
with dark red lipstick, but she was butch enough that even
Chris found her attractive. He was surprised, though, to see
she was tan wherever her skin was showing; most of these
late-night ghouls cultivated the ashen corpse look. Chicago
suffered no dearth of her kind. Among his friends, Chris
jokingly referred to them as New-Waveos Rancheros, although he secretly found them interesting and perhaps even
envied them a little. He enjoyed listening to their favored
high-grade industrial doom-and-gloom music, but knew he
could never adopt their fashion without laughing himself
silly. He could never get away with it, not with his Bright
Irish Lad's face . . . which he reminded himself he no longer
had.

"Listen, you can see that I'm sick. I don't know what
you're doing here, but I'm too exhausted to play games. If
you don't get out of my apartment right now, I'm going to
call the police."

She closed the robe back over her breasts and tied it in
place around her waist.

"I'm serious," Chris continued. "So get dressed and
beat it, will you? And take your pizza with you." He set
the box down on the coffee table, while the girl followed
him into the living room.

She laughed. "The pizza's for you, silly!"

"I didn't ask for any pizza, and I didn't ask for you,
either."

"Yes you did."

"When! What the hell are you talking about?"

Chris realized he hadn't locked the front door after Tim
had left. Tim should have thought of doing that himself.
Chris was in no condition to deal with people who wandered
in off the street.

"You must remember." Her smirk was very cool.

"I—I'm not sure," Chris said finally. He still couldn't
rule out having met her, somewhere.

"Come on, Chris, I said I'm here to help."

"Help, how? Did Tim send you over?" Chris wouldn't be surprised if she turned out to be a friend of Tim and Bob's. Maybe he had even met her at last year's Screamfest.

"You don't remember last night?"

Last night? "Frankly, no." Now Chris was getting scared. What indeed had he done last night?

She was staring straight at Chris with black, glistening eyes like those of a great hungry bird, or perhaps a bat.

"Now you do," she commanded.

Chris felt as if he'd been struck by a thunderbolt.

The cloud of uncertainty was suddenly lifted from his mind, and he knew exactly who she was, exactly what she was doing in his apartment, exactly what had happened the night before, exactly what those bruises were on his neck, and exactly why he'd been dreaming dreams of vampires.

MORDUS SECUNDUS

LAST night there had been a knock on the door.

Chris went to answer it, only to find a strange woman on the other side who looked even stranger through the fisheye lens of the peephole. With the chain still on it, he opened the door a few inches and asked her what she wanted. In her arms she clutched a rumpled paper bag. She said Tim Duffy had sent her over with a load of groceries.

"Since he and Bob are leaving for Houston tomorrow, he said he didn't have the time to come over himself," she explained.

That sounded legitimate enough, since Tim and Bob were indeed finally making that trip to Houston, so he unlocked the chain and invited her in.

She smiled pleasantly as she crossed the threshold and said, "Thank you." She headed straight for the kitchen, set down her bundle, and proceeded to remove from it two cans of tomato soup, a box of crackers, and a cellophane-wrapped package of liver. The last thing she grabbed from the sack was a videotape in a plastic case.

"I brought you one of your favorite movies," she said as Chris joined her in the kitchen. He sat on a bar stool and picked up the tape to examine it.

"*Dracula, Prince of Darkness.*" He looked at her quizzically. "How did you know this was one of my favorite movies?"

"Tim told me."

Her answer made him suspicious. Tim certainly knew of Chris's fascination with vampires, but Chris seriously doubted Tim could remember the specific title of a film that wasn't well known outside the circle of horror movie buffs, much less request that this woman rent it for Chris's pleasure. Tim had always tried to disabuse Chris of his vampirish tendencies.

"Anyway, I'm Beth."

"Chris," he offered. He shook her hand and found it chilly; she'd just come in from outside, yet Chris knew it was a warm, muggy evening with no breeze to speak of. At least that's what they'd said on the six o'clock news. "How do you know Tim?"

"I met him at mass."

This answer made him doubly suspicious, and with the smirk Beth now had on her face, Chris didn't believe it for a second. She didn't look like the type of woman one would find at mass, unless it were ever held in the cavernous depths of the Smart Bar at Cabaret Metro at one o'clock in the morning. Beth seemed far too hip to be Christian, and Catholic was out of the question. At best, she might be a born-again Bauhaus fan.

"Come on, who are you, really?"

It was then that Beth turned to look Chris in the eye. He found himself gazing, utterly rapt, into her dark luminous pupils. The smirk remained on her face but seemed more sympathetic than before. Chris felt he could trust her. She would tell him nothing but the truth.

"My name *is* Beth," she maintained. "But I don't really know Tim Duffy. I've come because you need me, Chris. I'm a vampire, and I'd like to make you one."

"I see." Chris was laconic. If it weren't for her eyes, he would be convinced she was crazy. Vampires didn't exist, and that was that. Except her eyes kept pulling him in deeper, and the very fact he couldn't look away from her told him something was afoot.

"Look at this," said Beth, taking out a small hand mirror

and holding it up to her face. "See if you can find my reflection."

Chris turned the mirror every which way, but found very little of Beth reflecting back at him. The coating of lipstick on her lips hung in the air beneath faint black wisps of mascara, but other than that he saw nothing but an empty shirt, open at the top where Beth's neck should have been.

"Well, fuck me!" Faced with this evidence, Chris felt compelled to believe her.

"Notice the fangs." Beth raised her upper lip in what looked like a painful grin, and displayed her pair of long, pointed canines. "You've already felt my skin. Cool, isn't it? Roughly room temperature, I'd say. I'm cold-blooded, like a lizard. I go out only at night, like a predator of the desert, searching for moisture. But what I drink is blood, and unlike a lizard, I can live forever. Unlike you in your present state, correct?"

"Yeah." Chris remained transfixed. Not only was Beth telling him the absolute truth, but Chris found himself unable to lie himself, as if she were Wonder Woman wrapping him with her golden rope. He couldn't escape, but strangely didn't wish to.

"How long did they give you?" asked Beth.

"Five years max."

"And you'll be ready to die then, right?"

"Are you kidding?"

"How do you like being sick all the time?"

"Oh, it's peachy."

"How do you like being alone?"

"It sucks."

"Please, Chris, let's have none of your mordant wit. This is serious. Now I want to know what you think your chances are of finding a lover in the few years you have left."

"Roughly, zero."

"What sort of a family life do you have?"

"None whatsoever. My father hates me, and my mother is afraid of my father. I wouldn't be surprised if she hates me, too."

"That's rather harsh, don't you think?"

"No."

"At least you're looking forward to going back to work, aren't you?"

"You're crazy."

"Don't you like being in financial services?"

"It's the worst."

"Do you mean to tell me you didn't enjoy being a customer service representative?"

"No way."

"Talking on the phone all day? Straightening out your cardholders' problems? Making all those accounts nice and tidy?"

"I told you what I thought of it."

"There must be something you'd like to do instead."

"Sure, travel."

"After your insurance has run out and you've gone into debt paying your medical bills, how much money do you think you'll be able to scare up for traveling?"

"Zilch."

"Which means you'll have to spend the rest of your short life in Chicago."

"I suppose."

"Don't you think that's unfair? A young man like you, twenty-two years old, condemned never to see the world, while your more fortunate peers snort some cocaine and go flying off to Rome on their mother's gold card just so they can eat an American hamburger at an Italian McDonald's? Where's the justice in that? That's a rhetorical question— no need to answer."

"Thanks."

"What you need is eternal life."

"If it hadn't been for that mirror, I'd be thinking that you're a very clever insurance salesman."

"That's the idea. I have to try to sell it to you, Chris. I'm not going to force you to buy a policy. Don't you see it's for your own good?"

"To become a vampire? How would that do me any good?"

"Eternal life, eternal youth, no more leukemia, no more worries. You'll look like yourself once more. You'll be very difficult to destroy, and as long as you learn how to survive, as long as you play by the rules, as long as you use a little common sense, as long as you watch your back, you can live as long as you like. No more five-year death sentence. No more chemotherapy, do you understand? Disease can't kill vampires. Not leukemia, not syphilis, not AIDS. No more common cold, no more hay fever. A slight allergy to garlic, yes, but you can exist with that."

"I admit it does sound tempting."

"Tempting! Are you kidding? It's literally the chance of a lifetime. Allow me to change you into one of us. What have you got to lose?"

Chris couldn't answer; she was right. He would miss nothing of his present existence. His parents wouldn't even notice he was gone. Tim could get on with taking care of Bob. Chris wouldn't have to deal with the idiots at work.

"See? You're the perfect candidate. Why else would I have come to you? Besides, you've always wanted to be a vampire."

"How do you know that?" Chris realized it was true; ever since he was a kid he'd fantasized about it.

"That's what you said to your friend Emilio two or three months ago. Remember the conversation you had with him?"

Chris suddenly recalled the conversation perfectly. He had presented to Emilio all the benefits of being a vampire and how much more romantic and exciting it would be than this silly human existence. Emilio had thought Chris was playing devil's advocate, but Chris had spoken from conviction. Of course, he hadn't honestly believed at the time there were such things as vampires, but the fact they existed didn't necessarily rule out the arguments in their favor.

"You're right," said Chris. "I know you're right. But I

could never kill anybody. I don't think I could make it as a vampire.''

"Who do you think we are, the Manson family? You've read *Dracula*, naturally; don't you know it takes three bites to turn a human into a vampire? Well, why should we bite everyone three times and make more vampires? Too many vampires, and everyone will be after us. Either that, or they'll want to join us. We try not to make new vampires. It's part of our code. For feeding, all we need is to bite the victim once on the neck. They'll forget they were ever bitten, and the wound will heal more rapidly than usual so that it's virtually gone. We don't have to kill our food. I've been a vampire for ten years now, and I've not once had to kill anybody.''

"Then how can you be sure about this eternal life business?''

"Chris, I've met some who are over a thousand years old. Of course, no vampire can remain undead forever, but even a thousand beats twenty-seven any day, which is as much as you might be able to expect if you don't let me change you.''

"Okay, you've got me, so to speak.''

"Got you? You're hardly mine to get. I can't make you do something you don't want to do. That is, I could, but it would practically be rape. I'm not going to take you by force. You have to come willingly—but see, you are already. You've always wanted to be a vampire. You've admitted to that. It's there for the taking. All you have to do is reach out and grab it.''

"All right. Come on, let's do it. I want you to bite me.''

"All three times?''

"Yes, of course.''

"Only checking. But you must realize, it will take three nights to finish the job. I chose this weekend to come to you because your friend Tim will be leaving town tomorrow. The process won't be disturbed.''

"Fine. Let's just do it.''

"That's my Chris. I knew you'd come through. I think

you'll enjoy it. It's a fun way to meet boys.''

"That sounds excellent.''

Beth released Chris from her probing gaze. Then she cooked up the liver she'd brought—''To feed your blood,'' she said. Beth made him eat the liver, and then they went into Chris's bedroom.

Chris had never gone to bed with a woman before, but Beth was masculine enough that he could tolerate it. They stripped and lay on the bed together, but there was little passion before she finally plunged her razor-sharp teeth into his neck and began to suck his blood. Chris squirmed in ecstatic pleasure as his blood flowed down her gullet, though he found Beth to be cold and methodical in her sucking.

Chris's last thought before he passed out was that Beth was probably a lesbian herself.

The entire memory of last night came back to Chris in a flash, where before it had been locked away. Beth had made certain he wouldn't remember. No one remembered being bitten by a vampire the first time, she had said. That was how they could get away with biting so many people without getting caught. It was all a trick of hypnosis, an art the vampires had apparently mastered.

"See, Chris? You remember perfectly well who I am.''

Chris nodded. He was speechless, but unafraid.

"You know why I've come.''

Again Chris nodded.

Beth made Chris eat as much of the pizza as he could manage, to feed his blood once more. Then she asked, ''Shall we?''

"Yes!'' Chris's reply was emphatic.

Smiling sweetly, wide enough to show her sharp canine teeth, Beth motioned toward the bedroom. Chris walked ahead of her and lay down on the bed, eager for what was to come. He thought it amazing how he had gone all day without realizing what had happened to him the night before. So it was true vampires didn't have to kill their victims, but simply bite them once and mesmerize them into ignorance. This Chris could live with, especially considering the pleasure he'd be giving his victims as he bit them and drew blood from their veins.

Beth reached into a canvas book bag she had brought and pulled out several lengths of rope.

"Wait a minute," said Chris as she approached. "What are you doing?"

"Calm down. Before I bite you again, I must tie you down. Otherwise, you'll become violent. You would go out and harm others, and likely cause injury to yourself as well. Once I bite you, you'll have to remain secured to your bed until I return tomorrow evening. This is simply part of the process."

"Are you sure?"

"Trust me." Beth's wolfish grin returned. "Now get yourself spread-eagled. Belly up."

On top of the rumpled bed covers, Chris shifted to the center of the bed, stretched out his arms, and spread his legs. Beth tossed the strands of rope on his chest; the rope's texture was soft and smooth, probably clothesline. She grabbed Chris's wrist and coiled a length of rope around it four times, then tied it up with a couple of firm square knots and tied the opposite end around the nearest bedpost. Chris yanked on it and found it was secure. When that was finished, Beth grabbed another length and performed the same procedure on Chris's other wrist until his arms were stretched taut. Chris thought she needn't be so thorough, but kept his mouth shut. He flexed his fingers and felt his wrist bulge against the bonds; there would be no wriggling free. When Beth had coiled and knotted a rope around his ankle, she pulled it firmly and stretched Chris's leg as far as it would go.

"That's a little uncomfortable," Chris complained.

"It's supposed to be, boy."

Beth secured the leg to the bedpost, then finished off the other one, stretching it as much as before.

"There," she said. "Now you aren't going anywhere, are you?"

"Guess not." Chris forced out a chuckle. Beth was right, of course, he would never be able to get himself out of this. But if it was for his own good as she'd said, then he supposed it was all right. He could put up with twenty-four hours of bondage. It wasn't as if she were going to torture him. He would receive a nice, pleasant bite and then probably fall asleep, and when he woke up, he wouldn't have to wait long until she returned.

Beth turned off the lights. While Chris's eyes tried to adjust to the sudden darkness, everything seemed black and cloudy. He felt Beth's weight depress the mattress as she sat beside him.

"Now open your mouth," she said.

"What fo—" As Chris spoke, Beth poked a leather ball into his mouth, part of the gag she was now fastening around the back of his neck.

"That's good enough."

Chris tried to speak despite the gag, but found all he could produce was a low, muffled buzz in his throat. His tongue coated the gag with saliva, and he found he couldn't help gnawing on it.

Beth's hands caressed Chris's body, squeezing his biceps, stroking his torso, following down his flank to his toes and back up again, until they clutched his hardening penis.

"You're enjoying this, aren't you? Well, enough teasing. I'm not here to take advantage of you."

Chris felt her breasts press down against his chest as she stretched out on the bed, placing one of her legs in between Chris's widespread thighs, the other dangling off the edge of the mattress. Beth reached up and stroked the few wisps of hair that were left on his head, planting a chaste kiss on his lips. Chris felt the sharp edge of her fingernails as her fingers made their way down to his neck, poking and prodding until they found the right blood vessel.

Beth's bite this time was swift and deep, but the initial pain quickly dissipated, leaving in its wake the throbbing, intense sensations Chris remembered from the night before. His heart beat faster as it pumped the blood out of his body.

Some of it was trickling, warm and wet, down his neck, but Beth seemed to be getting most of it. His excited cock was growing rigid against Beth's cool pelvis. He moaned against the gag, thinking to himself, Oh, yeah! Come on! Deeper, harder! Suck me, baby! Suck my fucking blood!

Chris grew dizzier and dizzier by the minute. The pleasure was growing too intense. Reflexively, he pulled against the bonds, but to no avail. If his arms were free he would try to push Beth away. Surely this was enough blood! Chris couldn't take it anymore; it had become exquisite torture. But Beth went on. Chris's toes and fingers curled up as he flexed his wrists and ankles; these were the only parts of his body he could move besides his neck, which he was keeping perfectly still. He could imagine Beth's cold teeth ripping through his skin if he were to thrash his head to the side. Because of the gag, he could only breathe through his nose, and his breath grew quicker as she went on and on drinking and lapping up blood with her tongue. By now whenever he exhaled he let out a feeble moan, thinking, Stop! It's too much! Don't do this to me! It's enough blood, already!

Beth held his head steady in her hands.

Chris felt himself ejaculate a long, wet stream onto his stomach as he screamed against the gag. The world began to drift away and he finally passed out, while Beth finished her private feast.

SOME OF YOUR BLOOD

WHEN Chris awoke, his eyes sprang open and his brain immediately kicked into gear. He breathed in deeply, but the air came in only through his nose, because something had been stuffed in his mouth. He tried stretching his limbs, but found they were stretched already, and tied to the bedposts. He was completely nude, and cold as well.

In a sudden panic, Chris tried to remember what he had done last night, but his mind was a blur. The last thing he could remember was the face of the pizza boy holding up a box of pizza and demanding money. After that, nothing.

The pizza boy must have done it. Chris hadn't ordered any pizza. When he refused to pay, the boy must have rushed in and subdued him. Chris would have been an easy target in his weak condition, and wouldn't have been able to put up much of a fight. It was a cruel joke to play on someone. Chris had lain here all evening, sleeping bound to his bed, gagged with something that tasted like leather. Of course, it *was* leather, a leather ball gag of the sort Chris had seen advertised in gay magazines. But Chris didn't own one; he wasn't into bondage. Why would a pizza boy go around carrying a leather ball gag?

Maybe Chris wasn't the first one the kid had done this to. It was probably some kick of his, finding vulnerable customers, especially unruly ones, muscling his way in, and somehow forcing them onto the bed and tying them up.

33

People would be unlikely to report him because they would be too embarrassed—especially if all his victims were male. But when Chris got out of this mess, the first thing he'd do was call the police and have them arrest the guy. If the police wouldn't do anything, he'd call the pizza place and inform the manager of his employee's escapades. At least the kid would be fired.

Chris yanked at his bonds, to little effect. It was impossible. No way could ever be found to get free from these ropes. The pizza boy had certainly known what he was doing. But if Chris ever did get free, he suddenly decided, he'd skip going to the police or the manager and simply kill the stupid kid instead.

It wouldn't be too hard to track him down. All he had to do was catch him working at the pizza parlor some evening and follow him once he'd gotten off work. Then, an approach from behind, a tap on the shoulder, a turn of the pizza boy's head, and a flick of the straight razor in Chris's hand, and it would be all over. The guy's blood would come streaming out in a nice thin line across the throat, then spill over down the neck, despoiling the open collar of his shirt—all this before the body hit the ground. Maybe then Chris could get a taste of some of that pizza boy sauce, some of that gushing red death juice.

Chris growled against the leather gag, pulling hard on both arms at once, trying to loosen up the rope. He tried again three more times, and failed. This stuff was tight. Aside from wiggling his fingers and toes, all he succeeded in doing was bucking his torso up off the bed using his back and buttock muscles, but that did him no good whatsoever.

I've got to get out of here, he thought. I've got to get that pizza boy. Got to have some of that blood. *Some of your blood, boy, that's all I want.*

Perhaps the kid had seen the gleam in Chris's eye and known what it was he wanted. Then somehow, the kid had gotten the better of him. That must have been what had happened. If so, the pizza boy would have gone to the authorities. *I tied him up, Officer. He was about to kill me!*

That meant they would be here soon, and they would untie him. Several policemen would be present, surely, and they would think Chris wouldn't try anything against that kind of numbers. But before they got the cuffs on him, he could swipe at the first, and maybe get the second, before they knew what hit them. And there would be plenty of blood. Plenty of blood for everybody, though today Chris felt disinclined to share the drippings.

Testing the bonds once more, Chris realized it hadn't necessarily been the pizza boy who'd done this to him. If that were the case, no police would be coming to set him free. The culprit would likely return, either to undo the ropes or to take further advantage of Chris. That sure was sick of him, whoever he was, to want to molest someone suffering from leukemia. Something was wrong with this guy's brain.

Though, surprisingly, Chris felt stronger today, less sick in general. So far, he had taken no medication to his knowledge, yet he could feel no pain in his bones, much less the general fatigue and malaise he constantly had to put up with. Today, Chris felt aware, awake, alive, for the first time in a long time.

Of course, Chris realized, the man who'd tied him up could still be in the apartment. Chris couldn't see past the door to the bedroom. He moaned as loud as he could, trying to get the attention of anyone who might be out there.

If there was no one there, and if no one returned, he would have to wait a few days until Tim got back from Houston and looked in on him. Tim would quickly untie him, and then Chris could find a knife or a razor blade and slice open Tim's neck, because by then he'd be simply ravenous and it would take too long to call the pizza parlor and order a pizza boy.

Oh, I can taste it now, Chris thought. And just imagine how much blood Tim would have in that corpulent body of his! *Come on, man, some of your blood, that's all.*

If that failed, he could go down to a bar, or maybe a dance club, and find a suitable person there, perhaps two, or three, or more. It didn't matter who they were, only that they were alive and had some of that warm, salty red stuff pumping through their veins. Corner some guy in the bathroom, that would be easy. If there were no weapons at hand, break a mirror, grab a shard of glittery glass, then take the Nestea plunge, or a chugalug of blood. Find some empty beer pitcher somewhere and fill it with the guy's blood, then pour it down, letting it splash all over you like in the commercials on TV. If anyone asks, you tell them it's V-8. Then they'll slap their heads and say, "Aww, I could have had one!" And you'd say, "Yes, but I got here first. He's mine, all mine!" Then you bring what's left of the blood in the pitcher to the bar and ask the bartender to fix you a Bloody Mary, and you insist on Stoli because this is the ultimate Bloody Mary of all time, though in all likelihood it's a Bloody John or a Bloody Steve, knowing your predilections. And when he served it to you, it would taste damned good. Damned, bloody good, thank you very much.

Now, Chris thought, struggling against the bonds yet again, what the hell time is it and when do I get out of this?

The sun had gone down by the time Chris heard someone entering his apartment. The door slammed shut, sending a brief draft of cool air all the way into the bedroom. He could hear the soft padding of footsteps making their way across the living room carpet.

A young woman stood in the doorway. If it weren't for the curves of her figure, Chris might have mistaken her for a boy. Her black hair was short, but well coiffed and attractive against her dark skin. She wore a black, baggy sweatshirt and a distressed pair of blue jeans.

"So how's my Chris getting along today?" she asked with a smirk.

So she was the one who'd tied him up!

Chris growled, still gagged and immobile. This girl had better be careful, he thought. If she lets me loose, she's in for a big surprise. That delicate neck of hers won't last long. . . .

As she came closer, he tried once more to rip his arms away from the bedposts.

The girl laughed and began staring him down. Chris's eyes were locked in her gaze, and he found himself calming down. His breathing became more steady. He no longer felt like killing her.

"You remember me now, don't you, Chris?"

His memory came flooding back to him all of a sudden, and he knew this was the evening for the third bite from Beth, the bite that would transform him into a vampire.

Chris nodded. He knew now who she was.

"Don't worry, Chris. Be calm. Until I've finished biting you again, I won't be able to undo these ropes or remove your gag. You could still be dangerous and possibly hurt yourself. So just relax and lie still. It'll all be over before you know it."

Behind the gag, Chris smiled. He found once more that he trusted her implicitly. Beth must have been able to read his face despite the leather strip covering his mouth, because she said, "Your eyes have a nice smile."

Chris needed this third bite badly. He already had a great hunger for blood, a hunger he would never be able to fill as a human. Once he was transformed, everything would be fine.

Beth turned out the lights, but the bright moonlight shining through the bedroom window provided ample illumination. She pulled the sweatshirt up over her head, revealing no bra but two healthy-looking breasts. She didn't remove her jeans, but instead came over and sat down on the bed next to Chris.

This time Beth jettisoned the preliminaries and went straight to the biting. Her teeth glimmered wetly as her gaping mouth flew down and clamped onto Chris's neck, entering the skin through the same wound she'd made last night. She began sucking out the blood, and Chris felt the familiar sensations spread again throughout his body. Beth continued at it for a while, but it never quite reached the crescendo of the second bite. Chris sensed somehow that this third bite would be less practical and more ceremonial. She had to bite him, but not necessarily suck out all the rest of his blood, which would certainly happen if she repeated the lengthy suck of last night.

Beth finished and withdrew her fangs, a pleasurable sensation Chris had been unable to experience the other two times because he had passed out already. This time, however, he was fully aware. He could feel the blood already drying up on his neck as Beth smiled down at him with red lips.

Quickly, she unstrapped the gag and removed it from Chris's mouth, the leather ball wet and dripping with saliva. Chris took in a few deep breaths, but said nothing. Within a few minutes, Beth had untied all the ropes on his various limbs. He was free.

"What's going to happen after I'm one of you?" Chris asked. The thought had only then entered his head. "What do I do then?"

"Relax. We'll be there to help you."

Chris stretched his arms and legs. His knees and elbows had grown stiff after enduring an entire day of bondage. Joints popped and ligaments were pulled taut as he flexed his muscles.

But now, without warning, Beth was back at his neck, sucking more of his blood.

"Wait! What are you doing?" Chris found it painful to speak while her teeth were sunk in his throat.

Beth gave no answer, but continued on.

Chris's heart began beating uncontrollably as the blood disappeared from his veins. It seemed to grow faster every second until, suddenly, it sputtered a few times and then stopped. Chris felt himself breaking apart, the way he'd divided in two when he'd dreamed he was a lymphoblast. It seemed as if a part of himself were now missing, cast off like an extra skin. He found he was no longer breathing. But despite that and his silent heart, he was apparently partly alive.

Beth stopped drinking from Chris's neck and turned his

head to face her. She locked her eyes on his and told him, "Now it's your turn."

She climbed on top of him, straddling his waist, and pulled him up so he was propped up against the headboard. Using one of her sharp fingernails, she cut a deep slice down her chest, in the hollow between her breasts. Blood flowed forth, dripping down toward her navel.

"Come on, drink!" she commanded. She grabbed Chris's head and thrust it between her breasts.

Chris's tongue darted out and began lapping up the blood. Beth pressed him harder against her, and he found himself cupping his mouth around the wound and sucking deeply. Her blood flowed into his mouth, and he gulped it down eagerly.

Chris's heart began to come back to life, pumping tentatively at first, then beating with slow regularity. The more blood he drank, the healthier the beat became, until he was again breathing normally, deeply through his nose. As the air came in, Chris could now taste the blood he was drinking; it was sweet, salty, and bitter all at once.

"More," said Beth. "Drink more. Don't be afraid."

He clutched his arms around Beth's waist and kept feeding for many more minutes, until at last he was satiated and passed out, collapsing safely against the pillows.

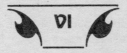

CHRIS GOES UNDERGROUND

CHRIS was vaguely awake as his body searched for a more comfortable position in which to sleep. He rolled on his side, but as he tried to curl up his knees struck the wall, and his shoulder met some surface above him. He backed away to allow more room, but his buttocks bumped up against the other wall behind him. Still half conscious, he inched forward, but once again his knees hit something. When he moved back this time, he could feel one wall against his backside while his knees stayed firm against the other.

Strangely, someone had put shoes on his feet.

His mind flickered slowly to awareness, but when he opened his eyes he saw darkness.

"Yeeow!"

Chris's eyes were in excruciating pain; like an idiot, he had gone to sleep still wearing his contact lenses. The stinging caused his eyes to tear up, yet the extra moisture did little good. He had to get to the bathroom and get these fucking things out and get them into a contact case. Even if morning was far off, Chris would never be able to get back to sleep. His eyes would keep him awake. It was the absolute pits.

Someone had turned on the air conditioner; the cold air was damp enough that he could feel it creep into his lungs.

Chris shivered as he rolled onto his back in the dirt.

41

In the dirt? Wait a minute, where am I?

Chris jolted up from where he lay, but his head ran into something hard, a wooden shelf or something.

"Ow! Shit!"

As he lay back down, small sprinkles of dirt fell onto his face, dislodged from the board above. His hand raced up to rub the bump on his head, but he banged his elbow into the side wall. He reached carefully behind his head and found another solid piece of wood a few inches away. Stretching his feet out, he felt yet another at the far end. His hands searched upward for what his head had smacked into, and confirmed that it was long and wooden with a glass insert . . . some kind of lid.

A lid, you dummy, and this is a coffin!

Chris's heart began to thump madly as if someone had given a few sharp turns to a giant key sticking out of his back.

They think I'm dead!

"Hey!" he shouted. "Hey, what is this! Get me out of here!"

Now wait a minute, he told himself. Settle down. Just hold your horses. Maybe you're in the back room at the funeral parlor, waiting for the ceremony. Then again, you could be in the middle of "services." If so, they're going to be in for a big surprise. Get your hands back up there and try the lid. See if it's locked shut. See if maybe you can get it open. That's it; now *push*!

The lid held fast, no matter how firmly Chris pressed against it. It was so close he had no leverage. All he succeeded in doing was dislodging more flecks of dirt, which fell down through a small crack onto his coat.

He was dressed in a smooth suit coat, he discovered, and a stiff shirt and a thin necktie, and he didn't need any light to know the shirt was white and the rest black. These were funeral clothes . . .

Vampire clothes.

Shit!

Finally, Chris was awake enough to remember what had

happened. That weird woman, Beth, had gone and done it. She'd bitten him three times, and now he was a vampire. Or so he'd been led to believe.

Chris's tongue felt its way along the upper ridge of his teeth, but found his canines were no larger than they had been before. His heart was beating, his breathing was okay, he wasn't dead; but he wondered, how could he ever tell if he was undead? He had no mirror to look into and see whether or not he cast a reflection, but no light could penetrate the confines of the coffin anyway, so it hardly mattered.

It was, Chris decided, within the realm of possibility that this girl who called herself Beth was playing some huge practical joke on him. No, not practical—*psychotic!* Just the sort of thing he might expect from a late-night club-going high-energy doomy-gloomy ghoul—a morbid, depraved, psychotic joke. After all, she had sucked his blood on three separate occasions, and if that wasn't psychotic . . .

But then, he had sucked hers.

If you suck mine, I'll suck yours.

"Hey! Hey, goddammit! Someone get me the hell out of here! The joke's over!" Chris yelled his loudest, the necktie constricting his throat, rubbing the sensitive bite marks. He pounded on the lid as best he could in the confining space, but only managed to create a cacophony that reverberated dully around the casket. His poundings were muted thumps. From the lack of resonance, he could tell he was packed tightly in earth on all sides. More bits of dirt trickled down through the crack, onto Chris's face, into his eyes already wracked with pain.

Goddammit!

Chris turned his head and tried to blink the dust from his eyes. They still stung like a son of a bitch. *To hell with it*, he thought, and carefully removed his contact lenses, damning them to the linty pocket of his suit coat. Only it wasn't his suit coat. He owned no suit like this. Beth must have picked it out especially for the occasion.

Chris was resting on his side now in a bed of earth that

covered the base of the coffin. His shoulder rubbed against the lid. Digging with his hands, he eventually found the wooden base beneath. It was solid. That was no way out, but he wondered suddenly if perhaps he could break the glass window above and claw his way to the surface. This time, though, he would protect his eyes before he caused any more damage. With a great deal of difficulty, he managed to squirm out of the suit coat and then covered his face with it.

Once Chris had found his target with his hand, he punched his fist firmly through the window, shattering the glass and causing a small shower of broken shards and dirt to fall. He had cut his hand, yet felt little pain. He could feel with his left hand that his right was sliced up and bleeding, caked with clods of earth.

He shook off the coat, shoving it into a corner of the coffin, and tried to examine his hand, but of course he could see nothing. Bringing it up to his lips, he stuck out his tongue and licked the wounds; the blood, however, was already coagulating.

That was strange. With his leukemia, it took forever for any wounds to heal because his blood lacked the necessary platelets, and even without leukemia, no one's wounds could begin to heal that fast. But then, the same thing had happened with the bite wounds on his neck. Chris should have bled to death after the first bite, yet there had been no blood on the pillow the next day, and he'd been alive. Beth had definitely done *something* to him.

Chris felt his face and found that his cheek and jaw bones were close to the skin. His face lacked the puffiness that had plagued him ever since beginning chemotherapy. Miraculously, he was losing his Cushingoid features.

As he felt his hand now, it seemed as if the bleeding had stopped and each of the long gashes along the back of his hand had closed up. He could feel them smoothing out, returning to normal, becoming once more undamaged skin.

But nothing about it was normal. No amount of reasoning could possibly explain what was happening to his body.

Little doubt existed in his mind now; he had indeed, incredibly, become a vampire.

Unless this is one of my Demerol dreams, he thought. But no, his situation lacked the surrealistic quality of those drug-induced reveries. All around him, everything within reach of his hands was undeniably real.

Down-to-earth.

I've got to get the fuck out of here.

Chris moved his head out of the way before he began digging at the dirt past the knocked-out viewing window. The dirt was packed hard enough that it made things difficult. He continued for only a few minutes before facing the reality that he was buried deep underground. Six feet under, no less.

"Hey, come on! Can anybody hear me?"

He heard nothing from outside. He could sense, somehow, that night had fallen.

Someone was tightening the giant key in his back once more. His heart ticked—thumped, rather—more rapidly, as he came to the realization that absolutely no means of escape could be found. One simply couldn't claw one's way through six feet of earth, no matter what the zombies in the movies did. This was the real world, dammit, and those kinds of things didn't happen.

I'm totally fucked!

Chris had snapped readily at Beth's bait, believed every word she'd said. He'd bought her whole story about vampires being so benign they only bit their victims once, while she'd found in Chris a regular nightly food source that she could dispose of at her convenience. So she'd locked Chris away in a coffin and lowered him into a grave, never to be seen or heard from again. She would have no reason to care if her victims lived past the burial. Even if they lived forever, trapped in a box, it wouldn't matter to her. Once she'd fed, that was it. The rest, as the Bard said, was silence.

The closeness of the space was bothering Chris ever more as the minutes wore on. He felt like the toad he'd buried alive when he was a kid, back at the old house on Racine

Avenue. He'd captured a toad in the garden and put it in a margarine tub. The toad had been large and warty, and filled up most of the tiny space without room to move around. Chris's mom had called from the house, wondering what he was doing out there in the garden. Quickly, before his mom could come out, he had dug a small hole in the earth and hid the plastic tub there, as the toad scraped the slippery sides with his feet. Chris couldn't have let his mom find the toad; she would have made him set it free, and she'd have warned him never to bring anything like that into Her House. She had appeared in the garden just as he'd finished filling in the hole. But she hadn't paid any attention to what he was doing; she'd asked him to come inside and help her with the dishes. Chris could hardly have refused, so reluctantly he had followed her into the house and set to work. By the time they had finished, he'd forgotten about the toad. Hours later when it had come back to him, he'd forgotten exactly where he'd dug the hole. He had gone out into the garden with a small trowel and dug wherever he could, but it had taken several hours to find the container. When at last he had unearthed it, the garden had looked like a disaster area, and when the lid was opened, he'd found that the toad had suffocated and was now quite dead.

A musty odor permeated the casket, an odor separate from that of the damp earth. When Chris scratched at the wood, he found it to be brittle. This was old, weathered lumber, dried out and cracking, though from its texture it seemed to have once been good-quality hardwood rather than pine. No one used wood for coffins anymore; they were all aluminum with polyester lining. Only paupers got wooden ones these days, but those were made of pine and lacked viewing windows; no one needed to view a pauper. Chris could feel shreds of coarse cotton still tacked to the sides of his coffin, remnants of the lining that had once graced the interior of the box and cushioned the previous occupant.

Beth had buried him in a used coffin.

Get me out of here *get me out of here GET ME OUT OF HERE!*

Chris knew yelling would be pointless. No one could hear, and if they did they would dismiss it as the wind.

The night was wearing on. It was almost as if he could feel the motions of the earth as it rotated, drawing the world farther into darkness. The moon would be high up in the sky by now; Chris had seen it last night, bathing Beth's dark skin in a cold blue light.

That fucking dyke bitch! This is her revenge against men. Probably a man made her a vampire and she's out to get all the rest of us while she's got the chance. (Oh come on, Chris, that makes no sense. If she were after men, you'd be the last guy on her list—well, second to last, next to Tim. You're thinking too hard. All she wanted was your blood.)

Which reminds me, I'm hungry.

Chris wondered what Beth had done with the other body, the one that had lain where Chris now lay. He wondered how long the missing corpse had occupied this domain— one hundred years? Perhaps it hadn't been a corpse at all. Perhaps it had been one of the undead, another vampire like himself. Perhaps the same trick had been pulled on it a hundred years ago and it had remained safely sealed away all this time, until Beth had dug it up and kicked it out.

Chris Callaway, you're an idiot!

He realized he had made a gigantic mistake.

No matter how tempting the idea had sounded, he should never have allowed Beth to turn him into a vampire. He was in way over his head, past the point of no return. How could he ever return from the grave?

Right then, he would have given his left nut to be back in his bed or on his couch with his leukemia, suffering from excruciating bone pain and being waited on hand and foot by Tim, but where at least he would be safe and sound. As it was, here in this tiny box, he was doomed.

Buried alive.

Or was that buried *undead*? But this was no time for semantics! He had to get a grip on himself.

Chris's eyes were feeling better. Now that he'd removed his contacts, his eyes seemed to be healing as well, like his hand. They were no longer as teary, and the puffy swelling seemed to have dissipated. But that was little consolation compared to the problem at hand.

He began to make out shapes in the darkness. He could identify his hands, and he looked down to see his feet in their shoes. It was another impossibility: seeing in the total absence of light. A quick scan of the coffin proved that no light was creeping in from anywhere. He seemed to be developing terrific night vision.

Whatever good that would do him stuck in this hole.

From off in the distance, above ground, Chris heard a brief noise, muffled and unrecognizable. It happened again, and yet again, until it began repeating itself with a certain regularity, finding a rhythm that seemed comfortable. This was no machine-generated noise; the lapses in the rhythm implied a human element.

Chris chose to ignore it; it couldn't have anything to do with him.

As the sound persisted, ticking away like a slow clock, it grew louder, until Chris, interested once more, could nearly recognize its source. It was a sharp, swift, slicing sound, like someone scraping the ground with a rake. But it sounded as if it were coming closer, heading toward the coffin.

It was someone digging with a spade!

Chris got his hopes up for a second, then realized the prospect was doubtful. It couldn't be someone coming to dig him out. Beth would never have told anyone where she'd buried her victim. If indeed the sound was digging, it was probably Beth digging a fresh grave nearby for some other lucky stiff.

Chris wondered if he would have to endure listening to this digging throughout eternity: a spade forever getting nearer, but never finding him. It would be torture.

He wondered what he'd been thinking when he had agreed to let Beth turn him into a vampire. Most likely, he had been spaced out on Demerol the whole time, ready to believe anything she said, ready to tell her anything she wanted to hear. The way her eyes had captivated him, she had probably hypnotized him into doing her bidding, making him think he was doing it willingly when in fact he was far more sane and rational than that.

The digging continued up above, and for the first time he thought he might be dug up.

But the thought wasn't necessarily reassuring. If vampires existed in the world, it only followed that vampire hunters would be around as well. If they had spied on Beth as she buried Chris, they would be able to find him and destroy him. He wondered if the people up there had brought along some wooden stakes and an axe to pound them home with and to cut off his head. It would be a fitting end to a perfect joke.

Chris would have laughed, if he weren't the butt. The whole thing had been well executed. He only hoped he wouldn't be.

The digging pressed on. It sounded as if they might strike him soon.

A spider skittered across Chris's face, making him gasp; he tried shooing it away with his hand, but failed to locate it even with his improved vision. It had probably disappeared into a crack somewhere.

The digging sounds grew nearer. Soon they were directly overhead.

Right as Chris realized someone actually was trying to unearth the coffin, a spade jutted down through the broken window—and would have cut off his head had the opening been wide enough.

They're going to kill me!

Chris screamed.

A sliver of moonlight slipped into the coffin.

"Here he is!" said a voice on the other side. It was a man's voice—the man with the spade.

"Don't kill me!"

Chris had a sudden, terrifying thought that it was his father, but knew that couldn't be true. Still, he had no problem picturing his own father driving a stake through his heart. Chris would rather remain buried alive for eternity than be discovered by his asshole father.

"I ain't gonna kill you," said the man's voice as if that were the funniest thing he'd heard all day.

"Step on it, guys. Get him out of there fast." This voice belonged to a woman. It was Beth.

At least it wasn't a vampire hunter, but Chris wondered what Beth wanted with him this time. Maybe she had decided she hadn't drunk enough of his blood already.

The scraping and digging continued in earnest, until Chris felt the coffin being lifted clumsily out of the ground, feet first. His body slid downward, and before he could catch himself his head had banged into the top of the box. Then he was tipped back level again, up and out of the grave, and set to rest on a sideways-slanting pile of dirt.

Slowly, the lid was opened.

Against the starry, moonlit night sky, four interesting and interested faces, belonging to Beth and three males roughly the same age as himself, stared down at Chris.

Chris was too petrified to speak.

With a smile Beth reached out, offering her hand. Shaking, Chris grasped her hand with his own, and she pulled him up, helping him climb out of the coffin. He looked warily at the faces surrounding him as he rose to his feet, not knowing what to expect from this bevy of strangers.

Chris saw he hadn't been buried in a graveyard at all. Where they stood was a vacant lot infested with weeds that sat behind an old brick warehouse that also appeared vacant. Turning to look toward the city's skyline, he could tell he was roughly due west of downtown, probably somewhere in the area of Maxwell Street. In the immediate vicinity were lots barren of anything except weeds and garbage, and a few warehouses similar in size and character to the one looming behind them. The moon, nearly full, sat in the sky directly above the roof. It was a cool, pleasant evening.

"How's it going?" said one of the men, a tall Hispanic fellow with a short flattop haircut. He, like Beth, offered a smile, displaying his sharp fangs in a subtle, endearing manner. He extended his hand, and Chris shook it, amazed at the strong grip. "I'm Luis."

"C-Chris," he said with a stammer.

Chris could see a small rabbit scurrying now, about fifty yards away in an unlighted lot near a crumbling bridge. It was amazing that he could discern such distant details in this darkness, but even more fantastic was that his contact lenses were gathering dust in the pocket of the suit coat, which still sat rumpled in the casket. For the first time in his life, he had perfect vision, perhaps better than perfect, superhuman.

The other two men shook hands with Chris, introducing themselves as Del and Jamie, and he began to relax at last. He felt a smile begin to take over his face, and as it did, his canine teeth suddenly extended themselves; when he relaxed his smile, the fangs drew back to their normal places among the rest of his teeth.

Hot damn, they were retractable!

"Sorry you had to go through that," Beth said, motioning toward the coffin. "But it happened to each of us when we made the transition."

"Now you tell me." Chris's anger was tempered with his relief at being released.

"I'm not allowed to speak of it ahead of time. It's all part of the ritual. Like I said, we've all had the same experience."

"Then you're all vampires."

"Of course," said Beth. "And now so are you. These guys are friends of mine from the Underground. But enough of this standing around out here. Let's go inside."

Chris followed Beth and Luis into the warehouse, while Del and Jamie carried in the coffin.

SOME NEW FRIENDS

"I know you'll find it hard to believe, but you're looking great." Beth stood in front of Chris and surveyed him from head to toe. "I wish you could see yourself, but as you've no doubt realized, you're going to have a little trouble with mirrors from now on. Still, you're turning out splendidly, and it's a shame you can't see how good you look. Oh well, there's nothing you can do about it now. So how do you feel?"

"I can't believe it. I feel perfect! It's almost as if I've never been sick!" By poking around his torso, legs, and face, he could tell much of the fat he'd gained in recent weeks had disappeared during his stay in the coffin, which Beth had told him had lasted twenty-four hours—most of it thankfully spent in slumber. His pain had vanished entirely; he felt rejuvenated. "I bet I could do a hundred push-ups."

"How much do you want to bet?" asked Beth, amused.

"I don't have any money."

Beth extended her hand. "Gentlemen's bet." They shook hands. "Go on, Chris, prove it."

Chris shrugged sheepishly, wondering if he really could do it. "Okay, here goes."

Chris lay prone on the Oriental rug and got into position, supported by his toes and arms. As recently as two days ago, he could never have even attained this position. He had tried exercising while he was sick, but all he could manage were a few brief walks. He'd been unable to perform push-ups, sit-ups, knee bands, or any other major calisthenic. His arms had been too weak to support him during push-ups. He could lock his arms in place at the very beginning, but once he began bending them at the elbows he would invariably collapse. He hadn't been able to perform such simple exercises for months now.

"Go on," Beth said, "don't be afraid."

Carefully, Chris allowed his arms to bend, and found to his amazement that his muscles actually worked! There was no pain, no weakness, no dizziness. He was easily able to lower his body toward the ground, nearly close enough to touch his nose to the rug. Then, miraculously, he pushed himself back up, with little effort. He had hardly felt a thing.

"I don't believe this," he muttered.

"That's only one, Chris. I thought you were going to do a hundred."

His confidence renewed, Chris proceeded with the exercise, increasing the pace so that he was pushing himself up and down like a pro. He felt his arm muscles tighten and loosen in rhythm, working like well-oiled pistons in some great machine. He breathed calmly and steadily, exhaling and inhaling comfortably. Overhead, Beth counted out loud, and Chris was stunned to find that before long he was up to fifty, then sixty, then seventy, and he hardly even felt tired. He'd never done this many push-ups in his life, not even before taking ill.

"Ninety-seven . . . ninety-eight . . . ninety-nine . . . one hundred. Congrats!"

Chris sprang to his feet, only mildly perspiring. "I bet I could do even more."

"That's all right. You have nothing to prove to me."

"I guess not."

Chris sat with Beth and Luis in the spacious living area of the converted warehouse. The whole of the building had not been made habitable; the second and third stories remained vacant, as did much of the first floor. The place was rather large, and Beth and her friends had no need for all that space.

The old coffin in which Chris had been buried now sat against the far wall, where Del and Jamie had set it down.

"Where did you get that crappy coffin?" Chris asked.

" 'That crappy coffin' happens to be an antique. I got it at the White Horse Gallery on South Halsted, and if I had bought it instead of stealing it, it wouldn't have come cheap. They had several others, but yours was the only one with a window. I thought it was nice. I'll get Luis to fix that before tomorrow."

Luis was punching out a number on the phone; it seemed to be long-distance. He sat waiting for an answer with his eyes rolled up at the ceiling and his lips in a pout.

"You look nervous," Beth said to Chris.

"I'm hungry." Chris was ravenous, but he didn't want to sound more than marginally hungry. He didn't want them to think he was complaining.

"Thirsty." Beth corrected him. "You won't be eating anymore, only drinking."

"Yeah, I know."

"Ah! But what exactly do you know? A lot of what you think you know about us may not necessarily be true. I know you've read novels and seen movies, but most of those have little or nothing to do with reality. From this moment on, you'll be starting from scratch. You've got to learn how to survive, as if you'd just popped out of your mother's womb."

"Only you're my mother this time," Chris interjected.

"After a fashion." Beth was amused.

"Fucking phone," muttered Luis as he repunched the long number over again.

"My point is," Beth went on, "don't expect to know everything by instinct; most of it has to be learned. By now you've accumulated twenty-two years of human experience, and you'll have to unlearn much of it if you want to succeed as one of us. You'll find it difficult at first. You're adjusting to an entirely new life-style, and an altogether different physiology. It will take time, and the first thing you'll have to master is patience. At this point, if you were to act without thinking, you could very easily destroy yourself. Caution should be your watchword, now and forever.''

Forever. Chris pondered the meaning of the word. It seemed impossible that he might actually exist throughout eternity in this human form, which he was beginning to understand was no longer very human. His arms tingled from the exercise, as if they were begging for more.

Luis spoke rapidly into the receiver, then hung up the phone. ''No answer at Temsik's,'' he told Beth. ''I went ahead and left a message on his machine. He's supposed to call us back.''

''Great,'' Beth said in exasperation. ''By the time he calls, we'll be gone. I'll have to call him again tomorrow. Or, Luis, why don't you call him back and leave another message? Tell him we're bringing him a new recruit tomorrow night.''

''I don't think he'll like that very much,'' said Luis. ''Springing it on him all of a sudden and everything.''

''It hardly matters whether he likes it or not. He has an obligation. Anyway, he owes us one after sending us Del, if you read me.''

''Gotcha. But would you mind making the call yourself? I wouldn't want Temsik pissed off at me. He'll be less mad at you, anyway.''

''Sure, you're right. I'll do it.''

Chris had been gazing with interest at one of the bookcases, and although he had heard Beth and Luis's conversation, their words hadn't registered in his brain. All Chris had gathered was that this Temsik fellow wasn't anyone to dick around with, but he failed to realize what it had to do with him. At his former job, where he and his co-workers had been packed tightly together in tiny modular cubicles, he had learned to tune out selectively other people's nearby conversations and had carried that habit over into his private life. He was very good at hearing a person's entire lengthy discourse without actually listening to it.

Presently, Chris's interest was focused entirely on what the vampires had done to the interior of the warehouse.

He had been given a tour by Beth and Luis while Del and Jamie had excused themselves to clean up and change into some fresh clothes after having done all the digging; Chris had been shown the empty upper floors, along with the comfortable living area on the first floor, and the boiler room and sleeping quarters in the cellar. The individual sleep chambers were well protected, each having a series of locks on its door to keep out anyone who might have succeeded in getting past the locked cellar door after first managing to get past the two heavily bolted doors at the first floor's rear entrance. The other entrances to the building had been walled over, as indeed had all the windows. From the outside, it appeared as if all openings had simply been boarded up from the inside, yet beyond the boards were studded walls, insulated and covered with drywall. Within the converted space, no windows existed.

The living area was tastefully appointed, with sleek Scandinavian furniture, Oriental rugs, chrome lamps, oak bookcases, and a state-of-the-art stereo system with four tower speakers that Chris found particularly appealing. The place had bathrooms but lacked a kitchen, though Chris had noticed a working refrigerator in the laundry room. Curious, he had asked why they needed one. Luis had opened the door to show him, and where Chris had expected to see plastic packets of blood there stood instead bottles of tonic water, seltzer, grape juice, apple juice, cranapple juice, mineral water, Wisconsin beer, Finnish vodka, Polish vodka, Russian vodka, and various white wines.

"How did you guys get all this stuff?" asked Chris.

"Well," said Beth, "some of it is stolen. It's pretty easy for us to rob stores and warehouses. We don't show up on their surveillance cameras, and if we run into anybody, we can hypnotize them. We can make people forget what they've seen, or even hand over the money in their till. It's always a good idea to rob your victims. Take their cash and credit cards. Make them tell you their special code numbers for the automatic teller machines. You'll find you can scam a lot of money off a victim that way. It's also been easy for us to convert electronics equipment into cash. We know a few good fences, and they prefer to work nocturnally, anyhow. We have no problem getting money.''

''But what about the people you steal from?''

''Chris, you can't afford to be squeamish about ripping them off, any more than you can afford to be squeamish about sucking their blood. It wouldn't be wise to find gainful nighttime employment somewhere—you'd eventually be found out. You have to make money somehow, and unless you're independently wealthy, you'll have to do what we do.''

''Okay, I guess you're right. I was also wondering about the first night you came to my apartment,'' said Chris. ''How did you happen to know so much about me? Are you a telepath or something?''

''Hardly.'' Beth's laugh made Chris's question sound ludicrous. ''I overheard your conversation with your pal Emilio a few months ago at the Smart Bar, and the rest was simple spy work. Luis assisted me. I do it all the time. Anyway, you said you were 'hungry.' Dinner is next on our agenda, once Del and Jamie have made themselves presentable.''

''Sounds good.'' Dinner meant blood, and Chris was sure he needed some desperately. Although he felt truly alive and full of energy, some inner craving was gnawing at him and wouldn't let go. He felt as if he could run for miles, but was also certain his energy would soon run out unless he had some blood.

''What am I thinking of?'' said Beth. ''We've got to get you into some decent clothes, too. You're about Del's size—why don't you go down and borrow some of his?''

''Why, where are we going?''

''How does Avalon strike you?''

''Fun place to dance.'' Chris couldn't wait to go dancing.

He used to do it all the time, but his leukemia had kept him from it for several months now. He knew that with his renewed strength, he could dance all night long without a break. "Never went there much, though. I always used to go to the Smart Bar."

"Good. We'll go to Avalon, then. We want to avoid any club where you might have been a regular. It wouldn't do for people to see you out and about if they knew you were supposed to be laid up sick in your apartment. You look a million percent better—"

"Thanks."

"And there's no way you could ever explain that to any-one. You don't look sick at all. Of course, that's because you aren't. Though there's still the matter of your hair. I expect you'll find it growing back pretty soon."

"It already is." Chris could feel the stubble poking up through his scalp, and almost felt as if he could feel it growing. The thought produced a broad grin on his face.

"But that doesn't help you much tonight. Well, Del's got some cute hats, and I'm sure he'll let you borrow one of those, too. Why don't you go ahead. I've got a phone call to make." Beth rose from her seat on the couch and grabbed the phone from its place on an end table.

Chris raced down the cellar steps and found Del's quarters at the end of the hall. The air was warm with steam. Del's door stood open.

"Hello?"

"Hi!" said Del. "Come on in." His voice betrayed a slight southern twang, as if he were from a border state like Missouri.

"Beth thought you might let me borrow some clothes."

"Sure, no sweat. My closet is your closet."

Del stood naked except for a towel around his waist. His body was indeed much like Chris's: lithe, lean, and poorly muscled. Now that Chris had shed some of his flab, he imagined his body looked much like its former self again. The main difference was that Del's skin was a dark bronze, while Chris's remained sickly pale. Water dripped from

Del's blond shoulder-length hair; he had obviously taken a shower, which Chris found astonishing.

"I thought there was something about running water—" Chris began.

"Oh! Don't believe everything you read. That's just one of those silly myths. Sometimes they say we can't cross running water. Then they say we can't tolerate *any* water of *any* kind, *period*, end of story. Others say it has to be holy water. But let me tell you, that's all bullshit. Go ahead, take a shower if you want, it won't destroy you. You look a little disheveled. We're going clubbing, you know. Better look your best. What's this?"

Del grabbed Chris's hand, the one he'd smashed through the coffin window. Flakes the color of rust still clung to the skin, though the wounds had healed completely, without any visible scars.

"You must have cut yourself," said Del. He rubbed Chris's hand with a few rough strokes, and the flakes were gone. "There, how's that?"

"I didn't know that was blood," said Chris. "It was the wrong color—too orange."

"Oh, it wasn't blood, at least not the kind of blood you're thinking of. I just call it vampire blood, but don't tell Beth I said that! Everyone else around here calls it *kroba* because Temsik does, which I think is the silliest thing I've ever heard, because Temsik's a Russian and *kroba* comes from their word for *blood*. Temsik calls it that because he's Russian. That doesn't mean we have to. But we're lazy, I guess. Anyway, none of us are rocket scientists, so what else should we call it?"

"So my blood isn't really blood, it's something else?"

"Boy, you're quick. It's what your body makes out of the blood you drink, but it's really very different. Listen, you'll learn about this soon enough. Now go get cleaned up so we can go dancing. Dancing will do you some good. Good way to let off a little steam, after the way you woke up this evening!"

"You're not kidding." Chris felt restless. The push-ups

had primed him for more exercise, and dancing was the best possible remedy for the situation.

Del led Chris down the hall to the bathroom and left him there. Chris set the water temperature for the shower and let it steam up the room while he undressed. He climbed into the shower grinning uncontrollably while the hot water streamed into his face. Everything was certainly different from what he had expected, and all for the better. These vampires were nice people. Chris had a feeling he was going to like it here.

He worked the soapy lather all over his body, loosening the dust and grit that seemed to have crawled into every nook and cranny. He was pleased with what he saw, his old trim self, not muscular but youthful and well shaped.

Suddenly, he saw a shadow appear on the other side of the shower curtain. Someone had entered the room.

"Who is it?" Chris asked with apprehension in his voice. Although he didn't think anything dangerous was about to happen, he still didn't know these people very well, and disliked having a stranger in the room while he was showering.

"It's me," said the voice. Over the roar of the shower, Chris failed to identify whose it was.

"What do you want?"

"It's me, your new friend."

Oh, Chris realized, it's probably Del.

"I haven't showered yet," said the voice. The shadow pulled the shower curtain partly aside and revealed itself to be Jamie. Until now, Chris hadn't got a good look at Jamie. His stout figure was muscular to an almost military readiness, his face masculine with an icy blue pair of eyes and hair closely cropped. Despite this, he looked less like a marine than he did a punk rocker. The anarchy symbol, an encircled letter A, was tattooed on his left pectoral, and marines were unlikely to have such a tattoo. His penis was thick and hard, jutting straight out from his crotch. He beamed a smile at Chris while the water splashed his face. "Could I join you?"

Chris was stunned by Jamie's forwardness, yet couldn't help but say, "Sure, come on in!" *What the hell*, he thought, *why not? I don't have to worry anymore about catching anything*.

As Jamie hopped in and closed the curtain behind him, Chris discovered he was already getting an erection himself. Sex, of course, was up there with dancing among the great exercises, and Chris's body craved a workout. After all the changes that were happening to his body, he was glad to find that his favorite organ was still in perfect working order.

THE SECRET MISSION

THEY drove a minivan north on Halsted on their way to Avalon, passing the flea market district known as Maxwell Street. Chris was pleased with himself for having pinpointed the location of the warehouse. It had turned out to be at Sixteenth and Morgan, just a few blocks from the Maxwell Street area, as he'd predicted; and for a city the size of Chicago, that wasn't half bad.

Del had loaned Chris a snappy pair of cotton twill slacks, a striped crewneck shirt, and a Cubs baseball cap to cover the wasteland of his scalp. Del had said he looked terribly cute, and Jamie had grinned at him lasciviously.

Chris looked out the window and watched all the black people hocking their wares. Nearly anything could be found at Maxwell Street: bootleg audio tapes, Day-Glo women's shoes, cheap men's cologne, cheap jewelry, small appliances, hosiery, "vintage" clothing, old copies of *Hustler*, baseball caps, T-shirts, hair-care products, hubcaps, hubcaps, hubcaps, and more. The men and women standing behind their tables of goods exerted a great deal of energy trying to get people of similar economic station to buy things none of them wanted. Seller and customer alike had queer looks on their faces, as if this moment were the only moment they could ever believe existed, or might exist. Chris had come down here before, shopping for junk. One never knew when one might find an interesting lamp, some old jazz

45s, or a brand-new pair of high-priced men's shoes for about ten dollars.

But the best reason to come was for the Polish hot dogs with relish and peppers. Strangely enough, the Polishes on Maxwell Street were the best in the city.

"Luis," said Chris, "do you think we could stop so I can grab a Polish? I'll only be a minute."

Jamie elbowed him in the ribs.

Beth, riding shotgun, turned around in her captain's chair and smiled sympathetically at Chris. "No food allowed, remember? Besides, I'm not sure if you can get a Polish here at one in the morning."

Chris felt like an idiot, forgetting something as basic as that. He didn't fully understand the reason vampires couldn't eat normal food. All he knew was that countless Draculas on the movie screen had never touched any food, and always begged off any offers of beverages with the famous phrase "I do not drink . . . wine."

Beth and her friends did, apparently, drink wine, if their refrigerator was any indication. But food remained off-limits for some reason.

Chris had never come down to Maxwell Street by himself, despite the bargains that could be had. He wasn't as worried about being robbed as he was uncomfortable being the only white face for as far as his eyes could see, not counting the Poles working behind the hot dog stands. Chris didn't consider himself a racist, however. The fact that Maxwell Street was an alien world had little to do with the color of its denizens' skin. Whether they had been black, Chinese, Mexican, Polish, or Ukrainian, Chris still would have felt as if he'd walked onto the set of *Invasion of the Body Snatchers*. He'd never before seen the place at night, and was glad he hadn't. Even though it was May and pleasant outside, men were still huddled over oil drums, burning garbage in the leaping flames. Their faces were cast in an eerie glow. Since he couldn't have a Polish anyway, Chris was glad Luis was driving the minivan right through without stopping.

"How come we can't eat, anyway?" Chris asked.

"It's not really my place to tell you," said Beth.

"Why not? Union regulations? Whose place is it?"

"Your mentor."

"My what?"

"It's part of the way the Underground works. You'll be assigned a mentor, who'll train you in the art of survival, rather like an apprenticeship. Until we get you hooked up with your mentor, you're in our temporary care. Tomorrow we're sending you to Wisconsin. We didn't have the time to do it this evening, so for now you'll stay with us."

Heading up Halsted, they passed the infamous Cabrini Green projects, a crack-infested place whose residents were notorious smash-and-grab artists. Unwary people who drove their cars in there were liable to be smashed into by vehicles at both ends and boxed in so they couldn't escape. Both their car and their person would be stripped clean of all valuables.

Chris felt right now as if his vampire friends were doing a smash-and-grab on him.

"What do you mean? I thought I was going to be staying with you guys." Chris turned a quizzical eye upon Jamie, who must have known this all along, even before their brief tryst in the shower. Jamie merely shrugged.

"You'll be sleeping with us today," said Beth. "But come nightfall you go to Wisconsin. After you've finished training, you can go where you like."

"But I like it here," Chris pleaded, trying not to sound like a whining brat. "I like you guys and your warehouse. I like Chicago."

"When your mentor's finished with you, you can always come back. We'll have room."

"Wisconsin!" Chris was incredulous. "What could there possibly be for me in Wisconsin?"

Chris hadn't expected an answer, but Luis gave him one all the same, with what sounded like a sadistic chuckle: "Temsik."

"What?"

"Vasily Kirilovich. But we just call him Temsik," said Beth. "He's originally from Russia. We're arranging for him to be your mentor. And he lives in Madison, which I think you'll find an interesting place."

"Great. Marvelous. Fantastic." Chris scowled.

Jamie put his arm around Chris's shoulders. "Hey, man, cool off. We ain't responsible for the rules. They been like this a long time. The Underground's been in America since before Ben Franklin was puttering around in his little workshop, and they been in Europe long before that. It's all for your own good. The only way we can insure your safety is by you following the rules."

"Rules?" Chris laughed. "I thought you were an anarchist!"

"Hey, I just want to survive. Much as I might hate it, there's rules that gotta be followed, or I could be destroyed. Stick with the Underground and you'll be safe. If you ever leave, you'll be in a heap of trouble. You need us, we need you, we gotta stick together, all that crap. For tonight, it's just best if you do what we say and don't do anything without talking to us. You may think you could survive on your own, but you can't. That's why we gotta hook you up with Temsik. But until then, if something happens to you, our collective ass is collective grass, if you know what I mean."

"What he's saying is don't fuck up," said Beth. "We won't be letting you bite anyone tonight. Temsik will have to teach you that. We'll find someone for you and do the biting ourselves, and let you suck the blood. So stay with us and do what we say, and don't do anything on your own initiative—that is, besides dancing and general socializing. Feeding won't last all night, you know."

It was a long ride up Halsted. As they came closer to their destination, they passed a plethora of gay bars and dance clubs, until they reached Belmont and took a left. Avalon, which wasn't really a gay club, was in the west nine-hundred block, right near the El tracks. Chris had forgotten that Avalon was right across the street from Berlin, a gay dance club that, unlike Avalon, he *had* frequented.

A train passed noisily overhead as Luis drove down the alley and parked the minivan under the El tracks.

"Why didn't we take the El?" Chris wondered aloud. Ever since being kicked out of his parents' house, he had grown so accustomed to using the El that it felt strange to go anywhere by car.

"You ever ridden the El at night?" countered Jamie.

"Of course."

"Then you know why. At night, you can't see nothing but your own reflection—except you don't got one no more. And you can bet some prick will notice if you ain't reflecting the way you ought to."

"See why we're sending you away for training?" Beth added. "You can't afford to make a mistake like that for real. Stay close to us tonight and you'll be safe."

Chris would think twice now before he did anything, but he didn't think he needed Beth or Jamie to hold his hand. He had already decided he would pull the Cubs cap down over as much of his face as possible until they were safely inside Avalon, on the off chance that some regular at Berlin was walking down Belmont and happened to spot him.

Luis killed the engine, and they all got out of the minivan. The ground was muddy and sucked at the soles of Chris's shoes. The air outside was cool, but Chris's skin quickly adjusted, bringing his body temperature down into equilibrium with it.

Beth placed her hand on Chris's shoulder, holding him back.

"Luis," said Beth, "why don't you go ahead and take Del and Jamie inside? I want to talk to Chris for a minute."

"All righty."

Beth led Chris past the rows of parked cars, to the nearest of the El track's iron support beams, and stood close to him in the shadow cast by the moon. Chris gazed off in the direction of the moon, squinting his eyes.

"Bright, isn't it?" asked Beth.

"Yeah," said Chris in wonderment. "It almost hurts my eyes to look at it."

"Then don't. You might find you prefer wearing sunglasses at night, especially a pair that blocks out UV rays. Otherwise, if you stand around after dark and stare at the moon, you could damage your eyes."

Chris turned away from the moon and looked into Beth's shadowed face. Her hand came up to touch his cheek.

"I'm sorry if you're confused," she said. "I didn't mean to keep it a secret from you, about our shipping you up to Wisconsin. I only thought it would be better not to throw everything at you all at once."

"That's all right. I shouldn't have assumed I'd be staying with you guys."

Another train, going in the opposite direction as the previous one, roared past overhead. Chris looked up at it and smiled; the sound of the El was always reassuring somehow.

"I know you don't want to leave Chicago. I knew that even before you told me."

"You seem to know everything about me."

"That's because you're very important."

Chris smiled at the flattery, but then saw the earnest look on Beth's face and realized it had been more than an offhand compliment. This made his smile fall, because he had no idea what she was talking about. "What do you mean, important?"

"Haven't you wondered why I made you one of us?"

"It's because I was sick, wasn't it? And because I've always wanted to be a vampire. That's what you said."

Beth was shaking her head. "Compassionate as I might be, I don't go around turning sick people into vampires simply because they're sick and want to become vampires. If I did, I'd have my hands full. Besides, I didn't do it as much for your sake as for mine. I made you one of us purely for selfish reasons."

"Wait a minute," said Chris, thinking she had designs on him. "If you know so much about me, you must know I'm gay."

"Of course. I didn't mean I wanted you for myself. I've got Luis to keep me company. And I didn't want you for

Del or Jamie, either, though they both like you immensely. No, I needed you for a secret mission I had in mind.''

"Secret mission?''

"I don't have to send you up to Wisconsin for training. I could do it myself. So could Luis or Jamie. Del, as a matter of fact, is just finishing his training, under my tutelage. And there's nothing that says I have to send you away.''

"Then I'd like to stay here.''

"I'm afraid you can't. I made you what you are, and you must do what I ask. All I want you to do is carry out my mission.''

"Which means I have to go to Wisconsin.''

"Exactly. I'm sending you up to Temsik in Madison because I'm worried about him. It's hard for me to tell what's going on up there, but I've heard some strange rumors. I've heard that he's all alone now, that his companion, Laura, has been destroyed.''

"By a vampire hunter?''

"No one knows. We don't even know if it's true. But I'm worried about Temsik's health and well-being. I keep dreaming there's going to be some awful disaster.''

"How could he be in poor health if he's one of us?''

"That doesn't mean he can't destroy himself. And with what I've been hearing, that seems a distinct possibility. I haven't been able to get in contact with him, and it's rumored that he's depressed. He might do something drastic, like walk out into the sunlight, or try to starve himself out of existence.''

"And you want me to stop him.''

"Yes, but you don't have to do anything. I've already done it by apprenticing you to him. It's his duty to train you, and he can't back out of it. It'll take time to teach you, and he'll have to stay fit. I only hope that by then, he'll be out of his depression. If I know Temsik, the time he spends teaching you will help him get on with his existence, and perhaps in time he'll get over Laura. I've never known him to be like this. I'm counting on you to get him out of his slump by being there and getting his mind onto other things, and by making him get out once in a while. That's all you have to do. But remember, it's secret. Luis knows, but don't tell Del or Jamie, and please don't tell Temsik. He's a very private person, and would never forgive me for meddling.''

"I doubt if I can do anything, but I'll give it a shot. If that's why you made me a vampire, it doesn't sound selfish to me.''

"I love Temsik. He's extraordinary. I don't know what I'd do without him. Even though he's not here in the city, I always like knowing that he's around, somewhere. He's been around much longer than the rest of us, and he's often been helpful in sticky situations, because he's been there before. He may be a little ragged, and you certainly don't want to get on his bad side, but overall his bark is worse than his bite. And I should know.'' A tear made its way down Beth's cheek, and she grinned self-consciously, as if she were embarrassed by it.

Chris got her meaning, that Temsik was the one who had changed her into a vampire. He kissed the salty tear away and clasped her cool hand tightly in his own. "I think I'm beginning to understand.''

"Let's go inside,'' said Beth, and sniffed. "You're probably thirsty.''

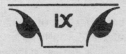

HAUNTING AVALON

AVALON was on the second floor of an old building, and was reached from the street by a long, narrow staircase. The club was divided into a few different rooms, one of which frequently featured live bands; the rest of the place was prime ground for dancing, with a darkly lighted dance floor and an excellent disc jockey who churned out one high-energy song after another over an incredible sound system. An elevated platform was provided along the sidelines from which one could stand, sit, drink, and watch other people dance.

Chris was sitting at the bar near the front of the room, downing the last of his Rolling Rock.

After one beer, Chris was already dizzy. Jamie and Del had assured him that drinking was perfectly all right, whether it was blood or Budweiser. They said that most of his formerly human digestive system had shut itself down, so that he could no longer process solids. In addition, he would be pissing pretty much what he had been drinking, since little of any liquid besides blood would make it into his bloodstream. Alcohol would still affect him, but, they pointed out, the effects would wear off rapidly and he would sober up fast. Unfortunately for Chris, one beer had promptly put him on the road to plasterdom, only because he was drinking on an empty stomach.

"When are we going to get some blood?" he asked Del,

whose face was having problems keeping itself in focus.
Del was presently splitting into two Dels, both of them
grinning crazily and pouring twin gin and tonics down their
throats.

"Not until that beer gets out of your system. But don't
worry, fifteen minutes and you'll be fine." The two Dels
were shouting in Chris's ear, and their combined voices
were just loud enough to be heard over the music.

"In that case," said Chris agreeably, "let's dance while
I'm still feeling goofy."

"Okey-doke!" Del, returning to his usual singular self,
tossed back the last of his drink and set the empty glass on
the bar. He grabbed Jamie's arm, and the three of them
went out onto the dance floor.

Beth and Luis were already there, dancing in the midst
of a small throng of people. Although over the weekend
Chris had lost track of what day it was, Jamie had told him
it was Monday night (by now, technically, Tuesday morning), which explained why the club wasn't packed wall-to-
wall with people trying to prove their hipness. Jamie had
said the best nights to dance were the weeknights anyway,
because on Fridays and Saturdays all the best clubs—including Avalon, Cabaret Metro, and Esoteria—were filled
with suburban kids trying but failing to become a part of
the scene. On weeknights it was not only less crowded but
the crowds themselves were composed of more true bohe-
mians. The suburbanites came to the high-energy clubs to
watch the people, but the regular weeknight-goers *were* the
people.

The song being blasted from the speakers had been pounding its beat for five minutes already and would probably
continue for five more, doggedly repeating its aggressive
synthetic drum track along with a throbbing, deep bass line
and gloomy vocals interspersed with digitally sampled
sound effects and bits of old movie dialogue from some
obscure and unidentifiable source. It was moody music, but
hard-driven and wild. The total aural effect was hypnotizing,
inviting, and something Chris had never been able to resist.

Although he was closer himself to being a suburban kid than a New-Waveos Ranchero, he liked this Chicago-style high-energy music as much as any of the ghouls who haunted Avalon. It felt great to get out on the floor and finally dance, after having been sick for so long. This alone was worth his having become a vampire.

If he had tried this a few days ago, his knees would have collapsed and he would have fallen in a heap on the floor in great pain. He could have done nothing but sit at the bar quietly, and even that would have caused him to grow dizzy.

But now, Chris felt stronger than he'd ever felt in his life. He was out of practice, but quickly fell into the overpowering beat and let the music guide his movements. He felt like a giddy schoolboy, already becoming less drunk than a few minutes ago, yet he was still tipsy enough to have been loosened up. His style of dancing was rather jumpy and awkward; his arms would thrash around with little control, and on occasion he would accidentally elbow a fellow dancer in the ribs and quickly apologize even though his victim both couldn't hear him and wasn't paying attention, anyway. He figured people either never expected the apology or actually enjoyed the elbowing in the ribs.

Chris was dancing opposite Jamie and Del, though none of them were truly dancing *with* one another. Del was a smooth dancer wrapped up in himself, while Jamie's style was more antagonistic, like toned-down slam-dancing. Jamie kept deliberately bumping into Chris in a friendly manner, unlike Chris's frequent people-bumping, which was purely haphazard.

Chris was slightly mad at Jamie for having joined him in the shower when he'd known all along that Chris would be gone in a day's time. It made Chris feel as if Jamie had taken advantage of him.

As the song finally neared its end, the disc jockey skillfully merged it with the beginning of the next tune in such a way that the beat wasn't lost. The new song turned out to be one that Chris happened to know, "You Often Forget," by the Revolting Cocks.

The strobe light began flickering, catching all the dancers every split second in a still, stark pose. In the first flashes, it caught Beth with her hands reaching up near her head, her nose high in the air, her seductive mouth open and her eyes closed. Luis was caught slightly bent over with arms held close but going in opposite directions. Jamie's fists were clenched against his chest, while Del was caught smiling, the beam from the strobe light glinting off one of his fangs. The figures of Chris's new friends looked suddenly as if they had become animated cartoons flickering their way through the dark.

As the strobe flashed, a young man joined the circle, worming his way in between Jamie and Chris. Chris tried to meet his eyes during the white lightning flashes, and soon they were dancing in sync with one another, playing off each other's moves. Chris began to feel more in control of himself; he preferred having someone he could dance with/ against. And this guy, he discovered, was really good, even better than Del or Beth. He was also better looking.

He looked as if he might be a model for one of Chicago's top agencies. His face seemed to have catapulted itself out of a high-fashion ad in a men's magazine, and here it was within feet of Chris's face, only it was genuine flesh and blood. His chin and cheekbones were perfectly defined, his skin tan (but possibly made up), and his sandy blond hair long but combed back loosely in a thick wave over his forehead, the way all the models in the magazines were wearing it. Under his clothing, which Chris could tell was overly expensive, he appeared to have a terrific body as well, though one couldn't be sure, at least not yet.

When the song was over, the model followed Chris to the bar, while Chris's friends remained on the dance floor, not noticing he had left.

"I like the way you dance," said the model as they sat on two empty stools, facing one another.

"Thanks." Chris couldn't believe his luck. No one this gorgeous had ever given him the time of day. He wondered if he were emanating some sort of animal magnetism as a result of having become a vampire. Besides being hungry, Chris didn't feel worn out in the slightest after all his dancing.

"Frankie Stannard," the model announced as they shook hands. "Francis, really, but I like Frankie."

"Chris."

"Chris what?"

He stopped himself before giving his last name, and decided he'd better provide a false one. He was beginning to figure out this game, without any help from Beth or the others. "Wilson. Chris Wilson."

"Are you here alone?"

Chris couldn't stand it. Frankie was obviously working his way toward a pickup, but this evening of all evenings, sex was the last thing Chris wanted. He was starving, and even beginning to feel weak inside. He needed nourishment, and would have loved to go somewhere with Frankie and plant his teeth in his neck and drink some of his blood, but Beth and the others would never let him. They didn't want Chris out of their sight tonight, and they weren't going to let him do anything on his own. Perhaps he could get them to bite Frankie for him; he looked as if his blood would taste exquisite, the Dom Perignon of hemoglobin.

"No, I'm not alone," said Chris. "I'm here with friends." He motioned toward the dance floor. "That's them over there."

"You're a friend of Beth's then." It was a statement, not a question.

"How do you know Beth?" Chris asked. Frankie had caught him by surprise, leading Chris to wonder if perhaps Frankie was a vampire as well. He certainly had dark enough skin. So far, every vampire Chris had met was dark-skinned, rather than ghostly pale as they should have been, an anomaly he failed to understand. If they never saw the sun, they couldn't possibly get suntanned, yet they were. He would have to ask one of them about it.

"I met her last week, right here," replied Frankie. "She's . . . fascinating."

If Frankie were indeed a vampire, he was playing a game with Chris. He certainly acted knowing, or was that all in Chris's head? It probably was; Chris was simply getting paranoid, like a teenager wondering if his dad could tell he was stoned. Frankie was simply a friendly guy trying to strike up conversation and/or take someone home with him this evening. The fact that he knew Beth didn't necessarily mean anything. Beth's friends didn't all have to be vampires.

"Yeah, I like her a lot," said Chris.

"Are you her boyfriend?"

"Me? No." Chris laughed. "That's Luis, I think."

"That would be the tall spic."

"That's right." After living here all his life, Chris was used to the bigotry of native Chicagoans. No sense in raising a stink about it and scaring away this hunk.

"Good. Whose boyfriend are you?"

Chris wondered if he knew Del and Jamie as well. "I don't have one. I mean, I'm not anybody's."

"Ah, a little slip of the tongue," Frankie said, getting closer. His knee touched Chris's. "This is getting interesting."

"What about you?" Chris was bold. "Do you have a boyfriend?"

"Not right now . . . not yet."

Interesting indeed, thought Chris. But at the same time his bladder suddenly cried out for relief. That Rolling Rock had snaked through his system fast. If he remained sitting at the bar another minute, he'd be in agony. He needed to take a piss.

"Frankie, I've got to go to the bathroom. Will you stay here until I get back?"

"Better yet, I'll come with you."

They left the room together and headed down the hall to the men's room. They passed people who looked similar to Beth: flat black hair, dark eyeliner and mascara, ruby-red lipstick, loose black clothing. The Beth clones were all smoking and staring into nowhere. The air in the hallway was thick with smoke, and Chris caught a whiff of pot smoke amidst the smell of Camels and Marlboros.

"Are you a model?" Chris asked as he followed Frankie into the men's room.

"A model what?" Frankie looked over his shoulder with a self-satisfied smirk on his face and gave Chris a wink.

Past the men's room door, they turned a corner and Frankie headed straight past the sinks, toward the pissoirs. Chris abruptly came face-to-face with one of the mirrors above the sinks, and gasped when he saw that it was empty, reflecting the pale wall behind him but not his face. Even though he'd known this would be true before seeing it for himself, the sight of it was a genuine shock. He was lucky Frankie had passed the sink area without glancing at the mirrors and seeing nothing behind him where Chris should have been.

"What's the matter?" asked Frankie. He must have heard Chris's gasp.

"Nothing," Chris answered quickly. "I . . . I look terrible, that's all."

"You must be drunk—you're cute! Especially with that Cubs cap. I'm not much of a fan, myself."

Two feet showed from underneath one of the stalls, but other than that the bathroom was empty of people. Chris claimed a spot at a pissoir, opened his fly, and dug around for his cock. He wondered why it was that his need to piss always increased geometrically whenever he approached a waiting toilet. Chris aimed and let loose a warm stream, but looking down discovered he was essentially pissing tepid beer, as Jamie and Del had said he would. It foamed up as it hit the drain. Chris moved closer to the pissoir, hoping Frankie wouldn't examine the quality of his urine-that-wasn't-really-urine from his vantage point at the neighboring unit.

"Still, you look like a model," Chris said. Surreptitiously, he sneaked a peek at Frankie's exposed cock, and found it met his satisfaction. He doubted that tonight he would get any closer to it than this, but perhaps on some future evening . . .

"Flattery will get you everywhere," said Frankie, "but I'm no model. Just a professional rich kid."

Ah, this was one of those types Beth had warned him about, the kind who would use his mother's gold card to fly over to Italy for lunch. The thought was not without its appeal. Chris might like to get to know this guy—and his pocketbook.

"Nothing wrong with being rich." Chris was diplomatic.

But he kept forgetting he was being moved to Wisconsin tomorrow. This was the only night he'd be able to spend time with Frankie.

Frankie finished pissing, zipped up his pants, and withdrew from inside his shirt a small black cylinder hanging on a rawhide necklace. "Are you into poppers?"

"No, I'm not." *Poppers! Good God!* Chris had never done poppers and didn't want to. Sniffing amyl nitrate fumes up his nose was toward the bottom of his list of things to do. Mostly, it seemed to be a psychological block against most things having to do with the previous generation of gay men. Poppers, tight Levi's cutoffs, bandanas hanging out of rear pockets, chin-strap beards, roller skates, old disco, and Judy Garland all made Chris think of death. Perhaps he was more tuned in to the dark vibrations these things emitted because he had been so close to death himself, but on the other hand, he wouldn't be surprised if others of his generation felt the same way. There was nothing inherently gay about any of these symbols; they had merely been fads enjoyed by one generation. Chris saw no need for them to be passed down to successive generations, as if they were grand contributions to gay culture, which they decidedly were not.

Chris tucked his cock back in his briefs and zipped up his pants.

"Come on, Chris, it won't kill you."

That word! Chris wondered if Frankie had been reading his mind. Chris had also shied away from amyl nitrate because he'd heard it increased the heart rate, among other sensations. He'd long suffered from a rapid heartbeat to begin with, and had never sought out further stimulation for what might have been an already weak organ. The very idea of sniffing poppers had always been terrifying to him. He'd read the stories about people sniffing too much and having heart attacks in the middle of sex. And even though Chris knew that nothing but the tried-and-true classical methods could destroy him now, his old prejudices against poppers held fast, and he had to refuse.

"Sorry, Frankie. I'm not interested."

Frankie unscrewed the cap of the small cylinder, put it to one nostril, shut the other one with a finger, and took a whiff. A manic gleam came into his face as a satisfied smile also spread across it. "Whoa! It's a rush, Chris, are you sure you won't try it?"

Just then Jamie burst into the men's room, sweating from all his frantic dancing. Dark spots of perspiration clung to the front and back of his shirt. He was out of breath.

Frankie hurriedly capped his capsule and tossed it back down the front of his shirt. His quick movements were suspicious, the way one would act with an illicit drug, which amyl nitrate was not. Chris wondered if it really was amyl nitrate after all, or if it were cocaine that Frankie had been trying to force on him. After all, he had only met Frankie this evening, and couldn't necessarily trust him.

"There you are!" said Jamie, grabbing Chris by the arm. "We been looking all over for you. Come on!"

"Go ahead," said Frankie. "Go with your friend. I'll find you again sometime."

"I'm moving to Madison tomorrow," Chris blurted, but didn't know if he said it to deter Frankie from looking for him or because he wanted Frankie to find him. Jamie pulled him past the mirrors and through the doorway. From where he stood, Frankie could never see that neither of them cast a reflection.

"I'll still find you," Frankie said, but Chris couldn't tell if it was a promise or a threat. Frankie looked even more the model in the bright light of the bathroom, but he was sending off dark vibrations similar to those Chris had picked up from the poppers. A part of Chris found it enticing, but another part was decidedly grateful to Jamie for coming in and rescuing him, which was what it was beginning to feel like.

"That was stupid. You gotta watch yourself better than that. Public rest rooms are bad places for you to go."

"But I had to take a piss."

"You should've taken it outside, in the dark somewhere. What if he'd looked in the mirror, or someone else, even?"

"I don't know."

"You don't want to know. People are smarter than you think. They can surprise you."

"I'll be more careful."

Jamie took Chris down Avalon's front steps and out of the club, whispering into his ear as they passed the bouncer. "All right. So nothing happened to you. We're going outside for a while. Luis has found you some blood."

Chris found his body once more adjusting to the cooler air, and within a few seconds it was no longer chilly at all. Beth had said they were cold-blooded, but Chris had a feeling the process was more sophisticated than that. His circulatory system had to be slightly more complex than that of a lizard.

Across the street, the door to Berlin was open, and pouring out of it was the dance mix of a song by Bananarama. No one was leaving the club who might recognize Chris, but he yanked the baseball cap down over his face all the same.

Jamie led him down the alley beneath the now quiet El tracks, past a long line of shadowed cars parked diagonally along its length. Chris could see Luis clearly, standing on the other side of an iron support beam just up ahead. He was talking to a girl whose back was up against the beam. Chris could make out her curly blond hair and the curve of her hip protruding past the thick column of metal, but all else was obscured.

Jamie whispered in Chris's ear once more: "Luis is gonna sell this girl some crack. We're his suppliers."

"What do you mean?" Chris gave him a quizzical look.

"Not for real—jeez, Chris!" Jamie made it sound as if Chris's naïveté was beyond the pale. "That's what he told her so she don't get suspicious when she sees us coming. Try telling someone 'I vant to bite your neck' and see how far that gets you. Christ!"

They tramped through the mud and came around behind Luis, and Chris got his first glimpse of their intended victim. She was younger looking than any of the vampires, probably about nineteen. Her wild mop of bleached blond hair was teased into a big but stylish mess, and her tight jeans hugged hips that were slightly too full. Since she was lacking in the chest department, her hair served to balance out her figure, which would otherwise be too hippy.

"Are these the guys?" she was asking Luis.

"That's them."

The girl appraised Jamie and Chris, and her face caught a square of moonlight streaming through the tracks above. She was painted to excess, with swaths of rouge that made her look less like a whore than like a clown, and were complimented by the bright colors elsewhere on her face, from lipstick to eye shadow. She probably isn't a whore, Chris thought, but with proper teasing, her hair could be made to look like Bozo's, and her clown look would be complete.

"Let's see what you've got," she said, her voice a high-pitched whine.

Jamie got closer to her and removed something from his jeans pocket, holding it up in front of her face. Chris craned his neck around Jamie's shoulder so he could see. Jamie was holding his fist just past his own nose, so that the girl was looking directly into his eyes. Chris saw her clown-face transforming from animated curiosity to a mere passive stare, entrapped by Jamie's eyes.

"This here's an excellent rock," Jamie said, unfolding his fingers. Yet the girl's eyes remained on Jamie's, not on the object he was revealing. It was a sugar cube.

"Wow!" said the girl. "It looks excellent."

"Fifty dollars."

"Sure, man." Without turning away from Jamie's gaze, she reached into her front pocket and pulled out a crumpled wad of bills with some difficulty, due to the tightness of her jeans. She handed him the entire crinkly ball.

"Okay, that's fifty," Jamie said while he handed it to Luis without even glancing at it. Then he placed the sugar cube into the girl's hand and closed her fingers tightly around it. She jammed it into her pants pocket, grinning. "Now let's have a kiss," Jamie added, smiling wide to reveal his fangs.

The girl took a step forward, entranced, yet Jamie placed his hands on her shoulders and pushed her back gently against the iron beam. She parted her lips, but he ignored them and went straight for her neck.

She cried out briefly as he sank his fangs into her flesh, but her hands gripped his back more tightly, pulling him closer. "Yes," she muttered amid Jamie's wet, sucking sounds.

But Jamie didn't drink long. "All right, Chris," he said. "This blood's for you."

As Jamie left her leaning there, blood trickling from both wounds on her pale neck, Chris was reminded how thoroughly clowns had frightened him as a child. Strange, how he had loved vampires and yet been mortally terrified of clowns. He had hated going to the circus for that reason alone; the lion tamers, trapeze artists, and fire-eaters had been thrilling and marvelous, but whenever a clown had come up into the audience to make the children laugh, Chris had always screamed. His nightmares had been filled with hideous clown faces and brightly colored gloved hands, often disembodied. Chris had always associated the hands with the clowns, though he couldn't remember why. Right now, he had to take a moment to remind himself that this girl wasn't a clown at all, but simply a whorish drug addict garishly painted.

"Hurry," Luis prodded, "before the wounds heal up. You have to use those same holes."

It's now or never, Chris thought, but in the end his terrific thirst exceeded his fear of clowns; he smiled wide, feeling his sharp canine teeth stretch into position, and placed his mouth against the girl's neck, tasting the blood Jamie had left behind. The tips of his teeth quickly found the soft, raised puncture wounds and plunged in to open them farther. He began to suck.

"That's it," said Luis from one side of him. "Slow and easy." Luis grabbed one of Chris's hands and placed it against the girl's chest. "Feel the pumping of her heart. Get into rhythm with it. That's right. Good, real nice."

Her heartbeat was steady. Chris could feel it easily through her cotton shirt. Her blood spurted split seconds after the thump of her heart, and Chris's sucking quickly became synchronized with it. At first it was difficult timing the swallowing in between sucks, but once he let it come naturally instead of thinking so hard, he found it was easy: a long suck followed by a brief swallow, like the syncopated rhythm of the girl's heart. The wetness drenched his gullet, warm and salty. Breathing came only through the nose, and each intake of breath was accompanied by the musky, tangy scent of her blood.

Chris kept at it, filling himself up, until his thirst was finally quenched. He discovered it didn't take much.

"There, that should do it." Luis pulled Chris away from her neck and wiped his bloody lips with a handkerchief. "You're as good as new, at least for now."

Jamie grabbed the girl, who had passed out, and lay her down gently on the ground, where Chris knew she would wake up the next morning bewildered as to how she got there and what she had done the night before. Not to mention fifty dollars poorer, or however much money she'd had in that wad of hers. And all she would have to show for it would be two wounds on her neck (which by morning would look like large pimples), a general malaise from her lack of blood, and, in her pockets, a tasty cube of sugar.

"How come you didn't have any?" Chris asked Luis as they headed back down the alley.

"There wouldn't have been enough of her to go around for the three of us, not in one night, at least. Also, Jamie and I have already fed this evening, before we dug you up. Beth and Del didn't, which is one reason they stayed behind in the club when we came out here."

"They're still trying to get in their licks," said Jamie, and chuckled.

They showed their stamped hands to the bouncer at the door, who nodded and let them up the stairs.

A familiar beat met Del's ears: *bah doo doo BAH doo BOP BOP*. The song was "Everyday Is Halloween," by Ministry, a song the Chicago clubs had played to death over the last several years, but that remained one of the best dance tracks Chris had ever heard. Tonight it seemed to have pulled people away from the other rooms, because the dance floor was packed with flailing arms and bodies, a thicker crowd than before. Del was out in the middle of the dance floor, but Luis went in and pulled him away from it. Del looked giddy with pleasure.

"You ready to go?" Luis asked him.

"Sure," said Del. "I've had mine." He nudged Chris and whispered in his ear, "A gymnast, no less. Hot stuff!"

Chris wondered if it had been Frankie Stannard, but on second thought, Frankie's body hadn't looked muscular enough to be a gymnast's, and he had described himself as a professional rich kid. No, if Del said it was a gymnast, it had to have been someone who truly looked like a gymnast, someone with firm, well-developed muscles. Chris scanned the dance floor, the bar, and the elevated platform across the room, but saw no sign of Frankie; unless he was in some other room, then he was gone, which was understandable considering it was three o'clock in the morning.

"Where's Beth?" asked Luis.

"Oh, she left with some guy. She said we shouldn't wait for her."

Luis grumbled, but told Chris, "She does this all the time. Nothing to worry about." It sounded more as if he were reassuring himself than Chris.

As they headed toward the stairs, Chris wondered if Beth had left with Frankie. After all, Frankie had said he knew her, and perhaps they had gone out to some other club to finish up the evening. But there was something about Frankie that bothered Chris, and the thought of his being with Beth made Chris uneasy.

"What did this guy look like?" Chris asked Del as they left the club.

"What guy?"

"The one Beth went off with."

"Oh, I don't know. Just some guy. I didn't really notice him."

That in itself allayed Chris's fears, which were ill-defined and probably irrational to begin with. The fact that Del hadn't noticed the guy meant that it couldn't have been anyone as gorgeous as Frankie Stannard. Del would have noticed *him*.

Beth was safe, then, but *from what?*

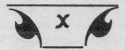

THE THING IN THE CHAIR

SLEEPING in a coffin would take some getting used to. In the four years since moving away from home, Chris had grown accustomed to a wide double bed. At any given time of night, he could be found sprawled across it in strange positions. On the few occasions when he'd had guests in his bed, he'd been told he had a tendency to kick. A coffin allowed no room for kicking, not to mention guests.

Chris himself was a guest this morning in Del's sleeping quarters, though in his own coffin, a few feet away from Del's. The window remained busted; Luis maintained that he would fix it the following evening. Chris had picked the shards of glass from the bed of earth, and searched for spiders, finding none. Del had laid a blanket over the dirt for Chris's comfort, then given him a fraternal kiss before closing the lid on him.

Aside from having no room to move around, however, the coffin wasn't all that uncomfortable. Sleeping on an earthen bed with a blanket for padding was not unlike lying on the ground in a sleeping bag out in the woods, and Chris had always found he got his best sleep whenever he went out camping. The only difference lay in the lack of stars overhead and the presence of wooden walls on all sides of him. Still, sleeping on such a firm surface would probably do wonders for his bad back; though his back, like his eyes, had no doubt already been taken care of.

Chris felt like a kid again, sleeping over at a friend's house and playing some weird game.

"Del? Are you awake?" Although Chris spoke through the empty hole of his viewing window, he was unsure if Del could hear him in his own sealed coffin.

Del's coffin lid creaked on its hinges, sounding as if it had been opened a crack. "Sure, what's up?"

"Do you know Temsik? What's he like?"

"That's not an easy question."

"I get the impression he's going to eat me alive."

"Temsik? No way, hon."

"I thought he was . . . difficult."

"Difficult, yes. Cannibal, no." Del laughed. "Temsik is going to be your trainer, and while you're in training you'll be protected. He's there to see you don't get eaten alive by anyone else."

"What I mean is—I'm kind of a nervous person by nature. I don't get along with everybody. Especially over-bearing personalities. At my last job, I had to deal with some guys who were real assholes, business types all the way, and it drove me crazy. I'm not very competitive. I don't fit in easily in that sort of environment. I was just lying here worrying that Temsik's going to turn out to be like those jerks in the office, some kind of obnoxious brute."

"Oh, he really isn't like that at all. I know you've probably been getting strange signals from us, but once you meet him you'll see for yourself. He's a good guy."

"How well do you know him?"

"Not all that well, I suppose, but I know him. He's the one who sent me down here for my training."

"He's the one who bit you, then?"

"No, that was Laura. She's his significant other."

Laura. Del spoke of her in the present tense, but she was the vampire Beth had mentioned, the one who was rumored to have been destroyed. Beth had said that Del knew nothing of Chris's true mission in Wisconsin, so he must not have

heard this rumor, either. Chris would have to make sure his
tongue didn't slip.

"I guess I needed some reassurance. Beth said Temsik's
bark was worse than his bite, but I think she's got a thing
for him, so I figured she was a little biased."

"A thing for him?"

"Well, he bit her, didn't he?"

"Really! I never knew that!"

Chris hoped he wasn't supposed to have kept that a secret
as well, but it was too late now.

In fact, it was getting late in the morning. Despite their
being sealed off from the world down in the cellar, Chris
could sense the sun ascending above the horizon, stretching
its rays across the land. He yawned; he was exhausted. As
the minutes wore on, he could feel his energy slowly evap-
orating.

The whole evening had been amazing. It felt so good to
get out in the world again and have some fun. Push-ups,
sex, dancing, these were things he wouldn't have dreamed
of doing during his remission therapy. But now he was
effectively cured. Not only that, but he possessed greater
strength, hearing, and eyesight than he ever had before.
Chris began to wish he had become a vampire sooner. Then
again, he had all eternity to enjoy himself now, so it hardly
mattered.

"Chris," said Del, yawning himself, "I'd love to keep
talking, but we've got to get some rest. I'll see you this
evening, and we'll talk some more, okay?"

"All right. Good night, or good morning, or whatever."

"Yes," Del said with a chuckle, "good morning."

Del's hinges squeaked once more as he lowered his lid.

Chris felt like turning on his side and curling up, but the
coffin wouldn't allow it, so he remained on his back, his
arms folded across his chest like Boris Karloff in *The
Mummy*. It was the most comfortable place for them; leaving
them at his sides made him feel too much like a corpse.

Of course, in a way he *was* a corpse, a walking corpse,
a creature of the night, a *nosferatu*, one of the undead.

But within minutes he was neither dead nor undead, he was sound asleep.

That evening, Luis replaced the window in Chris's coffin and rigged it with a sliding wooden panel beneath, to provide added privacy and to protect Chris if ever the sun's rays accidentally landed on the coffin while he was inside. Chris got in to try it out. Luis had screwed a wooden knob into the small plywood panel and fixed it on two runners. Chris grasped the knob and slid it in place, blocking out Luis's smiling face looking down from above.

"Works great," said Chris when he got out.

"Good. Now we just have to crate this thing up."

They spent the next half hour assembling a solid crate around the coffin. Before hammering down the lid, however, Chris threw several of Del's shirts, pants, socks, and pairs of underwear into the coffin, with Del's blessing. The vampires wouldn't let Chris return to his apartment to get any of his own clothes. His disappearance had been duly noted by all concerned parties and reported in Tuesday's *Tribune* and *Sun-Times*; it would be insane to risk exposure for the sake of some personal effects.

Tim Duffy had been quoted in both articles, and it was obvious he felt partially responsible for Chris's mysterious disappearance. "I was out of town for the weekend," he had told reporters, "but when I got back I knew something was terribly wrong. People in Chris's condition simply don't get up and walk away. If he did, he couldn't have gotten far." Tim had gone on to speculate that a second party might have been involved, and that perhaps it had been a kidnapping. Police said there was no evidence of a kidnapping at this time. It was being investigated as a missing-persons case. It wasn't front-page news, but it was a story weird enough to have piqued the media's interest. The *Sun-Times* had run a current photo of Chris with his Cushingoid features, no hair, rings around his eyes. Del assured him he no longer looked anything like the photo, and said that he doubted if anyone at Avalon the previous night would notice the similarity. Still, Luis said it was yet another good reason for him to be going to Wisconsin.

Luis wanted to get on the road as fast as possible because he had to drive Chris up to Madison and come back the same evening, and he wanted to allow some extra time in case of car trouble or any other unforeseen circumstance. All things considered, it was unsafe for him to be three hours away from the safety of his own coffin. So, as soon as they were finished with the crate, they hefted it up the stairs and out the back door. They removed the back row of seats from the minivan and slid the crate inside.

The physical labor invigorated Chris. He was proud of being able to lift heavy objects without even working up a sweat.

Chris sighed heavily as he stared at the wondrous lights of the Chicago skyline, knowing he might not see them again for a long time.

He hugged Jamie and planted a kiss on his lips, in a gesture of friendship. He couldn't blame him for their both being so horny in the shower together the night before, and besides, it had been fun.

"Come back soon," said Jamie.

"As soon as Temsik lets me." It struck Chris as odd that this proto-punker could be so sentimental, but then, he still didn't know him very well.

Del received the same kiss and hug, but Del's strong arms threatened to knock the wind out of Chris. Del's lips were softer, and tasted of gin.

"We never finished that talk," Del said. "But don't you worry. Everything's going to turn out fine. Actually, I'm glad you'll be with Temsik and Laura. I won't have to worry about you that way."

"Del, you're a sweetheart."

"Come on, let's go." Luis was impatient. He got in the minivan and started the engine.

"Call me when you get there," Del said, giving Chris a final peck on the cheek.

"I will. I want to talk to Beth anyway. I didn't get a chance to tell her good-bye."

"I'm surprised she isn't back already. She would have wanted to see you off."

"Are you sure nothing's happened to her?"

"What could happen to her? She's the smartest one of us all. If anything had happened to any of us last night, it would have been me."

Maybe it had, Chris thought all of a sudden. Beth had left the club with only Del as a witness, and at the time he had probably been dancing, drunk on his gin and tonics, and satiated with the blood of his "hot" gymnast. If Chris had been a vampire hunter, he would have had an easier time abducting Beth in front of Del than Del in front of Beth.

"I hope you're right," Chris said, and did. He hoped his conjectures were mere fantasies, drummed up by the mind of an ignorant neophyte. After all, these guys knew Beth better than he did, and they weren't worried. Chris was probably getting all riled up over nothing. It wouldn't be the first time. The smallest thing could get the gears spinning in his head and send him toward wild conclusions lacking any basis in reality. This had happened just yesterday when he had been buried and thought Beth had tricked him, when in fact she had promised him he would be fine. This aspect of Chris's nature had also paved a rocky path for his few attempts at relationships with other men, and had led to suspicion and jealousy on his part, often without cause. One boyfriend had even accused him of being paranoid, which probably wasn't far from the truth.

So Chris would keep his mouth shut about Beth. The others knew what they were doing.

Chris thanked Del for the clothes, said good-bye to him and Jamie, and told Luis he was ready to roll.

On the way up to Madison, they listened to Luis's salsa tapes and worked on a six-pack of Meister Braü. Chris found that the beer didn't affect him as severely as the night before,

and Luis said it was because of the fresh blood he had inside
him. Luis remained his usual level self behind the wheel,
despite the alcohol. He wore a pair of Ray-Ban sunglasses;
the moon shone brightly, low in the sky just off to the left.

"We'd better do something about that squinting," said
Luis as they approached the outskirts of Rockford.

"What squinting?"

"You've been squinting all night. Sky too bright for
you?"

"I guess, a little."

They stopped at a PDQ service station to gas up. Luis
handed Chris a fifty-dollar bill and told him to buy himself
a pair of sunglasses and to keep the change as "walking
around money."

Chris chose a black pair of mirrored glacier glasses with
leather eye protectors, which looked almost like a pair of
goggles such as the first race car drivers used to wear. But
when he put them on and looked at himself in the small
mirror on the display rack, he found the Invisible Man
staring back at him. The glacier glasses floated in midair,
like Claude Rains without his wrappings in the old movie.
Chris wasn't startled this time, but he was annoyed with
himself. This was the second time he had made the same
dumb mistake. Luckily, no one had been standing behind
him, able to witness it.

The sunglasses made the trip to Madison more enjoyable.
The night looked more as it should have, and Chris's eyes
were more comfortable.

On the way up, Chris found out that Luis's family had
fled Cuba during the revolution, when Luis was ten years
old. They had been one of Cuba's wealthiest families, and
were still rich here in the United States, but Luis had severed
all contact with them twenty years ago, when he had become
a vampire while pursuing medicine at Berkeley.

"That was when Vietnam was happening, and the school
was full of protesters and crazy radicals. I wasn't a part of
any of it. To this day, my family thinks I was kidnapped

by the Black Panthers or the SLA and brainwashed or something.''

''You mean they're still looking for you?''

''You bet.'' Luis crushed a can of Meister Braü in his fist and threw it in the back, where Chris heard it strike the crate and bounce off, onto the carpet. ''I keep expecting to see my face show up on TV, you know, on one of those fucking Geraldo Rivera specials.''

''I'm glad I don't have to worry about that. My parents are probably happy that I'm gone.''

''Don't be so sure, Chris. The powers of darkness are everywhere.''

''Meaning . . . ?''

''Parents. What else?''

Once they left the interstate, they entered the city limits and headed up a north-going boulevard, toward the center of Madison. They passed the coliseum on their left, its sign advertising an upcoming concert by Kenny Rogers. They banked past a large mass of trees on their right, which gave way to a panoramic view of a vast lake reflecting the city's skyline in its black waters. Most of the squat buildings were darkened, yet Chris could make out plenty of detail in the bright moonlight. Standing taller than the others was the stark-white classical dome of what Chris took to be the state capitol, illuminated by floodlights.

The boulevard wrapped its way around the western shore of the lake, aiming for the capitol and what looked like the downtown.

''Not very big, is it?'' Chris asked.

''No,'' Luis answered. ''Not compared to Chicago.''

''The lake's kind of nice, though.''

''There's another one on the other side. Temsik lives downtown, smack-dab in the middle of the isthmus.''

''Isthmus. Like in Panama?''

''Right. But no canal.''

Chris was a Pisces, a water sign, so perhaps the move to Madison would be a good thing after all, if he was going to be living between two large lakes. Of course, Chicago had had Lake Michigan, but Chris had always lived away from it.

When they reached the downtown, Chris discovered that Madison, like all good American cities, was filled with one-way streets. The capitol was clearly the center of everything. Luis had to circle around it (one-way) to get where he wanted to go. They drove five blocks down Wisconsin Avenue, which shot straight off the capitol and took them up a small hill, and then they turned the corner.

"This is Gilman," Luis said, referring to the street. "And this is where you're going to live." Parked cars were packed in bumper-to-bumper along the street. Luis pulled the mini-van up behind a glossy black Jaguar, on a yellow curb; he turned on his hazard lights.

Chris didn't get a good look at the building until he got out of the car. It was a five-story Art Deco apartment building made of beige brick that looked like something out of the H. G. Wells movie *Things to Come*. Stylized horizontal shelves jutted out from the windows and wrapped themselves around the corners. The upper apartments had either curved balconies or squarish terraces, with canvas awnings and banks of potted plants. Chris was impressed.

Luis was already opening the back doors of the minivan while Chris gawked at his new residence. "Come on, man, give me a hand."

They removed their sunglasses before entering the building. With one person on either end, the crate wasn't that heavy, but it was cumbersome. Chris's newly strong muscles had no problem lifting his end; he felt as if he and Luis, together, could bench press it. They found they couldn't fit it into the old elevator, so they had to get it up the staircase. Chris took the top end, since Luis was clearly the stronger one, and backed his way up slowly. By the time they reached the fourth floor, Chris realized the job had taken very little out of him, and his arms weren't even tired. Chris chalked up another new accomplishment for himself and began to wonder how much weight he might be able to lift in his improved condition.

The stairs stopped at the fourth floor. Chris had to open a heavy metal fire door for them to get through. Then they stood the crate up on one end and knocked on the door to Temsik's apartment.

No one answered.

Luis tried again, but still they heard nothing.

"Just as I figured. He's out. Beth never was able to reach him on the phone. But she told him we were coming. She asked him to leave the key under the mat."

Chris reached down and lifted the straw mat at their feet; beneath was a small brass-colored key. "Here." He handed it to Luis.

Luis fit the key in the lock and turned it twice over, unlocking the deadbolt. He opened the door. "Hey, Temsik! You home? Hey!"

Chris wondered what Temsik would look like. Naturally, Beth had had no photos to show him, since no vampire could ever show up on film. Would he look like Frank Langella? Christopher Lee? Bela Lugosi? Lord Byron?

They hauled the crate inside, setting it down in the living room beside the leather sofa. Chris closed the door behind them.

The lights were on in the apartment.

"Shit!" Chris was in awe as he surveyed the room. To his left lay an immaculate kitchen, its floor and walls done in alternate rows of black and white glossy ceramic tiles. The kitchen opened up to a small dining area with black lacquered table and chairs, which gave way to the living room with its high ceiling, where the gray carpeting began, and where sat furniture that looked comfortable enough to spend the rest of one's life in. Tall ferns and exotic trees loomed up all around, framing the bank of windows that reached from floor to ceiling. To the right of the living room a staircase curved up to the second level, and beyond the foot of the stairs a door stood open, a crack, to a darkened room.

The smell of aerosol disinfectant hung in the air, as if it had just been sprayed around the place.

Luis set the apartment key on the dining room table.

"Listen," he said. "I don't know when Temsik will be back, but he'd want you to make yourself at home."

"You're not leaving?" said Chris.

"Yeah, I've got to run. I need to get back to Chicago, anyway. It's midnight already."

"Are you sure he knows I'm coming? I wish you'd stick around so you could introduce me."

"I can't."

"All right. But before you go, we should call Beth, at least."

Chris used the white rotary-dial wall phone in the kitchen. Luis prompted him the numbers as he dialed. After a few rings, he got the message on the answering machine, in Beth's voice, asking him to leave his name and number. This was followed by giddy laughter and the expected *beep*. It sounded as if Beth had been drunk when she taped it.

Chris left a brief message, saying it was him and Luis, and they would call again later.

"Nobody's home there, either," he said. "But it was Beth's voice on the answering machine."

"I should have expected them to be out at this hour. Oh, well. Now I got to go."

"I wish you'd stay, just until he comes back."

"He may not return until dawn. Sure, I could stay here tonight, but I'm much safer in my own coffin. They're expecting me back in Chicago, anyway."

"But I'm worried—"

"Nothing can hurt you here. And if you're concerned about Temsik—well, he knows you're coming. Otherwise, he wouldn't have left his key under the mat. Temsik's got to be expecting you."

"Then why is there no note or anything?"

Luis sighed. "You're reading too much into this, Chris. Trust me."

"Okay. You're probably right." Like he had been telling

Del last night, sometimes he could get a little paranoid, blow things out of proportion. He had to try to calm himself; Luis knew what he was doing.

"There you go. Nothing to worry about. Why don't you call me in Chicago before you go to bed this morning and tell me how things went?"

"Okay. Drive safely and all that stuff."

Luis took out his Ray-Bans and put them on, then swirled his key ring on his index finger and grasped the keys in his fist. " 'Bye, now." He left, closing the door behind him.

Chris was all alone.

The first thing he did was look for a bathroom. All that beer he had consumed on the drive up was screaming to be let out. In the foyer, he found two closets—one for coats and one for brooms and the vacuum cleaner. No doors in the kitchen, just a pantry. The pair of glass doors on one side of the living room (he would have called them French doors, except they were Art Deco) obviously led to a balcony. That left only the upstairs, or perhaps the darkened room beyond the staircase. Somehow, though, Chris got the feeling it wasn't a bathroom.

But he opened the door anyway, and stepped inside. He reached for the light switch and flicked it up.

It was Temsik's library, its walls lined with books both ancient and recent, red leather spines intermixed with brightly colored paperbacks. On the far end of the old Persian rug, in front of the windows, sat a large desk carved of mahogany, cluttered with papers and knickknacks. Facing the desk, with their backs turned to Chris, stood two high-backed padded chairs of dark brown leather, sitting atop wooden claw-feet.

An arm, *somebody's* arm, was dangling from the armrest of one of the chairs. The gray, bony hand protruded from a black sleeve and a white cuff, its long nails and curved posture causing it to resemble one of the chair's hideous feet. The hand hung there perfectly still.

Chris's heart skipped a beat, then began to race, acting like it had during his remission therapy in response to all those destructive drugs. But he was no longer sick, he reminded himself; he was staring at somebody's withered arm, and the sight was churning his stomach.

Chris made a great effort to hold his bladder as he moved closer, to get a look at the figure from the other side. Keeping his distance, he crept stealthily behind the other chair, clasping its wooden frame tightly in both hands.

This close, the disinfectant in the air wasn't strong enough to cover up the body's sickening odor.

It was sagging in the chair, dressed in a tuxedo with a white bow tie, gold cuff links, and a red silk scarf in its breast pocket. The long, white hair was sparse upon its scalp, its skin ashen in tone, covered with age spots. Its tightly wrinkled face resembled weathered, worn deerskin. The eyes and cheeks were sunken, lips drawn back over pale decayed gums and blackened teeth. A dark ooze had dribbled over the side of its mouth and dried there. A torn bit of flesh was flaking off at its right temple, exposing the putrescent muscle beneath. The jawbone looked as if it would burst through the brittle skin, while the Adam's apple was prominent on a thin neck that barely seemed able to support the head.

Chris's first thought was that Temsik had sucked someone dry and neglected to dispose of the body.

At least Temsik had had the decency to close the thing's eyes before going out on the town. But, Chris realized, this corpse's nails had been growing for some time; it had been killed days, perhaps weeks ago. Yet Temsik hadn't done anything with it.

Chris mustered up his courage and approached the corpse. He peeked under its collar, but saw no bite marks on the rotting flesh. However Temsik had gone about it, he had left his victim without a drop of blood. It was grotesque.

Chris was staring at the corpse's withered hand when he noticed that below it, on the rug, lay a golden ring set with a large emerald. As he bent over to pick it up, his peripheral vision picked up a slight movement. Something had happened. Swiftly, he snatched the ring from the floor and jumped back from the corpse.

Staring back at him from the skull-like face was a pair of dull, glassy eyes. They had sprung open when he wasn't looking.

Somehow, Chris still managed to hold on to his bladder. Dead people's eyes popped open all the time, didn't they? What did they call it, a reflex action? It was a common occurrence. Sure, a reflex action, that's all. Nothing to pee your pants over.

But then the corpse's mouth opened, and it proceeded to wet its lips with the ooze from its gray tongue.

"*Go . . . away,*" it whispered.

A voice like sandpaper.

"*Leave . . . me . . . alone!*"

BLOODTHIRSTY

CHRIS pissed a foamy stream of tepid Meister Braü down his leg.

"Leave . . . now!" said the corpse.

"Who are you?" Chris said, trembling and wet.

"Go, Chrisss . . . get out!" it hissed.

It knew his name!

Chris remembered what Beth had told him: *I've heard that he's all alone now, that his companion, Laura, has been destroyed. . . . I'm worried about Temsik's health and well-being. I keep dreaming there's going to be some awful disaster. . . . I've heard that he's depressed. He might do something drastic, like walk out into the sunlight, or try to starve himself out of existence. . . .*

"You're Temsik!" Chris's voice cracked on uttering the vampire's name. "You're him, aren't you?"

The corpse was silent.

"You're Temsik! My God!"

"God." A short guttural statement. "God. Hegh!" The corpse coughed up a green glob of phlegm that landed in its lap. "Beer."

"What?"

"Beer. I sssmell . . . warm . . . beer."

"Th-that's me."

The corpse laughed—a wheezing, dead man's laugh. His

101

eyes looked down at the wet stain along Chris's trousers.
"I . . . ssscare . . . you?"

"You are Temsik."

"Yesss."

"Good God! What happened?"

"Thisss?" Temsik wheezed more laughter. "I . . . did
thisss."

"But it's horrible! How could you possibly—"

"I did thisss," Temsik repeated.

Chris couldn't believe his eyes. By all rights, this man
should be dead. His body was decrepit, decaying, fit only
for vultures and maggots. He wasn't dead, however, but
undead like Chris himself, and that changed all the rules.
It looked as if Temsik were on the verge of crumbling into
dust, as Christopher Lee had done in *Horror of Dracula*
after Peter Cushing had lured him into the sunlight. After
Dracula had been destroyed, the wind had blown his dust
away, leaving only Dracula's great ruby ring.

Chris examined the ring that had fallen off Temsik's
finger. It was exquisitely crafted, apparently solid gold, and
displayed a beautifully cut emerald. It was not perhaps as
impressive as Chris imagined Dracula's ring to be, but it
was magnificent nonetheless. The inner side of the band
was inscribed: "To V.K.T.—Eternal Love—L.S."

Looking at Temsik, Chris wondered if eternity was all it
was cracked up to be. *Is this what's in store for me?*

Chris withdrew his glacier glasses from his jacket pocket.
He held their mirrored lenses at an angle beneath Temsik's
face and found that the rotting visage indeed cast no reflection.

"Goddammit!" Chris felt suddenly clutched with de-
spair. "Beth sent me up here! You knew that, because you
left the key under the mat! You're supposed to be my
teacher, for chrissakes! What the hell do you expect me to
do now!"

"Teachhh. Hegh!" Temsik coughed up another glob of
phlegm.

"Oh Christ!" Chris was reeling; he had to sit down. He

collapsed into the chair opposite Temsik, aghast that he was carrying on a conversation with a supposedly wise old vampire who was looking more like a zombie extra from an Italian horror movie.

"Chrissst." Temsik laughed. "Chrissst. Hegh!"

Chris couldn't let Temsik collapse into a pile of dust. If he did, he would have failed his mission. Beth would never forgive him, and then who knew what might happen? It might be unwise to tempt the wrath of a cunning female vampire. Chris was too much of a novice to know how to defend himself. The plain truth was, he needed Temsik.

And Temsik needed blood.

"Temsik, I'm going to help you."

"Help. Hegh!"

"I know about Laura." Chris realized he was already betraying Beth's confidence; she hadn't wanted him to divulge the smallest hint of his mission. But Beth hadn't foreseen such a drastic circumstance. Or, if she had, she had put it out of her mind. "Beth said it was a rumor, but I see it's got to be true. You can't let yourself wither away like this! Beth says you're duty-bound to be my mentor. I won't let you starve yourself if I can help it. I'm going out. I'm going to find you some blood. I'll be back as fast as I can."

"Fassst."

Chris was amazed at how he had been able to take control of the situation. Temsik must have been shocked at his impertinence. After all, Chris had only been a vampire for two days, while Temsik had been around for who knew how long.

"You wait right here until I come back." Chris was embarrassed at having said that; it was obvious that Temsik couldn't even get up from the chair. He felt as if he had told a blind man to watch his step.

Temsik's hand snapped up lightning-quick and clutched Chris's wrist in what seemed like a death grip. "Not . . . muchhh . . . time!"

Temsik's grip abruptly relaxed. Chris sprang from the

chair and fled the apartment. He had to find someone for Temsik to bite. He had to bring Temsik *back*, before it was too late, before his mentor was reduced to nothing. Of course, in the movies, a vampire could usually be resurrected from his dust, his ring, and a few drops of fresh human blood, but Chris doubted he could make it work, and hoped for his own sake that he wouldn't have to try.

As he slammed the door behind him, he realized he had forgotten to grab the key. He tried the knob, but it was no use. The door had locked by itself.

He had to get back in and get the key.

A landlord or building manager had to be around there somewhere. Chris went down the hallway and checked the peepholes in the doors. All were dark except for one, which displayed a small yellow bead of light. Somebody behind in that apartment was awake.

Chris knocked firmly against the wooden door. On the other side, a dog began to bark, a low deep-throated bark—perhaps a collie. Chris thought it sounded like Lassie.

A shadow passed momentarily on the other side of the peephole, and then the door was opened a crack, the chain lock still in place. Half of a woman's face was visible peeking around the door.

"Yes? What do you want?"

Chris broke out into a cold sweat, not knowing exactly what to say. He looked into her eyes in an effort to be as sincere as possible, and felt a burning sensation in his adenoids as he spoke. "Yeah . . . I'm a guest of Mr. Temsik's, you know, in 401? And I can't believe I did this, but I just locked myself out of the apartment. Temsik isn't home, and I was just going out, but I guess I left the key"—(Now where had Luis left it? on the dining room table?)—"on the dining room table. I didn't know the door was going to lock behind me like that. Anyway, I'm trying to find the landlord or building manager or whoever I need to let me back in. Where should I—"

The woman shut the door. Chris couldn't blame her. No one in their right mind would buy a story like that. They would only think he was some nut trying to get into the nicest apartment in the building.

But the woman opened the door again, wider this time. She had only shut it so she could remove the chain. The dog barked right at her heels. Chris managed to get a glimpse of it: a Border collie or a Shetland sheepdog, or something not quite as big as a regular collie. The dog began to growl.

"Hush, Rocky!" said the woman. She kept the dog back as she came out into the hall, closing her door behind her. In her hand was a fat key ring. "Landlord's out of town. What was your name again?"

"Chris."

They headed down the hall, back to Temsik's apartment.

"I don't know what's the matter with Rocky. He loves people. The landlord gave me a passkey for emergencies like this. Everyone's always locking themselves out of their apartments. All the locks in this building are the same. I mean, they all lock behind you, like in a hotel. Did you just get here today?"

"Yeah. Today."

"Thought I hadn't seen you around. Here we are." The woman fit a key into the lock and turned it over once. Luis had turned it twice, which must have unlocked both the door and the deadbolt. Since Chris hadn't locked the deadbolt, she had only to make one turn of the key to open the door. "Voilà!"

"Thanks!" Chris went in and grabbed the apartment key from the table, holding it up for the woman to see. He quickly left the apartment and closed the door behind him. "Right where I left it," he said, feeling a compulsion to prove to the woman that he was an honest guy.

But the woman was laid-back, as if she didn't care whether or not he turned out to be a burglar. "Nice to meet you," she said with a smile. "Hope we'll see you around."

Chris had already opened the door to the staircase. "Oh, sure. Thanks again."

As he started down the stairs, he wondered if he should have tried to bring her inside for Temsik to bite. But somehow, he couldn't imagine himself forcing Temsik to suck the blood of one of his friendly neighbors. He had been right to leave it alone.

But he still couldn't believe how easy it had been. The woman hadn't questioned a word of his story.

Chris ran down the steps two at a time, and realized as he looked down that his pants were still damp from the beer he had let go. He turned around abruptly to go back and change into some pants. Then he remembered all his clothes were crated up with his coffin, and he didn't have time to unpack it. He wondered why the woman hadn't noticed the long dark stain down his leg; she must have decided not to mention it out of politeness, or shyness. Chris would have to live with it, and hoped that it would air out once he got outside. He fled the building quickly.

He had to go out and find somebody for Temsik, and time was short.

If this had been Chicago, it would have been easy. Chris would have known places to go where he could have found suitable victims. But this was an entirely different city, a place where he had never been before, and he was all alone, and he hadn't the slightest clue where to start.

BITING TIME

THE place was called Paul's Club. Even at one o'clock in the morning, it was doing good business. It looked less like a bar than it did someone's living room, but thankfully there were no mirrors to be seen. A diverse assortment of people had gathered, sitting in sleek blue vinyl chairs that looked as if they had come from the Doctor's Office Surplus Store. Tall drinks sweated on glass-topped coffee tables. The oldest couple in the joint appeared to be in their sixties, while the majority seemed to be university students. But the students themselves were a mixed bunch, from long-haired T-shirted neo-hippies to conservative necktied proto-yuppies. The song playing on the jukebox was Glenn Miller's "Moonlight Serenade."

All in all, it looked more like a place for couples than for singles, although rules like that were never exactly written in stone. A few solitary souls were seated along the bar, ordering second or third or fourth rounds for themselves.

Chris sat at the bar next to a blond girl with a frizzy permanent whose squarish face gave her the look of an athlete, as if she might be on the campus volleyball team or something. She had overdone it on the rouge and eye shadow. Under a red University of Wisconsin sweatshirt, her shoulders were broad; her stonewashed blue jeans encased meaty thighs that did not look fat. She was drinking a Screwdriver, or a variation thereof.

The thing about Paul's Club that bothered Chris was the large tree that stood in the middle of the room. It grew out of the floor, up to the ceiling, its branches reaching out over the heads of the drinkers, and there was no denying that it was real. The place had obviously been built around it, with a hole cut in the floor right around the trunk. Without any sunlight, it couldn't possibly be alive, yet its limbs were filled with dark green leaves, and it looked, in fact, like one of the healthiest trees Chris had ever seen.

But what the fuck is it doing here?

Chris had never before in his life tried to pick up a girl. Even with the guys he had known, he had never picked them up in bars; he had always met them at parties, through friends, or through friends of friends. In fact, mulling it over in his head, he realized he had never before tried to pick up anything in a bar, male, female, animal, vegetable, or mineral.

Chris turned to the girl beside him.

"You come here often?" Chris cringed as he said it, but it had escaped his lips before anything could be done.

She stared at him as if he were speaking Gaelic.

"I'm sorry. I mean, can I buy you a drink?"

"Have one already." She turned back to nurse it.

Chris was a total neophyte, and these lines were going to get him nowhere. He tried to think of something nifty, like from a movie, but the only movie that came to mind was *Looking for Mr. Goodbar*—not a good omen. If he used that as his model, this girl jock might turn out to be a rapist.

Chris had to remember to stay in control. After all, he wasn't looking for a roll in the hay. A pint of blood was more like it, and anyway he was procuring for a friend. He had to keep in mind that he was more powerful than this weak creature at his side and ought to be able to make her do what he wanted. He had seen both Beth and Jamie work their hypnotic effects on unsuspecting humans. There was no reason why he couldn't get the same results.

"What is that you're drinking?" he asked.

"A Fuzzy Navel." She said it without turning her head.

Chris needed to make eye contact with her if he wanted to put her into a trance. He knew that much for sure. Once he had locked her in his gaze, he would have to make up the rest.

"Excuse me," he said. It failed to get her attention. "Excuse me, but could I look at your eyes for a second?"

With a sigh of exasperation, she turned and looked straight at him, as if this were the last bit of nonsense she was going to put up with.

Chris sat up a little on the bar stool and stared her down. He locked his eyes on hers and willed her into doing his bidding. He knew he had her in his power. In only a few minutes, they would be back in Temsik's study, saving the old vampire from self-destruction.

Making sure not to lose eye contact, Chris said, "You're going to come with me right now, back to my apartment."

"The fuck I will," she said. She tossed back the last of her drink, picked up her purse, and left Paul's Club in a flash.

It hadn't worked. Chris had failed to put her into a trance. He had to admit he didn't know what he was doing.

Now the jukebox was playing David Bowie's "Fashion."

"Buy you a drink?"

The melodious voice came from the other side of him, and belonged to another girl, this one utterly different from the jock. She had red hair that she wore long and straight, with no makeup on her freckled face. Her body was lean and spindly. Her flat chest hid behind a plain black T-shirt, and her jeans were loose on her narrow hips. Chris didn't normally notice such things on women, but in this case it was difficult not to see how lacking she was in the womanly curves department. Her face was not unattractive.

"Sure," said Chris. "I'll have a Rum and Coke—"

She shook her head and said, "I'm going to buy you a Firefighter." She ordered two of them from the bartender. "It's their specialty here. They keep the recipe locked in a safe. Only one bartender here knows how to make it. It's kind of special. You'll like it."

"Okay." How did she know what he would like?

"See that tree there?"

"Hard to miss it."

"It's not real. It's dead. Those are plastic-coated leaves. They replace them once a year. Glue them onto the branches. They have to close the place for a couple of days to do it."

Perhaps this girl was a regular. She seemed to become despondent at the idea of the bar being shut down for a few days each year. But Chris was thankful for the insight into the mysterious tree. The girl must have been able to spot that he was a first-timer at Paul's.

"I'm Mary."

"Chris."

They exchanged niceties and fell into a conversation. Mary seemed slightly drunk already, and kept trying to kiss Chris. Once, when his lips shied away from hers, she went ahead and kissed his ear.

"You're cute," she whispered.

For his part, Chris reserved judgment.

Mary was probably drawn to him because he resembled her, in a way. Same hair color, same freckles. His hair had already grown back enough that it probably looked like a fresh crewcut. Chris was one of her own kind, and not much of a threat.

Soon the jukebox was playing Frank Sinatra singing "New York, New York," and one of the bartenders was singing along into a microphone over the small PA system. The whole bar came to a standstill, everyone watching the bartender's performance with affection. When the song was over, there was much applause and cheering. The bartender soaked it all up as if he were headlining Vegas.

"He does that all the time," said Mary, as if Chris couldn't figure it out for himself. "They love it."

"This drink is excellent," said Chris. It had been served in a tall glass with ice, and was bright red in color, like the chairs. A cherry floated on top, and there was more than a hint of cherry in the drink itself.

"Yeah, it is. You got any drugs on you?"

"Nope."

"Are you sure?"

"Yes."

" 'Cause I want some drugs. I want to get high, and I want you to make love to me."

Chris nearly choked on his Firefighter. He had lost control of the conversation, and now Mary was trying to pick *him* up. And he had been trying to resist! He had to pull himself together. Even though he didn't want to get high or have sex, he needed her badly. Temsik needed her blood. If Chris didn't watch his step, he was going to lose this one like he had lost the girl jock.

"I think I've got some drugs back at my apartment," he said. "In fact, I'm sure of it."

Mary jumped off the bar stool. "Come on, lover, let's go."

After Chris had unlocked the door and led Mary inside, he didn't know what to do.

"What's this?" asked Mary, sitting upon the crate.

"Uh, please," said Chris, and scooted her off it. He motioned to the sofa, making sure she sat facing the kitchen so she couldn't peek past the doorway to Temsik's study. "This is much more comfortable."

"But what's the box for?"

"New shipment of drugs," Chris answered. When Mary's eyes lit up, he had to say, "Just kidding. It's really . . . It's a kit."

"You building something?"

"Yeah, a . . . a harpsichord." It was the first thing that had popped into his mind. But it would do; Mary's eyes widened, showing she was impressed. Chris felt an urge to leave the room. He had never been a very good liar. "You just stay right here while I go get the drugs."

Mary pouted. "Okay. But hurry."

Chris expected her next words to be something like, "My motor's running." She proved him wrong.

He raced into the study and shut the door.

Temsik was still intact. Chris was relieved that he hadn't become a pile of dust. Temsik's bulbous eyes stared at him expectantly. "Well?" came the raspy voice.

"I've got a girl . . . outside." Chris was suddenly out of breath. "What do you want me to do?"

"Bring . . . the poor creature . . . in." Temsik's mouth spread into a grin, a morbid death's-head grin revealing teeth and gums.

"But she'll freak!" Chris could see it now, bringing her into the room and letting her get a good look at that corpselike face. She would scream and run and go to the police. He and Temsik would be found out.

"If ssshe . . . 'freaksss' . . . then hold her . . . ssstill . . . for me."

"What do you mean?"

"Grab her . . . hold her . . . ssstill! . . . You got that?"

"Yeah. Sure." Chris didn't know if he would be able to do it, but he would try.

"I'll . . . do the ressst. . . . Jussst . . . bring her clossse . . . hold her . . . ssstill."

Chris nodded. It wasn't much of a plan. Temsik would have to make it work somehow or they would be in deep shit. Chris couldn't hold Mary indefinitely if something went wrong.

Chris went back to the living room, closing the study door behind him.

"Hey, Mary." Chris swallowed a lump in his throat. "I want to show you something."

"Where's the drugs?" Mary slurred, getting up. "I thought you said you were getting the drugs." She came over to him and leaned up against him, sliding her leg between his thighs.

"They're in here. That's what I wanted to show you." Chris tossed his head to one side, indicating the study. He threw his arm around Mary and turned the knob.

He kept Mary ahead of him as they went in, his hands on either of her shoulders.

Temsik had withdrawn his arm so that none of him could be seen from behind.

"Wow! Look at these books! You must be rich!"

Chris urged her forward across the Persian rug. She had not yet seen anything. But although Temsik was well hidden, his odor was not.

"What is that?" Mary stopped, turned her head over her shoulder, and crinkled her nose. "Rot?"

"My books are moldy. Falling apart." Chris's voice cracked. His hands were getting clammy.

"You're trembling." Mary placed her hand on Chris's, over her left shoulder. "Or are you just horny?"

They were about to reach Temsik. Chris didn't know what he was going to say (*I wonder who that is?*). He had to remind himself that despite Temsik's disgusting appearance, he wasn't going to kill Mary, just take some of her blood, like Chris had done with the blonde beneath the El tracks the night before. Mary would come to no significant harm.

Chris brought her before Temsik.

"What's tha—"

Temsik looked up and grinned.

Mary screamed.

Chris clutched her arms and held them behind her back. But she was still screaming. He had to shut her up. He managed to get both of her small wrists in the grip of one hand, and clamped the other across her mouth. His muscles gripped her tightly; with his new strength, she wasn't going anywhere.

Temsik simply continued to sit in the chair, so Chris had to force Mary down. He yanked on her arms and pushed her down on her knees. Her screams were muffled behind Chris's hand, but he could feel the vibrations in his fingers as her terrific noises yearned for escape. Mary's head struggled from side to side, so Chris clamped down harder, holding her steady. It felt good to have so much control over his muscles, and to be able to control someone else.

Mary's eyes bugged out as she was forced to look straight at Temsik's corrupt face. Some of her hair had fallen in her face from all her thrashing. Her teeth bit deeply into the flesh of Chris's palm.

"Ouch!" Instinctively, Chris drew his hand away.

But the instant he did, Mary stopped screaming.

Temsik had sat up slightly and was holding Mary in a trance. His eyes had lost their glassy look, and now seemed brimming with life. They were a cold steely blue, nearly glowing in their brightness.

On her knees, Mary stood stock-still, staring directly into Temsik's unearthly eyes. Chris continued to hold her arms behind her back, but she offered no resistance. Her breathing became steady and measured.

As Temsik came forward, Chris heard what sounded like bones snapping, but Temsik was undeterred. He brought up his emaciated arms and laid them on Mary's shoulders, opening his mouth, getting ready for the bite. But Chris noticed that some of his black teeth had fallen out. Temsik had only one fang.

Temsik's slimy tongue felt its way along the upper ridge of his teeth and discovered the gaps there. He stopped right before biting into Mary.

"Won't work," he said.

Chris's heart sank. All this work, for nothing.

"You mussst . . . Chrisss . . ."

"Huh?"

"Mussst . . . bite her . . . for me."

It seemed all right; Mary was still in her trance. Chris gathered that all he had to do was make the proper wounds in her neck and let Temsik suck her blood, like Jamie had done for him the night before. But Chris had never actually bit into a neck before, and didn't know how to proceed.

"Hurry, Chrisss!" Temsik hissed.

Chris swallowed hard and leaned over. He opened his mouth wide, drawing his lips far back over his teeth, letting his long canines spring into place. A drop of fluid dripped from his fangs onto his tongue; it had a sharp, pungent taste, like a strong cheese. Chris's mouth began to water. He placed the tips of his fangs along the girl's neck.

"No!" Temsik's voice suddenly gained power, perhaps in anticipation of what he was about to receive. "A little lower . . . to your right . . . that'sss it. Now!"

Temsik's command was powerful. Without hesitation, Chris bit down hard, using his bottom row of teeth as support. Mary's flesh was tough, but Chris's canines were sharp enough that they plunged through easily. An initial strong spurt of blood shot into his mouth. Chris drank it down until the spurting became less. Then he handed her over to Temsik, licking the spilled blood from his own lips.

Mary was moaning in ecstasy.

Chris stood up and watched as Temsik closed his withered mouth around the wound. Temsik's chest swelled as he sucked her blood within him. His bony fingers dug into her skin, his sharp fingernails ripping small holes in her T-shirt and tearing her skin, drawing more blood.

Chris had the beginnings of an erection, but he believed it was from his own brief taste of Mary's blood, not from watching Temsik having his turn at her. For a near corpse, Temsik went at his task with vigor.

Minutes later, the old vampire seemed to have had enough, and withdrew his mouth. Blood continued to run from Mary's neck marks.

"Close it up!" Temsik ordered. His voice had lost its hissing, raspy tone already.

Chris stared dumbly at him. He had no idea what Temsik wanted of him.

"Bite her again, Chris! So she doesn't bleed all over."

Chris did as he as told, sinking his teeth back into the wound. At first he didn't know what good it would do, but then his tongue tasted again the heady liquid that was dripping from his fangs. This must be what would help Mary's blood to coagulate. Beth had done the same to him each time she had bitten him, or his wounds would never have healed because of his leukemia. Since Temsik was in such bad shape, and one of his fangs was missing, he needed Chris to finish the job for him. It didn't take long. Chris withdrew his teeth, and Mary's wounds closed up in their wake. He licked the last of the blood from her neck and stood up. Around the puffy red marks, no bleeding could be seen, only the glistening wetness of Chris's saliva.

Mary had passed out. Chris picked her up and seated her in the other chair.

"Good," said Temsik. He cleared his throat. The blood seemed to have lubricated his vocal cords. "Good work. Now get rid of her. Quick, while she's still under. You can take my car. Keys are on the desk."

"Your car?" Chris asked in bewilderment, still stunned by what had taken place, and by what he had done.

"Yes. The black Jag out front. It's all right, my boy. I trust you implicitly."

Temsik's corpse-face grinned up at him. Some of the color was returning to his cheeks. Bones creaking, he slowly managed to rise from the chair and stand on his feet.

"Don't get arrested, and be sure to be back by sunrise. I'm going to bed."

 **XIII**

LOST SOULS

CHRIS was awakened by someone rapping on the lid of his coffin. He slid open the door to the viewing window and saw Temsik's face staring down at him. Temsik no longer looked like a corpse, but rather a skinny man of seventy. His jowls hung in folds below his lean chin. He had trimmed his hair, which seemed already to be growing back where it had been sparse before. His lips had grown fuller, less puckered, and some of his wrinkles had smoothed out, though many remained. The dangling chunk of skin over his temple had been shed, and had grown back afresh. But the most agreeable changes of all were the pink, healthy luster of his cheeks and the piercing quality of his eyes. If Chris could have looked only at his eyes, and ignored the rest of the face, he would have thought he was staring at the most beautiful and youthful pair he had ever seen.

"The keys to the Jaguar," Temsik said expectantly. He pronounced it "Jag-you-are." His voice bore no trace of a Russian accent, sounding more British than American.

Chris pushed open the lid to his coffin, continuing to stare at Temsik's somewhat renewed visage. He had set up his coffin in the first upstairs bedroom, the one Temsik wasn't using. The room contained a double bed, night tables, a dresser, a roomy closet, and a window that could be shuttered from within during the day. He wondered if Laura

117

had slept in this room, or if she had shared the other bedroom with Temsik.

"Are they on your person, or have you hidden them from me?" Temsik stood in a canary-yellow sweatshirt and a pair of chinos, his arms held behind his back. His tone sounded displeased.

Finally, Chris's mind began to work at the problem, and he realized the keys must be in the pocket of the pants he had worn last night. He had slept in a pair of sweatpants, without a shirt, and therefore the keys couldn't be on him at the moment, because he had no pockets.

"Try my pants," he said. "On the floor there."

"On the floor," Temsik repeated, bending over to reach the trousers.

Chris wondered if he had done anything wrong. He couldn't remember having brought the car any harm, even though his driving had been a little rusty. "Is something the matter?" He sat up and propped himself on his elbows.

"Not that I know of," Temsik said as he rummaged through Chris's clothes. "Ah! Here we are!" The jingle of keys. "So long as you tell me where I might find the Jaguar."

"I'm sorry. I couldn't find a space when I got back. I had to park it down the street, in front of some church or temple or something."

Temsik now stood, spinning the key ring on one finger. He had trimmed his fingernails. "A church or temple or something—which, exactly?"

Chris thought hard. Temsik was putting him on the spot, testing him, perhaps. He tried to visualize the building in his mind: large, bland, made of stone, with pillars and a bank of steps. Suddenly, he could see clearly, chiseled right above the pillars; TEMPLE OF FREEMASONRY. "Masons," he muttered. "The Masonic Temple."

"Good. I knew it would come to you. Now, here." Temsik reached behind himself and pulled out a pistol that must have been tucked in his belt. "Catch." He tossed it lightly Chris's way.

Chris snatched it out of the air with one hand. He was amazed at his own dexterity; he had never before been very adept at such impromptu feats. He hefted the black pistol in his hand. Its weight felt good against his palm. "What's this?" he asked.

"That, Chris, is a nine-millimeter Smith and Wesson automatic pistol with a fourteen-round clip. Standard Underground issue."

Actually, Chris had misphrased his question. Although he knew little about guns, he had at least been able to tell that it was a gun, and something other than a revolver. "I mean, what's it for?"

"Believe it or not, there are such things as vampire hunters. There are numerous ways to dispatch them, but I find that a gunshot wound to the head is most efficient."

"You actually kill them?"

"It's kill or be destroyed. I don't ask that you carry it around with you. Not unless you feel the need. It is unlicensed, and could get you into trouble. Get a switchblade for protection on the street. Keep the gun in your coffin, as I do."

"You sleep with it?"

"By all means. Leave the safety on and you'll be all right. Not that it can kill you; it can't. But if you manage to blow off your own toe, I can assure you it won't grow back."

Chris got out of his coffin and stretched, the gun still in his hand. "Is it loaded?"

"Of course it's loaded. Hard to blow the brains out of your nemesis with an empty pistol." Temsik stared at Chris as if this point were patently obvious.

"I get you." Chris removed his finger from the trigger.

"You may not need it today or tomorrow, but someday you will. Only a fool would fail to protect himself against hunters. Alas, the hunters themselves never seem to realize this."

"What do you mean?" Chris checked to make sure the safety was on. It wasn't.

"Oh, they all see themselves as Van Helsings in the great tradition. *Dracula* may be a grand entertainment, but it's also a silly one. I always find myself shouting at him, 'Grab your gun! Your gun, you idiot!' But of course, he hasn't got one! It's 1897, and with all his wealth Dracula doesn't even own a gun! That strains credulity a bit. But naturally, there wouldn't have been a novel if he had shot his enemies at the earliest opportunity."

"Good point." Chris put the safety on, and, pointing the pistol at the floor, put his finger back on the trigger.

Temsik went on. "Even with Dracula's aversion to crucifixes, he could still have gotten off a shot while hiding himself from the cross. He could have made mincemeat out of Van Helsing—or blood pudding, as it were."

Chris laughed. Perhaps Temsik wasn't that difficult to get along with after all.

"Why didn't you tell me you couldn't drive?" Temsik's tone was exceedingly pleasant. Chris wondered if he was pissed off.

"I can drive," Chris protested.

"You're quite sure of that? I saw you lurching away from the curb last night when I looked out my window." He sounded pissed off. He sounded like Chris's dad. "Did everything go all right?" Temsik looked at him warily.

Chris felt put on the spot again, like an amoeba being examined beneath a microscope. "Everything's fine."

I dumped her in the park.

"That's good to hear." Temsik brightened.

I dumped her in the park, beneath a scrawny elm tree. It was chilly outside for a human, and she had no jacket.

"No problems with the girl?" Temsik prompted.

"No. None at all." Chris's stomach turned in circles.

"Fine. I hope this room suits you. You've got a bed in case you need to bring someone back here. Throw a blanket over the casket so they don't ask any questions."

"But they won't remember anyway—"

"Yes, but you don't want them to cause problems while they're here." Temsik turned toward the door, jingling his car keys. "I'm going out on an errand, but I'll be back presently. Here's some money." Temsik tossed him a thin leather wallet.

"Did you steal this from somebody?" Chris opened it up; it smelled new and contained one hundred dollars in crisp new bills.

"Of course not. I've got plenty of money."

"How?"

"I'll tell you later. Why don't you go out and grab a bite?"

"You mean, on my own?"

"Why not? I showed you how to do it last night."

"But I don't remember how to—"

"Sure you do. Concentrate, and it will come back to you. Right here, on the neck." Temsik pointed with two of his fingers to a spot on his own loose-skinned neck. "The jugular vein."

"Which side?"

"Either side. It makes no difference. Don't worry, you'll smell it. Can't mistake it."

"But how do I hypnotize them?"

"Didn't I show you that?"

"No."

"Oh." Temsik frowned. "Then I'll show you now. Here, have a seat."

They sat together atop the bed's comforter.

"There is a certain power within you," said Temsik. "Call it supernatural, or even parapsychological. Call it what you will. We don't know its true nature. At least I don't. In time, it'll be like a second skin. But until then, you'll have to work to conjure it up."

"I tried last night," said Chris, "when I went to find the girl, but I couldn't get it to work. I stared down this other girl, but—"

"It's more than simply staring them down. There's a physical state that goes along with it, a condition you can call up. It's as easy as moving your arm. You have to lower your body temperature slightly. You'll break out in a sweat, your mouth will get dry, and you'll feel a burning in the back of your throat. Then you look into the eyes of your victim, and concentrate. You tell them what you want them to do, and they do it."

Chris remembered how he had gotten the neighbor lady to open up Temsik's apartment for him, and realized he had hypnotized someone already. The physical symptoms had been the same as Temsik had described, and she had done everything Chris had asked.

"All right," said Chris. "Sounds easy enough. But what if I—"

"Chris, you can't help but succeed. No need to worry." Temsik smiled at him. His teeth were no longer black but yellow, and his missing fang had grown back. He looked at his watch: a Rolex. "It's nine o'clock. Be back here by two. I've got something planned."

"Like what?"

"Like something, all right? You'll see soon enough. Now go out and have some fun. Explore the city. You'll find a great many pretty necks in Madison, waiting to be conquered."

It proved amazingly simple. Chris went barhopping down State Street, the downtown business and tavern district where he had found Paul's Club the night before. Eventually, he ended up at Jocko's Rocketship Tavern, a rowdy bar around the corner on Gilman, and met a college junior named Steve, who wore a T-shirt bearing the University of Wisconsin mascot Bucky Badger and reading FUCK 'EM, BUCKY! In this particular instance, Chris determined that the enticement of drugs would work better than the promise of sex, and he led his prey into the bathroom. He threw the bolt in place, locking them both in the one-toilet cubicle, and went to work. Steve fell quickly under his spell, and Chris managed to have a nice, quiet repast. When he was finished, he was pleased to discover that Steve had grown a healthy erection under his Levi's. He wiped his mouth and Steve's neck with wet paper towels and flushed the bloody rags down the toilet. Steve's wounds healed up nicely right before Chris's eyes, becoming large pimples that perhaps had been aggravated in a shaving accident. No one would be the wiser. Chris left him there, passed out on the toilet with a grin on his face and a stain in his crotch.

At two o'clock in the morning, when Chris returned to the apartment, he could smell the food before he had opened the door—not blood, but *food*. All over the dining room table, Temsik had laid out an enormous feast fit for a dinner party. Ovens had heated the air (though, anymore, one temperature was as comfortable as another), and the smells that filled the room were wondrous and exotic.

Chris was horribly confused as he closed the door behind him.

"What is . . . why are . . . ?" He hung his jacket in the closet and stood dumbfounded before the table. "The Chicago guys said we couldn't eat food."

"They're quite right." Temsik, one foot out of the kitchen, wore an apron and was holding a slotted spoon in one hand. He returned to his labors at the stove.

"Then why . . ."

"Not exactly the Socratic method, I'll admit." Temsik stirred the contents of a steaming pot. "But my job is to teach, and yours is to learn. I've no time to dillydally, so tonight is your first lesson. Have a seat."

Chris sat at the far end of the table, gawking at the assortment of dishes.

"A movable feast? Perhaps not," said Temsik as he brought a large bowl to the table filled with some kind of red soup. "An implacable feast—that's more like it!"

"I don't get you."

"You will, Chris. Believe me, you will." Temsik sat down beside Chris and grabbed a crystal carafe from the middle of the table. "We'll start with some vodka." He poured from the carafe into two shot glasses, and handed one to Chris.

"Uh, I don't really like straight vodka."

"You'll like this." Temsik held up his glass. "*Vasheh Zdorovyeh!* Your health!" He threw back the shot in one big gulp.

"Ditto." Chris followed suit, reluctantly. He expected a sharp, foul sting upon his tongue. Instead, the vodka was icy cold, smooth, and slightly sweet. "Whoo! What is this stuff?"

"You were expecting shit?"

"It must be Stoli, then."

Temsik shook his head. "Stolichnaya is fine. But this is better. Our comrades in Soviet Union send it to me. It brings me back to the 'good old days' in Petersburg. Leningrad, to you."

That was the first hint in Temsik's speech that he was a true Russian. Russians never said "the Soviet Union"; it was always simply "Soviet Union."

"Do you send them anything in return?" Chris asked.

"Videotapes. They love our movies. My friend Polina Ivanovna has a Japanese VCR. I just sent her a copy of *The Hunger*, and she says she's watched it eight times already. So drink up, Chris, courtesy of Polina Ivanovna!"

"Do you ever go over there?"

"No. I haven't seen Polina in eighty years." Temsik set up another round. "*Vasheh Zdorovyeh!*"

Chris smiled. "*Vasheh Zdorovyeh!*"

"What you see before you, most of it is *zakooski*, which are sort of hors d'oeuvres that Russians eat before dinner, while they sit, drink vodka, and chat. Here, this ground-up mixture is 'Herring Vorschmack'. . . ."

Temsik showed Chris the various appetizer dishes and told him what they were. There were two varieties of fried hard-boiled eggs with different ingredients stuffed inside (eggs 'Princess Olga' and eggs 'Zoloto Grebeshock'), various smoked fishes, gray caviar, lobster in mayonnaise, radishes in sour cream, herring marinated in wine, herring salad, pickled herring, chopped herring with eggs, herring with mustard sauce, pickled beets, pickled red cabbage, hot mushrooms in sour cream sauce, chicken livers in Madeira, and small meat pies called *piroshki*.

"This would be a good *zakooski* table for a modest dinner party," said Temsik. "You eat a herring or two, have a shot of vodka, try some herring salad, drink some more vodka. It's very conducive to conversation. But you and I can only sit and drink vodka. Come, another shot!"

"Please, Temsik," Chris begged. He could already feel the effects of the first two.

"What's the matter? You've eaten, haven't you?" Temsik poured again from the carafe.

"Of course, but—"

"I did as well. A bag boy, behind the Sentry food store. Whom did you have?"

"Uh, a college student, at a bar called Jocko's."

"Ah, fine!" Temsik raised his glass. *"Vasheh Zdorovyeh!"*

Temsik seemed awfully cheerful for one who had just tried to commit suicide.

"Vasheh Zdorovyeh." Chris was sullen as he and Temsik downed their glasses at the same time. Chris winced. It still tasted good, but was not without its own special bite.

"What you wouldn't give for one of those pickled herrings right now, eh?" Temsik chided. "That would feel nice in your mouth, wouldn't it? Soothe your palate, get it ready for the next shot. In fact, I bet you've never tasted eggs 'Princess Olga' before, have you?"

"No."

"Then you have really missed something! You know, back in Petersburg, my friends and I missed *zakooski* so much, we once set up a human *zakooski*. We were celebrating a long, cold winter night in December, and gathered together all kinds of people. I believe we had a Kirghiz there, and a Siberian, a Mongol, a Ukrainian, a Georgian, a Finn, a Pole, and a Petersburg civil servant! We put them to sleep and laid them out on tables around the room, drank vodka, and sampled a bit of blood from each of their necks. The saltiness of blood goes a long way toward replacing pickled herring, but we still found it wasn't the same.''

Chris tried to imagine the scene, but could not. It sounded too horrible. Simple peasants and regular citizens, laid out like—well, like mushrooms in sour cream sauce!

''But *zakooski* is only the beginning of a meal, Chris. Over here I've got the entrées. First, a good Ukrainian borsch. Have you ever eaten borsch?''

Chris shook his head. They stood up and went to the other end of the table to look at it. It was the rich, red soup Temsik had been finishing when Chris had come in.

''Ah! Too bad. And now you never will. Look, in it we've got good stew meat, some smoked pork, beets, cabbage, beans, onions, potatoes, tomatoes, garlic, butter, and of course, sour cream. See how red it is! There's nothing more beautiful than a good borsch. And I put it to you that this one is excellent. Here, take a whiff!''

''I don't think I—''

''Go on, Chris,'' Temsik prodded.

Chris leaned over the hot soup and took in a deep breath through his nose. ''Mmm!'' he said with reluctance; he had hoped he might be indifferent to it. ''This smells fantastic! Now what's that over there?'' Chris pointed to a dish beside the borsch, with some variety of beef swimming in a dark, rich-looking sauce.

''Veal kidneys in Madeira. We used to eat this on occasion for lunch when I was growing up. The railway station restaurant at Tsarkoe Selo was famous all over Russia for its kidneys in Madeira. I was never able to try it, myself, because by then I was already a vampire.''

The dish smelled incredibly tasty.

''What is the point of all this?'' Chris was blunt. ''Are you trying to show me what I can't eat? Is that it?''

''Precisely.'' Temsik placed an arm around Chris's shoulders, and they sat down again at the table, in front of the eggs ''Princess Olga.''

''I don't think it's very nice.''

''Good. Then you'll listen to what I have to say. But first, more vodka!''

They toasted each other's health and drank another round. Chris had lost count of how many had preceded it; he was getting drunk.

"My point, Chris, is that you've given up a great deal. I presume you've become one of us on your own accord. Beth never takes anyone against their will."

"That's right. I was dying of leukemia, or at least I would have been dead in five years. . . ." Chris told him the story of how he had become a vampire, and how much he liked his vampire friends in Chicago, and how much he was enjoying his new existence.

"Then I've read you very well. You have some very romantic notions about vampires, my friend. Perhaps some are valid. Then again, perhaps not. I don't believe you fully realize what you're in for. You asked me earlier if we actually had to kill hunters who crossed our path. You were shocked that I slept with a gun. You enjoy the fact that you aren't required to kill for your blood. Your heroes are Christopher Lee and Frank Langella. You love the idea of eternal youth, good health, sexual freedom, leisure time, moontans."

"Moontans! Is that why everyone's got a tan?"

"Didn't they tell you?"

"They only told me to buy some sunglasses to protect my eyes from UV rays."

"It's those same rays that tan your skin. If you go out into the night, and the moon is out, you will gradually develop a tan, or a burn if you're not careful. We're acutely sensitive to ultraviolet rays. The moon reflects an infinitessimal fraction of the sun's light, and yet we respond to it. You know, of course, what would happen to you if you went out into the daylight. You would fry in an instant. Well, the same would happen to an ordinary human if the ozone layer were to disappear. Without that layer to protect them, they would sizzle into a heap of dust, just like us. So go ahead, go out on my balcony if you like and catch some rays. But not now."

"That was the one thing I couldn't figure out. I always thought vampires were deathly pale."

"See how excited you are by this idea? This is exactly what I'm talking about. You are too much the romantic. That's why I cooked these dishes, to make you suffer. Do you realize that I have not had a bite of real food since 1808?"

"You're kidding."

"No. I remember it well. The last food I ever ate was a bowl of sauerkraut *s'chee* soup, which I promptly threw up, because I was sick from being bitten the second time and couldn't keep anything down. What I wouldn't give to eat a genuine bowl of *s'chee*!"

"What is it?"

"Cabbage soup. Simple fare, to be sure. But what could be simpler than what we must drink, time and again, night after night? It begins to wear on a person. But, of course, I'll never taste *s'chee* again. You see, by now your whole physiology has undergone a complete change. Some of your digestive organs have ceased to function. Namely, your bowels. Solid foods are absolutely out of the question. There is nothing in your stomach to break them down, and no means of egress for what you've eaten. Food won't do you any nutritional good whatsoever, anyway. Your body can tolerate only one food now, and that's blood."

"Let's have another round," said Chris. This vodka had been a good idea after all. He grabbed the carafe himself and poured the shots. "*Vasheh Zdorovyeh!*"

"*Vasheh Zdorovyeh!*" A look of bliss passed over Temsik's face after he tossed back the vodka. "As you know, you can still drink. It still passes through your kidneys and out your bladder, but without being broken down. The alcohol will get absorbed into your bloodstream, so you can still get drunk, although the effects are short-lived. You've probably noticed already that every vampire you've met is an alcoholic. I've personally met over a thousand vampires, and out of that, I'd say that two or three were not complete lushes. And even they drank on occasion. It's one of our few formerly human pleasures left us: getting smashed to kingdom come. That and sex. Sex is very much the same, except that males are sterile and females infertile. And if you think that hasn't caused a few vampires some grief, you're sorely mistaken.''

"The way I see it," said Chris, beginning to slur his words. "It's all give and take. You give up having children, but you get to live forever. You give up food, but you get to drink all the booze you want. You give up looking in the mirror, but you gain eternal beauty. So you have to give up a few things. Big deal!''

"Well, you're young. Someday you'll know what I'm talking about. You won't take so much for granted. At least you had a choice in your own destiny, and I must say I probably would have made the same choice if I had been in your shoes. But as it was, I was made a vampire entirely unbeknownst to me, and it was anything but pleasant. I don't want to give you a hardship speech about how I had to walk ten miles to school every day through a raging blizzard, but you must realize that you've got it easy. I had no one like me to help me make the transition. I had to learn it all the hard way.

"I didn't know at first about my altered physiology, but I managed to figure it out. You see, Chris, the functions of your organs have all been altered. Either that or they've become useless. You still breathe, and your heart still pumps blood, so perhaps *undead* is a misnomer. When you suck a victim's blood, that blood is in turn converted into vampire blood, what I call *kroba*.''

"Del told me about *kroba*." Chris put in.

"It looks different. It's rust in color, and keeps your body from decaying, keeps you healthy and young in appearance, wards off all diseases, and heals most injuries. But the fundamental difference between human blood and *kroba* is this: human blood transports food around the body, while *kroba* itself *is* the food. Your body consumes *kroba*, but has no way to replenish it. A human's blood is manufactured in his bone marrow. Our bone marrow is useless. We manufacture nothing, and in that sense, we are nothing more than bipedal parasites.''

"So if I were to sit around without biting anybody, like you did, I would use up all my *kroba*?"

"Exactly. I probably had none left when you found me last night.'' Temsik shifted uncomfortably in his chair. He seemed eager to change the subject. Another round of vodka was in order. They toasted each other's health, and drank.

"You already know that it takes three bites to turn a human into a vampire, just like in *Dracula*. But Bram Stoker didn't know the half of it. The first bite will cause the victim little harm. He will forget the incident, though he might have a mild taste for blood afterwards. You know, if he cuts his finger, he will put it in his mouth and suck on it rather than reach for a bandage. That sort of thing. Now, it is imperative that we bite our victims once and only once. The reasons for this are quite obvious.''

"They go crazy.'' Chris knew this firsthand.

"That's right. The second bite causes an enormous bloodlust to take over in the victim's brain, a powerful craving that he can only fulfill by cutting people up and drinking their blood. He doesn't have a vampire's equipment or resources. All he does is run around, slashing throats, doing whatever he can to get at fresh human blood. It is not uncommon that psychopathic serial killers turn out to have been bitten twice. A twice-bitten human is a violent, dangerous individual with enormous strength and great cunning. Many go on murder rampages, but just as many end up killing themselves, just to see the blood come flowing out of their veins.''

"That's disgusting! I remember wanting to kill when Beth tied me down to my bed. I wanted to kill the pizza boy, and my best friend, and policemen.''

"Beth is smart. She knows how to go about it. Of course, we try to avoid biting anyone twice, since it can lead to so many unnecessary human deaths. Since ours is essentially a master/host relationship, we try to inflict as little pain as possible on human society. To have unleashed a maniac upon the world is a heavy burden to bear. That is perhaps the main reason that we bite our victims on the neck. Sure, the jugular veins are rich sources of blood, and historically that may be the reason for the tradition. But in modern times, the biting on the neck has become the means by which we mark our victims. Even if the wound heals completely, it leaves a trace that any vampire will notice readily. That mark tells him not to bite this person. Even if the victim was first bit thirty years before, to bite him now would still constitute a second bite and unleash his unquenchable bloodlust.

"But on occasion mistakes do happen, and a victim is accidentally bitten twice. In that instance, you have two choices: either kill him or turn him into a vampire. Killing him will keep him from murdering others. Making him one of us will lead him to a responsible existence. It's always a judgment call. And if you're biting a person twice on purpose, you must do what Beth did to you, and make sure your victim won't get away from you, kill himself, or kill others. We very seldom set out consciously to turn someone into a vampire. I guess you were one of the lucky ones—at least the way you see it, with your 'give and take.'"

"Sure, I think I'm lucky. My family had ostracized me, and I was sick. I had no future. I would have been dead in five years. You can't possibly tell me that I made a mistake."

"Can't I? Well, I'll do it right now, all the same. Chris, you did make a mistake. And I'll tell you why, after one more shot to calm your nerves. *Vasheh Zdorovyeh!*"

"*Vasheh Zdorovyeh.*" They tossed back their drinks. The carafe was considerably less full by now, and the vodka was beginning to grow disagreeably warm.

Chris kept his besotted mind at the ready, so that he could defend himself against whatever Temsik had up his sleeve. He was positive that nothing Temsik could say could possibly cause him to question his decision to become a vampire.

"Are you ready, Chris?"

"Sure, I'm ready."

"What would you say to me if I told you that in becoming a vampire, you gained a somewhat questionable immortality by forfeiting your immortal soul?"

"I'd say you're full of shit. I've never believed that I had a soul to begin with, and you can't prove that I did, or that I ever lost it, for that matter."

"You've never believed in the afterlife?"

"No. I've always thought that when we die, we die, and there's nothing after. So I haven't given up anything, have I? I didn't have a soul then, and I don't have one now. Big hairy fucking deal, as we say in Chicago."

"All right, Chris, I can accept your answer. But for purposes of discussion, let me tell you the way of things. Humor me, okay? All right. You started out, you were sick with leukemia, you were perhaps dying, yet you had a soul. Then, you get bit the first time. This damages your soul only slightly. It becomes less pure than before, but who's to notice? Then, you get bit the second time, and with that your soul becomes horribly corrupt. You've read *The Picture of Dorian Gray*?"

"Yes."

"After the second bite, your soul looks like the painting in that book, diseased, decayed, and depraved. But at least you still have a soul. This means you will still go somewhere when you die. Where, I don't know. But you still have a soul. But when you're bit the third and final time, your soul utterly disintegrates. It doesn't go to Heaven or Hell or Hades. It doesn't go off to haunt a Victorian mansion or participate in séances. Your soul becomes fully, irrevocably destroyed."

"So, if that were true—and that's a big if—what does that really mean?"

"It means that when you're destroyed, as you will be someday, you will simply cease to exist, and that will be the end, just like you've always thought anyway. It means that you can look forward to nothing, in the most literal sense."

"That's all very interesting," Chris said, yawning. "But it's still bullshit."

"Call it bullshit if you like, but someday you'll realize the truth, which I'm telling you now. The truth is, you would have been much better off living your life to the fullest and dying as a human and going on to some kind of afterlife than having any sort of existence as a vampire and being snuffed out. When you learn the truth for yourself, you'll wish that Beth had never turned you into one of us. Frankly, you'll think that she ripped you off."

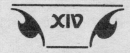

FIENDISH ENDEAVORS

THE next night, Temsik looked younger still. He was gaining muscle on his arms, and his face had become fuller. The wrinkles were now little more than lines on his forehead and chicken scratches at his eyes. His hair, though mostly gray, had developed streaks of black. All in all, he looked like a man in good health, somewhere around his fifty-fifth birthday. Overnight, the blood from the Sentry bag boy had transformed Temsik from grandfather to uncle.

Chris asked Temsik where he could find the gay bars in Madison. Of the five Temsik knew about, the New Bar sounded the most promising. The New Bar was a modern, loud dance club located in the old Hotel Washington building, six blocks southwest of the capitol. Chris decided to go check it out. He hadn't been to a genuine gay night spot since he had first taken ill with leukemia, and he was eager to get his feet in motion and dance to some disco.

Chris walked the eleven blocks down to the Hotel Washington, but had trouble finding the New Bar among all the other restaurants and bars in the building. He could see that it was no longer a hotel but a complex of cafes and bars. The New Bar appeared to be unmarked. So Chris waited around until he saw two pretty guys open a door to an atrium and descend the staircase within. Chris followed them inside and found himself at the New Bar. Finding the bar in this fashion reminded him of when he had been in high school and he and his buddies had followed pizza delivery cars around the neighborhood, hoping they would lead to a wild party somewhere. The party in the New Bar this evening was not yet very wild, but then it was nine-thirty by his watch, and a Thursday night at that. At least there was no cover charge.

The interior of the place was decorated in crisp chrome and neon, with a bar and dance floor on the main level and a balcony and another bar upstairs. Chris was disappointed to discover that a wall of mirrors surrounded the dance floor. He would have to stay by either bar and forgo the dancing altogether.

But, Chris did manage to meet a young cute guy named Patrick. The name reminded him of his own long-dead older brother, which earned this new Patrick a vote of sympathy. Anyone named Patrick deserved to be treated with kindness. Since Patrick was unable to coax Chris out onto the dance floor, they went back to Patrick's apartment "for coffee." One thing led to another, and Chris bit him on the neck and sucked his blood.

By then, it was only midnight. He had the whole night ahead of him. But he decided to return to the apartment and check in on Temsik. On the surface, at least, Temsik seemed to be doing well; after all, two nights ago he had been little more than a corpse. But Chris could not forget the purpose of his mission, and realized it would be a good thing to figure out what was really going on in Temsik's head. Last night, despite Temsik's outward cheerfulness, his cynicism had come through boldly. Chris perceived this as a warning flag, and he was determined not to let anything happen to him. If Temsik did anything drastic, Beth would never forgive Chris for failing the mission.

So, when he returned to the apartment, he decided to find out all he could about Laura and what had happened to her. The destruction of Laura had started this whole affair to begin with, including Beth's decision to turn Chris into a vampire.

Temsik was still doing the dishes from last night's uneaten feast.

"Why do you even have dishes to begin with?" asked Chris.

"Sometimes it's nice to wine and dine someone and spend an entire evening together, have sex, and bite them only at the very last." Temsik put the last plate in the rack to dry, and removed his rubber gloves. "That's also why I'm such a phenomenal chef. I never cooked a meal in my life until I became a vampire."

They went to the living room and sat together on the leather sofa, with a bottle of brandy between them on the coffee table. Temsik put a recording of Vivaldi's *La Stravaganza* on the compact disc player and poured them each a snifter of brandy.

"If you don't steal it, where do you get all your money?" Chris asked.

"I've been around a long time. I've got money stashed away in Swiss bank accounts, and I live off the interest. Back in the old days, when I became a vampire, I took some of my family's money and eventually wound up in Petersburg, where I set myself up as Count Pirogov. I frequented the gambling salons and expanded my money into a small fortune. It wasn't very difficult. I usually played card games—faro, whist, *Boston*, and so on—and I found I could influence the other players into making stupid mistakes. I made quite a bundle of rubles that way. I spent a great many years gambling all over Europe, but I haven't done much of that since the turn of the century. I've hired accountants and brokers to conduct some of my financial business. But with automatic tellers, I can do most of my day-to-day banking myself. I also keep a stash of money lying around the apartment in case I somehow lose access to any of my other funds."

"Can you tell me what happened to Laura?"

"I believe I can." Temsik swirled the brandy around in his snifter. "It's not a very pretty tale. But you should pay attention, lest the same thing happen to you."

"I'll be all right. I'm a cautious guy."

"Even the most cautious fellow can make mistakes. The man who destroyed Laura is no ordinary vampire hunter by any stretch of the imagination; indeed, he's no ordinary man. His name is Franz Stadler. Remember it well. He is an entity of his own creation, and the worst enemy that vampires have ever known, discounting the sun, of course."

"Franz Stadler," Chris repeated, as if the name should hold some significance for him. "What makes him so different?"

"The typical vampire hunter is on a search-and-destroy mission. He's an ordinary human who has somehow stumbled onto our secret, and he hunts us down out of fear and ignorance, with only one purpose: to eliminate us. But Stadler is anything but typical. When he learned about us, he also learned about the unique properties of *kroba*. He experimented and found that it produced similar effects on him as it did on us. By applying it to his skin, his wounds would heal miraculously. But to get *kroba*, he had to get vampires and take it from them. The more of us he destroyed, the more *kroba* he got. Then he realized that our blood not only healed his wounds but also kept him from aging, so he began to bathe in it. By now, Stadler is no more human than we are, but he's not a vampire, either. He's an immortal being who captures vampires and milks them of their juices, just to keep himself alive, and young, and beautiful."

"Isn't that what we do, with humans?"

"Absolutely not!" Temsik was adamant. "Each of our victims survives and is let go. But every last one of Stadler's victims is used up, destroyed, and disposed of. That, Chris, is what happened to Laura."

"What do you mean, used up?"

"Laura was abducted somewhere in Madison. I'm not sure exactly where. But Stadler took her back to his lair and drained her of her *kroba*. Then, he must have set her out in the sunlight to finish her off."

"How do you know that?"

"Because he sent me her ashes, in a porcelain urn, which I keep in my bedroom."

"But how do you know it's Laura?"

"By the smell. Believe me, it's her. Stadler also returned her ring."

"Were you and Laura married?"

Temsik laughed. "No. Laura Stevens was my companion. I met her in New York in 1957. She had already become one of us, in Kansas during the Great Depression (you'll find that most who have come willingly did so during times of great personal desperation). There's not much to tell, nothing relevant anyway, until the very end. We were together for over thirty years, and then she was taken from me in the most horrible and cruel fashion that you could possibly imagine. There was not one thing I could do about it."

"I'm sorry," said Chris.

"Don't be. It was all my fault. My only consolation is that I'm quite positive Stadler destroyed his own soul long ago from his excessive contact with *kroba*. Someday, when he's finally dead, he'll be nothing more than a pile of dust like the rest of us."

"How is it that you know so much about him?"

"Stadler has crossed my path many times. He's been a vampire hunter for as long as I've been a vampire. But we knew each other even before that. I first met him in 1798, when I was sixteen and he was seventeen. You see, we were both students together at the University of Leipzig. Later, I invited him to share my apartment. In fact, we were best friends, thicker than anything."

"Best friends! What happened?"

"Quite a lot, actually. We remained best friends even after I completed my studies and moved back to Moscow. Years later, after I had been turned into a vampire, he learned my secret. From there, he became what he is to-day—a monster. Stadler has chosen not to destroy me, so he can torment me instead. It's entirely my fault that Laura was destroyed, as well as Stadler's five thousand other victims.''

"Five thousand?'' Chris was incredulous.

"That's a conservative estimate. If it hadn't been for my stupidity, most of those five thousand vampires would probably still be around today. Stadler is the only truly effective vampire hunter I have ever run across. The rest are imbeciles, but Stadler is a genius in his own insidious way. And I am the only reason that he ever found out about us. Someday I'll tell you the whole dreadful story.''

Chris poured himself another snifter full of brandy and drank half of it in one gulp.

He thought he understood now why Temsik had tried to starve himself out of existence. It wasn't merely the loss of his longtime companion; all of Stadler's crimes were weighing on Temsik's conscience.

"Well, how do I protect myself?'' asked Chris. "What does he look like?''

"I personally haven't seen him in over forty years. He has this habit of tracking me down despite my best efforts to be rid of him. He takes great pleasure in destroying my friends, so be careful. All I can recommend is that you watch your back, carry a knife, and be careful who you go off with. Three months ago, he arrived in Wisconsin and started up operations. Five vampires have disappeared from the region since then, all of them acquaintances of mine from the Underground. But I don't know what Stadler might look like now. I can only give you a general description. He has a squarish jaw, very German features. He always used to have sandy blond hair, but I wouldn't be surprised if he has changed its color. His eyes are dark brown, but anyone can change the color of their eyes these days with the right lenses, so you can't go by that, either. He's tall, with a good build, very good-looking. I was in love with him when we were students at Leipzig. But that is an altogether different story.''

Chris's attention suddenly reached a second wind. "I'd like to hear it."

Temsik told Chris his tale.

"My father sent me to the University of Leipzig in 1798, one of very few Russians the tsar allowed to go. I was sixteen and ignorant, having learned French and German but little else. I had been tutored privately all my life, and had taken or left my studies as I pleased. More often than not, I pleased to leave them to play games with the serf children in our Moscow household. I paid little attention to my tutor, and by the time I was sent to Leipzig, I knew precious little. Yet my father was wealthy, and our family had enough pull to get me sent out of the country for my schooling.

"I met Stadler a week after my arrival. Though my father wanted me to learn languages and economics, I had entertained thoughts of becoming a physician. I was exploring the medical college when Stadler came up and introduced himself to me. He stood tall and was well built for a fellow his age, and fair of face, with long sandy blond hair tied in a bow at the nape of his neck. We took a quick liking to one another. Stadler was going to become a physician himself, and proved eager to point me in the right direction. He invited me to come with him to an amputation that was about to take place in the other wing of the building. It sounded exciting. I had never before seen a man lose his limb.

"So we went. The small dark room was crowded with students, some sitting on a long bench, most standing behind and trying to peer over their fellows' shoulders. A single window offered some light through its dusty panes, which was augmented by a few nearly spent candles on the walls. The smell in the room was sickening. The short wooden table in the middle of the room was dark with bloodstains, some of them fresh, and the floor was equally bloody. Franz and I squeezed in among the crowd, toward the front. The surgeon walked in wearing his apron, which was almost wholly stained with blood from his recent operations. The patient was brought in on a stretcher and laid out on the table, the lower halves of both legs dangling over the edge. He was barely conscious. The surgeon explained that the patient had been drugged with opium to lessen the pain. They had tried to knock him out with a blow to the head, but it hadn't worked, so the opium would have to suffice.

"The physician asked a few students to help him by holding down the patient's limbs. Among them was Franz. He asked Franz to take the right leg, the one being severed, and hold it straight out. The students donned grimy aprons, rolled up their sleeves, and grabbed their respective limbs. The patient's gown had been pulled up to his waist, exposing his lower torso and both legs. I could see the large infected wound right above his ankle, the dried blood, the running pus, the red streaks reaching up his calf, marking the spread of the infection. It was clear the wound was already causing him great pain. A wooden dowel was placed between his teeth for him to bite into when the real pain began. With one student on each limb, the physician went to work, while the patient's head lolled around on the table.

"What I saw of the operation lasted less than a minute. Using a long, skinny, curved blade, the surgeon pierced the muscle just above the knee and ripped upward, slicing through the entire muscle in one stroke. Blood spurted all over his apron, and the patient howled in pain, clamping down on the dowel. The students had their hands full holding him down as he tried to thrash around, but Franz had little difficulty keeping his injured leg still. Then the surgeon plunged the same knife into the muscles below the femur bone and ripped downward. In a few rough strokes, he had cut entirely through the muscle on the underside, which now left him with only the bone to do. He exchanged his blade for a small serrated saw and immediately went to work. He threw his muscles into it, sawing back and forth quickly and deeply, producing a great grinding noise. But within thirty seconds he had cut through, and the lower half of the patient's leg came off into Franz's hands. Both the severed leg and the stump bled profusely. Franz grinned with satisfaction at having witnessed the skillful operation so closely, and finally dropped the leg into the bucket below, where it belonged.

"But before the surgeon could begin to sew the hanging flap of skin around the meat of the stump, I tasted bile in my throat and felt my lunch begin to come up. I pushed my way past the students and ran from the room, vomiting outside in the hallway. I didn't return to see the remainder of the demonstration, but waited outside for Franz, considerably down the hall to get away from the patient's horrible screaming. That put an end to any notion I might have had about becoming a physician, but it marked the beginning of my friendship with Franz."

Chris interrupted to ask, "Why is he *Franz* all of a sudden instead of *Stadler*?"

"My memories of those days are good ones. Franz and I were very close. But I haven't truly known him for over a hundred-fifty years. Today, he's a mere stranger, so I think of him as Stadler. But when I used to know him—and love him—he was always Franz. It would destroy all my good memories if I were to imagine him then the way he is now."

"You keep saying you loved him. Were you gay?"

Temsik cringed, and his answer was evasive. "That's such a silly term! When I met Franz, I had never had sex with either a man or a woman. He decided to correct that, and introduced me to the pleasures of the flesh by taking me to a brothel. We paid for two whores, and they screwed us both in the same small room on one large bed. I watched Franz to see how it was done, but found myself unable to remove my gaze, even with my chosen girl beneath me. I was fascinated by my schoolmate, and utterly disgusted by the two prostitutes. My first sexual experience was a failure, except for the fact that it awakened feelings in me that had, until then, remained dormant. I began to lust after my best friend in my every waking hour. It was an obsession.

"In Leipzig, Franz became the most reasonable of men,

a product of the Enlightenment, a student of the natural sciences who sought, and found, justification for his ideas in nature, and in the classic writings of the ancient Greeks and Romans, rather than in the Bible. Germany in the eighteenth century had seen reason triumph over faith, and despite my strict Russian Orthodox upbringing, I fell easily under Franz's sway. He was capable of defending any idea on any subject, as long as he could find the proper books or cite the proper example from the natural world. I envied his talent—and his single-minded passions.

"And so, following his example, I sought justification for my 'unnatural attraction' wherever I could find it. I knew from the start that my lust defied God's laws, so I rejected God, as Franz had done, though for different reasons. Nature failed me, as well. Yet through the course of my education, I easily found what I sought in the Greek and Roman writers. Plato, Xenophon, Plutarch, Anacreon, Virgil, Horace, Petronius, Juvenal—the list was practically endless. I found many passages that spoke of and praised the noble qualities of love between men, and succeeded in lessening my fears. However, these works were from the ancient, pagan world that had been overthrown by glorious Christendom, which I could not then wholly abandon. Then, by chance, I happened upon an English novel, *Vathek, an Arabian Tale*, by one William Beckford, in which no great distinction had been made between the love of girls and the love of boys. The fact that this had been written in the modern era, and presumably by a Protestant, made a great impression upon me, and caused me to dream at night of lustful encounters with mysterious Muhammadan men.

"I yearned to show Franz how I felt about him and to present my case as rationally as possible. Being a reasonable man, he would be convinced when I showed him that the greatest minds of ancient Greece and Rome affirmed what I had to say. Then he would fall into my arms and be mine forever.

"But I never developed the courage. During all our years at Leipzig, we never became physically intimate, except for certain winter nights when we slept closely together because of the cold in my apartment. Aside from that, we remained friends only, and I don't believe Franz ever suspected the true nature of my interest in him, at least not then.

"After Leipzig, I called upon Moscow's young ladies and danced with them at the balls. I even became infatuated with some of them, however briefly. Yet I knew that what I really needed to attain perfect happiness was to be with Franz forever.

"But that proved to be my undoing. Someday I'll tell you how it all happened."

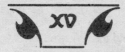

THE HEAT OF PASSION

THE following night was a Friday, and Chris had a feeling that the New Bar would be chock-full of cute gayboys dancing their ever-loving hearts out. Even though he couldn't allow himself to dance because of all the mirrors, he could still watch and try to meet an interesting fellow.

Dancing wasn't the only thing he hadn't done since his leukemia had struck. He hadn't had a meaningful bout of sex in over six months, and the tryst in the shower with Jamie didn't count. That had been a quickie, just some kissing, foreplay, and mutual jacking-off while the water streamed over their bodies; it had lasted less than fifteen minutes. What Chris needed tonight was a good, long fuck.

And he didn't even have to worry about diseases.

No matter what Temsik had said the other night, Chris firmly believed that in becoming a vampire he had gained more than he had given up. He was immune to any and all disease, whether it was leukemia, AIDS, herpes, or the measles. If all of America would only become vampires, he mused, then we wouldn't have to worry about health care, and we could spend our time and money on other problems—such as where to find human blood to suck. No, Chris realized, that wasn't the answer. Everyone couldn't become vampires, because humans were a necessary and vital part of the whole equation.

Quite a few of these necessary and vital parts were packed

into the New Bar this evening, drinking and dancing.

A cover charge of three dollars had been taken at the door, but that was a bargain compared to some Chicago clubs. The stereo system, with its huge sets of speakers hanging from the ceiling, was blasting the Depeche Mode dance track "Behind the Wheel/Route 66," one of Chris's favorites. It was all he could do to prevent himself from going out on the dance floor, but everyone around him would be freaked out to say the least when they saw a black Bundeswehr T-shirt, a pair of Levi's, and a pair of Nike running shoes, without anyone inside, boogying their way across the floor in the mirror's impartial reflection.

"Bud Light!" Chris shouted at the bartender over the loud music. He found that the drink prices were also considerably less than those in Chicago.

The oval-shaped bar was full of men, many of whom seemed to be in their thirties. All the younger guys were standing, wherever a spot could be found. Most of the crowd looked like they were either college students or working stiffs in their mid-twenties, and they were generally well dressed and beautiful. They wore their hair either very short, like Chris's, or very long and tied at the back. The few in-between cuts were on the older men.

Chris decided to go upstairs, where there was no chance of his accidentally stepping too close to the mirrors. The upstairs had no mirrors, and it was equally packed with people, mostly guys. A few women could be seen here and there, but for the most part Chris failed to notice them. To him, they were either fat fag hags or thin fag hags, or perhaps transvestites, none of which held his interest.

Temsik had made Chris slightly paranoid about his every move. It sounded as if Chris was in direct danger of being abducted by this Stadler fellow, and once taken, no one had ever returned from his clutches. They had all been destroyed. Chris decided that he would be cool to anyone's advances, overtures, or offers to buy drinks. He had to remain in control and socialize exclusively with guys of his own choosing. If he allowed anyone to be the aggressor and pick him up, he could very easily be in danger.

That meant Chris would have to watch how much he drank. If he got too drunk, his judgment would fail him and he might fall prey to Stadler, or for that matter some other vampire hunter. He had to remain in control.

The Depeche Mode song faded into the Pet Shop Boys' cynical, snide, and brilliant disco rendition of "Always on My Mind."

Upstairs, all the tables and bar stools were taken, and there was more conversation going on than downstairs.

Chris spied a gorgeous guy who looked lonely standing at the balcony, watching the dancing down below, and nursing his drink. His features were Polynesian, with dark skin and silky black hair that hung loose just past his shoulders. His snug pair of Levi's showed off a perfect, firm ass, and his yellow T-shirt displayed a muscular back and well-developed arms.

Chris approached him and stood beside him at the railing. "It's really packed tonight, isn't it?"

"Yeah." The hunk turned his head and smiled at Chris. "You come here often?"

"No. I just moved to Madison. I came here last night, but didn't stay long. I was early, and there weren't that many people here."

"It can get pretty busy on Fridays and Saturdays. What's your name?"

"Chris."

"I'm Sheridan. Sheridan Cooper."

"Your name doesn't match your face."

Sheridan laughed and tossed back his hair. "No, I guess not. I'm Hawaiian. My mom's a native, but my dad isn't. He's from Wyoming. That's where he got the Sheridan. You look like a Chris, though. What's your last name?"

"Callaway."

"Irish. I should have known. All that nice red hair." Sheridan reached out and rubbed Chris's newly grown, bristly hair, scratching it lightly as if it were a dog's coat.

"Red hair doesn't necessarily make you Irish."

"No," Sheridan agreed. He drank the last of his drink. "But green socks do. Are you wearing green socks?"

"Nope."

"Me neither. Hey, I need another drink. Do you want anything?"

Only you, Chris thought, imagining what Sheridan might look like without his clothes on. *Only you*.

Sheridan had a small studio apartment with a double futon on a pinewood platform.

They had stayed talking together at the New Bar for a few hours. Chris had met with good luck in the fact that Sheridan didn't like to dance. So they had grabbed a table at the first opportunity and sat down to talk. Sheridan had several Rum and Cokes, and Chris drank more beers than he should have.

But it was obvious from Sheridan's features alone that he wasn't Stadler. A German could fake this hair color, and perhaps the skin color, but never the round face and broad cheekbones, full lips, and sleepy eyes. Chris had nothing to worry about. He was being paranoid, anyway; it was highly unlikely that Stadler would be the first guy he ran across.

Sheridan put on a Bryan Ferry album, lit some candles, and turned off the lights. His apartment began to flicker in the dancing glow of the candle flames. Chris sat on the edge of the futon, admiring the shelves of books along Sheridan's wall. Sheridan was a junior at the university, studying history. He lived alone in the apartment, but said that it had been months since he had last had sex. Normally, he spent his time studying for class and didn't allow himself much time for socializing. But finals week had just ended, so he had gone out to have some fun. He was glad he had met Chris.

"Come here," Sheridan said. He took Chris's hands in his own and pulled him up off the futon.

Chris wrapped his arms around Sheridan's broad back and held him close. Sheridan stood slightly taller than Chris, which made Chris feel as if he were being protected. Sheridan's arms roamed around Chris's back until his hands reached Chris's ass and clutched it through his jeans.

"You've got a nice ass," said Sheridan.

"So do you." Chris was exploring it now, enjoying the way Sheridan's Levi's hugged the contours of his body. His hands traveled up and pulled Sheridan's shirt out of his jeans and up over his head. A dark, well-developed chest faced him now, and Chris couldn't resist bending down and licking one of Sheridan's brown nipples.

Sheridan removed Chris's shirt, and now they were pressed chest against chest, their warm skin feeling electric. Sheridan opened up his mouth and planted it against Chris's, prying his tongue deep between Chris's lips. They held each other tightly, and the kissing seemed to go on forever. Before Chris knew it, he could feel Sheridan's sizable erection pressing against him, and they were both at each other's jeans, unbuckling belts and unbuttoning flys. Chris slowly pulled Sheridan's jeans down just over his buttocks; his pants were so tight that they came inside out as they were pulled off, as if Sheridan were a giant banana being unpeeled. But once Sheridan stepped out of his jeans, Chris came face-to-face with the true giant banana, an erect cock about nine inches long, fatter at the engorged head than at its hairy base.

Chris got out of his own pants, and they fell entwined together onto the futon, exploring each other's bodies and kissing like crazy. Every muscle of Sheridan's was nicely proportioned, but nothing compared to his exquisite ass. They got into a sixty-nine for a while, which was almost too much sensation at one time for Chris. He took Sheridan's cock into his mouth, while Sheridan reciprocated, and meanwhile Chris fingered the smooth rosebud in the cleft of Sheridan's ass. This produced the expected low moans from Sheridan, which provided a nice vibration along the length of Chris's throat-embedded dick.

"Roll over and I'll give you a massage," said Sheridan.

He got up and came back with some baby oil. "That's it, on your stomach."

Chris lay facedown upon the futon. Sheridan grabbed both legs and spread them apart, so he could sit between them right near Chris's buttocks. Then he spread some oil along Chris's back and kneaded the muscles along his spine. Sheridan took care of the shoulders and thighs as well. His fingers dug deep; he obviously knew what he was doing. He spent an inordinate amount of time massaging Chris's ass, rubbing the oil over his cheeks and into his hairy cleft. Then, a lubricated finger made its way into Chris's hole and spent a great deal of time massaging the tight muscles there, eventually relaxing them. Sheridan put on a rubber and entered Chris slowly, until it was comfortable.

Chris was fucked longer and harder than ever before in his life, and it was magnificent. The hot Hawaiian bucked and ground his pelvis into him, thrusting fast and deep, sometimes slapping his buttocks, which made Chris's muscles tighten. When it was over, after what seemed like an hour, Chris was exhausted. It was the best fuck he had ever had.

But Sheridan rolled over on his stomach, and reached behind to grab his own cheeks and spread them wide—a tacit invitation to even greater pleasures.

Chris couldn't believe that the most beautiful ass he had ever seen in his life was being offered for sacrifice. He got behind Sheridan, licked his sweaty buttocks, and nuzzled his nose in the crack, scraping the sides with the stubble of his face.

Sheridan's musky scent was overpowering. Chris clutched the two muscular globes in his hands, and before he knew what he was doing, his fangs had sprung forward, and he was biting down into the meat of Sheridan's ass.

Sheridan cried out, and said, "Oh, yeah! Oh, Chris, that is fantastic!"

Chris sucked Sheridan's blood as best he could, but it took longer, because it didn't flow as easily through the muscular tissue as it did in the jugular vein. Sheridan's muscles tensed beneath Chris's mouth, but he continued to moan, and told Chris never to stop.

It seemed to last nearly as long as the fucking had, and when Chris was finishing, he had the most intense orgasm of his life, sending shivers and quakes throughout his body.

Sheridan had already passed out.

Chris collapsed beside Sheridan, one arm draped across the hunk's back.

Chris stared at Sheridan's face in its contentedness and brushed a lock of hair from off his cheek. It was only then that Chris saw, for the first time, the marks on Sheridan's neck. Someone else had already bitten him.

XVI

A THIEF IN THE NIGHT

"**H**OW could you be so manifestly irresponsible!" Temsik was undeniably pissed.

"It was an accident, I swear," Chris pleaded. "It was in the heat of passion, and I couldn't help myself. I didn't think he'd turn out to have already been bit."

"Heat of passion I might be able to understand. But you must learn to control yourself. Even if you had been the first to bite him, future vampires would have had no way of knowing, short of ripping off his underwear!"

"I'm sorry."

"Sorry is the worst thing you could be. You simply can't go around biting people on the ass. Not even 'hot Hawaiians.' I suppose you've got him tied up now."

"Yes, I secured him to his futon frame while he was asleep."

"And you gagged him?"

"Yes, with two of his sweatsocks tied together."

"We don't want him rousing the neighbors and getting himself released. Now what are you going to do?"

"I'll go back tomorrow night and bite him again, and everything will be okay."

"Oh, you think so? You'll simply turn him into a vampire and everything will be fine. Did you ask him if he wanted it? Is he coming to us willingly, as you did? No, Chris. He's a college student, with another year to go, with parents in Hawaii, and a full life ahead of him that you have just ruined through your stupidity.''

''It was an—''

''I know, an accident. But I would think long and hard if I were you on whether or not to take the final step and bite your friend a third time.''

''What are you saying, that I ought to kill him instead?''

''It's up to you. He's your responsibility.''

''What would you do if you were me?'' Chris asked.

''I would kill him without hesitation. In fact, I would have done it already. There's nothing for him in an existence like ours. He obviously had everything going for him. To bite him once more would only add insult to injury. If I were you, I would be merciful and shoot him in the head tonight while he's still asleep.''

''I can't!'' Chris was unable even to entertain the thought. He could never kill anybody, and he had already made up his mind to go ahead and bite Sheridan, and complete the process.

''Then go ahead, do what you will.'' Temsik sighed heavily. ''Accept the responsibility. But you'll also have to face the consequences, whatever they prove to be.''

The following evening, Temsik drove them over to Sheridan's apartment. They brought with them a ''traveling'' coffin in the back seat, a hardwood box that was collapsible like a Boy Scout's drinking cup, in four segments, each one fitting snugly into the larger one before it, so that it could be pulled out to accommodate the length of a grown person. The lid on top was in four pieces, hinged together so that it could open out and lay flat atop the box in its uncollapsed state. Temsik had procured the item from some enterprising young vampires, the Gladsø brothers, who operated an exclusive mail-order business in Amsterdam that catered to the needs of the undead.

Temsik killed the engine. He had driven behind the building and parked in the back parking lot, near the rear entrance. They would take Sheridan out through that door.

"Can't you wait out here?" Chris asked. Last night, he learned how erotic bloodsucking could be, and he would be embarrassed to bite Sheridan again with Temsik looking over his shoulder.

"If you had ever turned anyone into a vampire before, I wouldn't have bothered to come along. But you haven't. You could wind up killing Sheridan after all if you don't do it right. So I'll be on hand to ensure your success."

When they reached Sheridan's apartment on the third floor, Chris opened the door with the key he had taken the night before, and they went inside.

Sheridan was awake, tied spread-eagled on his futon in his underwear, and growling against the sweatsock stuffed and tied in his mouth. Chris had secured him with lengths of nylon cord that he had found among Sheridan's camping gear in his closet. When Sheridan saw Chris and Temsik enter, he began to tense against the ropes. His thigh muscles and biceps bulged and relaxed as he tried to wrench his way free. He cast an evil glance at Chris, and shook his head violently from side to side, trying to shake loose the gag. But Chris had done his job well, and none of the bonds had come loose all day.

Chris could tell that Sheridan wanted to slit his throat, as Chris had wanted to do to Beth under similar circumstances.

"Don't even bother to hypnotize him," said Temsik. "Since he never knew what was happening to begin with, there's no need to tell him now. It'll be much easier to tell him once he's one of us, when it's too late for him to do anything about it."

Temsik stood nearby as Chris went to work.

Chris removed his shirt, to keep it from getting stained with blood. He looked down into Sheridan's frightened, angry eyes, and realized that Temsik was right, that Chris had thrown a gigantic monkey wrench into Sheridan's life. The only consolation Chris had allowed himself was the fact that Sheridan would soon be a vampire as well, and perhaps they could become friends. But now he realized that Sheridan would hate him for what he had done to him.

And for what he was about to do.

Chris lay on top of Sheridan, who tried to wriggle away from him, but to no avail. Acutely aware of Temsik's presence, Chris dispensed with any preliminaries and bit into Sheridan's neck, over the old bite marks left by some previous vampire. As the blood began to flow, Chris wondered if Temsik had been the one.

When it was done, Chris cut the half-dead Sheridan from his bonds. He took a razor blade, cut a long gash between his own pectorals, pressed Sheridan's head between them, and ordered him to drink his *kroba*. As Sheridan lapped it up, his body came back from the brink of death. His strong arms clutched Chris's back, pulling Chris's chest tightly against his face. Finally, when he had drunk enough, he passed out with a satisfied grin across his Hawaiian face.

Chris wiped the blood off both their bodies and dabbed at his own wound with a towel. His *kroba* was already coagulating, forming the beginnings of a long orange scab.

"Good work," said Temsik encouragingly. "That went off without a hitch. You catch on fast."

Chris found no solace in Temsik's words. Aside from the immediate gratification of drinking Sheridan's blood, he had found little satisfaction in what he had done. As Beth had said to him, to take him unwillingly would have been rape. Chris now felt like a rapist, and Sheridan would awake feeling truly victimized, unlike Chris, who had felt wholly liberated. Becoming a vampire, Chris realized, was not for everyone.

"Come on, Chris," said Temsik, handing Chris his shirt. "Don't look so morose. What's done is done. Sheridan will have to make the best of it, but he'll survive."

"That's some help." Chris couldn't look Temsik straight in the eye. First Temsik had told him how he had fucked up Sheridan's life, and now he was saying that everything would be fine in the end. Temsik seemed to be a perennial devil's advocate.

"All right. We need to make Sheridan decent and get him out of here. I'll find some clothes."

"Do we really have to bury him?"

"Yes, absolutely. There's a certain power down in the earth that helps accelerate the transition process."

"It's only that, when he comes to, he won't have any idea what's happened to him," said Chris. "He'll think he's been buried alive."

"Exactly. And when we dig him up, he'll be relieved to find out that he's become a vampire instead, and he won't be nearly as upset."

Looking at Sheridan's big muscles, Chris hoped for his sake that Temsik was right.

They had gotten Sheridan into some clothes, then grabbed his limbs and carried him to the waiting Jaguar. Temsik had claimed that if he had allowed himself to grow even younger, he could have slung Sheridan's large body over his shoulder and carried him out himself. But Temsik was keeping at his outward age of about fifty-five, like a person on a diet who wanted to lose a certain amount of weight and no more. He wasn't getting any older, but neither was he getting younger. Chris wondered why.

No one had seen them put Sheridan in the car. Temsik had been very careful about that. Now he was slumped in the back seat, leaning against the collapsible coffin.

"Where are we going?" asked Chris.

Temsik gave the key a twist, and the finely tuned engine roared to life. "To the Arboretum," he said.

The Arboretum took up much of the southwest side of town, a man-made forest and wilderness owned and maintained by the university. Along the winding Arboretum Drive, Chris noticed a few private homes tucked in among the dark trees. They drove on past the houses, to a more secluded part of the main forest, where Temsik pulled over to the side of the drive and parked.

Temsik grabbed the traveling coffin and asked Chris to

hold the small end, where Sheridan's feet would go. Together, they stretched the box to its full length, which tapered from the widest segment at the top to the smallest at the bottom. They set it down in the gravel at the side of the road, and Temsik unrolled the padding that would line the coffin.

Chris suddenly remembered reading about the four collapsible lifeboats on the *Titanic* that had failed to function properly. He was developing a bad feeling about what they were doing, yet Temsik maintained that it had to be done, and Chris was in no position to ask questions.

Sheridan fit nicely. Temsik tucked a small pillow under his head, then unfolded the many-hinged lid across the top. He grabbed a pickax and shovel from the trunk of the car and set them on top of the coffin.

"All right, let's get to work," he said.

They grabbed either end of the coffin and went off into the forest. No matter how quiet the woods were tonight, Chris couldn't shake the feeling that they weren't alone. The Arboretum was still a part of the city, and cities were full of people, and people were liable to wander around, or come to the forest for clandestine activities, as Temsik and Chris had done.

Navigating through the woods was easy with Chris's improved vision. When they reached a small clearing far from the road, Temsik said this was the place to dig.

Temsik began the digging with the pickax, but barely managed to get through the first layer of topsoil before handing the duties over to Chris.

"I'm in no condition for this kind of work," he said.

Chris took the shovel and dug out large clumps of earth. Occasionally, he struck a root and had to jump onto the shovel to slice on through it. If he was supposed to dig six feet deep, it was going to take forever. He wished Temsik were operating at the same age he was, so he could help him.

"Why aren't you letting yourself get any younger?" Chris asked, already beginning to tire.

"Because I don't want to." Temsik was matter-of-fact.

"But you said yourself, you're in lousy condition."

"Listen, Chris, I have no doubt that Beth sent you up here to 'save' me from myself. Her motives are abundantly clear, and I'm deeply touched. But I won't have any part of it. I was hoping to waste away before you arrived, but of course I fell slightly short of my goal. Now that you're here, I'm obliged to help you. I wouldn't have been much use to you as a ninety-year-old, so I've allowed myself to grow younger, enough that I can at least train you. But there's no point in my going all the way back to being a twenty-year-old. I don't want you to have any illusions about your role here, Chris. Once your training is complete, I'll no longer be under any obligation toward you—nor you toward me. You can go back to your friends in Chicago, and I shall go back to wasting away, as before."

Chris continued his digging, and chose neither to look up nor to respond to what Temsik had said, because if he did, it would come out something like, *Fine, see if I care.*

By the time they had finally finished burying Sheridan, it was four o'clock in the morning. Chris drove a stake into the ground to mark the spot, and then they headed back to the apartment. Chris was exhausted, and wanted nothing more than to crawl into his coffin and go to sleep.

The next night, they waited until midnight to return to the Arboretum. It was Sunday night, heading into Monday morning, and no one would likely be anywhere near where they were going.

They found the grave exactly as they had left it, a low pile of dirt in a clearing beneath a shadowed canopy of birch trees, with a single stake marking its head.

Chris had calmed down by now, and was no longer worried about anything going wrong. The only thing that concerned him was what Sheridan would say when they let him out.

Temsik had already decided that they would send him down to Chicago for his training. Chris had tried once again to reach Beth, or anyone else for that matter, but continued to get Beth's same recorded answer. He had left a message, asking them to call at their earliest opportunity.

Chris was sore from last night's digging, and now he had the same task to do all over again. Once they had Sheridan, they would get out of the Arboretum and take him back to the apartment.

It took two hours to unearth the head of the traveling coffin six feet down. Temsik had forced him to bury Sheridan at regulation depth. Although Chris was tired from all the digging, he doubted if he could have ever lasted this long as a human. Even before his leukemia, he had been out of shape. Now, as a vampire, he seemed to be much stronger than ever before.

Chris dug out more dirt at the head of the coffin, expecting to hear Sheridan cry out from inside. But no noise came from within. The woods were silent.

Temsik jumped into the grave to help Chris dig out the rest of the coffin and lift it out, but they both soon discovered that Chris didn't need any help; the box had been collapsed to its traveling size, each segment fitted into the other.

They lifted the lid, and were at once horrified and relieved to find no one inside.

"He's gone!" Chris jumped to his feet, staring at the shortened coffin containing nothing but the rolled-up pad and the small pillow.

"Stadler must have been spying on us all this time," said Temsik. "He's taken Sheridan. I'm sure of it."

XVII

GIVING BLOOD

MONDAY night, Chris left the apartment without saying a word to Temsik.

It was the warmest night of the year so far, and many of Madison's college students were going about town in shorts and tank tops, even after the sun had gone down. Chris followed suit, donning a pair of Del's baggy-legged khaki shorts and an extra-large salmon-colored tank top that hung low across his chest and that he barely tucked in, so that it would drape loosely over his waist. He also wore his glacier glasses and a pair of plastic flip-flops on his feet. The moon was beginning to wane but still shone brightly; now was as good a time as any for Chris to start on his tan.

After Sheridan had been stolen, Chris had wanted to go after Stadler, but he could never do it without Temsik's help, which the old vampire refused to give.

They had searched the ground around Sheridan's grave, looking for footprints, but found none except their own. Stadler must have erased his tracks with a tree branch. Even so, he had likely driven away in a car, and Chris and Temsik were unequipped to trace a vehicle's tire tracks, even if they could find the proper treads along the much-traveled Arboretum Drive. Based on this lack of viable leads, Temsik had claimed that there was nothing they could do.

"I haven't the faintest idea where his lair is," he had said as they were driving back to the apartment. "After he got Laura, I tried to find it, but failed. Stadler employs a small band of thugs for his protection. Any time I've gotten close to finding him, he's been tipped off in advance by one of his guards. The same thing used to happen to Eliot Ness down in Chicago, during Prohibition. At first, whenever he tried to raid Al Capone's warehouses, he found them empty of all liquor, because Capone had been tipped off. That's what keeps happening with me and Stadler. Once, I managed to track down one of Stadler's locations, but by the time I got there, it had already been abandoned. It was an old two-story building on the east side, and all of the windows in the back rooms had been freshly bricked over. I could also smell that vampires had recently been kept there. But it proved to be a dead end, and I was perhaps weeks off his trail. Since then, I've found no more clues, and that puts us back at the proverbial square one.''

Which, in a nutshell, meant that Temsik had given up and didn't want to help Chris find Stadler and try to save Sheridan, or anyone else who might fall into Stadler's clutches. Chris wondered if Temsik would bother to do anything if Chris himself were ever captured.

"If Stadler did take him," Temsik had said, "then we're too late already."

Chris hadn't liked Temsik's fatalistic attitude, and had asked, "What chance is there that it wasn't Stadler?"

"Alas, none." Temsik had sighed, but whether it had been a sigh of sorrow or of boredom, Chris couldn't say. "As I've said already, Stadler is not your run-of-the-mill vampire hunter. I always manage to find out about the others long before they can ever get near me. Laura and I used to make it easy for them, and lure them to our apartment, so that we could play our games with them."

"What sort of games?"

Then Temsik had laughed, briefly, in remembrance. "Once we enticed this hunter, an old man who was brighter than most. We set up our coffins in the same room, so that we could protect one another if anything happened, which was a remote possibility. We got inside our coffins and waited for him. The old man arrived, as expected, picking the lock on the front door. We had left the deadbolt unturned so he wouldn't have much trouble breaking in. We heard him stumbling about downstairs. He must have been nervous. I heard him drop his bundle of stakes. I could hear Laura giggling over in her coffin, and I told her to keep quiet. But I found it difficult to keep a straight face myself. Finally, the old man made his way up the staircase and came into the room—this was Laura's bedroom, the one you're in now. Neither of us knew whom he would go after first, so we were both ready. I heard him toss some of his gear onto the bed between us. Then, he started to open Laura's lid. I hoped she had calmed down and gotten the smile off her face; if we gave the game away, all the fun would have been ruined. But apparently, the old man noticed nothing out of the ordinary. Then, I heard the sound of a mallet pounding the head of a stake.''

Temsik paused long enough that Chris found himself blurting out, ''Well, what happened?''

''Nothing. Not to Laura, anyway. I opened my coffin and sprang out in time to see him try once more, but he simply couldn't drive the stake into Laura's heart. He couldn't even get it past her clothing. He whirled around in shock and confusion when he heard me, and he saw that I was pointing my gun at him. 'I've got you,' I said. He dropped his mallet and stake, grabbed the crucifix from around his neck, and held it out, but of course it did no good, and I simply laughed at him. 'Put your hands up,' I told him. There was always the chance he could have a legitimate trick up his sleeve. He whimpered a little, but did what I asked. Then he said, 'I don't understand.' At which point, Laura sat up in her coffin and unbuttoned her blouse, showing him the bulletproof vest she'd been wearing underneath. She gave him a sly look and said, 'Come, Professor, don't tell me you've never heard of Kevlar!' And then I shot him twice in the chest.''

''Where did you get the vests?'' Chris had asked.

''From the Gladsø brothers.''

"The traveling coffin guys." Chris had thought once more of when they had discovered it empty, back at the gravesite. Otherwise, he might have enjoyed the ending to Temsik's story.

"Precisely," said Temsik, all cheerfulness.

They had brought the collapsible coffin back with them to the apartment, when they should have been bringing back Sheridan.

And now Chris was mad, both at Temsik and at himself, for what they had both done to Sheridan. But mostly, he was mad at Temsik for being unwilling to try to find Stadler's hideout. Chris wondered why Temsik was so afraid. There couldn't be much harm in trying.

Chris didn't know yet what he might be able to do about Stadler, but that wasn't going to stop him from doing something good for a change. And that was why, in his tank top and shorts, soaking up the moonrays, Chris was heading downtown, to the Madison Public Library, which was open until ten o'clock on Mondays, and was the perfect place to do a little research.

By looking through the faculty/staff directory for the University of Wisconsin, it didn't take Chris long to find the name he was looking for: Dr. Ronald F. Sunstrom, Head, Department of Human Oncology, Room K4/666, Clinical Sciences Center.

Using the microfiche index to the local newspapers, he came upon a listing for a relevant article from the January twentieth issue of *The Capital Times*. He found the article itself on microfilm; it proved to be an interview with Dr. Sunstrom. Primarily, the doctor discussed the vital research he and his team were doing into possible new treatments for leukemia. Sunstrom sounded as if he were campaigning for more money for his laboratories, but that was mere subtext. It was obvious that he believed in the importance of his work and was proud of some of the pioneering research they had done at the university. Chris took out a pencil and made a few notes on a scrap of paper.

Then he went to a pay phone in the foyer of the library.

A recorded voice came over the speakers in the ceiling, telling him the library would be closing in ten minutes, and anyone wishing to check out materials should do so at once. Chris knew he wouldn't find Dr. Sunstrom at his work number at this hour, but in a research lab like that, he was bound to find somebody.

Chris waited on the line a long time while it rang and rang. After the fifth ring, he heard a brief *click* before it continued to ring, as if the call had been automatically transferred to another line. Two rings later, a young female voice answered, "Hi, Clive!"

"Uh, this isn't Dr. Sunstrom, is it?"

The woman cleared her throat. "Oh, no. I'm just a grad student. Sunstrom's gone home."

"Of all the rotten luck," Chris said. "Just as I figured. And here I am with a deadline."

"Is it anything I could help you with?"

"Probably not," Chris said. That would get her goat, and she would end up all too eager to help him.

"Give me a shot. I'm Sunstrom's assistant."

"Well, I don't know. I'm here at *The Capital Times*. We were getting some copy all set here for tomorrow's edition, but somehow we lost a couple of paragraphs. The reporter who did the story"—Chris scanned his notes—"Sam Hoover, well, er, Sam's on vacation, and we can't find the original copy or any of his research. Our features editor was hoping that maybe I could piece together the missing parts of the interview, and—"

"What interview?"

"The one with Dr. Sunstrom. Sort of a follow-up to the thing of Sam's that we ran in January. We've been delaying it for weeks now, but we promised Sunstrom it would go in tomorrow's paper. So, I'd like to get this finished before we put the thing to bed. If we have to pull the story, we'll have to redo the whole layout, and—"

"What do you need to know?"

"Well, I'm not entirely sure. The description of the lab

is missing, and the tail end of some of the doctor's quotes. Actually, you know, it would be easiest if I could come over there and take a look for myself. Then I can do the lab description myself, and I'll just show you what we've got of the interview, and maybe you can fill in the doctor's missing words. Or better yet, I could simply quote you."

That would be an ego boost, Chris figured.

"Sure, why not?" the girl said. "As if I had anything else to do."

Chris found the door to the Clinical Sciences Center open and went on in, but he saw no people in the halls.

He met the girl in front of the department office door. She wore her hair in a ponytail, and was not unattractive, probably a year or two older than Chris. She wore a white lab coat, jeans, and Top-Siders on her feet.

"You don't look like a reporter," she said.

"Oh," said Chris, looking down at his tank top and shorts. "I guess not. I'm really just a copy editor, but I was the only one they could get for the job, I guess. Kind of like in the movies, when the prima donna has a disfiguring accident and the understudy finally gets her chance."

"I see," she said. "Anyway, I'm Kate."

"Chris."

"Follow me, and I'll show you the lab."

Chris had wondered, on the walk across campus, why it had been so easy to convince her to see him. He had never been a good liar, but he had given it his damndest tonight. Still, he didn't think that he would want to entertain a strange male if he were a woman working alone in a lab at night, especially when he was dressed as casually as Chris. But he soon discovered why she hadn't been worried about being assaulted. A tall, very black man who looked as if he were probably an African foreign exchange student was also at work in the lab.

Chris had to get her alone, and convinced her to take him to Dr. Sunstrom's office.

Once the fluorescent lights came flickering on, and they

were inside, Chris worked himself up into his hypnotizing state. He felt the cold sweats come, and then the burning sensation in his adenoids. Then he turned his gaze toward Kate, shutting the door behind him with the bottom of his flip-flop.

She was at once trapped in his gaze, her eyes bulging wide and staring at him, unblinking.

"Sit down," he commanded, pointing at one of the two chairs before the doctor's desk.

She did, and Chris sat in the other chair opposite her.

"Do you have any hypodermic needles around here?" he asked.

"Yes."

"Can you go get one? One that you might use to draw some blood?"

"Yes, I think so."

"Then go get it, and come back here."

Entranced, Kate rose and left Sunstrom's office. The room was decorated with diplomas and posters of waterfalls and trees under which lurked inspiring quotes from the New Testament.

Chris failed to be inspired by them, yet he felt good about what he was about to do. After the Sheridan fiasco, he had felt helpless in being unable to do anything against Stadler, and frustrated in dealing with Temsik. Every move Temsik made, and every word he spoke, was maddening. Chris found him unfathomable, a difficult, irascible individual whose every decision seemed affected by his overwhelming desire for his own destruction, at the expense of everyone and everything else. He had clearly put Chris's life in danger, or at least he was doing nothing to protect it. If Stadler could snatch Sheridan so easily, he could do the same to Chris. Yet Chris, almost as new at this game as Sheridan, simply had to protect himself and look out for someone he had never met, or for one of his "thugs," the existence of which Temsik had only bothered to divulge last night.

Now Chris was going to right some wrongs.

He would leave a sample of his *kroba* with the leukemia

researchers. Even before they analyzed it, they would see it was something unique. And once they made their analysis, anything could happen. If *kroba* had been able to keep Stadler alive all these years, ward off his diseases and heal his wounds, as it did for vampires, there was no reason why other human beings shouldn't benefit from it. Cancer patients, AIDS patients, leukemia patients, any number of people could probably be cured, once a suitable drug had been developed based on what they would find in Chris's *kroba*. For all Chris knew, it might save all humanity from disease and famine.

Kate came back with a syringe and an empty vial.

"I'm not trained to do this," she said.

"That's all right. Do your best." It wouldn't really matter if she missed a vein, because Chris would heal immediately anyway. As long as she got a vial full of blood, he would be satisfied.

He made a fist, causing one of his veins to bulge out, not blue but slightly brown in color.

Kate poked him inexpertly, but drew the blood like a professional.

"These lights must be funny," she said. "It looks orange."

"Yes, isn't that strange?" said Chris.

When she was finished, Chris told her that once he was gone she would forget everything that had happened, except that she would make sure that Dr. Sunstrom got this blood sample and would urge him to examine it under a microscope.

Chris left the Clinical Sciences Center feeling a true sense of accomplishment.

When he returned to the apartment, he discovered that Temsik was out and he had the place to himself. He broke out a bottle of Polina Ivanovna's vodka, to celebrate the Nobel Prize in Medicine he had just won for Dr. Sunstrom.

Chris awoke the following evening when Temsik opened the lid to his coffin and threw a newspaper in his face. Chris wondered what was up. Dr. Sunstrom couldn't possibly have made his discovery already.

But then he sat up and read the headline in the afternoon edition of *The Capital Times*: LAB ASSISTANTS MURDERED. The article was accompanied by photos of Kate Wister and Kwadwo Belele, the two victims.

"Did you honestly think I would let you get away with that little feat of subterfuge?" asked Temsik.

Chris was dumbstruck. All he could do was stare at the photos and read how their throats had been slit from ear to ear, right in Dr. Sunstrom's laboratory.

"It was the only way." Temsik held the vial of *kroba*, along with the used syringe.

"I can't believe you killed two people," Chris finally managed to say. He climbed out of the coffin and stood before Temsik, unable to take his eye from the newspaper.

"You should be thankful that I managed to get to them in time, before they could show your little gift to anyone. Otherwise, you might have had a mass murder on your hands."

"On *my* hands! I didn't kill them!"

"Sure, you didn't kill them, but you made it so that I had to, and that's close enough."

"I only wanted to do some good." Chris felt a clutch in his throat, as if he were about to start sobbing, yet no tears came. He tossed the paper aside. "Why did you have to do it?"

"Because *kroba* is the most fundamental secret we have. Give away *kroba* and you destroy us all."

"But Stadler knows about it," Chris countered.

"Yes, and he's killed thousands of vampires to get it! True, he hasn't shared the secret with anyone, out of his own selfish vanity. I dare not think what would befall us if *kroba* were ever to fall into the hands of someone like your Dr. Sunstrom. The whole world would learn about us, instead of a handful of ineffectual hunters and one mad genius."

"I only wanted to save some lives," said Chris. "You

don't know what it's like, being sick. Knowing you're going to die before the age of thirty. I still can't forget it. I thought about death all the time, when I should have been living. Everyone else my age was out having fun, and I had to go to the hospital and take all those drugs and have other people take care of me. I'd never even had a real boyfriend. Never anyone special, no one who lasted more than a month. And once I got sick, I knew I never would. I knew that I'd die alone, kicked out of my family, shunned by my friends, with no one at my side but a lousy doctor. I figured guys my age shouldn't have to think about things like that. They should be out dancing, whooping it up.''

The tears finally came, and Chris couldn't hold them back. He hadn't intended to pour his heart out to Temsik like that, but now that he had, it felt good. He wanted Temsik to hold him, or at least put an arm around his shoulders and tell him everything was going to be okay.

But Temsik offered no such signs of affection.

''That's all very well and good, Chris,'' he said. ''But you can no longer be concerned with the health and welfare of human beings. You're one of us now, and there's no way you can forget that. What you did might have helped humans, but at our expense. But you're not a human anymore, you're a vampire. You no longer have a life, you have an existence, and you must exist according to the agreed-upon rules. Don't you see the Pandora's box you nearly opened?''

''I guess I wasn't thinking.''

''No, and I suppose I shall have to continue doing your thinking for you for a while. And I thought I was making some headway.''

''I'm sorry.''

''Please, Chris. The last thing I need is a sorry pupil. Don't keep saying you're sorry. You simply made a mistake, and I corrected it. Since everything turned out all right, all I ask is that you realize what you did and refrain from making similar mistakes in the future. So I had to kill a couple of people. I've done it before, and I would do it again if I allowed myself to go on much longer. It is an unpleasant business, but sometimes necessary. As a rule, we try to kill humans only when they threaten our survival, or in the case of the twice-bitten, when they threaten the survival of other innocent humans. The sooner you learn this, the better off you will be. If you had allowed yourself to kill Sheridan, he would have met a better fate than he's getting at the hands of Stadler, believe me. One of these days, you will have to kill a man or be destroyed yourself, and you must be prepared for it."

"In that case, I'm glad you did what you did. At least I didn't have to." Chris was reeling as he realized the magnitude of his mistake, which he had thought so heroic less than a day ago. "Could it have worked?" he asked.

"You mean, could *kroba* have wiped out diseases in men?"

Chris nodded, sullen as he thought about how the leukemia had ravaged his body and made him think he was close to death on more than one occasion.

"Yes, it could have worked. But at what cost? As I've told you, I believe that Stadler's soul, like ours, has been destroyed through his constant use of *kroba*. If humans were ever to use *kroba* on themselves, they would lose their souls as well, and perhaps fall to the same level of evil and depravity as Stadler."

"I still don't buy into this business about souls," said Chris. "But are you saying that when a man loses his soul, he becomes inherently evil?"

"Yes. That's what I believe. I cannot explain Stadler otherwise."

"Then, by your logic, you and I are both evil."

"Not at all," Temsik answered. "You and I are not men."

PARTING WORDS

IT was Womyn's Wednesday at the New Bar the next evening, which meant there would be practically no men present, and the music would most likely be mellow women's stuff like Joni Mitchell rather than ten-minute extended dance mixes of Rick Astley (at the scientifically tested, Giorgio Moroder–approved international standard of 120 beats per minute), so Chris decided to return to the rustic Jocko's Rocketship Tavern, where he had bitten his first victim exactly one week earlier.

He drank beer with some guys at the bar and watched the final innings of a game between the Detroit Tigers and the Milwaukee Brewers. Then, using the same promise of drugs that he had used before, Chris lured a blond guy named Matt into the bathroom. Matt was stocky but well built, with massive arms and a thick neck; he was probably a football player or a weight lifter. Whatever he was, he seemed not to be in training, because he was very interested in buying a quarter-ounce of pot from Chris.

Chris hypnotized him and handed him a sandwich-sized plastic bag holding tea leaves, for which Matt gave him forty dollars. After pocketing the money, Chris examined Matt's flesh to make sure he had never been bitten. Seeing that it was virgin meat, he sank his teeth into the muscular neck and sucked out the blood. As he drank it down, he wondered whether or not blood contaminated with steroids would have any effect on a vampire.

When Chris returned to the apartment, he found two presents waiting for him on the dining room table.

"What's this?" Chris asked in bewilderment.

"Open them and find out," said Temsik, stirring up martinis, most likely made with vodka rather than with gin, in a glass cylinder. "Care for one?"

"Sure, why not?" Chris sat down in front of the gifts. Both were wrapped in purple marbleized paper, one the size of a matchbox, the other slightly larger than a hardcover book.

Temsik sat across from Chris, poured him a glass, and dropped a green olive into it, then waited expectantly.

Chris took a large sip. The drink stung his tongue with more bite than mere alcohol. "Jesus! What is this?"

"You've never had a martini made with pepper vodka?"

Chris made a face. "Not a very nice joke to play on a guy."

"I didn't mean it as a joke. I thought you might like it."

"It's awfully hot."

"Give it a try. It'll grow on you." Temsik seemed amused by his little experiment. "Go on, open your presents."

Chris opened the smallest one first, thinking there might be a heavy vampire ring of his very own inside, set with a colorful stone. But when he lifted the lid of the box, he discovered a tarnished key. "A key," he stated. "What's this for?"

"For your new apartment."

"You're kicking me out?" Chris was alarmed. This was unexpected. He wondered what was going on. His mind began spinning.

Temsik reached out and lightly touched Chris's wrist. "Not at all. This is all part of your training. It's always a good idea to let the pupil live on his own for a while. You're going to have to do it someday anyway. The apartment is only about ten blocks from here, on East Gorham Street. If you get into any trouble or need help, you come get me. It's not as dangerous as it may sound. I'll come and check in on you a few times. After a week, we'll sit down together and evaluate how you've progressed. Then, I'll decide whether or not you need any more training. If so, you'll stay with me a little longer. If not, you'll be free to go your way, back to Chicago if you like. How does that sound?"

"What about Stadler? What if he snatches me?"

"I'm afraid that on that account you're no safer with me than without. After all, he got Laura, didn't he? Of course, she wasn't here when it happened, but you can't stay cooped up in here all night, every night. You have to get out. The risk is the same wherever you keep your apartment. Stadler could be anywhere, and he could be nowhere. For all I know, he could be in Milwaukee or Chicago, and only come to Madison on odd occasions. You'll have greater freedom in your own place without me telling you what to do all the time."

"Bullshit," said Chris. Temsik was manipulating him like an expert puppeteer pulling the strings of a marionette. Chris felt the sudden rush of adrenaline that comes with intense anger, or perhaps Matt had been taking steroids after all and Chris was feeling their effect. "You're up to something, and I don't want any part of it."

Temsik laughed. "If you believe that I'm being less than candid with you, you're right. But if you think I'm going to tell you what it is that I am up to, you're out of your fucking mind."

"Do you think I'm an idiot? I know what your plan is. You want to get rid of me so you can go back to starving yourself. You don't care what happens to me, or to any other vampires. You'd rather destroy yourself than go after Stadler, and I'm the only thing currently standing in your way. You're nothing but a coward. That's the honest truth, isn't it?"

"As opposed to the dishonest truth, which is that I'm setting you up in that apartment for your own good. Oh, you can call me a coward if you like, if that pleases your sense of propriety. But don't lay a personal claim to the honest truth. The honest truth is much worse than you could possibly imagine."

"You're shortchanging me, you know that? I'm not ready yet, and you know it. When I first came here, I didn't think I needed your training. But over the last few days, I've learned that I don't know the first thing about survival. And now you turn around and kick me out!"

"Chris, you haven't even opened your other present."

Reluctantly, Chris unwrapped the box, scowling as he did so. Temsik looked harried. The box, from a copy shop, contained a hundred-odd pages of typescript.

"What's this?" asked Chris, still wary of Temsik's intentions.

"That, Chris, is a portion of my memoirs."

"Your memoirs." Chris stared at them in disbelief.

"Not that you would ever find them interesting. The chapters you have in your hands constitute the most complete information you could ever find on Franz Stadler."

Chris felt a grin creep its way across his face. "What good will that do me if you refuse to help me find him?"

Temsik spread his hands. "Make of it what you will."

"But I'll need your help."

"A coward of my magnitude wouldn't be much help."

"Hey, don't twist my words back around."

"Who's twisting? You called me a coward. Or were you perhaps mistaken?"

"I don't know."

"Go off to your new apartment and read what I've given you. Try to learn as much about Stadler as you can. Think long and hard on the problem. You're a bright fellow. You ought to be able to think of something, once you know how Stadler's mind works. After a week, come back to me and we'll work out a plan together. Then we'll go after him together and fry the son of a bitch."

Chris rifled through the pages and smiled up at Temsik. Once again, his paranoia had gotten the better of him, and he had blown up at Temsik for no good reason. Here he had thought that Temsik wanted him gone so he could go back to wasting away into nothingness, when in fact he had come around to Chris's point of view all along. Temsik must have been wanting to make up to him for the killing of the lab assistants, over which Chris was still shaken up. But even though Chris remained mad at Temsik, it would be an egregious error to turn down his offer. Chris couldn't possibly get Stadler without Temsik's help.

"You'd better not be lying to me." Chris swirled the last of the martini in his glass and tossed the whole thing down, then winced as it burned its way down his throat. A burst of pepper vapor in his sinuses abruptly made his eyes sting.

"Or else what, Chris?" Temsik was intrigued. "Do you dare to make a threat against me?" He grinned, baring his yellow teeth and fangs, with a sinister gleam in his eye.

"That's not what I meant," said Chris, backing down. "I only meant that I hope you don't go back to starving yourself. I need you, or I'll never find Stadler."

"Come back in a week, and we'll talk."

"Okay," Chris said, suddenly relieved. He was beginning to think that he might already have succeeded in his mission after all. If he couldn't trust Temsik, then who could he trust? "It's a deal. Let's have another martini."

They shook hands.

"That's my boy." Temsik refilled his glass.

They filled Chris's coffin with his personal effects, crated it up, and hired a Four Lakes cab (a Chrysler station wagon) to transport it to the apartment on East Gorham Street.

The place was furnished, in the basement of an old house that had been converted into student apartments. Temsik explained that he had been renting the place for a few years and that it had been used by other vampires in the Underground when they were passing through, or coming to stay for a few months. He said that Beth and Luis had lived in it for six weeks the previous winter because they had needed a break from Chicago.

It had a couch and some chairs in the living room, a separate bedroom, and low ceilings. The few windows had been painted over with black paint and then shuttered closed.

Over the next five evenings, Chris spent little time in the apartment, spending most of his time out at the bars, either at the New Bar or at the nearby neighborhood tavern, the Caribou. Each night, he found someone interesting to bite, and spent the rest of the evening drinking, dancing, chatting with people, or playing darts (at the Caribou, at least).

But he made sure to set aside time each night to lounge around the dusty apartment and read from Temsik's memoirs. . . .

ODESSA, 1808

From the Memoirs of V. K. Temsik:

UPON my graduation from the University of Leipzig, my father, Kiril Kirilovich Temsik, set me to work as an agent at his Moscow trading company, to which I had been destined since birth. My father, however, failed to appreciate what I had learned at school. "A fine education," he said, "for a Petersburg fop—not for a Moscow business man!"

Napoléon's conquests in eastern Europe had greatly diminished my father's expected profits over the last few years, and rendered my German education practically useless in his eyes. On the whole, Moscow cared little what Napoléon might do next; he remained a meager threat to the glory of Russia. Muscovites were, almost as a rule, entirely disinterested in foreign affairs. Yet the French emperor remained a thorn in my father's side, disrupting trade and ruining longtime clients in the west.

The solution to my father's problems came from the unlikeliest of sources: my mother, Akulina Pavlovna. She wanted us to build a dacha in Odessa on the Black Sea, a summer home to which we could retreat from the seasonal crowds (and accompanying smells) of summertime Moscow.

"What!" Spittle flew from my father's lips as he erupted in anger. "What need do you have of another dacha, in addition to the estate at Smolensk?"

My father's idea of a grand holiday was to drink vodka and smoke cigars with his chum, the ancient Count Uzhassniy, on the veranda of our crumbling country home outside Smolensk, where they could watch our three hundred serfs at work in the fields beneath the hot August sun.

"But—" my mother began.

"The answer is no," my father said.

I came to my mother's defense. Tsar Alexander was developing Odessa as an important port, "the Saint Petersburg of the south," and I therefore suggested to my father that he set up a company office there to help reduce his recent losses. Odessa's reported exports were numerous: everything from wheat and timber to horsehair brushes and caustic potash. My father said he would examine the prospect, but I quietly doubted his sincerity. He was conservative in all matters, and antipathetic toward change.

But after a journey to Odessa in August of 1807, my father's outlook changed.

"Met with Prince Trubetskoy, their customs fellow," he said. "Their exports are trifling compared to Moscow's or Petersburg's. Right now they're faring poorly because of this war with the Turks."

"But we'll soon beat the Turks," I chimed in.

"Of course. And I'm convinced that Odessa can become a major port. I said as much to Trubetskoy—crafty son of a bitch! Had a gleam in his eye like a Jewish usurer. I wanted to speak to Governor Richelieu, but he was off somewhere fighting the bloody Circassians, so this other Frenchman, de Castelnau, showed me their plans for the city, which I admit are ambitious. He and Trubetskoy were eager for me to commit some capital down there. I've decided to make a go of it, though it could be risky."

This was unexpected. I had been certain he would reject

the idea out of hand. My father was a stubborn man, and not known for taking risks.

"So your mother will get her dacha, and I'm putting you in charge of the Odessa office, since it was your idea. I always knew your education would prove beneficial someday."

I stood there in shock, my mouth hanging open, wondering what in Odessa could have had such power to cure my father's irascible disposition.

In June of 1808, my parents decided I should make the trip to Odessa to oversee the completion of our dacha and get to work setting up our company office.

It was fifteen hundred *versts* from Moscow to Odessa, a long and tedious journey by hired coach across the Ukrainian steppes, by way of Kiev. I spent my time reading bad French novels (something I was afraid to do in the presence of my father, who considered them womanly), but my groom, Maximych, being practically illiterate, had no such luxury, and proved restless and talkative the entire trip. After only three days, I was amusing myself with plans of his murder.

Maximych was a few years younger than me and dark-complexioned, the only son of our old serf Rurik, who had run our household when I was a child. I remembered Rurik best for his terrifying tales of evil vampires who snatched the souls of naughty children, and of the great witch Baba Yaga, who flew through the air in a mortar and pestle and feasted upon children's bones. But while I was away at school, our Rurik had suffered a fit of apoplexy and died while administering hair tonic to my father's scalp, leaving behind Maximych and his two sisters. The mother, Marfa, was our laundress, a dependable and hardworking peasant woman.

The green summer steppeland was all we could see for days on end, and continued with us until we finally rode up the gentle slope on the outskirts of Odessa. The town was enclosed by a modest limestone wall over which could be seen the spires of several churches, and was quite small compared to Moscow. Riding in on the Tiraspol Road, we entered through the Gate to the Waters, and were able to gaze down the length of the broad avenue before us and see the ocean at the opposite end. My first impression of Odessa was of an island unto itself, surrounded on the one side by a sea, on the other by a sea of grass.

After eight blocks, we reached a cliff high above the ocean. The town was situated on a rocky promontory two hundred feet above the shore and at the southern end of a semicircular cape. The vista from atop the promontory, along the seafront, was a sight to behold. The steep hills led down to the quay below, where tall-masted brigs and schooners, stripped of their sails, were docked close in, in the process of being loaded and unloaded. Two stone breakwaters thrust outward into the sea, the northernmost marking the military port, the southernmost the commercial port. Around the docks, several beaches sloped gradually into the ocean.

Maximych was in awe, as he had never before laid eyes upon the sea.

Having previously seen only the glassy, gray waters in and around Petersburg myself, I was unprepared for the shocking play of color upon the ocean in the deep harbor, a rippling indigo blue giving way to lighter cerulean shades. The harbor was magical, seemingly alive, with an air of mystery, beckoning me to explore it. The surf rolled in calm and steady due to the man-made breakwaters, absent the violent poundings of the shore one would expect at such a rocky place. I saw myself, in my mind's eye, running down the hillside, stripping off my clothes like some African savage, and running down the beach into the enveloping waters, which I imagined to be bottomless and as cold as death.

Over the next few weeks I found Odessa *charmant*, as my mother would have been wont to say. The place stirred in me a sense of freedom not felt since my days at Leipzig. I often found myself thinking of Franz. I had no way of knowing whether he had survived Napoléon's invasion of his homeland. I had lost track of him four years ago. I tried not to brood about it; yet the atmosphere along the seafront was conducive to such pensive behavior.

The family dacha was progressing nicely. The exterior was of the classical design favored by the architects in Petersburg and Odessa and abhorred by those in Moscow: two tall stories of pale limestone quarried from the promontory (from, strangely, *underneath* the town!), with white Grecian columns in a half circle surrounding the front portico, topped with an austere half dome. The roof slanted sharply and was graced with three squat chimneys. I bought several well-crafted furnishings from a Neopolitan merchant, G. Vitalis, for a price remarkably low by Moscow standards. I was certain my mother would be pleased with my taste, my father with my frugality.

The gardens around the dacha, however, were nonexistent, save for eighteen white acacia saplings, a gift of the duc de Richelieu, governor of Novorossiysk Territory. I soon learned to keep the windows shut tight, due to the frequent and strong winds that blew clouds of dust all over town.

The Khvostovs were my neighbors on the adjacent property. I dined with them nearly every day, at the request of Sofya Ivanovna, whose invitations were not solely for the benefit of my stomach, for she inevitably sat me beside her daughter Tatyana Gerasimovna, an agreeable but simple girl in whom I failed to develop even a shred of interest. Yet I made polite conversation with the girl, for the food was good and I did not wish for Sofya to think me ungrateful. Sofya never seemed to notice that Tatyana had as little interest in me as I had in her.

More enticing to me was the Khvostovs' maidservant Anyuta, whose full bosom was always worth a glance or two as she carried in the *zakooski*. More than once I caught Sofya's husband, Gerasim Trofimovich, making a similar assessment of Anyuta's breasts. All in all, I found the dinners enjoyable. Yet life in Odessa was making me fat.

* * *

On the afternoon of the first day of August, I had sent
Maximych to the post office and was reading Goethe at my
desk when I looked out the window and saw a disheveled
man crouching before one of our white acacia saplings in
the "garden." The man's back was turned to me, the tails
of his yellow waistcoat dragging in the dirt. I was displeased
to see a stranger wandering about the property, so I ventured
outside to see what he was doing.

"You there!" I shouted.

"Ah! Vasily Kirilovich!" Armand Emmanuel Sophie
Septimanie du Plessis, duc de Richelieu, governor-general
of Novorossiysk, mayor of Odessa, rose from the ground
and offered me his dusty hand.

"Monsieur le duc." I was taken aback, but quickly recovered myself and shook his hand firmly in the European
manner.

In spite of his dusty habiliments, the duke was the very
picture of French nobility. His sleepy eyes were dark and
long-lashed, beneath slim eyebrows raised in a perpetual
question. His was a round face with a nose like a falcon's
beak above full, healthy lips. He resembled every portrait
or engraving I could remember having seen of a French
duke, count, or king, except that instead of a long wig of
black curls or a short white powdered one, he wore atop
his head his own graying hair, in an unruly shock like the
coat of a sheepdog. He was at least ten years older than I.

"I have but a few minutes, Vasily—my afternoon
rounds." Richelieu spoke in flawless Russian.

It struck me as odd that the duke would *walk* around town
to conduct his affairs rather than ride in a carriage—odder
still for him to be unaccompanied by any secretary, servant,
or hanger-on. Richelieu's second aide-de-camp, Comte
Léon de Rochechouart, was forever at his side; I had never
previously seen the one without the other.

"So happy you could make the time—" I began.

The duke interrupted, but his manner was pleasant. "It
is the matter of your trees . . ."

"Oh! Perhaps I haven't properly expressed our thanks—"

"No, that's all right." The duke dismissed the thought with a wave of his hand. "You've been most appreciative. My dear Vasily Kirilovich, I made a point of seeing you today because of your poor saplings. They demand better care."

I examined the closest white acacia, no taller than myself. Its leaves were as full as one might expect in a tree so young. "They seem perfectly healthy to me."

"Ah, but see how this limb droops?" asked the duke. "This tree is begging for water!"

"I'll see that Maximych attends to it."

"And where is your Maximych?"

"At the postmaster's."

The duke frowned. "My friend, these poor saplings need water at once, and if you don't fetch it, I shall have to do it myself."

At that moment, I happened to espy Maximych approaching leisurely down the avenue, past stone houses that were for the most part still under construction. Maximych's dark skin was taking to the sun in a way that mine could not. In his hand he carried a small bundle of letters.

"Please, Monsieur le duc. You can see my groom is heading this way. He can water the trees. There's no need for either of us to dirty ourselves."

Finally, Maximych appeared and handed me a sheaf of letters. Six were from my mother, one from my father. The last had been forwarded (in my mother's own hand) from Moscow to Odessa, having been sent originally from Königsberg, East Prussia, without a name on the envelope. Yet I recognized the careful German script—it belonged to none other than Franz Stadler!

Forgetting the duke's very presence, I ripped open the letter at once, carelessly letting my parents' letters fall to the ground. Franz's letter was brief and to the point: he was coming to Moscow to visit me. Tears of joy sprang to my eyes as I read it. I would write my mother at once and ask her to send him here to Odessa.

Meanwhile, the letters I had dropped were blowing across the yard; Maximych was chasing after them. Richelieu, returning to his original mission, had found himself a pail of water and was going from tree to tree, giving each a good drink. I was oblivious to the action around me as I read Franz's note over and over.

FRANZ

From the Memoirs of V. K. Temsik:

ONE week after writing my mother to tell her of Franz's impending arrival and to ask her to arrange for his travel to Odessa, he appeared without forewarning on my doorstep. Although his letter had been dated 25 July 1808, I had in my excitement neglected to take into account that he was on the Gregorian calendar, which was twelve days ahead of the Julian calendar we still used in Russia.

I had just returned from an early dinner with the Khvostovs. The sun was setting, and I was reading Schiller by candlelight in my makeshift study when he arrived. Maximych let him in. Yet before Franz's presence could be announced, I was upon him, already embracing my old friend in the Russian manner and kissing him fraternally on the cheeks. The stubble on his face scratched my own clean-shaven skin.

"Vasily!" he said, his low voice squashed by the strength of my great bear hug. "So good to see you." He spoke in German. His greetings had always been rather cool, lacking in excessive sentiment, something I had always attributed to his nationality. He patted my back with one arm, holding the other close to his side.

"Franz, my German brother!" I shouted in his language,

quite emotional and un-German myself. "I hardly believe it is you!" I released him and stood back to examine him.

His appearance had changed. His hair remained dusty blond, but was cut much shorter, military-style, and was already beginning to thin on top. If anything, his square Teutonic face had grown more striking, and now sported a long pink scar across his cheek, adding a certain distinction. His dark brown eyes were as luminous as when I had known them in Leipzig, but they now hid behind a pair of spectacles that distorted them greatly. His frock coat was shabby; he looked exhausted from traveling. Indeed, such a journey from Königsberg to Moscow, from Moscow to Odessa, required an almost Russian tenacity!

I instructed Maximych to take Franz's trunk upstairs to my bedroom. Until I could procure another bed, Franz would have to share my large Italian four-poster, as Maximych's small bed would have been unsuitable, and in any case I could not force my groom to sleep on the floor. I doubted Franz would mind the arrangements; we had always been fond of one another, and accustomed to close company from our student days.

I asked him about his trek through Byelorussia and the Ukraine as I led him into my study. He complained that his backside was sore from weeks of travel; it had rained throughout most of his trip to Moscow; my parents had told him I was in Odessa, had put him up for the night, and had loaned him the money for his trip south. He had many kind words for my parents' generosity.

"Say, Temsik, isn't that my Schiller you have there?"

I picked up the book from my desk and handed it to him. "I don't believe so. I've had this for some time."

A loud *thump* came from the foyer; poor Maximych was struggling with Franz's trunk.

"Vasily, you had never heard of Schiller before you met me. I rather think it is mine. I recognize it distinctly." He turned the book over in his right hand. "It was pilfered from me in Leipzig. I never realized you were the culprit!"

"Perhaps you loaned it to me."

"Not likely." Franz's smile was abrupt. "Well, it's no matter. I'm not asking for it back. If you hadn't stolen it—"

"I never stole it, Franz. If it is your book, I have it purely by accident."

"If you hadn't stolen it, neither of us would now be looking at it. All I have left to my name is what's in that trunk. When I left Leipzig in '06, I was in a hurry."

Suddenly, there came a crash from the stairway.

"I think I should give your servant a hand," said Franz, getting up. I rose and followed him into the vestibule.

Maximych was standing on the fifth stair, his grip on the bulky trunk having failed, which had allowed it to slide to the base of the staircase, scraping the new varnish along the bottom four steps. I sighed, knowing I would have to call back the Albanian carpenters for repairs to their handiwork. Maximych had rolled up his sleeves for the job. Sweat glistened on his olive skin in the light from the wall candles and trickled down his forehead. A lock of his dark greasy hair had fallen in his face.

Franz threw me his frock coat. I noticed he had removed it using only his right hand; his entire left arm remained stiff and motionless. I removed my own coat, laid his and mine upon an enshrouded chair, and joined the two of them on the staircase. Franz grabbed the bottom end of his trunk using only his right hand, propping the lid of the trunk beneath his chin and throwing his back into it, while Maximych took the top end and I attempted to hold up the middle. But as we ascended the curving stairs, I found I was merely in the way. Franz took to the task with vigor, his muscles straining along his arm and back. It was obvious by now that his left arm was unusable. All the same, he nearly toppled Maximych backwards twice. I had to admire his strength, especially in one already so tired from travel.

When they were finished, Maximych brought the samovar into my study; the sparsely furnished dining room was having its walls plastered, and though the workmen had gone home for the day, it was a great mess and hardly a cozy place for tea. Maximych served Franz and myself some strong black tea in glasses with silver holders, which I had indeed pilfered—from my mother. Maximych brought in plates of cold cuts and sliced cheeses; a basket of rye bread, with a dish of unsalted butter; and *pastilla*, *marmelade*, and other sweet confections, each in their own small glass dish.

Having just eaten, I had little room for more food, and simply drank my tea and nibbled on a piece of cheese. But Franz devoured everything in sight, even though he admitted the confectionery he had eaten was too sweet for his palate.

Afterward, I offered him some amontillado newly acquired from a Milanese by the name of Luchesi, and Maximych brought our chairs out onto the portico, where the night air was brisk and refreshing. I dismissed Maximych, saying I would call him if he was needed.

I discussed my father's plans for our office in Odessa and my own eventual role in it. Franz seemed impressed. We talked of the beauty of the night sky, and of Odessa's darkened buildings, and of the fresh smell of the breeze from the sea.

Finally, I asked him about his arm.

"This? I have Napoléon to thank for that, and the stupidity of the Prussians." Strangely, Franz's tone was mild when he mentioned Napoléon, and became derisive on "the Prussians."

"What happened?"

"It was during the Battle of Auerstadt. I was attending to a wounded officer, when—"

"You fought in the Prussian army?" Until that point I had had no idea he had been a soldier.

"Not exactly. I mean, I didn't fight. I joined them as an army surgeon when I fled to Berlin two years ago. So, as I was saying, I was at Auerstadt, and we were in such rapid retreat the French artillery was suddenly able to reach the tent where I was working. I was amputating an officer's arm when—"

I immediately recalled the amputation Franz had taken me to at the beginning of our friendship, when I had briefly entertained the notion of becoming a physician. My stomach became queasy, and despite the sweet amontillado on my lips I could suddenly taste the borsch I had eaten earlier at the Khvostovs'.

"—when we were struck by a cannonball. Bits of metal embedded themselves into my arm, and I was thrown to the ground, covered in dirt. Someone dragged me out and dressed my wound. The injury was slight, yet it left my arm enfeebled and utterly useless."

"That's horrible." I downed the last of my glass and asked Franz if he required any more amontillado.

He declined, saying he was exhausted and wanted only to go to bed. I called Maximych and instructed him to close up the house, and Franz and I retired upstairs to my bedchamber.

After changing into his nightshirt, Franz fell asleep immediately and slept peacefully for twelve hours.

On my side of the bed, I had difficulty finding sleep. Ever since leaving Leipzig, I had felt a constant emptiness that I knew could be filled only by my German friend. What puzzled me now was that this emptiness persisted. Franz's presence at my side should have made me whole again, yet I felt little changed from all those years in Moscow.

My heart beat quickly, and my excitement remained heightened all evening. The mere presence of Franz next to me prevented my getting more than two hours' sleep. I couldn't help but remember those winter nights in Leipzig, when we had slept flesh against flesh for warmth, when I had felt so protected and content in his brotherly arms, and had hidden my arousal from him. I couldn't help but remember, because I was now equally aroused, and yearned to be held once more in his sheltering embrace.

The night lasted an eternity. But once the sun had risen, I spent the morning hours staring at Franz's prone figure, remembering how wonderful life had been when we were students, until finally he awoke.

* * *

The next day, I took Franz on a small tour.

We crossed the dry ravine behind my family's property by means of a wooden footbridge and climbed the hill to the great citadel, which now functioned as the port's quarantine facility. The stone walls of the fortress stood at a steep incline to the ground and jutted out to form seven points around the perimeter. Richelieu had recently shown me a map of the town on which the citadel resembled the Hebrews' Star of David in its configuration, save the seaward wall, which extended straight along a sharp precipice high above the bay.

The wind on the hill fluttered Franz's open frock coat as he gazed upon the battlements. A guard atop the wall looked down at us and waved a greeting. I waved back and smiled, but Franz ignored the soldier, and we continued on.

From the hill, Odessa lay before us, its avenues straight and broad, lined with Richelieu's precious acacia trees. The more magnificent homes and buildings had been erected close to the seafront, two- and three-story classical structures reminiscent of Petersburg. Reaching above the uniform rooftops were the many and diverse churches, some still under construction. Nearer the walls of the town sat the flimsy shacks and mud huts of the many poor immigrants and state peasants.

Franz still seemed out of sorts, which I now attributed to his journey. I believed him to be the same Franz I had known, yet his manner was more reserved, and he struck me as aloof and unhappy, as if some hideous spell had been cast over him. I was determined to break the spell, whatever the cost.

Together, over the next two days, Franz and I explored the whole town, from mud huts to palatial homes, from the customs house to the military barracks. He was impressed by the newness of the buildings and by the Greek-inspired architecture. Franz, of course, had never been to Petersburg, and had therefore never seen the houses and government buildings that had been the models for Odessa's.

One morning, Franz and I took a stroll down the rocky

terrain to Arkadia Beach at the southern end of town. The wind off the bay blew dust in my eyes. Milky breakers rolled in swiftly along the expanse of fine sand. It was a weekday, and most people were at work, so the place was overrun with children and older youths, chasing each other around the beach and dunking their fellows beneath the waves in innocent play. Nearly all were dark-skinned foreigners, and the youngest, both boys and girls, were naked. The older youths playing farther down the beach were all boys. Of them, the Albanians and Turks were completely immodest, as naked as the children, while the Greek and Italian boys wore small bathing trunks.

As we neared the end of the beach, we came upon two Albanian youths who were sitting atop a third of unknown nationality and laughing like mad hyenas. I thought at first that their victim was being tickled, but quickly realized they were instead playing some kind of erotic game. The two on top looked our way and smiled; the third's face was obscured by a skinny bronze thigh. The perpetrators waved at us, but not in greeting; they were beckoning us to join them. They said something in their native language that neither Franz nor I could understand. One stood up and made lewd motions with his hips, displaying to us his dark, erect member.

"Disgusting!" said Franz as he turned away.

"They're only boys," I countered, still watching. "They probably want our money."

"They didn't get any money from their friend, Vasily, I assure you."

I tried to lessen Franz's criticism: "At least he seems to be enjoying himself. I don't see him struggling, do you?"

"You sound as if you condone it."

I had no answer for him, but he saw how I continued to regard the youths. They were possessed of an extraordinary beauty.

"Come, turn away," said Franz, imploring, placing a hand on my shoulder. We didn't speak any more of the incident as we retraced our steps along the shoreline of Arkadia Beach, and returned to town.

Each evening, I continued to get little sleep as Franz snored beside me. I wished these were the coldest nights of winter, so we might sleep closer together. As it was, the nights were warm, and he remained a safe distance from me.

We dined a few times at the Khvostovs'. Sofya Ivanovna took to Franz at once and seated him next to Tatyana Gerasimovna, having given up on my ever showing any interest in her. I was stuck talking trade with Gerasim Trofimovich on the other end of the table. For distraction I regarded Anyuta's breasts whenever she entered the dining room (she finally caught on, and smiled discreetly at me while the others busied themselves with their food).

On the fourth day of Franz's stay, I turned down Sofya's dinner invitation with feigned apology; alas, we would be dining later that evening with the governor-general. I had told Richelieu of my friend's arrival, and he had requested that we join him for a late dinner.

A few minutes before nine o'clock, Franz and I arrived at Richelieu's home, directly across the street from the Theatre, at the heart of town, near the seafront. Franz was surprised by its modest size, and I informed him in a whisper that it was, in fact, smaller than my family's dacha. A manservant let us in, and we were met in the entry hall by Comte Léon de Rochechouart, whom I had by now learned was Richelieu's cousin, which helped explain their constant attachment to one another.

I introduced Franz, and we shook hands. Rochechouart's thin arms were hidden beneath the billowy sleeves of his linen shirt, but his similarly thin legs were readily visible in their tight beige pantaloons. The count wore a thin, immature mustache that seemed but a shadow upon his upper lip. His curly black hair sat tousled atop his head and grew downward in thick sideburns that stopped just short of his chin. Aside from his attempts at facial hair, Rochechouart's countenance was decidedly effeminate, with heavy-lidded eyes, thin eyebrows, and a dainty mouth. If I had not told Franz this man was a soldier, he never would have seen it for himself.

"Ah! It's Temsik and his friend," came Richelieu's voice from the small dining room. "We were about to serve *aper-itifs*."

I introduced Franz to Richelieu; his physician, Dr. Scudery; the Marquis de Castelnau; and the Abbé Labdan, our company for the evening. Franz seemed alarmed at the withering Abbé's cautious stare, although I had given him warning on the way over.

Sofya had told me the gossip about the Abbé, which I had dutifully related to Franz. As I knew already, he had been Richelieu's tutor in France before the Revolution. Another of his pupils, however, had been the young Duc d'Eighien, who had later fallen prey to the guillotine. After learning of the duke's execution, the Abbé Labdan had lost his senses, whereupon Richelieu had invited him into his household in Odessa, safe from the horrors of France. Apparently, the poor Abbé had not yet recovered from the shock of the incident. Sofya was convinced he belonged in an asylum, though he seemed perfectly harmless to me.

Richelieu greeted Franz in German: "Shall we consider you a refugee, Herr Stadler?" Richelieu poured us both a glass of golden Madeira.

"In a way, yes." Franz took a tentative sip and nodded his approval. "Fine Madeira."

"Are you a Mennonite?" asked Rochechouart, eyes agleam.

Franz laughed. I detected a note of condescension, though no one else seemed to notice.

Richelieu looked embarrassed for his cousin and gave him a reproving glance. "Come, Léon, does he look like a Mennonite to you?"

"I suppose not."

"I must apologize for my aide-de-camp, Herr Stadler. It sometimes seems as if all our Germans are Mennonites."

Now it was Rochechouart's turn to look embarrassed. A

bright red flush rose to his cheeks. Yet he threw the duke an affectionate glance.

"That's quite all right, Monsieur le duc," said Franz. "If you will excuse my common dress, I will excuse the error of Monsieur le comte."

"Hear, hear!" Dr. Scudery raised his glass.

"In Odessa we are all commoners," said the Marquis de Castelnau, gesturing at his companions.

"True enough," agreed Richelieu with a sad chuckle.

Rochechouart flinched, as if offended by the marquis's democratic remark. But the ordinary surroundings of the duke's home lent credence to what he had said.

Although Rochechouart might have been adept at soldiering, he struck me as possessing half the intelligence of Richelieu, and appeared every bit the fop my father had once accused me of becoming.

We made polite conversation around *aperitifs*, and much of the discussion concerned Germany. I was on my fourth glass of Madeira when Richelieu proceeded to tell us a funny story.

"I was in Germany in 1790—the name of the town escapes me at the moment—when I decided late one evening to take a walk and explore the outer ramparts of the village. I happened upon a young officer on patrol and began speaking to him in German. The poor fellow stared at me as if I were an idiot; he hadn't understood a single word. So I repeated what I had said, in Italian this time, but he still comprehended nothing. I tried again in English, and met with the same bad luck. Finally, thinking it was my last hope, I resorted to Russian, yet he continued to give me his blank stare, now coupled with a look of utter pity. By this time, the officer seemed completely disgusted with me, and inquired, in a rich Gascon accent, 'But monsieur, do you not know a word of French?' "

The room broke out into laughter. The Marquis de Castelnau, tears in his eyes, seemed about to fall off his chair. Even the Abbé was laughing. Rochechouart laughed politely, eyeing the duke, although it was clear he had heard this story before. Richelieu himself could not keep from laughing at his own story.

I found myself staring at Richelieu for several minutes while the conversation continued around me.

"Temsik," said Dr. Scudery, looking aghast. "What the devil's wrong with you?"

"Pardon?"

"I was asking you what you thought."

The whole table was now staring my way. I tried to remember the subject of conversation and realized, looking at Franz, that it was of course Germany. I would have to attempt an intelligent comment.

"I think," I began, directing myself at Richelieu, our host, "that there are altogether too many Frenchmen in Germany at present."

"Hear, hear!" echoed Dr. Scudery. The whole table joined him in raising his glass, except for the Abbé, who was not paying attention. Scudery proposed a toast. "To the inevitable defeat of Napoléon."

Hearing the toast, Franz withdrew his glass and did not drink, while the Abbé raised his own and joined the rest of us in the toast.

"I wouldn't be so sure of its inevitability," said Franz. "Who do you suppose will engineer this defeat? England? Russia? Or is it a job for the Turks?" Franz's chuckle expressed his contempt for any army that might try.

The room was suddenly silent. Everyone in it, aside from Franz and myself, was in one way or another employed by the Russian army.

I tried to repair the damage. "Come, Franz, it's not that hopeless. I'm sure Russia is up to the task. The French will be out of your homeland before you know it, and Germany will once again be in the hands of Germans."

Richelieu and Rochechouart concurred with me.

"I'm afraid you miss my point," said Franz. "I can think of no better way to sign Germany's death warrant than to put it into the hands of Germans."

"But you're German yourself," Rochechouart reminded him.

"Precisely. Who at this table could argue that they know the Germans better than I?"

Richelieu looked as if he were about to make an attempt.

"Germany doesn't really exist the way you think," Franz continued. "It's nothing more than rival princes in a continual struggle for power. If left to themselves, the greed of the nobility would bleed the people dry, and then there would be no Germany left."

"What exactly are you trying to say, my good man?" A pall had passed over Richelieu's face.

"That Napoléon is the best thing ever to happen to Germany. Prussia as well."

The Abbé Labdan abruptly began to choke. Dr. Scudery gave him three sharp slaps on the back. The Abbé coughed up a chunk of cheese and took a large gulp of Madeira.

But Richelieu's attention remained on Franz.

"If that's how you feel, why are you in Odessa?" asked Rochechouart dryly.

"Because the Prussians didn't want me. And if I had gone to the French, they would have thought I was a spy."

I wondered what Franz meant by that. *Could he be a deserter?* He had not yet told them he had been a surgeon in the Prussian army, but given his age, nationality, and scarred face, it was probably a tacit assumption that he had served either the Germans or Prussians. Now Richelieu was undoubtedly wondering if Franz was a spy working for the French.

"I, for one, refuse to believe that the Usurper's invasion of Germany could ever be construed to be a good thing," said Richelieu. "I spent over a year in your country and found it one of the most agreeable places on earth. I respectfully put it to you that the vast destruction caused by the Usurper could not possibly have improved upon it."

"Bonaparte is no usurper, Monsieur le duc. The nobility in France were already finished by the time he appeared."

"He helped finish them."

"I say that he's simply a man who knows what he wants and seizes it. The emperor is a common man who has made himself great by virtue of his actions, not by an accident of birth."

"Herr Stadler," said Richelieu, an edge creeping into his voice, "Napoléon has stolen the governance of France from the nobility. Even if he were the best thing to happen to Germany, as you maintain, I have no doubt he will destroy France unless he is defeated."

I agreed entirely with Richelieu. Russia's own nobility had lost much of their governing power during the reign of Peter the Great, and there were many of us in Russia who wished to see it restored.

I had never before realized Franz's affinity with the lower classes. Admittedly, his father was a Lutheran pastor in a small village near Leipzig; but at university, Franz had done exceedingly well and had always carried himself with a noble air, so I suppose I had never looked upon him as common.

"I'm not the only person who feels this way," said Franz. "Many Germans regard him as a hero, as does most of France."

"I needn't be reminded of that." Richelieu was plaintive. "You're quite right. Most of the French émigrés here revere the Usurper with all their heart. You can see I have to walk a pretty fine line to keep them happy. The Usurper once asked me to serve under him, but I refused, as a matter of principle. Odessa's French will never understand that."

"Nor will I," countered Franz. "I could never pass up such a unique opportunity."

"I doubt it would ever be extended your way." Once again, Rochechouart was dry as he defended his cousin.

"Léon!" Richelieu laughed uncomfortably, both embarrassed and amused. "No need to be rude. Herr Stadler and I are simply two gentlemen airing our differences on a highly subjective matter. Don't you agree, Herr Stadler?"

"I agree that we disagree, Monsieur le duc. However, if I remain in the present company much longer, I'm afraid I will continue to be insulted by Monsieur le comte, at which point I shall have to call him out. Since none of us want that, I believe it's best if I excuse myself from your table and bid you good evening.''

With that, Franz stood, downed the last of his Madeira, and left the room. I heard the front door close heavily behind him, as if it had been caught by the wind.

All of us were stunned, and I was pointedly embarrassed by my friend's behavior. I apologized vociferously for Franz, but had to excuse myself as well, as he was my guest. Richelieu understood, and asked that I go talk some sense into Franz's head and get him to come back. The manservant was already beginning to serve dinner: pork chops.

The Marquis de Castelnau sighed with displeasure as his plate was placed before him. "Do you think someday we might have something other than chops?" he asked.

Richelieu looked up, surprised. "My dear Gabriel, could it be that I have eaten them every day for three years? I must say, I haven't noticed."

Suddenly everyone was laughing again. "Please, Vasily Kirilovich," beseeched Richelieu. "Go get Stadler and bring him back here. He's going to miss these chops. I promise Rochechouart will behave himself."

Heartened by the duke's forgiving nature, I left his house in search of Franz. I found him a few blocks down the street, walking along the seafront wall.

"Franz!" I shouted.

"Ah, Vasily, it's you." He turned to face me, his face shadowed in the moonlight. Clouds were gathering in the darkened skies, and before I knew it, the moon had disappeared behind a gray veil. Franz's face turned even darker. The crash of the sea met my ears from far below.

"Richelieu is practically begging for you to come back. Rochechouart didn't mean to offend. They promise you won't be insulted, they only want to—"

"Vasily, I had hoped to get along with them, but I can't.

They're not my kind of people. I will not go back. But you go ahead, go enjoy your dinner party.''

The cool wind off the sea gave me a sudden chill.

"If you're that adamant, I'd rather walk with you back to the house. I can dine with them another day.''

"I'm not returning to the house.''

"You're not?''

"I'm going to take a walk—by myself. You go back to your friends. Have some fun.''

"But Franz, how can I—''

"Can't you get it through your head? I'm asking you to leave me alone. Now get the hell out of my way!''

XXI

MOY TSIGANOCHKI

From the Memoirs of V. K. Temsik:

I stood at the wall, gazing down at the Black Sea two hundred feet below, which indeed looked like a sea of pitch, its sluggish breakers the only discernible movement under a blanket of clouds that blocked out all the stars. I smelled rain. One solitary person wielding a lantern was walking along the quay, but the dockworkers were long gone. The unlighted streets of Odessa were devoid of people; everyone was either at home, at a dinner party, or at a tavern, all of them no doubt getting pleasantly drunk.

Franz had wounded me deeply. After my continued good friendship and generous hospitality, I couldn't fathom the reasons for his strange behavior.

I felt the first drops of rain on my nose as I headed back toward the governor's residence. But when I got there, I couldn't bring myself to knock on the door; after my failure with Franz, my embarrassment would be total. How could I ever explain to Richelieu and the others that my best friend refused to associate with them?

I couldn't face Richelieu, but I didn't want to go home, either, and face Maximych's questions. I set out to wander the streets of Odessa. The rain fell lightly on the cobblestones, which gave off the smell of wet dust and horse manure. Keeping the sea behind me, I turned the corner and walked down the acacia-lined central avenue leading away from the Theatre that marked its terminus.

Franz was clearly misguided in his reverence of Napoléon. I happened to find no great fault with Rochechouart's wry comment to him, for he had spoken the truth. Only an egoist could truly believe that Napoléon might make him an offer similar to the one made to Richelieu, who was, after all, a highly decorated lieutenant-general in the Russian army and a son of France. Franz was merely a common-born army surgeon for the defeated Prussians, and perhaps a deserter at that—hardly a useful asset for the ambitious French emperor. I failed to understand why he had caused such a row.

I had gone a few blocks when a faraway lightning bolt lit up the Catholic church on my right in three pale, rapid flashes. The rain had now begun in earnest, and I was becoming thoroughly wet. The sounds of a balalaika and a deep alto female voice were coming from some unseen tavern; it was the folk song "Moy Tsiganochki," "My Gypsies." I was unable to find its source before it disappeared in a loud crack of thunder and the lingering rumble that followed.

I wondered if I had personally done anything to offend Franz. Perhaps after our incident at the beach he found me as 'disgusting' as the Albanian youths. He had probably been able to read the desire on my face. Then again, it could have had nothing to do with that episode. Perhaps one morning he had only been feigning sleep and had spied me staring at him with lust in my eyes. But whatever the cause, Franz had acted as if I were anathema.

I was utterly confused. I walked with my head hanging, dragging my feet and watching the mud collect on my shoes.

It was only a matter of blocks before the cobblestones ran out and I found myself among citizens of lesser means. The ground was spongy beneath my feet. I passed small wooden shops whose paint was peeling and whose roofs were already sagging, even though they couldn't be more than twenty years old: S. SCHWARTZ, APOTHEKER; L. PICHKIN, TAILOR; A. PROKHOROV, UNDERTAKER. Nearby stood the new synagogue. But the Jewish neighborhood soon gave way to the Greek, and after that I found myself near the town walls, having walked a mere eleven blocks. In the darkness, the theatre was no longer visible at the avenue's end.

I turned up my collar against the rain. The wind was growing stronger, the rain falling harder. A shaft of lightning struck near a barracks house on this side of the wall, illuminating the clouds above and shattering my eardrums with its thunderclap. I jumped at the noise and decided I was a fool to be wandering the streets at this time of night in what was fast becoming a summer storm. I could be struck by lightning myself, or more likely be robbed by some immigrant. I decided at once to head home.

It seemed the quickest way would be to turn left, take a side street, and cut across, rather than retracing my steps all the way to Richelieu's first. I ended up on a short, narrow street that was sparsely built, and soon found myself among the flimsy shacks and mud huts of the poorest immigrants. If I turned left again, I would be heading in the proper direction, back to the family dacha. The way was dark, yet I proceeded.

Franz plagued my mind as I walked into the wind against the downpour, clutching my collar tighter around my neck.

I suddenly felt a great compassion for him. He had remained a common man despite his education, and I could see now that he, like Napoléon, desired some measure of greatness. He had clearly come to visit me in Russia because he had failed in his ambitions, whatever they were. The war had left him without the use of his left arm, which must have had some effect on his skills as a physician. Perhaps a life in medicine was no longer possible for him.

Oh, how I had failed him! Leading him on endless tours of the town, taking him to dinner at the Khvostovs', leaving him to converse with the feeble Tatyana (who could never understand his pain), showing him Arkadia Beach out of my own self-interest, taking him to Richelieu's home where every man was a success (except for the poor Abbé, whose crippled brain probably reminded Franz of his own dead limb)! I had failed as a host, paying no attention to the needs of my guest. I had only succeeded in alienating him, my one good friend, my German brother!

A whore accosted me from the shelter of a doorway, asking in poor French if I needed any company for the evening. I ignored her and continued on my way.

I decided Franz was no longer the strong, assertive man of reason I had known in Leipzig. He had grown weak and fragile in the chaos of the wars, grasping at the image of Napoléon for some ray of hope. But he didn't need Napoléon; what he needed was someone who cared, someone who could appreciate him despite his low beginnings. He needed someone like me to become his protector. . . .

Now where am I? I thought abruptly, looking at my surroundings. I had once more come upon the town wall, when I should have been back home already. All I knew for sure was that I was on the south side of town. If it weren't for the rain, I probably could have made out the silhouette of the citadel and gotten my bearings. But as it was, I was lost.

I followed along the wall until the shacks were behind me and I was crossing a field of grass. I had to be somewhere in the vicinity of the citadel. I trudged on, my feet sinking ever deeper in the mud. The wind blew head-on and was growing stronger. It began to feel as if I were taking one step back for every two steps forward. I was getting nowhere.

At last, I spied an orange glow a short ways ahead. As I neared, I saw that it came from a small wooden shack. A gypsy wagon stood nearby, but without a horse. I decided to go to the shack and ask directions.

Before I had knocked even once on the door, a young woman was opening it. "Come in, friend," she said in Russian.

I was taken aback. "How did you know I was out here?"

"One expects strangers on such nights." She spoke passably well and with a southern accent. I could tell she was not a native, but had learned our language from a Ukrainian. "You like tea, yes?"

"Thank you. What I'd really like are directions back to my house. I'm lost, you see."

"Of course you are," she said, as if that had already been established. She closed the door behind us.

The shack was lighted only by the bright glow from her roaring fire. The fireplace had been cobbled out of loose stones, without mortar to hold it together. Part of the room was hidden behind a sheet that hung from the ceiling; I presumed that a bed or mat lay beyond it. A flimsy pinewood table stood in the center of the room. A couple of kettles had been shoved to one side of the fireplace, while various pans hung from wooden pegs sticking out from the chimney. One whole wall of the shack was lined with shelves of glass jars, each containing a different variety of dried herb or spice, each labeled in some Slavic language I failed to identify.

Sitting by the fire was a scruffy youth perhaps sixteen years old, with long greasy hair, wearing a dirty workshirt and torn trousers. "This is Pasha, my helper. Pasha no speak."

I gathered from this that he was a mute.

She bade me sit on a sturdy three-legged stool beside Pasha, handed me a china cup of tea that had already steeped, and took a cup for herself. Pasha studied me intently, as if I might be the source of his next meal.

"You act as if you were expecting me."

"One expects strangers," she repeated. Then she frowned. "But you are wet! Give me your coat."

I gave it to her, and she hung it near the fire to dry. The fire gave off great heat; with my coat off, I was already getting dry myself.

The woman wore a long-sleeved blouse of embroidered silk, a pleated peasant skirt, and on her head a dyed orange scarf. Her face was youthful and olive-skinned, but plain.

Large golden earrings dangled from her ears, glinting in the firelight along with the gold bracelets on her wrists and gold rings on her fingers, some set with precious stones.

"I take it you're a gypsy," I said, hoping she wouldn't be offended if I proved wrong.

"You take it correct." She laughed. "I am *tsiganka* from Wallachia. One grows tired of Turkish men. So I come in search for new blood, is that not the phrase? Tell me, why you come here?"

"To Odessa, why to—"

"No, to me. Why you come to my house?"

"I'm trying to find my way back home, like I said. I'm looking for directions."

"This is lie. You come for other reason. You come for something else." Her green eyes gleamed like her jewelry.

"I don't understand you."

"You have problem, you come to me. You come not to my house on rainy night for being lost. You come to Madame Pescu because of problem."

She didn't look like a *Madame*. Although I could see only her face, she seemed younger than I was.

"You like my tea?" she asked, her voice lilting and soft. The rain drummed on the low roof of the shack.

"Yes, it's most peculiar. But delicious." I had no idea what it was. It was decidedly unlike the black tea to which I was accustomed.

"Is my own mix of herbs." Madame Pescu placed a hand on her bosom and gave a tiny bow. "I have many herbs and spices on walls. For many . . . recipes, heh-heh." She laughed knowingly, as if indulging in a private joke.

Pasha's persistent stare was beginning to disturb me.

I noticed again the many herbs and spices along her walls, and suddenly wondered if I had stumbled upon the home of a witch.

The herbal tea was making me drowsy, but not so much that I forgot the frightening tales our old Rurik used to tell me as a child, of the great witch Baba Yaga and her hut on chicken's legs. Baba Yaga flew through the air in an iron mortar, propelling herself with the pestle, and feasted upon human bones. The tales of Baba Yaga's evil doings were not easily forgotten and could still on occasion keep me up at night. I remembered how Rurik's eyes would grow large as he told of naughty children snatched by the witch. His tales of Baba Yaga had never ended happily.

I was suddenly apprehensive in the presence of Madame Pescu. *What if she's Baba Yagas in disguise?* I wondered. *Am I to be carried off in her hut on chicken's legs?*

"Forgive me, Madame Pescu, but I must be going." I rose so quickly that I knocked over the stool. Then I became dizzy, blacked out, and collapsed onto the grimy floor of her hut, bumping my head. Her wicked brew had cast a sleeping spell over me! I wondered if she were going to eat my bones herself, or feed me to Pasha.

My head throbbed. My vision returned, but I was seeing double. Suddenly there were two Baba Yagas swooping down upon me, and I cried out. But as my eyes came into focus, I saw that it was only kind Madame Pescu on her knees reaching down to embrace me. Her wide grin revealed two sharp fangs glistening wetly in the firelight, and I realized that she wasn't Baba Yaga after all but a vampire out to steal my soul! I screamed to the heavens as she bit into my neck, yet all I heard was a great crash of thunder.

The next morning my mind felt invigorated, but my body was exhausted. I awoke in my own bed back at the dacha, smelling food, and opened my eyes to find Franz handing me a platter with my breakfast upon it.

"Hearty German breakfast," he said, and indeed it was: sausages, eggs, potatoes, fresh milk, and hot tea. "I prepared it myself, by way of apology for last night."

"Last night?" I was still trying to wake up, and had difficulty remembering.

"The incident at the governor's house. I must have caused you some embarrassment. I'm sorry for the things I said."

Here at last was the old Franz again!

"You're forgiven, of course! What a nice breakfast this is!"

"I thought you might need it." He sat on the edge of the bed. "That must have been quite a dinner party. I didn't realize the governor kept such late hours. Your face looks washed out. Did you have too much to drink?"

"I don't think so."

Now that Franz was suddenly being so nice, I could never tell him that I hadn't returned to Richelieu's. I remembered wandering around town in the rain and getting lost in the storm. I remembered being taken in by a young gypsy woman who made herbal remedies. She had given me hot tea and sent me on my way. After that I remembered nothing until the moment when I awoke and smelled Franz's breakfast.

"How did you ever get Maximych to let you near the stove?" I asked. Maximych was ever mindful of his duties to the point where he was offended if I tried to help him or do anything myself. He would not easily give up the privilege of making his master's breakfast, particularly since it was often the only meal I ate at home.

Franz smiled. "Maximych and I have reached an . . . understanding. He obeys me implicitly, as if I were his second master."

I had a notion that Maximych must have obeyed Franz better than me, for he would never have let me get away with cooking breakfast. The usurpation of any of his duties seemed to make him feel unwanted or unappreciated. All I knew for sure was that he would end up sulking for days, and there existed no sadder sight in all the world than Maximych in a sulk.

"Seeing you like this makes me think of Leipzig." I spoke with a mouth full of spicy sausage. "I have nothing but good memories of those days."

"I'm sorry I've been so out of sorts," Franz said. "I suppose it takes time to get used to one another again. But I'm glad I came. It's good to see you again after so long."

There was a knock at the door, followed by the entry of

Maximych carrying a good Russian basket of sliced breads (both black and white, with a sweet roll), unsalted butter, and a dish of Sofya Ivanovna's homemade preserves.

"Why, thank you, Maximych. How thoughtful."

He gave Franz an evil glance, yet his sulky expression never wavered. "It is my pleasure, sir."

Shaving over the bowl on my night table, I accidentally dropped the mirror I was holding. As the mirror shattered against the floor, I flinched, and nicked two large pimples on my neck with the straight razor, drawing blood. I picked up a shard and regarded my wounds. When I had finished shaving, I patched myself up with some plaster.

The sky was clear once more that day. Franz told me the storm had blown over in a matter of hours. By mid-morning, the ground outside had soaked up all the moisture and was as dry as before. The white acacias looked healthy. It was another hot day.

After an early-afternoon dinner at the Khvostovs', Franz went off for a walk by himself at four o'clock to explore some nearby Roman ruins that he had heard about. He invited me along, but I was occupied with business, looking over some reports and registers that Prince Trubetskoy had let me borrow from the customs office. The Albanian carpenters had not yet hung the door on my makeshift study; they were repairing the damaged staircase in the adjacent vestibule, and I found it difficult to work amidst their unintelligible conversations.

After Franz had left, Maximych brought me a cup of tea, still looking as sullen as he had earlier. His shirt cuff crept up an inch when he stretched out his arm; red marks were visible on his wrist. I clutched his forearm. He tried to pull it away, but I held him fast. I pulled back the cuff and examined the marks more closely.

"You've got a rope burn," I said. "Let me see the other." Reluctantly, Maximych held out his other wrist, and I found identical marks on it. "How did this happen?"

Maximych looked surprised, as if I should already know

the answer to my own question. "Sir, it was your friend, Herr Stadler."

"When?" I demanded.

"Last night, sir, when you were dining with the governor-general. Herr Stadler came back here and punished me, as you told him to."

"As I told him to? I never said any such a thing."

Maximych looked as if he didn't believe me. "Herr Stadler said it was my master's express wish, sir, that I be soundly punished."

"What the devil for?"

"For dropping his trunk and scratching your staircase, sir. The damage was my fault."

"Nonsense! I would never punish you for such a thing."

"I caused the damage, sir, and I must take the blame."

"How is it that you got these rope burns?"

"It happened during the whipping, sir."

"The whipping?" I was horrified at what I was hearing.

"Yes, sir. In your bedchamber, upstairs."

I suddenly became conscious of the workmen wandering about the house, and desired to continue our discussion in private, so Maximych and I went up to that very bedchamber and closed the door.

"Remove your shirt, please, Maximych," I ordered.

Without a trace of modesty, he obeyed, laying his linen garment on the bed. As his back was turned, I saw immediately the long red streaks across his back, too numerous to count.

"*Bozhe moy!*" I said feebly. "Why didn't you cry for help? You might have raised a constable, or the Khvostovs from next door."

"The gag prevented it, sir." Maximych's reply was sober. He now turned to face me, displaying an equal number of lash marks across his lean chest. "But I was being punished, and it was not for me to question my master's methods."

I noticed small scuff marks on the varnish high atop the two posts at the foot of my bed, and realized at once what had happened. Franz had bound Maximych's wrists and secured him standing to either post, gagged him, and proceeded with the lashing.

"Maximych, believe me when I tell you I never asked Franz to punish you by whipping or any other means. And although Franz is my guest, he is not your master, and you do not have to obey him. You should not have allowed it to happen."

"But sir, Herr Stadler was right. I deserved it. My clumsiness—"

"You didn't deserve anything, Maximych. You're a fine groom, and I would never harm a hair on your head. The staircase is a trifling matter. Now let me have a closer look at you."

I examined him and saw to my relief that Franz's whip had not cut through to the skin. Maximych stood, stoic, as I poked and prodded him, asking where it hurt the most. He claimed not to feel any pain. But surely the whipping had been painful; the scuff marks on the bedposts and the rope burns on his wrists indicated violent struggling beneath the lash.

"You don't have to lie to me," I said. "Those abrasions can't be comfortable. We should put something on them."

Since Franz was a physician, I thought he might have a salve of some kind in his trunk. Opening it, I found his clean clothes folded neatly on top. I rummaged beneath, looking to see if he had a doctor's satchel down below. Among his possessions were numerous scientific works, and collections of Voltaire and Goethe. I found a heavy wooden box in which I thought I might find medicaments. I lifted the lid to reveal two fine dueling pistols; I took a whiff and smelled gunpowder. At the bottom of the trunk, I happened upon a small whip, a *nagaika*, with nine long knotted strands of hide dangling from its tip and a braided leather handle. I also found a riding crop, lengths of rope, and a wooden paddle very like the one my father used to beat me with when I was a child (the Bible tells fathers that if they love their sons, they must beat them frequently; my father loved me perhaps too much).

The only book at the bottom of the trunk was a large leather-bound volume in French entitled *Justine*, by the Marquis de Sade. I had never heard of it. The book was exquisitely printed, undoubtedly on a private press. Leafing through it, I discovered among the French text illustrations in black and red ink depicting naked young women in hideous acts of torture and violence, chained, caged, suspended, seared with hot irons, beaten, raped, whipped, eating human excrement. The red ink flowed freely on every page, dripping from the welts on the women's pale flesh, smeared on their lips and on their exposed sex.

I found no doctor's satchel among Franz's possessions, so I decided to procure a healing salve from Dr. Scudery, and if that failed, there was the Jewish apothecary I had stumbled upon in my wanderings around town.

"Maximych, you believe me, don't you?"

"Believe what, sir?"

"That I didn't ask Franz to whip you."

"Yes, Master. Of course I believe you. But, sir—" Maximych's face betrayed a look of utter confusion, as if I had somehow let him down.

"Yes?"

"Why then was I whipped?"

"That, my good Maximych, is what I intend to find out."

I was unable to locate Dr. Scudery, and by the time I reached the dilapidated s. SCHWARTZ, APOTHEKER, the little shop was closed and the sun was already setting.

I once again heard the woman's voice and balalaika, as I had the night before, singing the chorus of the folk tune:

Moy tsiganochki,
Moy tsiganochki ...

But as soon as it appeared, it vanished, snatched by a gust of wind off the sea.

The song put the idea into my head to seek out the kind gypsy woman who had helped me. What was her name— Pescu? Madame Pescu! She was some sort of herbalist, and indeed her tea seemed to have had a certain restorative power (I wondered if my father had partaken of a cup on his visit and thereby been cured of his disagreeable nature!). Madame Pescu was certain to have a salve or poultice that would help heal my Maximych.

I was unable to comprehend what Franz had done. I had never seen anything so vile as that book from his trunk. The book itself was very artfully crafted; it must have cost him a large sum of money, and he had obviously been willing to pay. I failed to understand how a modern man of reason like Franz Stadler could derive pleasure out of inflicting pain upon an innocent, helpless serf.

Crossing the bridge over the ravine, I walked south, the silhouetted citadel looming over my shoulder. The sky had grown a dark blue; stars were beginning to appear. The wind blew dust in my face this time, instead of rain. The air smelled of woodsmoke. I realized I should have brought a lantern with me, but I kept forgetting Odessa's streets were unlighted; one had little use for a lantern on the lighted boulevards of Moscow (at least in our neighborhood).

At last I saw the solitary light in the window of a shack across the field, not far from the town wall. As I approached, I saw the same gypsy wagon behind, still without a horse, and I knew I had the right place.

Again, the door opened before I had a chance to knock.

"So you come back to Madame Pescu." She was quick to let me in. "Have some tea."

This time I saw no sign of the mute Pasha. Perhaps he was lurking behind the hanging sheet.

I took a cup of tea, sitting again on the stool before her warm fire. Her brew was strong, but tasted sweet.

"I wanted to thank you for your kindness last night," I said. "Also I was wondering if you could make me a remedy. Something to heal abrasions of the skin."

Her jewelry tinkled as she went to her shelf of herbs. "I do this for you," she said. "Is easy."

Madame Pescu grabbed a crockery jug from the shelf. She poured some aromatic oil from the jug into a thin-necked glass jar, then plugged the jar with a glass stopper and handed it to me.

"Rub on your skin at noon and at midnight," she instructed. "But never during the new moon."

"Thank you," I said, finding her instructions eccentric. I put the salve in the pocket of my coat. "How much do I owe?"

I began counting out kopecks. I rose to my feet, but lost my balance. My vision became cloudy, and the coins fell through my fingers and landed upon the hardwood floor. I placed my hand against the wall to steady myself.

"Madame Pescu needs not your money."

The gypsy woman approached, and at first I thought she was going to kiss me. But then she smiled, and I saw her sharp fangs. Like a snake, she was poised to strike. I stood paralyzed; she had cast some evil spell over me!

In the next instant, she was biting my neck and sucking out my blood, and I was thinking: *Vampire!*

Then, nothing.

XXII

THE DUEL

From the Memoirs of V. K. Temsik:

I awoke back in my bed. From the sun's glare on my bedroom window, I could tell it was already afternoon. The curtains were open, but the windows were not; the room was far too bright for my weary eyes, and much too hot. The pillow and sheets were drenched with my sweat. My head throbbed, my stomach ached, and I wanted to stay in bed for the rest of the day. The hammering of the carpenters from downstairs sent my ears ringing.

Franz was sitting in a chair beside the bed.

"Welcome back to the living," he said.

"I feel awful."

"You're ill. I don't detect a fever, but your pulse has been far too fast, even while you slept. Your skin is pale. You look anemic. We ought to get some food in you. You've been asleep all day."

Maximych brought me a bowl of sauerkraut *s'chee* soup.

Seeing him reminded me of what Franz had done to him, right in this very room. I looked over at Franz, who had removed his spectacles and was smiling pleasantly at me. I thought of the illustrations in that book of his, the pen-and-ink drawings on which the blood had flowed so freely. I imagined Maximych bound naked to the posts of the bed,

219

legs and arms spread wide, taking his whipping front and back. His olive skin became streaked with red as I saw the whiplashes burn across his back, his torso, his buttocks and thighs. I imagined the lash breaking the skin and drawing blood, and could even hear Maximych trying to scream through his gag. I knew there had been no blood when Franz had done it, but my mind was conjuring up the image to match the illustrations in *Justine*. Franz's wooden paddle became stained with blood as he beat Maximych's buttocks. The whipping persisted until Maximych was broken, and Franz was laughing like a madman.

All this thought of blood had aroused my sex, and was making me hungry.

I ate some of the sauerkraut *s'chee*, but soon vomited it back out into the bowl on my night table. I was unable to keep down any food. All I could stand was a cup of tea.

Franz shaved my face with the straight razor, carefully avoiding the large pimples I had so expertly sliced the day before. Maximych brought me one of my French novels to read, but my eyes were unable to concentrate on it. The unappeasable hunger in my belly was keeping me preoccupied. Soon, I fell asleep once more, with Franz and Maximych seated on opposite sides of the bed.

When I woke up again, the bedroom was dark. The curtains were drawn, but a sliver of moonlight shone through where they didn't quite meet at the middle. The air was hot and musty.

I no longer felt ill in the slightest, though I was still possessed of a ravenous hunger. My mouth was parched. My eyes were wide open, my headache had vanished, and I didn't feel like staying in bed a minute longer.

I felt around on my night table, looking for the candle I kept there. I knocked the closed straight razor onto the floor before I was able to find the brass candlestick. But once I had found the candle, I realized I had nothing to light it with.

Clad in my nightshirt, I got out of bed in the darkness

and stepped with one bare foot directly upon the straight razor, which had come unclasped upon falling. I took in a quick, reflexive breath through my teeth and sat down on the edge of the bed, clutching my pain-wracked foot and crossing it atop my other knee. I swore under my breath, still unable to see the wound I had inflicted upon myself. Warm blood trickled from my foot onto the hand that held it. Its salty odor reached my nose, and I breathed it in deeply. My mouth began to water. *This* was what I needed!

I licked the blood from my hand eagerly. Then, with some difficulty, I managed to bend over and stretch my muscles enough so that my foot met my mouth. I found the small, dripping gash and began to suck out the blood, but I soon realized that it was far from enough. Instead of satisfying my hunger, it only made me yearn for more.

The energy was rapidly returning to my body. I rose from the bed and reached down carefully to find my razor. I grasped the ivory handle, closed the blade, and closed my hand over it.

"Maximych!" I called, loud enough that he ought to be able to hear me from anywhere in the house.

Suddenly, I heard a snort and a grumble from the other side of the room. "Master?" Maximych had been there all along, sleeping in the chair. "You're awake! Good Lord! What time is it?"

"The candle's gone out," I said.

"Oh, I don't think it was lit to begin with." Maximych cracked his knuckles and yawned.

I made my way over to the other side of the bed.

"Where is Franz?" I asked.

"I'm afraid I do not know, sir," came Maximych's voice in the darkness. "I can't understand German." I was close enough now that I could smell his musky scent; he had been asleep in this hot room for several hours, in his clothing. "I must open the door," he said. "I can't see a thing."

The chair creaked as I heard Maximych get up. He crossed in front of me and found the door, letting in the dim candlelight from the hall.

"Come here, Maximych," I said.

"Yes, Master," he said, stepping out of the direct light from the corridor. "How are you feeling now, sir?"

"Tremendous, Maximych, tremendous!"

"Would you like me to dress you?"

"Yes. Come here and remove my nightshirt."

Maximych stood before me, close enough that I could feel his breath against my neck, and began to undo the lacings at my chest. I could smell more than the musk of his body; I could smell the blood pumping just beneath his skin. I held my hands behind my back. My injured foot was throbbing. My stomach growled audibly.

Maximych chuckled. "Master is hungry," he said.

"Yes, indeed. But not for sauerkraut *s'chee*."

"No, sir." His hands were at my neck, ready to pull the nightshirt up over my head.

Suddenly, however, my hands were at his neck, caressing his skin. "Such a nice neck," I said.

"Master?" His voice was at once confused and excited.

I unclasped the straight razor and sliced deeply once, twice, across Maximych's throat. His blood spurted all over my hands and splattered my nightshirt. The only sounds were those of his blood gurgling forth and his convulsive gasp for air. I placed my lips against his neck and drank what I could. His arms clutched feebly at my sides, but then fell away. His legs gave out, and I carefully lowered him to the floor. When his blood stopped flowing, I licked my hands clean and lapped up the pool of blood from the dusty hardwood floor.

Franz was not in the house, so cleaning up proved easy. I burned my nightshirt in the fireplace, wrapped Maximych in a bedsheet, and took his body down to the root cellar. I gave myself a sponge bath using the water from the bowl on my night table; to take a bath in the tub would have meant having to venture outside to pump several buckets of water. I used the same water to scrub the last of the blood from the floor. I got most of it, and covered up any telltale remnants with an Oriental rug. I tossed the bloody water out the window, onto one of the white acacia saplings down below. Richelieu would have been proud of me.

When I was finished, not a trace of blood could be seen. But I was still hungry.

Franz came home not more than thirty minutes after I had finished cleaning up. I had gotten dressed, and was reading Tretyakovsky in my study, and waiting.

I had very nearly given up on Franz and gone out into the night. My hunger could only wait so long.

"Vasily!" he said, spying me in the study as he hung up his frock coat. "You look much improved."

"Maximych gave me something to eat." I went into the vestibule to greet him. "I feel like a new man."

Franz gave me an unexpected bear hug with his one good arm. I smelled vodka on his breath. "You had me quite worried. You mustn't wander around so late at night. You'll catch your death."

"I could say the same to you." I smelled the tang of blood lurking just beneath his collar. But his time had not yet come. I had something special planned first. "Where have you been?" I broke the hug.

"Not wandering, I assure you. There's this cozy tavern across from the public market, with some of the coziest women you'll ever meet. Had my fill of herring, I can tell you!" Franz patted his stomach.

"That goes without saying! I hope you didn't get into a drinking contest with a Russian," I said. But it would be so much easier if he had. The average Russian could put away twice as much vodka as any foreigner. I found it hard to tell how drunk Franz was.

"Don't worry about me," he said. "I was practically raised in a beer garden."

I put my arm around his waist and lured him upstairs.

"Remember how drunk we used to get in Leipzig?" I asked.

"We got so drunk that I *don't* remember!" he said, and

laughed. His foot slipped on a pile of sawdust. The carpenters hadn't yet finished their repairs. I caught him before he was able to tumble all the way down. "Whoops!"

"Come on, I think I should get you into bed."

"That's a fine idea, Vasily. Say, what have you done with Maximych?"

His question took me aback. "What do you mean?"

"Oh, he's always following you around, like a little schnauser. I knew a guy like that in the army."

"I let Maximych go for the evening. He's gone next door, to the Khvostovs', to pay a call on their maidservant Anyuta." This was my prepared answer.

"Maximych and Anyuta? I find that hard to believe!"

We had reached the bedroom. I had already lit the candles and brought in an oil lamp, so the room was well lighted. I had put fresh white sheets on the bed.

"You like my Maximych, don't you?" I asked. I felt in my pocket for the straight razor.

"He seems capable." Franz sat on the bed and removed his shoes and stockings, tossing them onto the Oriental rug I had only just laid down. "But he needs a little discipline, don't you think?"

"No more than you do," I said.

"What the devil are you talking about?" Franz glared up at me.

"I'll show you." Then I was upon him.

I knocked Franz back onto the bed and had him on his stomach before he knew what was happening. He kicked and twisted beneath me, but he was drunk, and clumsy in his movements. Besides that, he had only the one good arm. He was unable to get up.

"Vasily, get off! This isn't funny!"

I pulled his shirttail out of his trousers. I took the straight razor and sliced the shirt in half from collar to tail. Then I used it to slice the seat of his pants in half right down the seam. I ripped apart his undergarments with my bare hands, exposing his smooth buttocks.

"What the hell do you think you're doing?"

I'm going to have you like a woman, I thought. *And then I'm going to cut you and drink your blood.*

But as I moved to unfasten my own trousers and free my hardened sex, Franz managed to reach behind himself with his strong right arm and knock me off balance. He bucked me off of him, and I went tumbling off the side of the bed and onto the floor. When I looked up, he was standing over me, holding up his pants.

"I should kill you right now," he said, panting. Sweat beaded on his forehead. "But I'll give you a gentleman's chance."

I had lost my advantage. He wouldn't let me get close enough to slit his throat, at least not this evening. I wouldn't be able to taste his blood. "Are you calling me out?"

"That's correct. What manner of weapon do you choose?"

I got up off the floor. I tried to refasten my trousers, but found I had ripped off one of the buttons. "I rather fancy those beautiful pistols you have in your trunk."

Franz's face grew red with anger, or perhaps embarrassment. "How did you happen to be looking through my trunk?"

"I was seeking a salve for Maximych's wounds."

"Wounds?" He feigned ignorance.

"Instead, I found the rope and whips you used on him the other night."

"How dare you!"

"How dare I, indeed! Name your time and place, Franz."

"Meet me before dawn tomorrow, you and your second, under the footbridge in the ravine behind your property."

"That should do nicely," I said. "It is agreed."

I was restless that evening, still hungry for blood. I went out wandering, thinking I might find myself a whore to cut up. I headed toward the south end of town.

But once again I heard the sound of a balalaika beneath a woman's voice singing "Moy Tsiganochki." I followed the music and soon found myself back at the doorstep of

Madame Pescu's shack. The singing was coming from inside.

Pasha opened the door this time, smiling at me from behind a long strand of hair that had fallen in his face. He motioned with one hand for me to enter; his other hand held the neck of a small balalaika. I fumbled in my pocket for my straight razor, but something in me held me back and kept me from slashing Pasha's throat. I went inside.

Madame Pescu was there with her tea. She offered me a cup, which I took. I wanted to slice her up, too, but didn't. Something was keeping me from it.

"Welcome back," said Madame Pescu, her youthful face aglow in the firelight. She withdrew from her pocket a gold amulet on a chain. "Please take seat by fire."

I sat on the stool and took a sip of tea. Pasha sat beside me.

Madame Pescu brought her chair closer and dangled the amulet in front of my face. I watched it as it swung back and forth, glinting brightly. She told me to keep my eyes on it and count to twenty.

"Now, you remember!" she shouted, taking away the amulet.

Suddenly, I knew what had happened to me at Madame Pescu's on the two previous evenings. It frightened me. She had bitten me twice already. She was turning me into a vampire!

"Be not afraid," said Madame Pescu. "Is too late to go back. You become vampire now."

I was unable to move.

She leaned forward, baring her fangs. With the speed of a cobra, she lunged for my neck and pierced my skin with her sharp teeth. I cried out, briefly.

Madame Pescu drank my blood for several minutes, until I was nearly dead. Then she opened a vessel in her wrist and fed me her own blood until I had had my fill. I collapsed onto the floor. She and Pasha carried me into the small room behind the sheet and placed me in a coffin. There I passed out and slept for a few hours, knocked out as surely as if I had drunk too much vodka.

I met Franz before dawn, with Pasha as my second.

I was now a vampire, like Madame Pescu. Pasha, however, was not a vampire; he was merely the gypsy woman's "helper." Even at the stroke of dawn, the sunlight would not reach us down in the ravine. Once the duel was over, Pasha would put me in the back of the gypsy wagon (they had obtained a horse) and spirit me back to Madame Pescu's shack. This was, apparently, the sort of thing a vampire needed a helper for. Otherwise, said Madame Pescu, I would go up in flames if the sunlight touched my skin. On the other hand, she said, even if I were to receive a "mortal wound" in the duel, it would not destroy me.

The ravine was short in length, beginning as a level plain that cut deeper and wider through layers of limestone until at last it opened onto the Black Sea. Pasha and I drove the wagon by lantern light down the rock-strewn gully and brought the horse to a halt not far from where the silhouette of the footbridge stretched between the shadowed, craggy walls. The moon had already descended below the horizon, but I had no difficulty making out most details in the darkness. My sense of sight seemed to be heightened.

We arrived before Franz, and waited in the cool, still air. Pasha fed the horse an apple.

At last, I espied two dark figures making their way down the west side of the ravine carrying a single lantern. Their hasty footsteps echoed against the opposite wall. A few small stones came skittering down the side, dislodged by the men's progress.

I noticed the sky was beginning to lighten; the black, starry void had turned to a deep, nautical blue. We would have to complete the duel in a hurry.

When Franz reached the bottom, he stepped into the light of our lantern and introduced his second, who was carrying the wooden box containing the pistols. "This is Andronik

Palikarpovich Ogromniy, a sergeant with the Odessa garrison. I name him as my second.''

Ogromniy was a man of considerable heft. His military jacket stretched across his vast belly, looking ready to pop a few buttons. His dark beard was scraggly and unkempt, as if a sparrow had made a nest on his chin.

"I name my good friend Pasha," I said. I knew neither Pasha's patronymic nor his family name. Franz didn't seem to mind.

Ogromniy poured the powder down the barrels of the two pistols, packed it, and loaded the shots, under the inspection of Pasha. I doubted if Pasha knew the first thing about firearms, but everything had to look official. Pasha nodded his approval, and Ogromniy held out the guns.

"You may choose," said Franz.

Both pistols were identical, flintlocks with slightly curved handles of ebony that were carved with a checkered pattern to provide a good grip, and fourteen-inch barrels with large bores to accommodate the spherical shots of lead. I suddenly realized I knew as little about pistols as did Pasha. I had never fired a gun in my life. Seeing no difference between the two, and being satisfied that Ogromniy had loaded them properly, I chose the one closest to me, leaving Franz to grab the other. The weight of the thing surprised me.

The dimmest stars in the sky were already blinking out. If the duel dragged on too long, I would have to make a cowardly run for the wagon and be driven away by Pasha, or else I would disintegrate in the rays of the sun right before Franz's German eyes.

But Franz seemed ready to have it over with.

Ogromniy found a level spot in the dry gully. It would not have been a fair duel if one were aiming downhill and the other up. He positioned us back to back, Franz facing seaward, I turned toward the upward slope. We held our pistols pointing up at the sky, at the side of the face. I took in a deep breath.

Franz didn't seem nervous, but of course he was the one who knew how to fire a pistol. And despite what Madame

Pescu had said, I wondered seriously whether a lead ball lodged in the heart might not kill me anyway. I doubted if Madame Pescu had ever been shot.

"You will each take ten paces," said Ogromniy in his gruff, official voice. "Pasha, will you count off, please?"

I heard no counting from Pasha.

"All right," said Ogromniy. "One . . . two . . ."

Ten paces didn't seem like much. At that range, Franz ought to be an easy target.

"Three . . ."

I loved him and I hated him. We had spent so much time together at Leipzig, and deep down I wanted nothing more than to be with him always. When I was with Franz, I had always felt special. Any weak spots in my character that I exhibited around my parents vanished in his presence. He had always brought out the best in me and made me strive for more than I thought I could possibly attain. If I hadn't met Franz when I went to university, I would have received precisely the education my father had intended—the one for the Moscow businessman—instead of the one I fashioned for myself—Petersburg fop to the minds of some.

"Four . . . five . . ."

But Franz was no longer the man I had wanted him to be. Perhaps he had always been this way and I had failed to see it. The irrational devotion to Napoléon, the despicable treatment of Maximych, the indifference toward our friendship, all belied the man of reason I had always considered him to be and shattered the image in which I had long believed. In fact, Franz was a cad. I would be doing the world a favor, killing him now before he could get his hands on Anyuta, or Tatyana, or Sofya for that matter. Lusts like his could never be fully quenched. They would only grow in magnitude, corrupting him year by year, extracting from him every last ounce of humanity. I could not suffer him to live. I would have to aim straight, keep my arm steady.

"Six . . . seven . . ."

And yet, when I had fully become a vampire, I had been returned to sanity after a momentary dive into madness. The realization had come of what I had done to Maximych, and indeed, what I had tried to do to Franz, and would have done if he had only been a little more drunk. Franz's torture of Maximych was nothing compared to what I had done. At the time, I hadn't been able to control myself. He had been right there in the room when my hunger was strongest, and the scent of his blood had been impossible to resist. Now that I had my fangs, Madame Pescu told me I would not have to kill in order to feed. Not only that, but the blood I had drunk from Maximych would do me no good whatsoever. His life had been completely wasted, and there was no way I could bring him back. Franz had left no permanent scars on Maximych's skin. I had killed him.

"Eight . . . nine . . ."

The entire duel had come about because of my mad fit. If I hadn't attacked Franz, he never would have demanded his satisfaction. Franz wouldn't have wanted me dead if I had not tried to rape him. And since my own desires were seen as depraved in the eyes of the world, I was unfit to judge his own violent, bizarre lusts. I could not condemn him to death for whipping my groom. Indeed, Maximych seemed almost to have enjoyed it.

"Ten!"

I turned and stood, extending my arm and aiming my pistol. The sky was now light enough that both of us could get a good aim. With my improved eyesight, I seemed to have an advantage—if I decided I wanted to kill him.

I hadn't realized that ten paces translated into twenty when two men were walking away from one another. The distance between us seemed great. Perhaps Franz wouldn't prove to be such a good shot after all. I only presumed he could fire a pistol because he owned two of them, and because he had been in the army. But I wondered how often a surgeon was required to shoot at the enemy during a skirmish. Probably seldom.

Franz stood stock-still. His square Teutonic jaw was set firm. He was going to let me fire first.

I became slightly dizzy. The sky was turning to a lighter

shade of blue, and the stars had vanished. My energy was fading.

After a moment, I squeezed the trigger and fired my shot, deliberately aiming high above him. My pistol jumped back in my grip from the force of the powderblast. A small cloud of smoke arose from my weapon. Franz flinched to one side, and I saw some blood trickle from the left epaulet of his jacket. I had wanted the ball to go flying past his head, but instead it had grazed the shoulder of his bad arm. I had mistakenly wounded him.

I lowered my spent pistol and waited for Franz's shot. My wait was brief.

Franz stretched out his good arm and took quick aim. He fired. I heard the crack and was knocked to the ground. Pasha's horse whinnied in terror.

My stomach gurgled a pool of red-orange blood where the ball had struck me. It seemed an odd color to me, but I felt little pain. I felt as if I could get up, but I would not—not in the presence of Franz and Ogromniy.

I saw Franz leaning over me, tears in his eyes. He knew he had inflicted a mortal blow.

"Vasily!" he cried. "What have I done!"

"Too late for regrets, my friend," I said, and coughed up an impressive glob of blood and phlegm. I couldn't resist speaking to him in my "dying gasp." Then I let my head loll to the side, and pretended to be dead.

I wondered if he had also wounded me by mistake. The inaccuracy of pistols was well established, and the grazing of Franz's shoulder was living proof. But it didn't matter now. To him, and to everyone else, from now on I would be dead.

Franz grabbed me by the shoulder and shook me, looking for signs of life. "Vasily! Come back to me!"

Pasha pushed him away. The push turned to fisticuffs, but the scuffle was brief and Franz was soon running away with Ogromniy, down the ravine. He must have been worried about being discovered. If anyone had heard the shots and came to look into the ravine, they would have found that he had killed a man. Murder was a capital crime, and duels were illegal—officially, at least.

Pasha dragged me to the wagon. Franz and Ogromniy were now completely out of sight, so I rose on my own strength, climbed into the back, and settled into my coffin.

That was the end of my life as a man, and the beginning of my existence as a vampire.

PETERSBURG, 1819

From the Memoirs of V. K. Temsik:

THE salons of Petersburg knew me as Count Pirogov.
Our glorious capital was a vibrant city, full of gaeity
and innumerable excitements; seldom was the night when
I lacked an invitation to a ball, masquerade, dinner party,
or other function, which I accepted more often than not.
Yet I also managed to attend the theatre, ballet, opera, and
gambling salons. The only social events I missed were the
weddings, funerals, children's parties, ship christenings,
and frequent military parades down Admiralty Square, if
only because they took place during the daylight hours. I
was out to meet as many people as possible; for a young
vampire of means, Petersburg could be a fun hunting
ground.

The winter months were particularly joyous. Nights were
long; several in December lasted entire days, never growing
lighter than a late stage of dusk. The vampires of Petersburg
typically celebrated this time of year with parties that lasted
for days and gluttonous sprees of bloodsucking all over the
city. Indeed, our comrades came from all over Europe for
the festivities, a secret macabre Saturnalia through the dim
streets of the capital, amid the ornate Roman facades of
palaces, cathedrals, and government buildings.

The Petersburg existence was rich.

But it was not ideal. During the summer months, many citizens considered Petersburg intolerable. A disagreeable stench would waft over the city from districts such as the Hay Market, and from the outlying marshlands. The long summer days could grow very hot, a damp oppressive heat that served to magnify the unsavory odors of sweaty people and animals. Hence, those who could afford it would escape from Petersburg for the duration of summer to country estates, to the Black Sea, or to the capitals of Europe. Tsar Alexander retired to his nearby palace at Peterhof, the theatres closed, and the grand balls were placed on hiatus until autumn.

I normally traveled south to Yalta in the Crimea, a picturesque port city of less importance than Odessa but with a more pleasing, less dusty climate. I could never return to Odessa or Moscow for fear of being recognized by family or friends.

But I had my own reasons for escaping Petersburg during the summers: the nights were too short. Indeed, for nearly a fortnight every July the sun never set, creating the city's famous "white nights." To the vampires of the northern climes, however, these nights were infamous. In the past, many who had failed to flee south before the onset of the white nights had been trapped in their coffins and starved out of existence. None who stayed were known to have survived. It would be similar to being caught in a city under siege for which no supplies had been stocked. For a vampire to remain in Petersburg during July was tantamount to suicide.

Which was why, in late June of 1819, I was in a panic.

Human help on the order of Pasha was scarce, and I had so far failed to find even a suitable valet, much less a trustworthy accomplice. I had considered hypnotism, but had decided men could not be perpetually mesmerized and thereby enslaved. The peoples of Russia were a superstitious lot as well, and the divulging of my secret to anyone would be a risky undertaking. I therefore managed my own grand apartment on Gorakhavya Street near the Moika Canal, and had the entire five rooms to myself.

Loneliness was the primary reason I maintained a busy social calendar. It was also the reason I had courted the beautiful Elizaveta Ilyevna Demidova for the better part of the year. I had pursued her as a prospective vampire bride, intending to build a sound relationship before even biting her once. None of the existing vampires in Petersburg were to my taste as possible companions; we were of altogether different generations. I respected them as competitors, and we occasionally shared good times together, yet they were incompatible as possible partners.

Liza was a charming, witty young girl, possessing an uncommon intelligence that was worthy of a man. I had met her when we danced the mazurka together at the New Year's Ball at the Hermitage, and then courted her through June. Her twentieth name day had been celebrated in April; she was at the perfect age for marriage. In actual years, I was thirty-seven myself, which was considered an ideal marrying age for a man. However, the social set of Petersburg knew that Count Pirogov had come to the city six years before at the age of eighteen, and yet now I still looked younger than my supposed age of twenty-four. In the eyes of Colonel Demidov, I was barely a man. Liza's father also found my family background dubious (indeed, it was pure fiction), and believed that anyone who had been unfit to fight in the War of 1812 was unfit to have the hand of his daughter.

Many an evening I rode the boat across the Neva from Dvortsovaya Quay to Vasilevsky Island to call on Liza. The Demidovs lived in a grand baroque home on the Strelka, near the magnificent Exchange Building of Thomas de Thomon (the same architect who had designed the Theatre in Odessa). My pursuit of Liza was persistent, and even though the summer was on its way, I was determined not to abandon what we had invested in our relationship over nearly six months. I even grew a beard and mustache, hoping they would make me look older (to have allowed myself actually to have grown older would have only confused the issue). I was hoping that the colonel, seeing how happy we were together, would accept me at last. But he stood his ground, and Liza could not go against his wishes. Then, one evening in late June when I went to the Strelka, I was told by one of the Demidovs' serfs that they had left the city to summer at their estate near Voronezh. I was devastated.

The next night, I received a sad letter from Liza that ended both our courtship and my chance for a willing vampire bride. Liza had never learned that I was a vampire. Once I had gained her trust, and her commitment, I would have told her and taken her as my own. Now I would have to search anew for an agreeable companion.

That is how I found myself stuck in Petersburg with the white nights almost upon me. The other vampires had left the city weeks before. They felt no responsibility toward me, though they had tried to convince me I was insane to pursue this woman any longer. The evenings were now of few hours' duration, not even enough to make the journey south, little by little. I could not be guaranteed of finding safe lodging, or for that matter suitable victims, whenever I might happen to need either along the sparsely populated highway. I had to rule out sending myself south in my coffin as freight; that could leave me vulnerable to inspection by some overzealous civil servant. I could only hope to find someone in whom I could trust, who would personally transport me, without once exposing me to the sunlight, until we were sufficiently south of the Arctic Circle.

This, of course, was easier said than done.

The next evening, the sun set at ten o'clock. I rose from my coffin and dressed as fast as I could in gray cotton pantaloons, black leather boots, a white linen shirt, a high-collared blue velvet waistcoat, and a cravat of fine cambric. I left the apartment in a hurry and hailed a low two-horsed *drowska* in front of my building that was heading south down Gorakhavya Street. After crossing the Kameny Bridge over Ekaterinsky Canal, I instructed the driver to turn left at Sadovaya Street, then left again on Nevsky Prospekt, and there drop me off at the residence of Baron Behrens.

Nevsky Prospekt was the central boulevard of Petersburg, unevenly paved with flint in decorous geometric patterns, and lined with the steady glow of street lamps, which the policemen lit every evening at dusk. The monumental Admiralty Tower stood like a sentinel at the north end of the street, its tall spire reaching up from a squarish colonnaded base that sat atop a massive stone arch. My excellent night vision allowed me to see it in the distance, although to most it would have been a mere silhouette. Nevsky Prospekt bustled day and night with pedestrians and horse-drawn carriages and *drowskas*. It boasted the city's most expensive shops, as well as its most extravagantly dressed citizens. Boulevarding along Nevsky Prospekt was a daily ritual for much of the gentry. Husbands walked with their wives, bowing their heads in greeting to friends and associates as they strolled by. This occurred in the mid-afternoon, and was only known to me from the party chat of those who indulged in this activity. The evening saw few women on the *prospekt*; this was the time of the young bachelors, hurrying down the avenue on their way to unknown destinations. The early morning belonged to Petersburg's finest whores, but when they were caught by the police they no longer walked Nevsky Prospekt—they swept it.

Short summer nights were sad times for those of us walking the street that evening: gamblers, hustlers, whores, policemen, and the one solitary vampire left in all of Petersburg.

I went up the granite steps to the door of Baron Behrens's house, a three-story stone edifice done in the style that had been popular sixty years ago, as gaudy and German and baroque as the baron himself. I knocked with the great brass ring hanging from the mouth of a cherub, and was promptly escorted by Behrens's man Sevastian down the carpeted hallway to the doors of the salon. Once there, the fat, rosy-cheeked baron himself took over, greeting me with a hearty slap on the back. His cigar smoke drifted in my face.

"Pirogov!" Behrens withdrew his cigar and smiled, displaying his tobacco-stained false teeth of ivory. "Have a cigar!" He produced one from the breast pocket of his black waistcoat.

"No, thanks."

"What is your pleasure this evening?"

"Perhaps a game of *Bostón*." I pronounced it in the French manner, with the accent on the second syllable. Otherwise, poor Behrens would not have known what I was talking about.

"Splendid! We were trying to get another table going not five minutes ago, but we were in need of a fourth." The Baron took me by the arm. "This way, if you please."

In the main room, twenty-five gamblers sat at a long table playing faro, with Behrens's protégé, Tihin, sitting at the head as both dealer and keeper of the bank. Tihin was actually better at it than the baron; his reserved nature scared fewer punters away than did the boisterous personality of his mentor. His quiet, methodical way of tallying accounts had sent chills up many a spine.

On the other side of the room, a *zakooski* table had been set up, with three kinds of caviar, herring with roe sauce, pickled mushrooms, chopped chicken livers, calves' brains in mayonnaise, and *dragomir forshmak*. Carafes of icy cold vodka sat on silver trays surrounded by small, decorative vodka glasses. Several waiters flitted around the room bearing drinks, serving ices, and lighting pipes.

A waiter approached and asked if I would like a drink.

"Kvass, please." I wanted no hard liquor this evening. I only wanted to find someone who could help me.

"Kvass! Lemonade! Coffee!" Behrens spat out the words. "Are all my best customers becoming teetotalers?"

"Maybe it's the heat," I offered. "How is it that you managed to gather such a crowd this evening?"

"Because Chekalinsky has closed himself down for the summer, that's why. Got out of the city. Went to Vienna, I think."

"Lucky bastard," I said.

Two tables of old men were playing slow games of whist for high stakes; the gold coins were stacked high. I recognized Lieutenant-General Betancourt, chairman of the Committee for Construction and Hydraulic Works. His stack of coins was less high than the others; he seemed to be losing a bundle.

Behrens led me to a smaller chamber off the main room, where one game of *Bostón* was already in progress at one of two green tables. He sat me at the empty table, then left to get the other players.

The waiter brought my kvass, and then Behrens returned, bringing with him my friend Tomsky, who sat on my left. The baron himself sat on my right.

"Ah! You're joining in the game this evening, Baron?" I pretended to be delighted at the prospect; yet we could have done worse than Behrens. Some of his customers were rather shady.

"I need to keep my wits up," said Behrens with a knowing laugh.

"Good to see you, Pirogov!" said Tomsky, a pleasant fellow younger than I who, naturally, looked slightly older. He was from a well-to-do family, had served in the Guards, and was now a civil servant of the fifth rank. He had recently been transferred to the Ministry for Spiritual Affairs. I liked him. He was always full of outrageous stories filled with phantoms, magicians, superstitions, and incredible twists of fate. After eight shots of vodka, one could never shut him up.

I wondered if I could confide in Tomsky. If he ever told anyone about me, at least he would never be believed.

"Where is our fourth?" I asked Behrens, taking a sip of kvass.

"He's coming. He was on a winning streak at the faro table."

Then the fourth man walked in the room and sat down across from me.

Seeing him, I suddenly choked on my kvass.

Franz was our fourth!

"Herr Stadler, this is Count Pirogov and Captain Tomsky. Good heavens! Are you all right, Pirogov?"

"How do you do?" said Franz. He seemed to have finally learned Russian.

Tomsky slapped me several times on the back until my choking fit subsided; it saved me from having to shake Franz's hand in greeting. I drank more kvass to settle down.

Franz was now bald on top, his short blond hair graying at the temples. His clothes were now as fine as mine, but I noticed his left arm was still motionless at his side. He was not wearing his spectacles, and did not seem to recognize me. Of course, he thought I was dead, and my beard and mustache were perhaps sufficient to throw him off. From the way he squinted across the table, I could tell that I must have been little more than a blur to him.

Bostón had been derived from whist, but was more fast-paced and, to me at least, more enjoyable. As far as I was concerned, whist was a stodgy old game for stodgy old people. The variation we played in Behrens's salon was called *Bostón de Fontainebleu*, but differed from normal *Fontainebleu* in the respect that if a player were dealt no trump cards he could demand points from each player at the beginning of the hand. Other than that, the rules were the same. We kept tally with white, red, and blue markers, white representing ten kopecks, red fifty, and blue one ruble. Every hand, we would each stake the pot with one red marker apiece.

The baron dealt first. Sitting on his left, I possessed the "eldest hand," and began the bidding by passing. Tomsky passed as well, and so did Stadler. Once we had passed, we would be unable to bid again.

"Six hearts," bid Behrens cheerfully, still arranging his hand. He became the caller, claiming he could make six tricks with hearts as trumps. The way we played the game, anyone calling up to eight tricks was expected to call for a partner. The baron did, and Tomsky accepted. This meant they now had to make at least ten tricks as a team or they would lose the hand and pay up accordingly!

Franz studied his cards, holding them in his good hand only inches away from his face. He still hadn't noticed who was sitting across from him.

Much had happened in the last eleven years. I was a vampire and had developed a new identity for myself. Russia and England had defeated Napoléon, and the tsar had gone on to conquer Paris. Russia finally had political influence on the European continent. Napoléon lingered in exile, while the French king had been restored. Armand Emmanuel Sophie Septimanie du Plessis, duc de Richelieu, had returned to France and was currently its prime minister, as leader of the conservative Ultras. I wondered what Franz had been doing these many years.

Holding the eldest hand, I led the play, tossing down my best card, the ace of clubs, and making the trick. I made the next as well, with the king of clubs. After that, I held no cards of value, and played the deuce of spades. Tomsky tossed in the five, Stadler the king. But Behrens slapped down the ace with a sinister laugh and took the trick. He and Tomsky together made the next ten tricks, winning the hand with a trick to spare. They took the pot and won a total of two rubles and seventy kopecks from me and Stadler. Ten kopecks had been a bonus for the extra trick, plus an extra twenty for having honors in the trump suit (ace, king, queen, and jack) between them.

With only one good arm, Franz had necessarily taken more time to play his hand. He had had to pick out the card he wished to play and set his hand down each time upon the table top, picking it up again as the fast play continued.

We replenished the pot, and as I dealt the next hand, I remembered how sorry Franz had been after shooting me. I wondered if I could get him to help me. After all, what had passed, had passed.

And now Tomsky passed, followed by Stadler and Behrens. Except for two aces, my hand was full of low cards, a bad hand for taking tricks, so I bid a *piccolissimo* and became the caller of the hand. A *piccolissimo* round was a *grand*, with no trumps. We each had to discard one card from our hands, facedown. Mine was the ace of hearts. To win my bid, I would have to lose every trick but one. I was guaranteed to win one trick with the ace of diamonds if I played it at an opportune time, but losing all the others was a different matter entirely. I lost the tricks easily at first, always having a lower card in each suit than the ones being played. When Tomsky led the deuce of diamonds, the rest played low, and I took the trick with my ace, giving me the one I needed. Then I led the three of spades, and lost the trick, as well as the next two. Things were looking good. But finally, Franz led the deuce of clubs, followed by Behrens's three, my five, and Tomsky's four. I had won the trick and lost the round, and I had to double the pot and give each player one of my blue markers, a ruble apiece.

"Tomsky," I said, handing him the marker. "Here, Franz. And baron, this one is yours."

Franz looked up suddenly, a look of genuine shock on his face. At first I thought he had recognized my voice, but then I realized that I had called him by his Christian name, even though Behrens had introduced him to us merely as "Herr Stadler." I knew I had given myself away, even though I had not yet decided whether or not I ought to take him into my confidence. Yet Franz merely squinted at me again and continued to stare perplexedly, probably unable to believe what he was thinking.

We added to the pot, and Tomsky dealt. Stadler passed, and Behrens bid six diamonds. But once again I became the caller with my bid of *petite misère*, which Tomsky failed to top. This was another *grand*, similar to the *piccolissimo* that I had lost in the previous hand, but worth less. We each discarded one of our cards (in my case the king of spades), and my object as the caller was to lose every trick. Now that I was rid of the king, none of my cards were higher than a ten. I played the hand well, and won the pot along with seventy-five kopecks from each player.

As Franz dealt the next hand, I came to the decision that I could trust him, even though he had "killed" me once already. Once he saw that Count Pirogov was really Vasily Kirilovich Temsik, he would demand to know how I had survived such a fatal wound, and also how I had remained young after all these years. I would promise to tell him my secret, what I would claim to be the secret of eternal youth, indeed the secret to life itself—on condition that he follow my instructions to the letter and get me safely away from Petersburg. Once we were far enough south, I could easily overpower him and escape, or hypnotize him so that he forgot the whole incident, or kill him if it proved necessary. As a physician, a man of science and reason, who was crippled and growing ever older while his old university chum remained young, he would be only too eager to snap at the bait. All I had to do was get him to remove me to a safe distance, which could easily be done by promising him the fundamental secrets of the universe. Franz would do whatever I asked.

After twelve hands, the game was over, and I realized there were perhaps thirty more minutes of darkness left for the evening. In the end, I came out ahead by about four rubles. Stadler won about eight, but Tomsky had taken the game with total winnings of twelve rubles, sixty kopecks. Baron Behrens had posted a deficit.

I led Franz back to the main room, where we sat down together upon a purple velvet sofa.

"Franz, put on your spectacles. It's me, Vasily."

"I know it is," he said, but put on his glasses anyway. His accented Russian came across very cool. There were no hugs this time. "I knew it the minute I sat at the table."

"Yet you said nothing."

"Neither did you. I didn't want to stop the game any more than you did. I knew we could skim a few rubles off old Behrens. Now we're both richer."

"What are you doing here?" I asked.

"Chekalinsky's was closed."

"I mean, what are you doing in Petersburg?"

"I live here now. You know, you really caught me off

guard when you called me Franz. I was surprised you would make such a mistake.''

"Who said it was a mistake?"

"Come, Vasily. You didn't want me to know it was you. Admit it.''

"Yes, you're right, I didn't," I said, pretending to be glum. Actually, he was already falling for my little trap. "Now you know my secret."

We returned to my apartment. It was nearly midnight, and the sun would soon be rising.

I told Franz I had discovered the fountain of youth, an elixir of life that could heal all ills and keep a person young for all eternity. I was living proof that it had worked.

"You look even younger than you did in Odessa," he said. "Even with the beard. But how did you ever survive the duel?"

I explained that I had obtained the elixir weeks before from a Turk and that it had made me impervious to wounds of any variety. The shot from his pistol had been removed from my stomach, and I had healed rapidly (this at least was true). I showed him my stomach, and he saw that there were indeed no scars, no sign that I had ever been mortally wounded by a ball of lead.

In turn, Franz showed me the small scar on his left shoulder, the graze wound I had inflicted upon him. Black specks had become embedded in the pink scar, remnants of gunpowder, I supposed.

Franz believed everything I told him, and he agreed to follow my instructions implicitly in return for being given the "great secret." Franz wanted to look young again, to have the use of his bad arm, grow back his hair, and throw away his glasses. I assured him that all this was possible.

Little did I know that it was!

I had never before traveled in my coffin. Normally, I would ride by night, check into an inn, and sleep by day. But this journey called for new thinking. It was crucial to my plan that Franz never learn that I was a vampire, so I desired as little contact with him as possible until we reached the end of the journey. Therefore, I asked him to keep me shut tight in my coffin, which was in turn to lie sealed inside a wooden crate that was to remain nailed shut, even in the brief evening hours when Franz would stop for a few hours' sleep at an inn. Then, after four days of travel along the road from Petersburg to Moscow, no matter where we were, he was to procure lodging for the night, take the crate to our room, pry it open, and let me out.

I could stand (barely) to go for four days without fresh blood and still remain physically sound.

We left Petersburg the night after we met. I had given Franz some money with which to buy a wagon and horses. I told him to meet me an hour after sundown, which allowed me enough time to go to the Hay Market and bite a old Kirghiz peasant in an alley to keep me going for the rest of the trip. Franz arrived at my apartment at the appointed time in a good flatbed with two strong stallions harnessed to the yoke. I had packed only one trunk with clothing and other necessities; I would of course be returning to Petersburg once it was safe again. Once I had climbed into my coffin and closed the lid, it was packed in with straw and the lid of the crate was nailed shut. I had a lock on the inside of my coffin, to keep out unwanted intruders; in this case, Franz. He grabbed someone off the street to help him get the crate into the wagon, and then I heard him throw the tarp over me and secure it around the crate.

I had explained the coffin to him by simply saying that sunlight wrecked havoc on the effects of the elixir and I had therefore chosen to live only in the evening hours. This had also served as my explanation for wanting to get out of Petersburg in this fashion. Franz agreed that it was a small price to pay for eternal youth. I had him completely convinced!

Franz was fond of cracking the bullwhip. He drove the wagon at speeds faster than it was probably meant to go, which was, in theory, exactly what I desired. In practice, however, I found myself wishing that he had bought two aging, swaybacked mares and suppressed the urge to whip, so that we might plod along instead of fly onward in a mad rush. Of course Franz, sitting in the bench seat up front, was cushioned by springs, while I on the bed suffered a bumpy, uncomfortable ride. Thankfully, it was daylight for most of the trip, so I was either asleep or in a heady daze due to my normal daytime lack of energy. But on occasion, bumps along the highway proved jarring enough to jolt me awake, even at midday! My head often struck the lid of the coffin, and I would awake every evening battered and bruised. Repairing these bruises, my body used up some of the precious blood I was trying to store until the end of the journey.

As we traveled south, I already noticed the nights growing longer. At my request, Franz left me outside, under the tarp, on the bed of the wagon while he went into an inn to sleep. During those hours, I lay wide awake in the close darkness of my coffin, listening to the chirping of crickets or to the animallike grunts of people making love in rooms of the inn.

During the fourth day of travel, I dozed more than usual and was only vaguely aware that my freedom was soon at hand. I allowed myself a brief pang of fear as I wondered if Franz would, in fact, ever let me out. But I was so confident in the infallibility of my scheme that this unreasonable fear soon subsided. Franz would indeed let me out so he could learn my secret. Any man would have given anything to lift the veil off the mysteries of creation.

At last, I heard Franz prying loose the nails along the lid of the crate. I panicked initially, thinking it was still daylight outside, but soon realized that I had dozed off—besides, my energy was slowly returning, which meant it had to be past sundown. We had come to the fourth night, and Franz was, from the sound of it, yanking out each nail in great haste, eagerly awaiting the Moment of Truth.

I heard the lid of the crate crash to the floor, then the rustle of straw as he unburied the coffin. I turned the key in the padlock on my side of the coffin and allowed the lid to be opened.

Franz threw it back quickly and tossed several slit cloves of garlic at my head. At once, the pungent fumes sapped me of my strength, and I lay motionless, trapped. I could not even grasp the knife I kept at my side. Sweat broke out on my forehead as the garlic began ever so slowly to draw the fluids from my body.

"Franz!" I gasped, my eyes watering. The muscles along my back tensed up, and my nostrils flared, desperately trying to draw in unpolluted air.

Franz stood over me, holding a wooden stake at my heart.

"If you don't think I can drive this home with only one arm, you're sadly mistaken." Franz was sweating as well; the room was hot and musty.

I wouldn't have tempted him even if I could. Even in Odessa, his right arm had been strong, and he must have carried his end of the crate with it as well. I had come to realize that skin and bones were amazingly fragile; with a bit of effort, Franz could twist the stake through my ribs to get it started and then pound it home with the head of an ax. I was completely at his mercy.

"I've also got a machete." Franz grinned in triumph. "I can cut off your head, turn it upside down, and stuff it with garlic. I can utterly destroy you, if I choose."

"How did you know?" My throat was raspy. I needed to drink some blood and get away from these garlic cloves. I could feel one resting right on my neck, slowly burning my skin as if it were acid, and I wanted nothing more than to get it off.

"That you were a vampire? I figured that out long ago. You recall our duel down in Odessa."

"Of course I do. After you shot me, you came rushing to my side. You begged me to come back. You wished you hadn't done it. So why do you want to destroy me now?" I tried to reason with him. Reason was something he understood.

"You're quite right. I kneeled down and clutched your

body. I did want you back. I didn't want to be your murderer. But when I touched you, my bad arm dragged in the dirt beside me and became covered in your blood. It was the color of your blood that first tipped me off. I had done enough surgery and seen enough battles to know what blood was supposed to look like, but I had never seen anything like it. It was orange, like rust!"

"That couldn't prove that I was a vampire."

"No. The proof came a few hours later, though I still never figured out you were a vampire for several years."

"What proof? Pasha would have killed anyone who came near me that day. He had good reason to protect me."

"I swear, Vasily, I never saw you again until we met at Baron Behrens's. It was what happened to my hand that later proved you were a vampire. The fingers of my left hand had been soaked with your blood. Only it wasn't normal blood, it was something different, because within hours of our duel, even after I had washed the blood from my hands, my dead fingers suddenly came to life."

"Bozhe moy!" I gasped. "That's impossible! How could my blood bring your hand back to life!" I didn't want to believe it was true.

"It's no more impossible than you are, my friend. I was never entirely certain until this evening, when I saw your reaction to the garlic. That was the final proof."

"Show me," I said. "Let me see your fingers."

Franz shook his head sadly. "They're dead again. Just as dead as before. The effect your blood had on my fingers wore off two days later. I lost all the feeling in them once again and was unable to move a single one. I think that was what drove me on, to find the answer. If they had been restored to me outright, I might have simply accepted it and never sought the complete truth behind the miracle. But once their use had been taken from me again, I knew it was no miracle. It was something beyond the realm of known science. I spent my free hours searching for the answer, traveling to see mystics and magicians, witches, mediums, faith healers, anyone who might have a clue. Once the idea of a vampire was thrown my way, it stuck, and I knew that was the key. You see, I had found Maximych.''

"In the root cellar," I put in. My eyes were stinging.

"Exactly. He had been brutally murdered, and his blood had been drained. There was no question in my mind that you had done it. Vampirism also explained your sickened condition on those days before the duel, before you killed Maximych.''

"I had gone crazy. I wasn't responsible for my actions. I would never have attacked you otherwise—''

"With a straight razor, no less," said Franz with a chuckle. "And you berated me for my cat-o'-nine-tails! I count myself lucky to have escaped becoming one of your victims. I buried Maximych, by the way, right there in the root cellar. Your name was never implicated, because he was never found. Anyway, a withered old witch in Kiev hit on the idea that you were a vampire. She said your bloodlust explained it, and that the color of your blood fit her own knowledge perfectly. Don't ask me why I believed her. Deep in my gut, I knew she was right. When I compared the clues at hand with what I was learning about vampires, I knew that nothing else even came close. Then I had to track you down, which took the better part of five years. But I found you, living in Petersburg under the alias of Count Pirogov. You may think you stumbled upon me by chance, but I assure you, it was I who stumbled upon you. I hadn't expected you to be around at this time of year. I was going to wait until September to start looking for you in earnest.''

"What for?" I asked. "Why do you want to destroy me?''

"Vasily, my friend, that's the last thing in the world I want to do. I'm only keeping this stake over your heart so that you'll hear me out. I want you to realize that I could end your existence at any second. If I had wanted to get rid of you, I could have opened the crate at any time over the last few days and let you dry up in the sun. But it would have served no purpose. Instead, I'm going to allow you to do me a favor. You can keep yourself from being destroyed by letting me have some of your blood so that I can heal my arm."

"What good would that do?" I was beginning to fear that no matter what I did for him, he was going to destroy me. "You said yourself that the effect only lasted for a couple of days. To fix it permanently, you would have to bathe it in vampire blood every few days—"

"Now you're beginning to get the idea," said Franz.

Suddenly, my heart lodged in my throat. I thought again of the *Justine* illustrations showing women chained up in dank dungeons, and had a vision of Franz keeping me captive and milking me of all of my fluids so that he could have back the use of his arm. Yet if he wanted to keep me going, he would have to provide me with humans to bite and force me against my will to suck their blood. Eventually I would be used up and wither away into nothingness. A stake through the heart would have been preferable.

"First, you're going to let me have some of your blood." Franz had a mad gleam in his eye, much as I must have looked the night I attacked him. He was a man with an obsession, one that had lasted eleven years. Like Napoléon, he had seized the day and was demanding that the world treat him on his own terms. "Then, when my arm is restored, you're going to lead me to your vampire friends. After that, I shall say good-bye and let you go on your merry way."

I had little choice, and the idea was certainly preferable to the images of enslavement and torture that I had conjured up in my brain. But what he had proposed was hideously evil. What he asked of me in return for my freedom was that I betray my brothers. They, not I, would become his slaves, providing him with the fluids he craved so fiendishly.

But as I writhed amidst the garlic cloves, thirsting for even a drop of human blood, and with a stake at my heart, I would have agreed to anything.

And I did.

That, Chris, is how I created Franz Stadler, the scourge of vampires everywhere and for all time.

XXIV

REDNECK

E VEN after reading Temsik's narrative, Chris was unable to come up with a plan for tracking down Franz Stadler. The new clues to Stadler's character only seemed to make matters worse. Now Chris knew that he had allowed Sheridan Cooper to fall into the hands of a horrible sadist, and that Stadler had to be stopped at any cost. But Chris had never before been faced with such a problem, and could think of no way to win against a fiend who had destroyed thousands of vampires. Chris assumed that many vampires smarter than he had already failed against Stadler.

Temsik had allowed himself to be defeated, but Chris felt that his only chance was to get Temsik's help. Perhaps together they could come up with a viable plan to get rid of this "scourge."

Chris hoped that Beth and the other Chicago vampires would be able to help as well, but he was still unable to reach anything but Beth's voice on the answering machine. He finally came to the conclusion that he had been denying for days: all of the Chicago vampires had probably fallen prey to Stadler already. In fact, Beth had likely been abducted by him on the night they went to Avalon. After leaving with "some guy" (according to Del) she had never returned, and the rest of them had disappeared shortly thereafter. Somehow, she must have inadvertently led Stadler to the warehouse. Either that or the information had been pried out of her under torture. Chris couldn't easily imagine Beth betraying her comrades, except under dire circumstances.

As Chris walked the couple of blocks from his apartment to the Caribou Tavern, he suddenly realized why Temsik had wanted to destroy himself. Temsik hadn't merely been despondent over the loss of his beloved Laura, he had felt responsible for what had happened to her, as well as to countless other vampires over the years, at the hands of Stadler. Chris could almost understand why Temsik, having borne such a heavy burden, would have wanted to bring about the end to his own existence. The destruction of Laura had probably been the catalyst for his actions, but not the sole cause.

And if that were the case, Temsik might still be in danger of trying again.

Chris hadn't seen him in six days, and Temsik had failed to pay Chris a single visit, despite what he'd said about "checking in" on him. Perhaps it would be worthwhile to go see him this evening, even if it was one day short of their agreed-upon rendezvous. If Chris lost Temsik before he had an opportunity to solicit his help against Stadler, he would never stand a chance.

But right now, Chris was thirsty.

The Caribou was another rustic neighborhood bar with wood-paneled walls, a jukebox pumping out the tunes, air filled with smoke, loud men seated along the bar, and the occasional girl. But despite the preponderance of males, it wasn't a gay bar by any stretch of the imagination. It was the sort of place, like Jocko's, where men went out together to be men together, watch baseball on TV, bitch about women, play darts, and get plastered over a couple of pitchers of Old Style and a few shots of Jägermeister.

Chris sat down and ordered a beer.

He had been coming into the 'Bou (as everyone called it) every other evening this week, since it was so close to his apartment and had such an agreeable atmosphere. The men there were both younger students and older blue-collar types, whom Chris found friendly. Two nights ago, he had bitten the neck of a white student with greasy dreadlocks who had large bags under his eyes from excessive pot smoking. Chris had gotten the equivalent of a contact high from drinking the guy's blood. Tonight the student was absent from the crowd. But the pickings at the 'Bou were still good, plus Chris was finally catching up on the baseball he had been missing; he had a feeling in his gut that the Cubs might actually make it to the World Series this year. They were back on another winning streak.

But tonight, for some reason, the TV was tuned to something other than baseball. However, no one seemed to be paying any attention to whatever the show was. Instead, they were talking among themselves. Three students at the end of the bar were playing a game of Quarters and getting blitzed as a result. Chris pegged them as possible candidates for his next meal, though he would wait until later before he made an attempt at one of them.

"Isn't there any baseball on tonight?" Chris asked the man sitting next to him.

"Brewers' game was rained out," said the man. Chris had seen him in here before. He was about the same height as Chris, but much larger, with muscular arms and a sizable beer gut. He had a few days' growth of beard and an untrimmed mustache that covered his upper lip. Chris hated mustaches; every mustached man he had ever met had turned out to be an asshole.

"What about the Cubs?"

"Guess they're not playing." The man withdrew a canister of chewing tobacco from the back pocket of his jeans and put a pinch of it into his mouth. His jeans sat low on his waist as he slumped against the bar. Chris felt certain that if the man's T-shirt were to come untucked, his asscrack would be visible peeking out above his belt buckle. He wore a green cap that read: JOHN DEERE—HORICON WORKS.

"You work for John Deere?" asked Chris. He was decidedly uninterested in biting this man's neck, but since there was no baseball this evening, he had to entertain himself somehow until he could make a play for one of the drunken students at the other end of the bar.

"Nope," said the man. "I drive a Four Lakes cab. My wife commutes to Horicon. She puts the wheels on lawn mowers, every night, second shift."

After a commercial break, Chris discovered that what they were watching was some show on NBC called "Mysterious Disappearances," hosted by Raymond Burr. The sound was too low to be heard over the noise in the bar, but when Chris saw a toll-free phone number flash on the screen, he realized that it was one of those programs that re-created unsolved mysteries and asked their viewers for help, tempting them with the promise of a reward if their information led to the cracking of the case.

It was precisely the kind of show Luis had been worried about, thinking his parents would appear to re-create the circumstances surrounding his disappearance nearly twenty years before. Chris hoped he wouldn't see an old yearbook photo of Luis appear on the screen, but he wasn't worried in the least about himself. His own parents were probably happy to see him gone, and unless a stink was raised by his family, Chris doubted his case would attract anyone's attention, much less that of "Mysterious Disappearances."

"Hey, Geddy, turn up the sound, will you?" asked the cabdriver. The bartender reached up and turned the volume knob on the old set until the show was barely audible. "Thanks, man. I love these things. Like that thing on live TV where they opened up Al Capone's vault. Did you see that one?"

"Huh?" Chris suddenly realized the cabdriver was talking to him again. "Oh, yeah, sure. I used to live in Chicago. I remember a bunch of us got together at my friend Tim's place and had a little party that night around that stupid show. I was disappointed that they didn't find anything."

"Yeah," said the cabdriver. "Like some corpse or something."

"Sure," said Chris uneasily. "That would have been great. Excuse me."

Chris saw one of the drunken students get up from the game of Quarters and head for the men's room. Chris downed the last of his beer, got up from the bar stool, and followed the guy into the bathroom.

Dinner was served.

When Chris left the men's room, leaving the sleeping student behind on the toilet, he saw that the cabdriver was utterly transfixed by the TV screen, even though no one else in the bar was paying attention. Chris couldn't see the screen at first, but he could hear a voice that he recognized immediately: the high-pitched, effeminate voice of Tim Duffy.

". . . and when I entered his apartment," came Tim's voice amid sniffles, "he was gone."

Chris caught a glimpse of Tim's fleshy face before it disappeared from the screen, followed by an eerie pan shot of Chris's apartment, accompanied by Raymond Burr's baritone voice-over: "Tim Duffy conducted an exhaustive search of the neighborhood, but he found no trace of Chris Callaway. When the Chicago police arrived . . ."

Chris headed straight for the door, noticing happily that the cabdriver failed to notice his exit. Chris could have been in danger if he had stuck around much longer.

He turned around for one last glimpse of the TV and saw two photos of himself appear on the screen: one from before his illness, and one after. Then he got out of there fast.

He had gone half a block down well-lighted Johnson Street when he heard from behind him "Hey, you!" followed by the hasty footsteps of someone running. Chris turned briefly and confirmed that the cabdriver was indeed coming after him.

Chris ducked into a dark alley and grabbed onto the closed switchblade in his pocket.

He might have been able to outrun the cabdriver, but that would have done little good. The cabdriver would still call the toll-free number and report having sighted Chris. Chris couldn't think why the cabdriver had chosen to come after him first, unless he thought he would have a better chance at the reward money by nabbing Chris before calling the authorities. After all, the cabdriver probably figured he was bigger and stronger than Chris; a guy suffering from leukemia would be an easy catch.

Chris wished he could hypnotize the cabdriver, but that would be impossible under the circumstances. The cabdriver would never stand still long enough for it to work, and Chris would lose any advantage he might have had. No, he would have to work quickly once the cabdriver appeared around the corner. Perhaps he could conk him on the head with something.

"Hold it right there!" shouted the cabbie.

"What gives?" Chris's voice cracked. Despite his confidence that he could get out of this somehow, his hands were shaking.

"You're that guy on TV. The one they're looking for. The faggot."

The hulking silhouette of the cabdriver lurched closer, step by step.

"I don't know what you're talking about," said Chris, backing up against a brick wall. Leave it to Tim, he thought. Tim would have thought he was eliciting sympathy by telling the cameras that Chris was not only stricken with leukemia but gay as well. Poor Tim.

"I could tell you was a queerboy the first time I saw you at the 'Bou."

"You stay away from me!"

"Fag-assed bastards like you really stand out. But I didn't think you had AIDS."

"AIDS? Who said I had AIDS?" There, now he had done it. He had admitted he was the guy they were looking for.

"I did," said the cabdriver. "Little faggots like you don't get leukemia, they get AIDS. I know a good lie when I see one."

"Don't come any closer!" Chris shouted.

"Or else what?"

Chris drew his switchblade. The sound of the blade springing forth was unmistakable, and even the cabdriver could probably see the knife's blue glint in the semidarkness.

"You little shit!" screamed the cabdriver. "I'm going to tear your fucking head off!"

The big man lunged at Chris, his arms outstretched, aiming for Chris's neck.

Chris was caught off guard, but managed to poke him in the ribs with his knife. It went through the man's shirt and into his skin, but Chris didn't plunge it any deeper. He only wanted to scare him.

But it did little good. The man clamped one hand around Chris's neck and began to squeeze, while his other hand grabbed Chris's wrist, keeping the switchblade out away from their bodies. Chris gasped for air as the man's thumb pressed farther into his Adam's apple.

"You sick little queer! I'll show you what happens to fag-assed bastards!"

Chris kicked his leg up, as if he were punting a football, and wracked the cabdriver's balls with all his strength.

The man lost his grip on Chris and fell into a black puddle of water.

Chris fell upon him, out of breath, and held the switchblade at his neck.

"Get off of me!" screamed the cabdriver.

Chris worked up a wad of saliva and spat it in the man's face, causing him to writhe in terror and claw up at Chris. But Chris, using his knees, quickly managed to pin down the man's arms. He pressed the point of the switchblade into the fleshy neck, not yet puncturing it.

"Let me go!"

But Chris couldn't let him go. Even though his existence wasn't at all threatened by this man's violent acts, it was threatened by the fact that the man might yet call that toll-free number on the TV screen and report having seen Chris.

Chris really had no choice.

He looked up and down the alley briefly and saw that nobody was looking.

"You goddamned faggot!" said the man.

Then Chris punctured one of the man's jugular veins and drew the sharp edge of the switchblade across the breadth of his throat, opening up the jugular on the other side. Blood came gushing out onto the crotch of Chris's jeans. More of it gurgled out of the man's mouth, and his arms struggled briefly before they collapsed at his side, splashing Chris with mud from the little puddle.

ASHES TO ASHES

AFTER the cabdriver's body went through its final convulsions, Chris witnessed something extraordinary and terrifying.

A faint purplish light gathered itself around the corpse and *whooshed* past Chris, spiraling upward into the starry sky and vanishing in the distance.

Chris suddenly recalled not only Temsik's talk of souls but also the feeling he had experienced when Beth had bitten him the third time, as if he had been broken apart and, like Humpty Dumpty, not wholly put back together again. All the king's horses and all the king's men hadn't been able to do it for Humpty, so why should Chris expect anything different? It also brought to mind the dream he had had of being a lymphoblast down in his own diseased bloodstream, and breaking apart to form another lymphoblast like himself.

He wondered if that part of him that had broken off had actually been his soul, in the process of being destroyed, just as Temsik had talked about. Chris had been a fool to take his mentor's word so lightly. Everything else Temsik had told him had been borne out already, so why should his talk of souls prove any different?

If that purplish light had indeed been the cabdriver's soul, then it had met a different fate than Chris's. Chris was certain that his own purplish light hadn't spiraled up into the heavens. If he had had one at all, it would have simply dissipated and then blinked out, right at the point when Beth made him drink of her *kroba*.

And if Temsik had been right about the fate of vampires' souls, then Chris needed his help more than ever.

He was appalled at what he had done.

The survival instinct had come to the fore, and he had found killing the cabdriver both easy and exhilarating; now he hated himself for having enjoyed it.

He stared down at himself. His hands and his pants were wet and sticky, drenched with both mud and blood. It reminded him of a recent Chicago murder case where the victim had been stabbed twenty-nine times in the back with a butcher knife and the assailant himself had suffered innumerable lacerations of his hands. The killer's lawyer had claimed in court that the victim had originally come at the killer with the knife, and that the killer had cut his hands when he had grabbed the blade to try to get the knife away from the victim. But the number of cuts on his hands, coupled with the fact that the victim had been stabbed in the back and there had been no sign of a struggle, had suggested otherwise. Apparently, all the blood spurting from the victim's back had lubricated the weapon, causing the killer's hand to slip and get cut every time he thrust the knife downward. Until hearing of this case, Chris had never realized how much blood a knifing victim could lose. Now the awful truth had been confirmed. Eastmancolor was never like this.

Chris was sure he would be caught before he could make it back to his apartment. Blood was splattered everywhere.

The lights of the houses along the alleyway were all dark, and he could hear no commotion, so he suspected there had been no witnesses to his crime. Still, he would have to cover it up as best he could.

With a little difficulty, he managed to heft the corpse up and into an empty dumpster. He could never have even lifted the body off the ground before becoming a vampire. When he grabbed the steel lid, it slipped from his bloody fingers and slammed closed with a bang, which set a dog to barking about a block distant.

Chris tore into his pants with his switchblade, cutting off the blood-soaked legs, until he was wearing a pair of cut-off shorts. A bloodstain remained at his crotch, but he covered that by untucking his shirt and letting it hang out both front and back. Except for a drop here and there, his shirt had remained clean. He wiped his hands as best he could with the clean parts of his discarded pant legs, and then shoved his still-red hands in his pockets. From what he could see, he had done a fair job of making himself presentable. All he had to do now was walk the two or three blocks back to his apartment, which he could do most easily by going through back alleys and entering his place through the backdoor.

Once he was back at his apartment, he would shower and change into some fresh clothes, and then he would get over to Temsik's as fast as he could.

In the shower, Chris felt as if time were standing still. When he was finished, he stood before the sink, and if he had been able to see his own reflection in the bathroom mirror he would have seen a murderer, but instead he saw only the dripping water that clung to his invisible hair and trickled alongside his invisible nose.

It was obvious to Chris that Temsik had made a mistake in letting him go after so little training. Temsik hadn't even bothered to prove his point about souls. All he had said was "Someday you'll realize the truth." That someday had come pretty fast, and the truth itself was too staggering for Chris to deal with. He was beginning to realize that he had lost a great deal when he had forfeited his humanity. He doubted he would have been able to kill the cabdriver before becoming a vampire, not only because he wouldn't have had the physical strength, but also because he would have been possessed of some moral sense that would have made him at least question what he was doing. Instead, the act had been simple, and it had essentially taken him over without his being able to control it.

That was what scared Chris the most. Without a soul, he wondered what horrors he might now be capable of, and how much control he really had over his own actions. More and more, he was beginning to understand the moral stance behind Temsik's wish to snuff himself out. Perhaps that was the best thing to do.

Once he had reached Temsik's apartment building, he found himself bounding up the stairs (forgetting the place had a fully functioning elevator), taking them two at a time until he stood before Temsik's door. He took a minute to compose himself before taking out his key and turning it in the lock.

"Temsik!" he called, stepping inside and closing the door behind him. "Temsik, it's me, Chris!"

No answer came; Temsik must have gone out.

The light in the foyer was on, but the rest of the apartment was dark. Chris could see his way perfectly, partly due to the moonlight shining through the French doors, so he didn't bother to turn on any lights as he headed for the staircase.

The door to the study was open, but the study was dark. Chris took the stairs one by one, looking down upon the eerie living room and dining room. The apartment was spotless and looked as if it hadn't been lived in for days. While Temsik seemed to be a tidy person, he wasn't obsessive about it, and there always seemed to be at least a bottle of liquor lying about somewhere with a couple of glasses nearby. But nothing at all was out of place.

Halfway up the staircase, Chris paused and took a listen.

He wondered if Franz Stadler had come and taken Temsik.

If he had, then Chris could be walking into a trap. He wished now that he had brought his pistol along rather than only the switchblade.

But Chris's ears could discern no noise other than his own labored breathing and the more rapid beating of his heart. That helped allay his fears. He felt confident that with his acute hearing sense he would have heard someone in the darkness, wherever they might be in the apartment. But he heard no one.

The place was dead.

Chris continued up the staircase and peeked into the first darkened room, what had been his own bedroom. Everything seemed in order, nothing out of place, shutters on the windows, bed made—it was just as Chris had left it. The whole apartment felt as if it hadn't been lived in since he moved out.

He walked on down the hall, and for some reason the old Doors song "The End" began running through his head, and he started to get truly frightened.

He wondered what he would find in Temsik's room if in fact Stadler had gotten to him already. He pictured Temsik's body lying there with a stake through its heart, the head cut off and turned upside down, with a head of garlic stuffed inside it. But Stadler wouldn't have done that, anyway, he would have taken Temsik back to his lair—if he could.

Temsik's door stood open, and all of the locks were still intact. At least no one had tried to break in.

The porcelain urn containing Laura's ashes still sat high on a shelf on the other side of the room. Temsik's windows were still shuttered, blocking out the night. At the base of the bookcase sat his coffin, sensibly shut.

Chris flicked the light switch, which turned on a small chrome table lamp near the coffin.

"Temsik?" he inquired, suddenly stricken with timidity. "Are you in there? It's me, Chris."

He paused again and listened to make sure no one was coming up from behind him. But he heard nothing.

Then he approached the coffin.

The simply carved lid creaked as he opened it and gazed upon its empty interior.

Empty, that is, except for a pile of ashes in the general form of a man, and Temsik's great emerald ring.

"Oh, God, no!" cried Chris, collapsing onto his knees beside the oblong box.

On an impulse, his hand reached out to touch the gray dust within. He grabbed some of it and let it sift through his fingers. This was all that was left of his mentor.

"It can't be!" His eyes welled up with tears.

At the side of the coffin, tucked in with Temsik's pistol, lay a green envelope addressed simply: "Chris."

Sobbing, Chris ripped it open and removed the note from inside. He had to wipe the tears from his eyes to clear his vision before he read it:

Dear Chris,

If you're reading this, then you already know that I am no more. I'm sorry for my chicanery, but it was the only way I could get myself alone. I hope my actions don't end up costing you. As long as you take to heart what I've already told you, you should do fine. Good luck to you.

I'm sure Beth will be sore at you for having failed your mission, but there was nothing you could have done. I had made up my mind long before our first meeting.

I couldn't go on any longer, knowing what horrors I've inflicted upon our brothers. I also have reason to believe that Stadler has been after me. It would have been the final indignity to fall prey to the monster I myself created.

With my last ounce of strength, I plead for you to leave Madison as soon as possible and travel far away, in the hopes that Stadler will never cross your path.

Take my money, take anything you like, but get out of Madison immediately, and don't come back.

I spend my last hours waxing triumphant!

Love,
V. K. Temsik

But Chris was damned if he was going to leave Madison, at least not until he had tracked down and killed Franz Stadler.

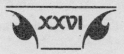

XXVI

LIVE BAIT

THE next night, Chris moved back into Temsik's apartment. For the moment, he didn't know what to do with Temsik's remains, so he left them where they lay and shut up the room, locking the door from the outside. He set up his coffin back in the first bedroom and put all his clothes back in the closet.

He wondered if Temsik could be brought back from his ashes, like Christopher Lee's Dracula had been so many times in the British horror movies. Chris would look into it sometime in the future and see if he could find anyone who knew anything about it.

But for now, he was all alone.

He tried again and again to reach the Chicago vampires, but continued to get the same stupid recording in Beth's voice. By now he had left several messages, and they had never once called him back. He had to resign himself to the fact that they had been abducted by Stadler or otherwise destroyed. Either way, they couldn't help him.

Chris was on his own against a man who had nearly two centuries of experience snatching vampires. Temsik had said that Stadler employed a gang of thugs to protect him. Also Stadler, or one of his men, had to have been spying on Temsik and Chris at one point to have known where to dig up Sheridan Cooper, and he had probably continued spying all this time, waiting for the right moment to kidnap Chris.

267

No wonder Temsik had felt ineffectual against Stadler and his gang. There was no way to make a move without it being telegraphed immediately to the man they were after. Stadler always kept the upper hand.

Chris remained in the same position he had been in ever since he had first heard of Stadler, and had no clue where to begin his search.

And that left only one option, the one most obvious to Chris's cinematic mind: he would act as bait and allow himself to be snatched, and then free himself somehow and kill Stadler.

As they said in the movies, it was risky, but it just might work.

On Thursday, Chris decided to go for a walk.

The night was cool and foggy, the streets and sidewalks glistening wet from the rains earlier in the day. The streetlights along Wisconsin Avenue were surrounded by glowing halos in the mist. At the end of the street, the capitol building was almost entirely obscured by fog. The broad paths of the arc lights that normally illuminated the dome were visible reaching up into the fog, but dissipated before they reached their target; the dome itself was shrouded in a thick veil of mist.

It was the perfect night to be abducted.

Chris realized that it was probably a suicide mission, but he also knew that Stadler was bound to catch up to him wherever he might go. Fleeing Madison would only postpone the incvitable. Stadler wouldn't want to let someone who knew so much about him run freely all over the world, warning other vampires about him.

Therein, it seemed, lay the key to the whole plan.

None of Stadler's other victims had known beforehand what was going to happen to them, nor did they know who Stadler was. That constituted Chris's advantage, but at the moment he failed to see how he could exploit it.

For now, he would walk around and hope that someone came along looking for him. He had his switchblade in his pocket and his Smith & Wesson nine-millimeter automatic pistol tucked into the waist of his jeans, hiding behind the zippered folds of the leather jacket Del had let him have. If he was lucky, Stadler himself would try to nab him, and then Chris could simply shoot him.

But one problem remained: Chris didn't know precisely what Stadler looked like. Wisconsin was home to many people of German, Swiss, and Norwegian descent; there were probably plenty of young men whose features matched Temsik's description of him. Chris could never bring himself to shoot unless he was certain that it was Stadler.

Walking through the fog was coating him with a layer of drizzle. The leather jacket was slick with moisture, and water was trickling down Chris's cheek, amidst the razor stubble.

Chris headed for the capitol and took a stroll around the square. Few people were out walking around. Finals week was over, so the university was between sessions, and the student population downtown had decreased accordingly. Those who were still in Madison were most likely at some bar and would flood the streets at bar time, but right now the city seemed empty.

As he walked along the slick sidewalk around the square, he thought he heard footsteps behind him. He stopped in his tracks and turned around, hoping to find an innocent pedestrian.

But when he looked in the direction of the footsteps the sound stopped, and Chris could see no one behind him in the gathering mist. A squirrel that had been scurrying around the lawn came to a halt and stared in Chris's direction, twitching its nose. But whoever had been following him must have ducked behind a tree, or behind the hedge that lined one of the walkways to the capitol.

Chris's heart began to beat more rapidly.

Calm down, he told himself. *This is what you wanted, isn't it? For someone to follow you around and take you away. Don't keep looking over your shoulder, or you'll scare him away and spoil everything. You don't want him to know that you know he's after you. So just stay calm, and don't blow it!*

Chris continued on his way, and after a minute he heard the footsteps begin again, keeping pace with him and trying successfully to match his own lazy pace.

He started whistling, both to act nonchalant and to calm himself down. At first he failed to recognize what he was whistling, but soon identified it as the ''Troika'' from Prokofiev's *Lieutenant Kije*. Nice happy music. It was already helping him to relax, although the pistol shoved in his pants added little to his comfort.

He left the square at Hamilton Street, which veered off onto West Wilson Street a few blocks away. Chris was leading his abductor to a neighborhood that was dimly lighted and poorly patrolled, an ideal place for a kidnapping.

Chris slowed his pace to let the footsteps catch up if they wished. He stifled the temptation to glance quickly over his shoulder; whoever was following him was probably talented enough to duck for cover, and would be convinced that Chris knew what was going on. But still, Chris wanted to confirm that someone was indeed following him.

Where he was walking, it was unlikely that a person out for a casual stroll would happen to be taking the exact same route.

West Wilson Street was lined with large trees whose leaves draped down to a height barely above Chris's head, and he had to duck the occasional branch. A few streetlights were burned out along the way. He had to stop at the intersection of Broom Street because the traffic was thick. The corner was well lighted, and Chris felt certain that his pursuer had stopped at least a half a block back. When at last the traffic cleared, Chris went on, and heard the footsteps recommence.

This is it, he told himself. *It's now or never. You could run away now, down Broom Street, where they wouldn't dare to snatch you. You could hail a cab and hightail it back to the apartment, and from there you could get yourself out of Madison. Stadler isn't your responsibility. If he was anybody's, he was Temsik's. There's nothing that says you have to be a hero, and who's to say you would succeed, besides?*

But Chris knew he couldn't escape. Stadler would track him down someday. He had to go through with it.

He walked two more blocks, which was the entire length of West Wilson Street before it became a dead end at the railroad tracks. The footsteps still hadn't caught up to him, so he turned the corner and went to Main Street two blocks over, heading back in the direction he had come.

Finally, he had had enough. He stopped at the large brick building on the corner, a pizza parlor that still sported an old, inoperable neon sign for MILLIN'S SUPERMARKET, along with a faded arrow painted along one brick wall, pointing out the supermarket parking in the rear. Hidden from the sight of his pursuer, Chris went to the far end of the building and ducked behind the corner to wait for him in the parking lot, which was empty except for a few pizza delivery vehicles.

This time Chris could hear the footsteps continuing on, coming closer through the fog.

Chris unzipped his jacket quietly and withdrew the pistol, holding it at the ready. He only hoped that no one from the pizza parlor would come out and see him. The smell of fresh-baked pizza wafted out through a nearby air vent.

Chris heard the footsteps turn the corner and then come to a halt, as if puzzled by which direction to turn. The soles of the person's shoes scraped the wet, gritty sidewalk as he stood there, apparently mulling things over. Chris leaned against the wall and held the pistol up by his face with both hands, like the cops did in the movies. His breath was visible in the humid air, swirling around amidst the pizza smell.

Then the footsteps resumed their pace. In only a few more steps, Chris's pursuer would be upon him.

Chris held his finger close against the trigger, ready to aim and shoot. Then he would have to run away as fast as he could to avoid being seen by anyone.

Suddenly, someone darted around the corner and lunged at Chris. The person was dressed all in black and wore both a beret and a mask. Two black-gloved hands reached out for Chris.

Chris brought down his pistol in the same instant and pulled the trigger just as his pursuer's hands reached his throat. But the trigger would not depress, and the gun failed to fire. Chris had forgotten to release the safety catch.

And now an extraordinarily strong hand was gripping his neck, and the other one was coming down hard on the other side, knocking him senseless and knocking his gun from his hands and sending him down to his knees, and he was collapsing onto his face on the wet asphalt of the parking lot, passing out while the figure bent over him and reached into his jacket.

When Chris came to, he was lying alone in the same spot. His pursuer had fled. Chris looked at his watch and determined that less than fifteen minutes had gone by while he was knocked out. He rose slowly to his feet, expecting to be aching and sore. But he supposed that in the time he'd been unconscious his body had repaired itself; he was feeling fine. He touched his face and could feel where the rocks on the asphalt had cut it, and where the cuts themselves had completely healed.

But the damndest thing was, he hadn't been snatched. His Smith & Wesson had been stolen, along with all the cash in his wallet, but that was all. His credit cards and identification had been left behind. He couldn't remember what his attacker had looked like, but it seemed now as if Chris had simply been robbed by a persistent crook who had had him pegged for blocks as an easy score.

If Stadler had been spying on the scene, he easily could have stepped in while Chris was unconscious and taken him. That meant that Stadler wasn't necessarily on his tail full-time. Perhaps Chris could make some use of that knowledge.

Right now, all he wanted was a beer.

He looked down at himself and was pleased to discover

that he hadn't landed in a mud puddle; he was still, on the whole, presentable.

Chris left the neighborhood of the pizza parlor, walking down Bedford Street, and found himself on bright Washington Avenue, within a block of the Hotel Washington building. So, after first stopping at an automatic teller machine to get some cash from Temsik's account, he headed for the New Bar, where he could find booze, boys, and blood.

Although it was Thursday, it was also past midnight, and so there was a good enough crowd at the New Bar, dancing and drinking. Chris went on upstairs to the balcony area, to hide out from the mirrors, and bought himself a Miller at the bar. A table overlooking the dance floor was open, so he grabbed it and sat down to watch everybody else having fun. The speakers were blaring the Pet Shop Boys' rendition of Stephen Sondheim's "Losing My Mind," with vocals by Liza Minnelli; it was an agreeable tune to listen to, but Chris would rather be down there on the floor dancing to it.

It was only a few feet away from here that he had met Sheridan Cooper. Then Sheridan had been snatched right out from under him, to meet some hideous fate at Stadler's lair.

If a big guy like Sheridan hadn't been able to do anything against Stadler, Chris figured his own plan was likely doomed to failure, which meant he would be history, just like Laura, Sheridan, Temsik, and perhaps Beth and all the rest. It was possible that there was simply nothing he could do about it. Stadler might be too powerful ever to overcome.

But if that was the case, there was no harm in trying.

Suddenly, Chris saw a good-looking blond head coming up the staircase, with a face like that of a fashion model, and he realized he had seen that face before.

It belonged to Frankie Stannard.

Frankie caught his eye and waved.

Chris nearly choked on his beer. He knew right away that

Frankie Stannard was really Franz Stadler. He was a perfect match for Temsik's description of Stadler, and the names themselves were too close for mere coincidence.

Now Chris had no choice but to follow through with his plan, armed only with a switchblade now that his gun had been stolen. The staircase was the only means of egress from the balcony, so he couldn't escape. Even if he could, Stadler would probably have some men waiting outside to nab him. But Chris couldn't take out his switchblade and stab Stadler, either. The bar was too crowded with people; he would never make it out the door. Not only that, Chris wasn't so sure he could kill Stadler anyway. If he had kept himself alive for all these years by using *kroba*, he might be immune to knife and gunshot wounds, as Chris himself was. An attack on Stadler would probably prove to be fruitless.

Chris was trapped.

And now Frankie was sitting down at Chris's table.

"Mind if I join you?" Frankie said with a winning grin.

"Go right ahead," said Chris, feigning friendliness.

"It's Chris, isn't it?"

"That's right, and you're . . . ?"

"Frankie." There it was, the sandy blond hair, the dark eyes, the chiseled features that, now that Chris thought about it, did look rather German.

"Frankie, of course. I remember now. We met down in Chicago?"

"At Avalon, a couple of weeks ago."

And that was the last night Chris had seen Beth. Del hadn't noticed the man she had left with, but now Chris was convinced that it had been Frankie. Everything added up.

"So what brings you to Madison?" Chris was annoyed to find that his beer was empty.

"Visiting friends," said Frankie. "You said you were moving up here. I thought I might find you some night at this bar, for some strange reason." He gave Chris a knowing wink.

"And sure enough..." Chris smiled uncomfortably. Frankie had him right where he wanted him. "Do you mind ...I mean, I need to get another beer."

"Oh, I'll take care of it." Frankie grabbed his empty can and headed for the bar, standing at the end near the staircase and blocking any exit Chris might have been planning.

Chris didn't have the guts to slip him the knife right here in full view of everybody, and it probably wouldn't do any good anyway, but the thought did cross his mind once more. Simply put, Chris was in big trouble.

"Here you are," said Frankie, and handed Chris a fresh Miller. He opened one for himself. "Glad I finally caught up with you."

So Frankie was going to sit and play games all evening. Chris would have to try and act as if he hadn't caught on to Frankie's true identity. He hadn't given it away yet. He would wait until Frankie did it himself.

"I'm amazed you could find me."

"Well, how many other places might you go for fun in Madison?" asked Frankie rhetorically. "Elementary, my dear Wilson."

"Pardon?"

"Your name." Frankie raised a quizzical eyebrow. "It is Chris Wilson, isn't it?"

"Oh, yes," Chris said, sweating. He remembered that he had, in fact, given Wilson as his last name. "I guess I just didn't get the joke. You know, the Sherlock Holmes reference?"

"I see," said Frankie with a smirk on his face. "And now back to sex."

"Huh?"

Chris wondered how Frankie was going to manage getting him out of there with all those people around. No one would stand by and let Frankie take him by force, and if Chris stood his ground there was nothing Frankie could do to get him to leave with him. Frankie might have some thugs waiting around the bar somewhere, but again that would be too obvious, and he could never get away with it.

"My friends and I always say that when there's a lull in the conversation: 'And now back to sex.' It's a good ice-breaker, don't you think?"

"Yeah, sure."

Of course, it was still possible that everything about Frankie was mere coincidence and he wasn't Stadler at all. He might be exactly what he had said he was, a professional rich kid, with nothing better to do than go visit some friends in Madison, which was, after all, within only a few hours of Chicago. The fact that they had both run into each other within a matter of weeks at two relatively popular night spots in two different cities wasn't all that improbable. Frankie Stannard might not know the first thing about what happened to Beth, and he might not be out to destroy Chris. Anything was possible.

Frankie withdrew once again the small cylindrical inhaler he kept around his neck on a string of rawhide. He un-screwed the cap, put the inhaler to one nostril, shut the other with his finger, and took a whiff.

"Mmmm!" said Frankie, rolling his eyes and smiling. "What a rush! Are you sure you won't have a whiff this time? I swear to God it won't kill you."

"I really don't want to." Chris waved it away.

Frankie removed it from around his neck and thrust it at Chris. "Go on! It's only poppers."

Chris decided Frankie was right. A whiff of poppers wouldn't kill him, and he didn't want to act as if he was afraid of Frankie. It was possible that Chris could still benefit from not letting on that he knew Frankie's real identity, if indeed it were true.

"Okay, here." Chris took the small black vial from Frankie's hands. Closing one nostril, he placed the opening at the other and inhaled deeply through his nose.

But it wasn't amyl nitrate fumes that he inhaled.

It was the pungent smell of crushed garlic.

Chris collapsed, dropping the inhaler and falling against the table, knocking over his beer and spilling it all over his hair. He remained conscious but incredibly weakened. He could barely move any of his muscles.

"Oh dear," said Stadler, picking him up and throwing one of Chris's arms around his shoulders. "I think you've had one too many!"

With one of Stadler's arms supporting his torso, they managed to get down the stairs together. No one paid any significant attention; they all thought Chris was stinking drunk, and Stadler and Chris weren't the first couple of men to walk out of the place arm in arm.

"Franz . . ." Chris mumbled, barely able to speak.

"Now you're all mine." Stadler laughed. If anyone had overheard him, they wouldn't have thought anything of it.

When they passed the bouncer at the door, Chris pleaded with his eyes for help. But the bouncer looked knowingly at the couple, probably thinking they were heading off for a night of drunken, sloppy sex.

"You . . . bastard. . . ." It took all of Chris's energy to say the words. He was sapped of nearly all his strength.

"I love you, too," said Stadler, and kissed him on the cheek, lightly licking off Chris's sweat. They headed out of the atrium at the bottom of the stairs and down the street to Stadler's waiting Mercedes.

IN THE DUNGEON

STADLER put Chris in the back seat and pushed him over onto his side, where he was unable to get up of his own accord. The effects of the garlic were beginning to wear off, but no sooner did the strength start to return to Chris's muscles than Stadler was putting a paper bag over his head that reeked with garlic fumes. This succeeded in rendering him immobile for the drive to Stadler's hideout, and also prevented him from seeing where it was located. He might as well have been handcuffed, hamstringed, and gagged.

Chris felt as if he were suffocating in the paper bag. The garlic was making him perspire; his face was dripping with sweat. His skin burned, and the more he sweated the more intensely it burned, as if he were being exposed to acid fumes.

By the time they came to a stop and the engine was turned off, Chris was thoroughly disoriented.

Stadler opened the back door and removed the bag from Chris's head, causing him to gasp for air that was fresh and uncontaminated. But as he was filling up his lungs, Stadler locked a steel collar around his neck, removed his leather jacket, and put his wrists in shackles behind his back. The collar was wide and kept his head from moving around too much. Chris felt a tug at his neck as Stadler yanked on the heavy chain that was attached.

"Come on, get up!"

A lone bright light bulb shone from the ceiling. They were indoors, in some garage somewhere.

Chris could barely move, but managed to drag his legs along the floor of the car in an effort to get himself out. But Stadler had to lift him by his shoulders and stand him up on his feet. Chris's knees gave way, but Stadler caught him, wrapping one arm around his chest to hold him up.

Stadler kicked shut the door of the Mercedes and led Chris through the doorway at the other end of the garage.

Chris's head lolled around on his neck as much as the collar would allow as they made their way through a series of rooms. He felt as if he were drugged, as if he had been given a big dose of Demerol that had knocked him for a loop. The feeling started gradually to come back into his legs, so that he could support himself with less help from Stadler, but he could hardly run away or hope to escape, not while he was cuffed and collared, with Stadler holding the chain.

Chris tried to think of what they said in the movies. *You'll never get away with this!* But he had no reason to believe that Stadler wouldn't get away with it.

Chris's mind returned to greater awareness when they passed through a heavy steel door into a large, hot chamber.

"This is your new home," said Stadler.

It seemed to be the back half of an old brick building, perhaps a small warehouse of some kind, lighted by five low-wattage bulbs that hung down from the ceiling. The walls were of bare, red brick; the rectangular window holes had been bricked over with much newer bricks of a brighter shade so that there were no places through which sunlight could shine. Two fresh brick walls had been constructed in one corner, forming a smaller room with its own metal door. Two squarish stacks of leftover bricks draped with clear plastic dropcloths sat nearby on risers, and next to them stood two unused bags of cement mix, along with a wheelbarrow caked with gray, lumpy residue of dried cement. Six thick support beams stood from floor to ceiling far apart

from one another; on two of them, Chris could see wrist
and ankle shackles dangling free, with no one in them. From
the other posts hung several varieties of whips and leather
straps.

But Chris and Stadler were not the only people in the
room.

Large wooden tables were lined up along the walls, like
beds in a military hospital. A few tables were empty, their
chains lying at rest on top or dangling over the edge, but
on the other tables lay Beth, Jamie, and Sheridan, naked
and firmly manacled to the sturdy woodwork. Intravenous
tubing had been stuck into their arms, through which their
kroba was being drained, drip by drip, into glass bottles on
the floor.

"Friends," said Stadler, "meet our new guest."

"Sheridan!" Chris said, elated to find that Sheridan was
still in existence. All this time, Stadler had been keeping
him here. But Beth and Jamie had probably been here for
longer.

Chris wondered what had happened to Luis and Del.

Jamie and Sheridan raised their heads from the tables as
far as their chains would allow, looked briefly at Chris with
expectant eyes, then laid their heads back down. They had
looked as if they were afraid to speak; or perhaps they were
distraught that Chris had been captured like them and would
eventually meet the same fate. Beth, however, remained
perfectly still. She was paler than Chris had seen her before,
and unbelievably thin, as if her body were consuming itself.
Jamie and Sheridan were thinner as well, but still looked
relatively healthy. Beth's *kroba* dripped less steadily than
did Jamie's and Sheridan's, as if she were trying to keep it
from escaping her body.

The room was easily over one hundred degrees Fahren-
heit, the air dry and smelly with the unique, sharp body
odors of the vampires. Around the room stood three braziers
heating pumice rocks, such as would be found in a sauna.
Near one of them sat an old-fashioned bathtub on claw feet,
but Chris saw no faucet nearby. He was already sweating,

his clothes sticking to his skin. His three friends in their chains were coated in perspiration, Jamie's and Sheridan's defined muscles glistening in the dim light, while Beth's wet skin looked all the more sickly, as if she had a fever.

"Can you stand, Chris?" asked Stadler.

"I think so." Chris spoke through his teeth. He despised Stadler for what he was doing to his friends.

Stadler attached Chris's neck chain to a hook hanging from an overhead beam and ripped his T-shirt off. Then he removed Chris's sneakers and socks and unbuttoned his jeans and pulled them down and off, followed by his striped bikini briefs. He felt more naked than he had ever felt in his life. Here he was, in chains and completely at Stadler's mercy, without any clothing or any of his weapons. The switchblade was in the pocket of his jeans, and his gun was now in the hands of some petty thief somewhere in Madison.

"All right, come on," said Stadler. He led Chris by the chain to a table across the room from the others. "Up on the table," he ordered.

Chris sat on the edge of the table, and then Stadler took over, swinging Chris's feet onto the tabletop and laying him out on his back. It was highly uncomfortable with his arms shackled beneath him. Stadler locked steel cuffs around his ankles, which in turn were attached to short chains that were bolted to each corner of the table, so that Chris's legs were now spread apart and firmly secured.

"Sit up."

Chris sat, and Stadler removed the shackles from his arms, only to lay him back down and fix new cuffs around each wrist, stretching him out between all four corners of the broad table. The chain attached to his collar was locked to some fixture underneath the table, allowing him some room to move his head and to sit up slightly, but little else. Chris was now Stadler's captive.

"That's better, isn't it?" said Stadler.

He went around and double-checked every lock, then added the appropriate keys to the hefty key ring that hung from his belt.

Although Chris's strength had still not fully returned, he tested his shackles and found that he would be unable to break them loose from the table. The tabletop was thick, butcher-block style, and every chain was affixed by means of thick bolts that had been driven in against the grain, probably at a depth of several inches. Even when he was feeling up to par again, he knew he couldn't get free.

He stared up at a moth that was circling the light bulb overhead, drawn by the light and the heat. If it got too close, it would fry, but perhaps that was exactly what it wanted.

The IV tube in his arm drained the rust-colored *kroba* from his veins. It disappeared down the clear plastic tubing, over the edge of the table, presumably to a glass bottle down below, just like the others.

Chris breathed the hot air into his lungs and felt the tickle of sweat dripping all over his body. Sometimes it felt as if insects were crawling across his skin and he could do nothing to brush them off, but it was only his own sweat.

Chris raised his head as far as the chain would allow and saw that on the other side of the room, Stadler was taking away full jars of *kroba* and replacing them with empty ones. He set down the jars near the brazier by the bathtub, where several other jars already sat, keeping warm.

"Ah, Sheridan!" Stadler's grin made him look ravenously hungry, as if he were about to dig into Sheridan's flesh. "And how are you today?"

Sheridan turned away his head, and Stadler slapped his face.

"I asked you a question."

Sheridan mumbled something.

"What was that?"

"I said I'm doing okay."

"Okay what?"

"Okay, sir." Sheridan spat out the words, betraying his repugnance of Stadler.

"I gather you don't care for me very much. I think it's time you received another bath."

Stadler removed his own shirt and tossed it on the floor by the bathtub. Chris was expecting him to unchain Sheridan and put him in the tub, but he did no such thing.

Instead, starting at the feet, Stadler began licking the sweat from Sheridan's body, while his captive squirmed beneath his tongue.

"Mmm! Tropical flavored," said Stadler, having finished Sheridan's leg and left none of it untasted.

"Stop it," Sheridan murmured. "Stop it."

Stadler merely laughed and continued on. He licked every last drop of perspiration from Sheridan's body, ending up at his face, licking his stubbly cheeks, his forehead, even his hair.

"You slimy bastard!" Sheridan shouted.

"Oh, you'll pay for that." Stadler ended his tongue bath and slapped Sheridan's chest, leaving a pale handprint that faded to red on his olive skin. Chris expected that Sheridan might be whipped next, or otherwise punished. "Now look over there—Chris has been watching the whole thing, and he looks like he's enjoying himself. Aren't you, Chris?"

Chris said nothing.

Stadler left Sheridan's table and came over to Chris.

"Aren't you, Chris?" he repeated.

Chris was afraid that he might be whipped if he failed to answer or if he answered wrongly, so he replied, "Yes, sir."

"What was that?"

"Yes, sir."

"Very nice. I think you'll fit in rather well among these guys, not counting Beth. But the rest of you are great ass-kissers. Still, I've got to teach Sheridan a little lesson."

Chris thought Stadler would reach for a whip from one of the posts, but instead he left the room, returning a few minutes later carrying a small plastic bag with something white lining the bottom, Chris couldn't tell what. Stadler took it over to Sheridan's table.

"Do you know what this is?" Stadler asked.

"No, sir."

Stadler put the bag up to Sheridan's face. "Recognize the smell?"

"Garlic," said Sheridan.

"Very good. Guess where it's going."

Sheridan stared in horror as Stadler put the bag over his exposed genitals, strapping it on with a rubber band.

Sheridan screamed in pain, writhing upon the table.

"Good night, all," said Stadler in the doorway. He turned out the lights before closing the door, plunging the room into total darkness.

Sheridan's cries continued for hours. Chris could imagine what the burning felt like, but could not imagine being unable to reach down to do anything about it. Sheridan must have been in agony, and it was all Chris's fault that he was in this mess to begin with.

But despite Sheridan, and the heat, and Chris's being chained to the table, he had no trouble finding sleep, as his energies disappeared with the rising of the sun outside.

When he woke up the next evening and opened his eyes, he saw in the dim light that Del was standing over him. Stadler was gone from the room.

"Del!" Chris was unable to hide his excitement. "Del, have you got his keys? Get us out of here, quick!"

But Del merely smiled down at him, his fingers tracing patterns in the sweat on Chris's torso.

"Del, don't mess around. Who knows when Stadler might get back!"

"Poor Chris," said Del. "I'm not here to set you free. I'm here to check on your progress. Looks like I need to set up another bottle." Del tossed back his hair and held up a full bottle of *kroba* that had come from Chris's arm.

"What did he do to you?"

"Who, Franz? Nothing. He's been my boss for a long time."

"Your boss?" Suddenly, Chris realized what Del meant. He had been in Stadler's employ all along, even before Laura had turned him into a vampire. No wonder Del hadn't noticed who had left Avalon with Beth; he had been part of the whole scheme, turned into a vampire so he could infiltrate the Underground and provide Stadler with new subjects to snatch. This sort of ingenuity must have been at least partially responsible for Stadler's success over the years. He had fooled everybody, including Temsik. Chris only wondered what Del had been promised out of all this.

"Don't act so surprised, Chris," said Del. "If Franz gave you the opportunity, you'd join him in an instant instead of withering away on this table."

"Is that how he got you?"

"Not exactly." Del took the end of Chris's dripping IV tube and stuck it through the stopper of a fresh, empty bottle. Chris watched the orange fluid drip until it coated the bottom of it, and then Del set it down on the floor. "I wasn't a vampire then. I was doing some spy work for him, but I screwed up once and he was displeased. Knowing what I knew already about his operations, he couldn't very well turn me loose upon the world, so instead he decided to offer me as a sacrificial victim to one of his captive vampires."

"Sacrificial victim?" Chris failed to comprehend Del's meaning.

"But instead, I struck a deal with him, and he gave me one more chance. We tricked Laura into biting me on the neck after one of Franz's captives had bitten me elsewhere. When she discovered I had been bitten twice, she chose to turn me into a vampire, and then I continued my work for Franz when I was sent to Chicago. You can figure out the rest."

"What do you mean, sacrificial victim?"

"Look over there," said Del, pointing toward the bottles of *kroba* stacked near the bathtub. "See all those? All of that has come from Beth, Jamie, and Sheridan in the last four days, although Beth hasn't been giving much."

"But they should be drained dry."

"Exactly, unless they've been feeding all this time."

"Even so——" Chris began.

"Even so," Del continued for him, "they couldn't have produced so much, you're thinking."

"Do you mean to tell me that Stadler provides us with human victims and forces us to suck their blood?"

"Boy, you're quick."

"But we'd have to—"

"You'd have to drain them dry. That's right. And that's exactly what Jamie and Sheridan have been doing, too. Beth is refusing to cooperate, and you can see where that's gotten her. Pretty soon she'll be all used up, just like Luis."

"Luis?" Chris was alarmed. "What happened to Luis?"

Del laughed. "Do you really want to know?"

Chris yanked on all his limbs at once, but the chains held firm. He felt like throttling Del right here and now. Del had betrayed them, and he deserved a worse fate than anything Stadler could dream up.

"Tell me what happened to Luis," said Chris through gritted teeth.

"No need to get testy." Del snickered, grabbing Chris's balls and giving them a tight squeeze. "Testy, get it?"

Chris cried out in pain.

"Well, if you put it that way," said Del, and continued on. "Luis followed the same path Beth is on now. He refused to bite any more humans, and then all his *kroba* was used up. It still would have taken a few days before he was fully destroyed. So I guess you could say we put him out of his misery. We took him into that room over there."

Del pointed at the brick-walled chamber in the far corner, with the steel door.

"What did you do, drive a stake through his heart?"

"No, nothing so pleasant. In fact, why don't I show you? It might be a good way to keep you in line, and I don't think Franz would mind."

"First-name basis, huh?" Chris didn't bother to hide the derision in his voice.

At first, he thought that this might be his opportunity to break free. When Del released him from the table, he could try to subdue Del, let the others go, and then they could battle Stadler together, if he was even around. But Chris soon realized it wouldn't be that easy. Before Del released the chains from his ankles, he put on a pair of leg irons attached by a short, heavy chain. He withdrew the IV tube from Chris's arm and then attached similar irons around his wrists, and then led him by his neck chain to the smaller chamber.

Hobbling his way across the room, Chris began to think there would never be any means of escape from this dungeon.

Before going in the chamber, Chris expected to find that a window or two might not have been bricked up. Perhaps when they had to dispose of somebody, they locked him in the room and waited for the sunlight to do its work.

The truth turned out not so simple.

"Here we are," said Del, opening the door and turning on the light.

Inside, Chris found no windows, but a few sets of wrist and ankle shackles set in the walls, and in the middle of the room, a tanning bed. It looked rather like a giant waffle iron in the form of an elongated clamshell, its upper and lower halves each containing a bank of ultraviolet light bulbs, presently turned off. The room was pervaded with the pungent odor of burned flesh.

Del took him up close to the machine. Chris tripped over himself, reluctant to approach it.

"We laid Luis out here, tied him down, left the room, and turned it on, and after a few minutes *poof!* he was gone. This thing is very effective."

"Ghastly," Chris murmured.

"But it can also be used for torture. We could chain you to the wall if we like, and turn it on for a few brief spurts aimed in your direction. After that, you'll do anything we like. So keep that in mind if you ever think of refusing any of Franz's orders."

"Yes, sir."

"Boy, honey, you're good at this 'sir' business! And

don't you ever try to escape, or we'll put you in here and provide you with an excruciatingly slow death by turning the tanning bed on and off at long intervals. Believe me, Franz has done it before, and you don't want it to happen to you.''

"Yes, sir.''

Del led him back outside and closed the door.

"It looks as if Beth might just end up in there pretty soon,'' said Del, shaking his head in mock anguish. ''Unless you can convince her otherwise. Ever since we got rid of Luis, she's been highly uncooperative.''

Chris looked over at Beth, who looked asleep, or else was so drained that she could no longer move. She hadn't aged the way Temsik had when he had tried to starve himself the first time, but then she had only been a vampire for ten years, so Chris figured she wouldn't have as much aging in her. Perhaps this was as far as she would go, and then Stadler would put her in the tanning room and fry her on the machine.

"Come on, Chris. It's time to get you back on the table.''

Now Chris realized his plan was an absolute failure. He would be stuck here in this dungeon until he was all used up, and then he would be fried on the tanning bed like Luis and, he supposed, like Laura. But he saw little point in refusing to suck blood, as Beth was doing. The longer he could keep himself going, the better off he might be. If worse came to worst, he might be able to strike a deal with Stadler, as Del had done.

But he still wanted to destroy Del for having betrayed them.

Chris imagined Sheridan wanted to do the same to him for putting him in his predicament. It must have been rough on him, having to learn about being a vampire here in this environment. Chris might have thought he'd had it bad with Temsik as his teacher, but Sheridan had had no teacher, outside of Stadler himself. Sheridan must have been seething with rage toward Chris, his mind a bundle of confusion and hate. But somehow, something in him was resisting Stadler, as evidenced by his being tortured the previous evening. Perhaps there still existed in Sheridan some innate goodness. Perhaps Chris hadn't completely destroyed him by turning him into a vampire. He could only hope.

None of the other vampires had said a word to him since he had arrived, and he couldn't stand it anymore.

"Jamie," Chris called. He raised his head and looked across the room. He saw that Beth's body was continuing to wither away. Her muscles had shrunk, and her skin had turned a flaky gray color and hung loose on her body. She looked as if she were asleep.

Jamie grumbled. "What do you want?" He didn't bother to look over at Chris.

"We've got to get out of here."

"You got any bright ideas?"

"No. But we can think of something." Chris lay his head back down. The weight of the collar and chains was too great a strain on his neck; the loss of a couple of pints of *kroba* was having an effect on his strength.

"When you do, let me know. Otherwise, leave me alone, or I'll get into trouble."

"Since when did you worry about getting into trouble? I thought you were an anarchist." If Jamie was going to be of little help, Chris figured he might as well harass him.

"Hey, man, I'm just trying to survive, same as you."

"But we've got to get Beth out of here as fast as possible. She doesn't look as if she'll last much longer."

"No thanks to you!" Jamie shouted.

"What did I do?" Chris rattled his chains. He wanted to go across the room and shake some sense into Jamie. "I haven't had anything to do with any of this, much less what happened to Luis."

"That's not what I'm talking about. Beth didn't blame Luis for choosing the path that he did. She started fasting when you allowed Temsik to destroy himself. That's what I'm talking about."

"How do you know about that?"

Jamie's chains clanked. "Then it's true, isn't it?"

"Yes, it's true. How did you know?"

"Stadler. That fucker knows everything."

"Believe me, Jamie, if I had known what Temsik was up to, I would have tried to stop him. I thought he was over it. The last time I saw him, he was talking about the two of us coming up with a plan to get rid of Stadler, and then, a week later when I went to see him, he was gone. Just a pile of ashes in his coffin, and that was it. I never thought he'd do it. But you can't hold me responsible. I don't think I could have changed his mind, even if I'd known."

"You still failed your mission."

"Then it wasn't very smart of Beth to entrust such an important mission to a neophyte like me. Maybe she should have sent you instead."

"Well, there's nothing either of us can do about it now. It's all the same to Beth, anyway. You're right, Chris, she won't last much longer. But with Temsik gone, I can tell you we don't have any chance of being rescued. So if you want us to get out of here with our skins before Beth gets fried, you'd better think fast."

Suddenly, the door opened and Stadler and Del came into the room.

"See how quiet it got all of the sudden?" Stadler asked Del. Then he addressed the rest of them. "Let me make it perfectly clear that there is to be no talking among you at any time. You may only address either myself or Del, but not one another. Jamie, you ought to know that by now."

"Yes, sir."

"It doesn't appear as if the whip has been able to get through to you so far." Then Stadler turned his gaze to Chris. "And it's about time you were punished for something, my little friend. So you and Temsik thought you might be able to get rid of me, eh?"

Chris realized Stadler had been eavesdropping, or perhaps the room was bugged. He should have assumed that to begin with.

"Answer me!"

"Yes, sir."

"Yes, what?" Stadler prodded.

"Yes, we were going to try to get rid of you."

"And now look where Temsik is, without my having laid a finger on him. He got frightened off, reduced himself to a few handfuls of dust. He knew he couldn't ever destroy me. The sooner you learn that, Chris, the better off you'll be. Meanwhile, it seems to me there's some punishment to be meted out."

Stadler grabbed a cat-o'-nine-tails from one of the posts, along with a riding crop. He tossed the riding crop to Del. "Here," he said. "You take that one over there. I want to work on Chris for a while."

Chris winced in pain as the first lashes came down across his chest, burning into his flesh.

He was turned over halfway through the whipping, so Stadler could do his backside and buttocks. When it was over, he was turned once more onto his back.

Chris knew he'd been beat. Stadler had him under his complete control, and there was no way to escape.

His body was covered in orange streaks and rust-colored welts. In a few places, the lashes had cut the skin. Stadler had licked the *kroba* from the wounds before they began to heal, and when he hung up his whip, he licked every inch of Chris's sweaty, tormented, bleeding body.

Because Chris had lost so much *kroba* already, his wounds did not heal as rapidly as they should have, so he remained in terrific pain for some time. Jamie seemed to be in a similar predicament, having been beaten with a riding crop that had also opened his flesh. They both writhed upon their tables, unable to tend to themselves.

Meanwhile, Stadler had gotten undressed and was now sitting happily in the bathtub.

Del took the bottles of *kroba* that had been amassed and, one by one, poured their warm contents into the tub, until Stadler was practically swimming in the rusty fluid.

"Ahh!" Stadler smiled in ecstasy, inhaling deeply of the aroma. He cupped his hands and splashed some of it onto his face, coming away orange-stained.

Del grabbed a sponge and worked the *kroba* into Stadler's skin, first on his back, then his front, then his legs. He squeezed some of it out into Stadler's wavy blond hair, then massaged it deep into his scalp. He smeared the *kroba* into Stadler's face, worked it into his ears, forehead, the back of his neck. He coated Stadler's arms with it, and scrubbed it in. When at last the work was over, he left the room, leaving Stadler alone to soak in the tub with a *kroba*-saturated washcloth draped over his face.

Stadler's laugh came from deep within his throat. "You fools," he said. "Such temerity! To think you could ever win against me! Without your precious Temsik, you're nothing."

The sad thing was, Chris knew he was right.

OUT FOR BLOOD

BY the next evening, Franz Stadler looked even more extraordinarily beautiful than before. His shoulder-length hair, swept back from his forehead, shone with more luster than ever. His skin was evenly smooth, nicely tanned. His face looked restful, his lips full and healthy. The *kroba* bath had restored him to a state of splendor, when Chris had thought he looked pretty excellent already. It was hard to believe that Stadler had been born in the eighteenth century. *Kroba* had done him well over the years.

But at what cost? Thousands of vampires, gone. At least that was what Temsik had said, and he ought to have known.

Stadler and Del had brought two new arrivals into the dungeon this evening, both of them human and drugged into a state of unconsciousness. One was a tall blond female, about thirty-five years old, in jeans and a polyester shirt; she looked like a housewife they might have snatched at some grocery store. She was laid out on the table on Chris's right, but was not restrained. The other human was a lanky man of about thirty, with a balding head over which he had tried to comb his last remaining hairs, and a handlebar mustache, wearing gray slacks, a blue shirt, and a red tie; he looked to Chris like a local politician, or at least someone who might work at the capitol. He was laid out on a table on the other side of the room.

"Jamie and Sheridan will have to share that one," said

Stadler, giving Del his instructions. "But give the girl to Chris over there."

"Yes, sir."

So Stadler had Del giving him the "yes, sir" treatment as well! Chris wondered if it were something he might be able to exploit.

Escape plans kept running through his mind, none of them the least bit workable. Even if he could get loose, he would only be recaptured and put on the tanning bed.

Stadler opened up a bottle of *kroba* and then took a large syringe out of a small black bag. He tipped the bottle a little and drew out enough *kroba* to fill the syringe. Then he rolled up his sleeve and injected the fluid into his veins, while a look of ecstasy spread across his face. When he was through, he repeated the procedure once more, then replaced the stopper on the bottle.

Stadler went over to Beth's table and examined her. Chris could see that she looked truly awful, her skin wrinkled and beginning to decay, her breasts shriveling up, her hair gray and falling out. She now looked as bad as Temsik had looked when Chris had stumbled across him on that first night in Madison.

"Look at this, Del," said Stadler. He withdrew the end of her IV tube from the bottle on the floor and held it in the air. No *kroba* was dripping from it. Stadler had gotten all he was going to get out of her. "Kind of sad, isn't it?" He seemed to be addressing everyone in the room. "Del, I want you to take care of it this time."

"But, sir—" Del stared, aghast, at Beth's withered figure.

"No 'buts' about it, Del. Take her to the chamber."

"Yes, sir," Del said grudgingly. Perhaps he was feeling a certain affection for Beth despite his own evil duplicity. Chris couldn't imagine anyone failing to respond to Beth's inherent warmth, at least in her former condition.

Chris felt distant from what was happening, perhaps because he could hardly believe that that decrepit body was indeed Beth. It looked like the corpse of some prematurely aged woman, a diseased, disfigured, disgusting thing. It bore no relation to the young, beautiful girl it had once been, no more than a week before.

Del unlocked Beth's shackles and carefully slid one arm beneath her legs, the other behind her back.

One of Beth's arms snapped up and clutched at his neck, and she spat a yellow glob of phlegm into his face.

Del jumped back, startled, but evidently Beth's grip on his neck was not so strong, because he simply removed her hand and laid it across her chest. He wiped the phlegm from his face with his sleeve, and picked her up off the table.

Beth spoke in the same hissing whisper that Temsik had used when he had been in similar shape. *"Bassstardsss!"*

But they hadn't destroyed her yet. Temsik had been brought back from the brink; perhaps they would give her a second chance, maybe let her bite the politician. But, Chris realized, if she hadn't given in by now, it was unlikely she would change her mind.

And it was soon obvious that Stadler wasn't going to offer her any more blood.

Del carried her into the smaller room, out of Chris's sight. In a minute, he was back outside, shutting the steel door. Then he threw a small black switch on the wall.

Beth screamed for five minutes, though the sound was greatly muffled by the brick walls. In another five minutes, Del turned the switch off and went inside, carrying a small whisk broom, a dustpan, and a paper bag.

Chris's wounds had completely healed. He looked as good as new, if somewhat thinner and weaker. Gases gurgled in his belly. He was starving. He hadn't had any blood in four days. Any longer, and he would begin to go the way of Beth, but he knew Stadler wouldn't let that happen.

The blond housewife was his dinner, and after what had happened to Beth, Chris wasn't about to refuse her.

The urge to stay in existence outweighed his need to escape from Stadler. It seemed the only way to escape was to deny him the *kroba* he most desired. Temsik, Luis, and

Beth had each escaped in this manner. Chris lacked the intestinal fortitude to go that route, no matter how much he might have sympathized with it in principle.

When Del had disposed of Beth's ashes, he and Stadler went to work feeding everybody. Del grabbed the politician, while Stadler took the housewife. Del laid out the politician next to Sheridan on his table, lining up the victim's neck with Sheridan's mouth.

Chris couldn't see what happened next, because the blonde was being laid out beside him on his own table, and her hair was in the way. He could smell the warm blood circulating beneath her pink flesh.

"Go on, Chris, bite into her!" Stadler commanded. He held the housewife by her shoulders, forcing her upon Chris. The woman was completely unconscious, probably heavily sedated. All it would have taken was a few Valium, which would have been easy for Stadler to procure.

Her neck was thrust into Chris's face. He hesitated only for a moment, but his thirst overcame him; he grinned wide, causing his canines to stretch into place, and then bit swiftly into the housewife's jugular vein.

Chris sucked hungrily at the wound, more anxious than ever to be filled up with blood. He felt his body going to work immediately, taking the woman's blood and transforming it into the *kroba* that he desperately needed. As he drank it down, his arms and legs clenched against their shackles. They yearned to be free, so he could grab this woman and control her himself. Instead, he was at the mercy of Stadler.

Chris pulled his teeth from the puncture holes. "That's enough," he said, breathing hard and smiling in ecstasy. He noticed he had achieved an erection.

"No it's not," said Stadler. "Continue!" He shoved the bleeding neck into Chris's face once again.

Chris knew, of course, what Del had said about Stadler forcing them to suck their victims dry, but until now it hadn't completely sunk in. Stadler was going to force him to drink every last drop of the housewife's blood.

"I won't do it," said Chris. Even he was surprised by what he had said.

"You won't, eh?" said Stadler. He left the woman for a moment and retrieved a large, glistening machete that had been hanging on the far side of the nearest post. He held it above Chris's foot. "If you don't obey me, you'll lose this foot."

"Okay, then." Chris capitulated.

"Okay, what?" Stadler tapped Chris's shin lightly with the blade, producing a small cut.

"Okay, sir!"

"That's better. Now get back to work." Stadler hung the machete from one of his belt loops and returned to his previous position, holding the drugged woman in place.

Chris could hardly bring himself to do it. Not only would he be taking this woman's life, he was also already full from the large quantity of blood he had consumed. But he didn't want to lose any appendage, so reluctantly he poked his fangs back into the wounds and began to suck.

It seemed to take forever. His sucking became slower and slower as his belly became further distended. His body couldn't process all this blood so fast; there was only so much *kroba* it could produce at any given time. Most of the blood sat within him, waiting to be transformed. He was feeling bloated.

"I can't," he pleaded. "I can't . . . drink any more."

"Sure you can," Stadler prodded. "You can take a little more. She's still got some left in her."

Chris could no longer feel a heartbeat. He had already taken enough of her blood that she was dead. Her skin had become white as linen.

Suddenly, an alarm bell rang in the room.

Two gunshots rang out somewhere in the building.

Stadler whirled around and looked up at the bell, which sat above the door. In doing so he lost his grip on the housewife, whose body rolled off Chris and off the table, landing with a thump on the floor. But Stadler paid no attention to it.

"Where are my guards!" Stadler shouted.

"I don't know, sir!" said Del.

Stadler grabbed the large machete from his belt and held it high in the air. "Find out what the trouble is, and report back to me!"

"Yes, sir!"

Del rushed to the door, leaving the politician lying atop Jamie, who must have had sloppy seconds after Sheridan. Jamie wriggled beneath the body, causing it to roll off the table and land on the floor.

But before Del could get out the door and find out what the trouble was, the trouble walked in carrying a pistol.

"Guards!" Stadler screamed.

"I've killed all your spies and all your guards, Franz," said the trouble. "And now I've come for you."

At first, Chris didn't recognize him, but when he heard the voice, he knew, incredibly, that it was Temsik. He looked about twenty-three years old, with a stony face, a head of thick black hair, and those same icy blue eyes that Chris had always thought were so beautiful.

In the commotion, Chris had failed to notice that Stadler was standing behind his table, holding the machete above his neck.

"Del, get him!" Stadler ordered.

But Del, unarmed, backed off from Temsik, even though Temsik's pistol was aimed solely at Stadler.

"Get him, you fool! He can't kill you with that!"

Del glanced over at Stadler, his face contorted into a look of fright and uncertainty. But he continued to back away from Temsik, falling onto his knees and cowering on the floor. "I'm sorry, I'm sorry," he sobbed over and over, but Chris wasn't sure whether he was addressing Stadler or Temsik.

"Drop your gun," Stadler said, "or I'll sever Chris's pretty little head."

Temsik's mouth was pulled back in a wicked sneer. He fired once. Stadler screamed and fell to the ground. Chris felt blood splatter across his chest. The machete fell to the ground with a dull clang. Chris turned his head and saw Stadler clutching his bleeding hand.

Temsik had shot three of his fingers off.

"I've had a few lessons since our last duel," said Temsik. "My mistake back then was shooting into the air, instead of suffering you to live, you snake."

Stadler was still wailing, staring at the blood gushing from his hand and desperately trying to get up off the floor.

Temsik stuffed his pistol in his jeans and grabbed Del roughly, picking him off the ground in a single quick motion and slamming him down upon the table that Beth had been on. He locked the steel collar around Del's neck and fastened his wrists as well, taking the key ring from around his belt, and left him there, sobbing.

The alarm bell continued to ring.

Stadler was rising to his feet and reaching once more for the machete, while red blood spurted from his wounded hand, forming a pool on the floor.

Temsik took his gun and fired once more, this time into Stadler's chest. Blood and fleshy matter exploded from the small hole left by the bullet, and Stadler fell once again to the floor, screaming.

Temsik must have been using hollow-point bullets to have caused damage of that magnitude.

"Way to go!" shouted Jamie from across the room.

"All right!" Sheridan cheered.

"How does it feel, Franz?"

"You can't kill me!" Stadler said, groaning and spitting up blood. "You know that!" Somehow, he managed a laugh.

"Then you have nothing to worry about." Temsik was mild.

Stadler lay upon the gritty floor, bleeding and unable to rise.

Temsik replaced his gun in his pants and hurried over to Chris. "Are you all right?"

"I'm stuffed," said Chris, and laughed. Temsik looked down at the spent woman on the floor and gasped.

"Let's get you out of this," he said.

Chris stared up at Temsik's face as he searched through Del's key ring for the right keys to the manacles. His was a rugged face, but somehow more beautiful than Stadler's. The difference lay in the eyes. Stadler's eyes were brown, nearly black, and lifeless. Temsik's crystalline eyes gleamed with some inner light. And even in the midst of all this confusion, Temsik's features were placid as he looked through the keys. No more was his skin wrinkled and old. It was smooth as silk, stretched taut around his cheekbones and square jaw. The heat in the room was causing him to sweat, and a few curls of black hair fell across his forehead.

Finally, Temsik found the right keys, and Chris was freed.

When Chris got off the table, Temsik hugged him tightly, and Chris in his bloated condition felt as if he might burst. But he appreciated the surprise show of affection.

"I'm glad you're all right," Temsik whispered.

"Me, too," said Chris. "I mean, the same to you." Chris still couldn't figure out how Temsik had fooled everybody. "They got Beth and Luis, though."

Temsik took the news without saying anything.

The ringing of the alarm bell was bothering Chris. "I'm going to see if I can shut off that bell," he said.

Chris found the alarm switch in Stadler's office, along with two dead guards with gaping holes in their chests. He turned it off.

When he returned, Jamie and Sheridan had been freed, and the first thing both of them did was grab Del.

"This one's got to go, too," said Sheridan.

"Please!" Del begged. "Give me another chance! Stadler forced me to do it! I had no choice!"

Temsik gave him a quick, appraising glance, then unlocked his shackles.

"He's all yours," said Temsik.

Del howled as Jamie and Sheridan grabbed his limbs and took him into the tanning chamber. Chris stood in the doorway and watched as they tied him in place across the lower bed of the machine. When Del was securely bound, they left the room.

"This is for Beth and Luis," Jamie said, and threw the switch.

Del's screams were louder than Beth's, but in due course they, too, died out. In another five minutes, Jamie turned off the switch and went inside. On the bottom shelf of the tanning bed lay a long pile of gray ash. Jamie took his hand and wiped the bed clean, spilling Del's ashes all over the floor.

Meanwhile, Temsik had put Stadler into leg irons.

"Look at this," said Stadler, breathing heavily. "My hand's already healing. Look! You can't kill me!"

Indeed, where his fingers had been blown off, new skin was growing, and the bleeding had stopped. The gash in his chest was beginning to repair itself as well. The *kroba* was having its effect.

"You can't kill me!" He laughed in triumph.

Temsik grabbed him by his shoulders and stood him up. Then he dragged Stadler into the tanning chamber.

"That won't have any effect on me," said Stadler. "It won't do any good, ha-ha!"

Temsik said nothing as he stood Stadler up and put his wrists in the shackles that dangled from the wall.

"What are you doing?" Stadler asked, suddenly desperate.

But Temsik ignored him, addressing Chris instead: "Go over there and bring me that bag of cement. Jamie, get that wheelbarrow. Sheridan, we'll need you to find a few buckets of water. Go to it, man!"

"Yes, sir!" Sheridan said, as if still under Stadler's control.

Jamie laughed, realizing what they were doing. "Holy shit!"

Finally, Temsik turned back to Stadler. "Franz, you don't know how much I've longed for this moment, when we could be reunited once again."

"Vasily!" Stadler screamed. "What the hell do you think

you're doing! Let me go! Get me out of here!''

"I gave you your chance long ago, Franz. Now you'll just have to suffer. Like Laura. Like Luis and Beth. Like countless others you've tortured through the years. We'll see how you like it.''

"Vasily, I beg of you—"

Chris had brought over both bags of cement mix. "Good, Chris. Now get me some of those nice bricks.''

From within the chamber, Stadler cackled hysterically as the wall went up. Temsik had removed the door and set the first row of bricks inside the door frame, with another row just outside. The cement had mixed well, and Sheridan had even managed to find a trowel in a toolbox somewhere.

"He might be able to survive those gunshot wounds," Temsik explained to Chris. "But without access to *kroba*, he'll surely die.''

"How long will it take?" Chris asked, laying a brick.

"Who knows?"

"You can't kill me!" Stadler shouted. "You can't do it. It won't work!''

Chris, Jamie, and Sheridan were so intent on their work helping Temsik build the wall that none of them cared that they were still naked. Chris, for one, decided to worry about that later. Their work was more important.

The wall looked as if it would be sturdy. If Stadler ever managed to break free from his shackles, he could never escape the sealed chamber.

"How did you know about these bricks?" Chris asked.

Temsik laughed. "Truth is, I didn't. Once I got to Stadler's hideout, it was a seat-of-the-pants operation.''

At last, one small hole remained unfilled. Sheridan applied the cement to the sides of the space, while Temsik held up the brick.

"Franz, this is where you're supposed to shout 'For the love of God!'" said Temsik.

"Fuck you!" came Stadler's reply. "Fuck you! Fuck you! Fuck you!''

"Come on, Franz, be a sport. Just say the words."

"I am immortal!" Stadler screamed. "Immortal! Fuck you all!"

"If you say the words, perhaps I'll reach within this old heart of mine for clemency and let you go."

"All right, then," said Stadler, suddenly becoming calm. "For the love of God."

"More feeling, old boy. Pour yourself into the role."

"For the love of God, Temsik! For the love of God!"

"Thank you."

With that, Temsik shoved the final brick into place.

A MODEST PROPOSAL

STADLER had disposed of their clothes, so Chris, Jamie, and Sheridan took some of Stadler's from his closet. They looted his safe and split the money four ways. Temsik took his financial documents, claiming he knew how to plunder Stadler's Swiss bank accounts.

Thcy dropped Jamie and Sheridan off at the basement apartment on Gorham Street, where they could stay for as long as they wished. Temsik assigned Jamie the task of training Sheridan, although he had already received something of a crash course.

Despite their euphoria over finishing off Stadler, Sheridan spoke not one word to Chris the entire time. Chris didn't blame him.

Temsik and Chris returned to the Gilman Street apartment building, and managed to find a spot directly in front where they could park the Jaguar. It was already late; the sun would be up in an hour or so.

On their way up the stairs, Temsik stopped at the second floor and led Chris down the hallway. At the end, near the backdoor, Temsik unlocked an apartment door and ushered Chris in. At first, Chris thought that perhaps Temsik was giving him this apartment, but he was wrong.

"This is where I stayed all this time," Temsik said.

It was a studio apartment, sparsely furnished, with a coffin in the middle of the floor. The shades were drawn over windows that had probably been blackened.

"The ashes in the coffin were Laura's. That was really the weakest part of my plan. If either you or Stadler had bothered to look in Laura's urn and found it empty, my cover would have been blown."

"But how did you manage to evade Stadler's spies?" Chris wanted to know.

"Let's go upstairs, and I'll tell you everything." Temsik's smile beamed with the same intensity as his eyes. He placed one arm around Chris's shoulders and led him out into the hall.

At last they were alone together, sitting in the living room with a cold carafe of vodka between them on the coffee table. Chris set up a shot for both of them.

"Vasheh Zdorovyeh!" said Chris.

"You remembered," said Temsik, as they raised their glasses. *"Vasheh Zdorovyeh!"* Together, they tossed back the drinks.

"Ahh!" Chris sank back against the leather couch.

"When you came into my study that evening, I thought my plan was ruined." Temsik's eyes twinkled. "After Laura was destroyed, I racked my brain trying to come up with a way to eliminate Stadler once and for all. But, as I've told you, every time I got near him, his spies were well ahead of me, tipping him off in advance. I could never get anywhere. So finally, I set on a course of trickery. I would pretend to starve myself out of existence to throw his spies off my trail. He had the apartment bugged, and had people looking in my windows. There was no other way to escape their scrutiny."

"How would starving yourself do that?"

"Stadler didn't employ his spies twenty-four hours a day. The spies were at work from one hour before sundown to one hour after sunrise. He may have monitored the bugging devices during the day, I'm not sure. But the men who watched me didn't watch while the sun was out. Stadler knew that our energies left us during the day and we'd be doing nothing but sleeping in our coffins, so why should he pay a few extra spies for doing nothing? Anyway, I allowed them to witness me growing ever more decrepit, until it was clear I was nearly destroyed. That's when you came in, and I thought you had screwed it all up."

"Somehow Beth found out about it," Chris put in. "She heard a rumor from somewhere."

"Yes, poor Beth." Temsik examined his empty shot glass. Then he snapped back to his train of thought. "But I soon realized that the plan could still go forth, but that you must know nothing about it. First of all, there were bugs everywhere. I couldn't have removed them without Stadler catching on that I had caught on to *him*. Second, I've learned that no one, no matter how trustworthy, is capable of keeping a secret. That's why not even Beth knew of my plan. If I had told anyone, it would have been her. Perhaps I should have." Temsik shook his head sadly.

"But if you had, she probably would have told Stadler after she was captured," Chris said, placing his bare feet upon the coffee table.

"Not probable," Temsik corrected. "But certainly possible, you're right. So I went on playing my part, telling you that it didn't matter how much you or Beth cared, I was going to do myself in once I'd got you trained. I had to throw you a bone when I gave you that section of my memoirs and suggest that perhaps you and I could come up with a plan together when you saw me again. Maybe I was trying to hint at what I was up to. But I still think it's best that you never knew. How do you think you would have stood up under Stadler's torture if you had known the truth?"

Chris didn't answer.

Temsik laughed and slapped Chris's knee. "It's all right. I would have done the same. No one is meant to withstand that kind of brutal treatment, whether vampire or human— although we do heal faster, at least on the outside."

"So you gave me your memoirs to buy some time—"

"I had to be alone. You would have found me out all too easily! I'd been renting that second-floor apartment for years, for the same reason I rented the one on Gorham Street, to provide a place for any of our brothers—or sisters, I should add—who were traveling or hiding out or simply needed a change of scenery. Stadler was mistaken in not watching me during midday. Our energies are greatly reduced during daylight hours, but not gone altogether. It took a great deal of willpower, especially in my frail condition, to leave, go down the hallway to the elevator, go down two floors, and vanish into the second-floor apartment. Thankfully, there are no windows in the hallways in this building, so I was safe. I crawled into the coffin I kept there. Then there was the matter of rejuvenation."

"I bet that was hard. You couldn't go out in your condition, could you?"

"No, I couldn't. Besides, Stadler's spies would have seen me. Instead, all they saw were the ashes I had left in my coffin. Since they couldn't account for me any other way, they were convinced that I had disintegrated from lack of blood. By this time, you had been off in your own apartment, and hopefully reading up on Stadler. I hoped with all my might that Stadler wouldn't get to you before I was ready myself. Down in the other apartment, I phoned out to find my victims. I ordered pizzas, flowers, even a strip-o-gram. I spent two evenings ordering people—and stacking up pizzas and flowers! I drank a great deal of blood, but never drained any of them. I always sent them on their way with an ignorant grin on their face and a good tip in their pocket."

"That's more than I can say for myself." Chris was suddenly sullen.

"Don't blame yourself. Stadler forced that woman on you. You had to do it, or he would have cut off your foot, like you said." Temsik reached out and patted Chris's bare foot.

"But she's not the first person I killed."

"I know, Chris. It's all right." Temsik scooted over to

sit beside Chris and threw an arm around his shoulders.

"You know?" Chris turned and looked him in the eye. "How do you know?"

"Because I saw it. You stumbled across my ashes before I'd expected you to, but even before then I was watching your every move, from when you went into the Caribou Tavern that evening to when Stadler took you with him from the New Bar. Once Stadler's spies thought I was destroyed—and once I'd grown a little younger—I would sneak out in my cloak and hat. His spies had stopped staking out my place, and they never knew to check the other apartment, anyway. I would leave out the back, slinking around like the phantom of the opera. I saw what happened in that alley. He was a genuine threat, Chris. You killed because you had to survive. There's no shame in that. I've killed many people, and I'll kill more in the future. Some people simply get in the way, but others might threaten your existence, and those have to be dealt with. You did the right thing."

Temsik squeezed Chris's shoulders, pressing him closer against him.

"I saw his soul go up," said Chris. "You were right about that."

"So what?"

"What do you mean, so what?" Chris was confused.

"So now you know that if you'd remained human, you would have gone on to some form of afterlife. And I say, so what? I harangued you about it before only because you refused to believe. Once you know about it, you can learn to live with it. Who knows what that afterlife might be? It might be a real bore compared to your present existence."

"I wouldn't doubt it." Chris laughed. The ice, at long last, was broken again.

"By the way, I have your gun upstairs." Temsik's grin was broad, self-conscious.

"That was you who attacked me?"

"I was only watching out for you. I didn't think you'd be able to hide from me like that. I lost your scent around the pizza parlor. All I could smell was pepperoni. I had to stop for a moment and get my bearings. But it wasn't until I came past the side of the building that I picked up your scent once more. I thought you might recognize me, so I had to attack you and pretend I was a mugger. But then I hung back in the shadows and followed you to the New Bar.''

''I should have known it was you.''

''Anyway, you did the right thing, defending yourself like that. If I had been a human, you would have had every right to kill me for attacking you like that, just like you killed the cabdriver.''

''Do you still think I would have been better off if I hadn't become a vampire?''

''Who's to say? Perhaps you should have stayed a human and allowed yourself to die. Maybe you would have been better off. After your leukemia was in remission, you could have lived as full a life as possible until, one day, you died and went on to be something else. But the honest truth is, now that you're a vampire, you shouldn't treat your existence any differently. You never know when you might make a mistake that will lead to your destruction. So live every night to the fullest! Rejoice in your existence! Make yourself a part of the night-world.''

''Maybe you're right.''

''Of course I am. But most importantly, if you hadn't become a vampire, I never would have met you. If you want to be sure you don't make any of those fatal errors in the future, you'll have to stay here for a while and complete your training.''

''I knew it,'' Chris said. ''I knew you'd shortchanged me! Now the truth comes out!''

''Time was wasting, and I needed to get Stadler. Yes, I gave you short shrift. I take full responsibility for the bungling of the Sheridan Cooper incident. I had no right letting you loose upon the world as ignorant as you were. I really had to clean up after you. I had to kill those lab assistants, do all kinds of things. But it was all my fault. I failed to teach you what you needed to know. But I won't fail you again."

"How much longer will it take?" Chris was really wondering how much longer he would get to remain in Temsik's company; he was finding him more endearing every minute.

"Who's to say?" Temsik said, twirling a finger in Chris's short bristly hair. "The training itself will probably take a couple of months. But don't think I'll let you go after that."

Chris's heart skipped a beat. "What do you mean?" he asked, wanting to make sure Temsik spelled it out for him.

"Stadler's taken too many of my loved ones away from me. Ten in Europe, three in America, and countless other friends and acquaintances." Temsik's finger stroked Chris's cheek. "You're the first one I've managed to save, and I don't ever want to let you go."

"Is that a proposal?" Chris looked into Temsik's steely blue eyes, so sincere, glimmering brightly even in the low light. Now that Temsik was back to his normal appearance, at roughly the same age as Chris, he was the most gorgeous thing Chris had ever beheld. And now Chris was holding him, draping one arm over his shoulders and the other around his waist.

"Yes," said Temsik. "That's a proposal."

"I accept."

Then their lips met. Their tongues entwined, and Chris cut his on one of Temsik's fangs. He tasted his own *kroba*, which he found sugary and sweet, like maple syrup.

Chris was the one to break the kiss. "Temsik, I love you." And, for the first time in his life, he meant it.

"I love you, too. But from now on, it's Vasily."

"Vasily," Chris said. "Vasily, I don't suppose the Gladsø brothers make a double-sized coffin?"

"As a matter of fact, Chris, you're in luck. Let's go upstairs to my bedroom, and I'll show you their latest catalog."

Avon Books presents
your worst nightmares—

...haunted houses

ADDISON HOUSE 75587-4/$4.50 US/$5.95 Can
Clare McNally

THE ARCHITECTURE OF FEAR
     70553-2/$3.95 US/$4.95 Can
edited by Kathryn Cramer & Peter D. Pautz

...unspeakable evil

HAUNTING WOMEN · 89881-0/$3.95 US/$4.95 Can
edited by Alan Ryan

TROPICAL CHILLS 75500-9/$3.95 US/$4.95 Can
edited by Tim Sullivan

...blood lust

THE HUNGER   70441-2/$4.50 US/$5.95 Can
THE WOLFEN   70440-4/$4.50 US/$5.95 Can
Whitley Strieber